ONE KIND OF
ENGLISHMAN

—— ONE KIND OF ——
ENGLISHMAN

a novel by
MICHAEL HODGES

First published in Great Britain 1996 by
Images Publishing (Malvern) Ltd,
The Wells House, Holywell Road, Malvern Wells,
Worcestershire WR14 4LH

British Library Cataloguing in Publication Data

A catalogue record for this book is available
from the British Library

ISBN 1 897817 75 4

Designed by Anita Sherwood
Cover design by Chris Redman
Produced by Images Publishing (Malvern) Ltd.
Printed and Bound in Great Britain by Bookcraft, Midsomer Norton, Bath.

To my father,
who taught me
the love of literature

PROLOGUE

When an old and dear friend dies one is left not only with an enormous sense of personal loss; but also, as my much respected mentor, Sir John Summerson, recognised, the essential futility of individual human endeavour. He was thinking of the fragility of man's artistic creations in a temporal universe, having seen buildings by Wren and Hawksmoor in flames during the bombing of London. I think, too, of the constant loss of experience hardly gained. If we were able to gather up all the wisdom of countless numbers garnered throughout the ages, what a treasure house there would be! Such a dream is, of course, quite beyond our reach. Nevertheless, there is a comparatively little store handed down in literature, and while it may be presumptuous it cannot be wrong to attempt to add a smidgen to it. For this reason, when I learnt of David Drummond's death, I collected some of his experiences together and set them down in writing. They provide, I venture to suggest, a useful record of just one Englishman's life between 1928 and 1990, reflecting one facet of our extraordinary island race in an extraordinary period.

He was my oldest friend in term of years. We attended the same preparatory school and kept in touch thereafter. He kept a diary, which, as his executor, I have been able to draw upon, although much of what follows is derived from my memory of what, from time to time, he told me himself. I have also consulted his children and grandchildren and shown them the proofs. They have raised no objections: indeed, they encouraged me to continue.

Life, as Henry Fielding observed at greater length, consists of tame periods interspersed with events. So, wryly entertained, as one should be, at least in retrospect, by the vagaries of fortune, I have taken experiences from David's life that I hope may amuse and perhaps instruct, and with some essential use of my own imagination within the bounds of facts, I offer these episodes as what might be described as "Images in an Interval", derived from George Santayana's profound aphorism: "There is no cure for birth nor death save to enjoy the interval". On the whole, I am persuaded that David enjoyed his.

CHAPTER 1

"As I was a pleasurin' my wife, as is my wont upon a Sunday arternoon, the accused put 'is 'ead in at the winder and says: 'Go it you old ram, go it!'"

FROM A REGIMENTAL SERGEANT MAJOR'S
EVIDENCE AT A COURT MARTIAL

It is a curious fact that one's distant memories are composed of clusters of pictures not unlike a series of strips of film recording pieces of life in clear though compacted form. Some of these can be drawn from the library of the brain as though they were thrown upon the screen of the inward eye as fresh and coloured as they were recorded, while others are blurred and faded, moving into that mysterious realm of the subconscious on their way, it must be presumed, to oblivion.

Everyone must be able to put together strips of this kind.

In David's case, some of the earliest had India as a background at a time when that fascinating land was one, its potentially fratricidal creeds tenuously controlled by a comparative handful of white men in the twilight of the British Empire. The Congress Party was shrill and active; and no doubt, there were many who foresaw what was to come about soon; though for him, a small English boy, all seemed very much as it must have done to several generations of children before him.

The Indian servants were many, and since Indians are very fond of children, who in turn respond with friendship and affection, he spent a good deal of time with them. Since he was the son of a Sahib they called him Chota Sahib, which means very roughly, little person of importance, and he accepted the epithet without consideration. The very young do accept such things at their face value in a world that seems at first sight both new and simple.

One afternoon David was sitting with a small friend called Terence under a brilliant sky, a sky that is blue as blue where you can look at it, but colourlessly bright towards the unbeholden sun that blazes down with astounding heat upon a brown and olive landscape. Behind them stood the small blue and white painted club house built for Europeans to change in for swimming in the creek that lay before them curving away to the Indian Ocean beyond their sight. Duckboards ran from the club house past them across the stony ground to a retaining wall of old railway sleepers. For a short stretch these divided the land from the water, which lapped softly against them, except when a daily steamboat passed and the waves from its rusty prow approached in a series of smooth lines that slapped and sucked at the blackened timbers causing the strands of deep green seaweed to toss and twist just beneath the surface. Not far out in the creek lay a raft, floating upon empty oil barrels, whose rusty brown matched the covering of coconut matting above. Against this sombre colour a life belt hung, long disused but significant owing to its whiteness. Some way out beyond the raft an Indian fishing boat was sailing slowly in from the direction of the sea, its elementary sail bulging and subsiding in a gusty breeze.

The two boys sat with their white topees protecting their small heads from the beating strength of the afternoon sun, examining an onion. It was Terence who had found it and it interested them because it was the first raw onion that either of them had seen.

"I think the brown part must be skin," said David.

Terence picked at it and it came off quite easily in light flakes disclosing what appeared to be another thicker white skin beneath. He picked this off too, pulling off another piece under it as he did so.

"That's another skin."

He peeled once more.

"I wonder when you get to the bit you eat?"

Terence said: "Isn't it funny how it stings your eyes!"

Their early and perhaps symbolic research was cut short by voices raised behind them. They turned to see everybody upon the verandah of the club house standing and gazing across the creek. Forgetting their onion, now no bigger than a marble, they stood up and looked in the same direction.

At first it seemed to them that all was as it had been before. There lay the brown ochre raft, lifting and sinking with the slight movement of the water and across on the opposite side of the creek lay the grey mudflats, backed by darker scrub and stunted trees with purple shadows. Then they saw that the Indian fishing boat looked different. No longer did it stand out with its sail silhouetted against the background of water the far bank and the sky: it now lay with the sail flat in the water and the black hull of the boat itself reared up in a dark curve. They thought they could hear high pitched cries from its direction, though it was difficult to tell at that distance with the increasing noise behind and around them; for, as always in India, people were gathering quickly. They formed brown-skinned, white-clothed groups, pointing and chattering.

Abruptly an authoritative voice spoke in English from the verandah.

"George, you are a strong swimmer: go straight out; and Eric and I will follow with the lifebelt."

There was a flurry as men took off their outer clothing and shoes, and a moment later the three were in the water striking out across the creek towards the sinking boat, two of them spending a short time at the raft unhooking the lifebelt which they then pushed before them while the other, unencumbered, moved steadily away from them.

David and Terence stood stock still as, enthralled, they watched the unfolding scene.

When the first swimmer was half way to the boat it disappeared, its mast rearing up out of the water for several seconds.

At that a hush fell upon the watchers, followed by cries of "Ahee! Ahee!" from the Indians and rapid chatter.

Several blobs were floating on the water where the boat had gone down, though whether they were heads of men or just floating objects they could not tell from such a distance.

The first swimmer reached the scene and seemed to splash about a great deal while the two with the lifebelt made slow progress towards him. One of the two left the other still pushing it and swam ahead. Shortly after, all came together again and slowly headed back towards the boys. As they drew nearer it could be seen that with the aid of the lifebelt the three white men were bringing back a limp dark form with black hair.

At this, to the two boys the most important point, they were hustled away by their mothers and put into the hands of their *ayahs* with instructions that they were to be taken away in spite of their heartfelt protests.

"Do you think that Indian was dead?" David asked Terence. The possibility was fascinating, though it gave him a queer feeling in his stomach.

"Dead as mutton I should say."

This reply impressed David, though the other boy's *ayah*, who was larger and more formidable than David's, chided him.

"That is no means a good way to speak, Chota Sahib."

"Do you think he was dead?" David asked his *ayah*, looking up into her wrinkled brown face framed within the usual white chudder.

"That is highly unlikely: the three Sahibs will have surely saved him, and thereby will have achieved much merit." Her sing-song voice was gentler though unconvincing. But David knew from experience that it would be useless to pursue his enquiries further with her.

They walked along the dusty road that flung the heat of the sun back up the body. On their right lay a large area of flat stony ground, on the far side of which lay the race course. On their left there was a ditch backed by a mud wall and an occasional stunted tree. From time to time, as they walked, they passed an opening with a driveway leading through it over a large drain pipe for water to pass through during the rainy season. These driveways led into compounds in front of bungalows occupied by Europeans. Each bungalow was fronted with a verandah with steps leading up in the middle. Here and there attempts had been made to grow a few flowers, whose colours were pitifully bleached by the sun.

At that time of day there was not much sign of life. A rough wooden cart creaked slowly by, its driver half asleep behind two ponderous, bony, cream-coloured bullocks. A dog sniffed enthusiastically at some fly-thick rubbish, retreating quickly, tail tightly tucked between its legs as they approached, returning furtively when they had passed. Beneath the shade of an ancient fig tree an old Indian sat cross-legged, wearing a *dhoti*, his long grey hair mingling with his beard. His eyes were shut and his skinny hands were folded in front of him. A kite wheeled slowly overhead. There was a brooding stillness and the slapping of the *ayahs'* sandals on the road seemed magnified.

When they came to a place where another road led off to the left towards where David lived, the two *ayahs* bade each other goodbye and Terence turned along it with his, while David's took him straight on towards the military cantonment. There was plenty of time left before they had to return home and David realised that she had decided to go onto Sergeant Major Stoner's bungalow, where one of her numerous relatives worked. It may have been her daughter – David never asked – but she often went there to sit and gossip while he was left to amuse himself as best he could.

At the beginning he had been dreadfully bored. Mrs Stoner was kind in a vague sort of way, but had not the least idea how to amuse a small boy. She was a slight pale woman with fading, reddish-blond hair always tied neatly in a bun at the back of her head. She seemed to spend most of her time sewing with the aid of a Singer hand-operated sewing machine or sitting talking to other soldiers' wives.

There were two daughters. Irene was nearly two years older than

David, and since that is a considerable difference when one is very young, she treated him with crushing superiority. The other, Madge, was much younger and her interest in dolls was not one that he could share.

But everything changed during one of these visits when the Sergeant Major himself returned.

On that particular afternoon Irene was reading a book in the shade of the verandah and Madge was in bed owing to some minor illness, while David was engaged in forming a miniature landscape in the front compound, smoothing the roads with a small piece of board, when the Sergeant Major walked briskly through the entrance of the compound.

David stopped his work in a kneeling position to look at him.

His first overriding impression was of the Sergeant Major's extraordinary smartness. From the top of his military cap to his gleaming boots he looked as if he had been taken from a mould and polished. He walked rapidly across the compound towards David with a shining silver-topped black stick under his arm, and as he drew near David saw that he had a black moustache neatly pointed at both ends above firm lips and a strong chin with a cleft in it. Piercing blue eyes beneath black eyebrows were set in a face that was brown and finely lined like leather.

He stopped sharply in front of David, his boots coming together with a click, and for a moment looked him up and down. David was oddly aware that his hands and knees were grubby. Then the Sergeant Major spoke and his voice was as crisp as his bearing.

"And you must be Master David Drummond."

David was not a naturally shy boy, but he felt awed and very small. He stood up saying: "Yes, Sir."

The Sergeant Major's eyes left him to inspect his recent handiwork in the dust and stones.

"If you 'ad some toy soldiers you could make 'em march up that road. 'Ave you got any?"

"Yes, Sir; twenty-four infantry and eight cavalry." It pleased David to be able to acknowledge ownership of such a considerable army.

"That's good. 'Ave you got a band?"

"No." David was crestfallen to have to admit to the deficiency, not considered before.

"You ought to 'ave a band." The Sergeant Major's leathery face creased into a warm smile. "Armies need bands." And he turned away as abruptly as he had arrived, quickly mounted the steps of the verandah and disappeared into the bungalow.

David did not realise it then, but that was to be the beginning of a relationship that quickly turned the boredom of visits to the Sergeant Major's bungalow to pleasure and interest. For, behind a stiff military exterior the man had a kind heart and it was probable that he wished he had a son of his own. In any event, he was very kind to David, whose initial awe soon altered to feelings of admiration and affection. He came to look forward to the times that his *ayah* decided to visit the bungalow in spite of the fact that the Sergeant Major was often away, for he was content to barter the periods of boredom in his absence for the times that he was there.

David learnt much from him: simple things of course because he was so young, and doubtless much that he was told went over his head, particularly when the Sergeant Major spoke of the Great War so recently ended.

The two of them would sit in the comparative cool of the verandah, the Sergeant Major upon a cane chair smoking a pipe, while David perched upon a wooden-legged, cane-topped stool. Occasionally the Sergeant Major would stand up, as for instance when he taught David to slope and order arms, using a walking stick taken from a polished brass shell case in the entrance lobby. Several times he brought out a real Lee-Enfield rifle in order to explain its working and how it should be cleaned, questioning the boy afterwards about the names of the parts and showing pleasure at his interest and answers when they were correct.

When he talked of the Great War he mentioned places in France such as Loos, Wypers and Vimy Ridge. David was much impressed by his description of tunnelling at the Ridge to lay mines beneath the German trenches and how, in order to escape the boredom and danger of the front line trench, he had volunteered to be in a digging party, which had taken a tunnel three-quarters of the way to completion before relief by another battalion took him out of the line: and how he had heard that the next day the Germans had blown up the tunnel by means of a counter mine, killing all the new party of diggers in it.

"I bore a charmed life," he said. "Even at the battle of the Somme, where a fine new army was thrown away and my battalion went in with over seven hundred men and came out with forty-four, I was 'it early on and got back to 'ospital quicker than most."

He produced an ugly jagged piece of metal that had been cut out of his shoulder and David began to understand what an exploding shell could do.

"The 'Igh Command didn't seem to understand the power of the machine gun, the condition of the ground and 'ow good a soldier the

Bosch is," he said. "Twas a war to end all wars, sonny, and I 'ope you'll never live to see the like of it."

Sometimes he talked of India. "They're a right mixed lot," he said, "and such a tangle of religions and castes that it's beyond the wit of man to sort it all out." Then, unconsciously prophetic: "There'll be the very devil of a blood bath if ever we go and leave 'em to it."

One day he asked David if he would like to go out with a Corporal who had been ordered to shoot a dog suspected of rabies. David agreed without showing hesitation because the proposal was made in the obvious belief that it would be a treat. Yet, the prospect of seeing a dog killed seriously worried him. They had a dog at home and David loved him. Nevertheless, he would never have admitted this to anyone and it is unlikely that the Sergeant Major suspected his intense apprehension as he introduced him to Corporal Trumper when the morning came.

Corporal Trumper was a tall, craggy soldier and a man of few words. Probably he was disgruntled at being saddled with a small boy. At the back of his head and beneath his cap between neat small ears, closely cropped fair hair showed, whilst the hair on his deeply tanned arms was almost white.

He told David to walk beside him on his left and to remain there. Although he probably kept his pace slow for his small charge, his long legs made it difficult for David to keep up with him as they made straight across open, stony ground in a direction that David knew led towards the sea: he obviously knew exactly where he was going.

The heat of the morning sun beat upon their backs while a warm sea breeze lightly fanned their faces.

After a time they passed an Indian working a small area of poor ground with a bullock and rudimentary agricultural instrument, and soon after a group of English on horses trotted by. They reached a cluster of brick and mud block buildings where white-clothed Indian women and for the most part naked small children were moving about. As they passed this settlement the familiar mixture of smells registered; a combination of curry, straw, goat and dung. Beyond was a small rocky hillock, which they climbed, and at the top Corporal Trumper stopped, arresting David with his left hand. He said nothing, and looking up at his bony face David saw that he was carefully examining the broken arid ground beyond, which sloped gently down towards grey mudflats and an inlet from the sea, the water gleaming in the bright sunlight. David could see no movement except for some sea birds on the mudflats. Away to the right was the creek and the town, while to the left the land undulated gently towards a line of sand dunes, on the other side of which was the open sea.

They remained like that for several minutes. Behind them the sound of the Indian women's voices mingled with the still higher pitched cries of the children, the bleat of a tethered goat and the creaking of some wooden instrument in use; and in front David could just detect the low roar of the surf as the Indian Ocean beat upon the invisible shore, above which the discordant cries of the sea birds formed a kind of descant.

Until, from behind a rock a couple of hundred yards in front, a small white dog appeared, its head turned sharply towards them, slinking away to the right. It seemed rather a nice little dog.

Instantly, though cautiously, Corporal Trumper placed his left foot forward and brought his rifle up to the aim. The dog moved slowly on, watching them intently all the time, ready to move off at full speed if they moved, supposing no doubt that it was safe at such a distance, far beyond the range of the familiar thrown stones. For a breathless moment David fervently wished he could warn the small animal which looked so harmless. If only he could have explained to it how important it was to remain behind that rock!

There was a violent explosion above and beside him – far louder than he had anticipated – and at the same moment the animal was hurled over and over, before with a few jerks of its hind legs it lay quite motionless upon the ground. Behind them the noises ceased abruptly, in contrast with the sea birds in front which rose into the air with raucous cries.

"That's it," said the Corporal, ejecting the spent cartridge and lowering his rifle.

The brass-coloured cartridge case glittered at his feet amongst the stones, as still as the small white and brown form in front of them. Each for a moment in time had been mysteriously linked and both were now dead; discarded.

The Corporal turned to leave, slinging his rifle.

"Can I go and look at it?" David asked diffidently.

The Corporal hesitated, probably anxious to return: then nodded.

"Don't touch it," he said.

The little dog lay on its side with legs extended, and David would have thought it asleep but for what he had just witnessed and its glazed open eyes. Its mouth was open and tongue slightly out. It was some sort of mongrel smooth-haired terrier. Just behind its shoulder was a small red hole.

Not long after, David's parents told him they were all returning to England for a holiday. His father was entitled to several months' leave to return there every three years, for in those days the journey was by sea and took three to four weeks. This time David was to be left behind at the end of the holiday in order to attend a boarding school.

When David told the Sergeant Major this he nodded and said it was a good thing that he should be educated. "And you'll see a bit of good old green England," he added. He pulled at his pipe, reflecting for a moment. Then he said: "I'll 'ave to teach you 'ow to box."

And sure enough, at David's next visit he produced two pairs of boxing gloves. David's pair were too big for his small fists, but he explained that they would do for a start. Then, kneeling upon a cushion, he proceeded to initiate David into the secrets of what he called "The noble art of self defence."

He raised his right arm in front of him, the forearm vertical, with his gloved fist at the top.

"Now," he said, "'ere is your opponent. See 'ow you can 'it 'im. No, not like that, sonny; if you stand like that and 'e 'its you, which 'e will do very quickly, seeing as 'ow you 'ave no defence and no balance, you'll be down on your back on the spot. Turn so that your left shoulder is towards your opponent and your right is away from 'im. Raise your left glove a bit forward and keep your right one tucked close to your mouth: that's your defences as well as your 'eavy artillery."

He stood up and demonstrated what he was saying.

"Keep on your toes like this and keep on banging away with that left glove of yours for a start."

He resumed his kneeling position and David did what he had been told while the Sergeant Major moved his right arm and glove about to make a moving target.

When he was satisfied with this he dropped his arm for a moment and said: "But you 'ave to remember your opponent is trying to 'it you too; so keep that right glove of yours ready to parry 'is blows with your right elbow tucked into your body to protect your belly. I'll use my left 'and 'ere to represent your opponent's left. Box on."

Within a few seconds David found himself sitting on the ground.

"There, you see, you weren't watching out, you were flat footed and you lowered that right of yours. Up you get now and keep a sharp look out."

And so the lesson went on until the Sergeant Major was satisfied that he had started David on the right lines.

The last time his *ayah* took David to the bungalow the monsoon was approaching and it was hotter that ever with a stillness in the heavy atmosphere. The exhausting heat was everywhere; in the shade and inside dwellings even with all doors and windows open and with fans whirring. There was no one on the verandah and they went as usual round to the kitchen at the back, where his *ayah's* kinswoman was sitting with the cook and *chokra* in the shade of the building, facing across the small rear compound of stony gravel to a mud wall boundary overhung at one corner by a tree growing in an adjoining compound.

Leaving them to gossip, David entered through the kitchen as was his custom when there was no one in the front of the bungalow.

From the kitchen he entered the dining room through a lobby and passed through an arched opening into the front hall, where a door on his right led to the sitting room and another on his left opened into a dark passage with the bedrooms and bathroom off it.

As soon as David was in the front hall he heard voices in the sitting room, where Mrs Stoner was entertaining two other women to afternoon tea. She was sitting facing the open door and saw him.

"Ah!" she exclaimed, "so you've come round this afternoon, Dave."

She and the two girls always called him Dave, though everyone else he knew called him David.

"Irene and Madge are playing in one of their rooms. Run along and join them. The Sergeant Major is out this afternoon."

Disappointed, he turned and went through the opposite open doorway, past the open door to a dressing room down the passage to Irene's room, where he found her with her sister.

Immediately, she proposed they should play a game of make believe.

"Not hospitals," said David emphatically. They had played at hospitals once before when Irene had been a surgeon intent upon taking our her sister's appendix, while David was appointed "the man who 'as to give the chloroform" with a brown lamp shade as his implement, which he had applied so diligently that Madge had taken fright and cried noisily.

"No, we'll play at getting married. You and Madge'll get married and I'll be the Padre."

Though not enthusiastic, this seemed innocuous enough, and David agreed.

But Irene's imagination and latent talent as a director dragged the proceedings out dreadfully, and after the intensely boring marriage ceremony a new scene had to be enacted in which Madge and David had to get on the bed together. David accepted this without demur knowing that married people slept in the same bed, though he flatly refused to take off his clothes in spite of Irene's crossness. And so the game dragged on under the control of Irene's dominant personality, until to David's alarm it seemed the wheel had come round full circle and they were back in hospital again where Madge was to have a baby. The argument that ensued was brought to an end by the arrival of David's *ayah* with the good news that it was time to return home and David eagerly went with her.

About a week after that David realised that the journey to England was to start in a few days' time and that there would be no more visits to the Sergeant Major's bungalow. It did not occur to him that he might never see him again, but he did wish he could have said goodbye.

The next day a brown paper parcel was brought to his home. It was rectangular and flat, and on the brown paper covering was written in capital letters: MASTER DAVID DRUMMOND. David's mother undid the string for him and he took off the brown paper. Inside was a sheet of white paper and a flat cardboard box. His mother read out the words written on the piece of paper. They were: "Dear David, I am sorry I was on parade when you came round the other day as I would have liked to have seen you before you leave and to give you this small token of friendship. Mrs Stoner and our girls join me in wishing you the best of luck. We may meet again. It's a small world. Remember to keep that guard up. Your old friend RSM Stoner."

Inside the box was a military band of lead soldiers.

That afternoon David's parents were invited to a farewell lunch by business friends and he was to go with them. There were two boys of about his age in this family and when lunch was over the three of them were sent out into the back compound to play while the grown-ups sat on the front verandah smoking and talking in the shade.

There happened to be quite a well grown tree in the corner of the compound and in a very short time they were scrambling about in it like monkeys. One branch reached out over a point where four boundary walls joined in the form of a cross, and it was while David was resting on this branch that he suddenly noticed that the back compound whose corner was diagonally opposite the one they were in was that of RSM Stoner. Young children do not have much sense of direction and he had not realised that he had just lunched in a house that lay behind that of his old friend.

His mother had talked of helping him to write a letter of thanks to the Sergeant Major, but it immediately occurred to him that here was a

20

golden opportunity to pay him a visit and thank him personally while saying goodbye. So he slid down the wall into the back compound and walked across the familiar stony earth to the back door.

It did not occur to David to try to enter by the front door: he had often done so by the back. Rather to his surprise the door was locked, but he assumed the servants had done this when going out since there was no sign of them. Indeed there was no sign of life at all.

Once before the back door had been locked and Irene had shown him how to climb through one of the kitchen windows by way of a low brick bunker and he now scrambled through in the same way. Inside the kitchen he was again struck by the quietness and began to wonder whether the whole household was out. He opened the door to the lobby and walked into the dining room. Still not a sound. He went on slowly across the dining room to the front hall while his eyes grew accustomed to the comparative darkness after the glare outside. There was no one in the sitting room, so he went into the passage opposite to see whether the girls were in. At least they would be able to tell him whether their father was out and if so when he was likely to be back. He stood still to listen just opposite the partly open door of the dressing room, and as he did so he distinctly heard a faint moaning sound coming from the other side of the door. It was a sepulchral sound and made his mouth go dry and the hairs at the back of his neck prickle as with pounding heart he looked cautiously round the door into the dressing room. Inside it was even darker than in the passage owing to thick curtains drawn across the only window opposite; but he could see enough to make out that no one was lying on the floor near death as he had anticipated. It was clear that the sound he had heard came from the bedroom through an opening in the right hand wall, across which a bead curtain was drawn. The moaning noise had now stopped and was replaced by a creaking sound. Filled with fear and curiosity he moved carefully to the bead curtain and looked through.

The bedroom beyond was lighter than the dressing room because the drawn curtains were of a thinner material. These curtains were green in colour with the result that the room was bathed in an eerie green light, as though looking into an under water cave. He glimpsed the dark shadows of several pieces of furniture round that part of the room in his view, though these made only a slight impression because of what lay almost immediately in front of him: for there was a double bed standing out from the left hand wall with its bed cover thrown back over the foot board, and on this bed lay a thing that turned his dread to terror.

21

It was a hideous creature of some kind, palely green with a very large head and four legs that writhed slowly like tentacles.

Our experience of time is relative, and this first fearful impression as David stood rooted to the spot just behind the bead curtain seemed to last much longer than the mere part of a second that it took him to understand that what he really saw were two naked grown-ups in close embrace.

The one underneath lay with thighs splayed and feet over the other's legs, the knees moving in time with the rhythmic rise and fall of the haunches of the one on top.

Instinctively he felt that it must be the Sergeant Major and his wife, and indeed he could recognise the latter's profile above her hair scattered upon the pillow, though the Sergeant Major's face was hidden, leaving only the back of his head in sight.

In an instant David's sensation of terror turned to a mixture of bewilderment, revulsion and disenchantment. What he saw was quite beyond his comprehension, but one thing was clear and that was that he had no business to be where he was. This was a grown-up phenomenon and he had to get away as quickly as possible without being discovered.

He had no recollection of his return journey to his parents, whom he found still sitting on the verandah with their friends, for his mind was in a turmoil. Nor could he recall the last few days before they were on a boat on their way to England. During that period all his thoughts revolved round the astonishing scene he had intruded upon in the Sergeant Major's bedroom. No doubt he should have confided in his mother, who could have reassured him, but a feeling of guilt and fear that he would be giving away a terrible secret about his friend prevented him. He must have seemed unusually quiet and subdued and remembered his mother's concern that he might be sickening for something. However, no one had much time for him owing to the packing and other preparations for the forthcoming voyage, and in the general hustle-bustle the letter of thanks to the Sergeant Major was forgotten. Later, when David was older, he much regretted this omission because he never saw him again and felt sure he must have been disappointed not to receive one word of thanks.

Of course, with the natural resilience of the young and with new interests his preoccupation with the amazing scene he had so briefly witnessed faded. Yet, for a long time after, when his thoughts were free of other matters, it floated back into his mind and he puzzled over what it might mean.

Above all, the mystery was confounded by his recollection of the back of the head of the man on top of Mrs Stoner, for the Sergeant Major was bald ánd the hair that he still possessed was black, while the head that he had seen was not bald and the hair was fair; very much like Corporal Trumper's.

CHAPTER 2

"My salad days, when I was green in judgement:
cold in blood, to say as I said then!"

SHAKESPEARE

In this world, into which we are brought without – as far as we can tell – our consent, yet, for the most part leave with reluctance, it is one of many disagreeable facts that quite minor errors of judgement can lead to awful consequences. Sometimes it seems that a chance and ill considered remark acts like a detonator, setting off a catastrophic explosion of unhappy experiences. I dare say that everyone can recall lessons of this nature.

Probably, David's first experience of this particular manifestation of the unhappy side of life was curiously, though directly, owing to his early upbringing in India.

In those days, soon after the first world war, white children in India were sent home to England by their parents or guardians at the age of about eight to go to boarding schools.

It was a serious separation dreaded by parents because it was for such long periods. There was no network of commercial airlines: instead, long distance travel was conducted by coal-fired liners; and since the journey from India to England took about three weeks there was no question of the children returning to India for their holidays, while those fathers like David's who were in business were only granted holidays in England once every three years. Thus, when David was left at a boarding school for his first winter term he would not see his parents again for three years, spending holidays during that period with relations and, perhaps, at the homes of school friends.

On the whole, I think, the children did not share the desolation of their parents, partly because a parting of three years is beyond the understanding of small children and partly because they simply had no idea what they were in for. Certainly, David experienced no dismay when his family returned to England for one of his father's triennial holidays with the knowledge that at the end of it he would be left at a Preparatory School where all the boys were boarders.

Perhaps this approach to such a new experience was due to the sense of pride and confidence he possessed in everything to do with England, which he regarded, in his innocence, as the home of everything that was superior and good. Indeed, everything he was taught and experienced led him to this belief, not least the attitude of the Indian servants, who in their own proud and dignified way treated him with affectionate respect as a 'Chota Sahib', the son of a 'Sahib'.

Before they returned to India David's parents took him in the train from Paddington station to the small town outside London where stood the school they had chosen for him.

Their taxi from the station wended its way through to its outskirts before entering the school drive lined with tall elms and dark green laurel bushes, sombre in the grey autumn afternoon, and deposited them with David's brown trunk and new wooden 'tuckbox' at the virginia creeper-clad front of the school building. The front door was opened to them by a maid in a white and brown uniform, who showed them in to the Private Side drawing room, where the headmaster and his wife were entertaining the parents of new boys to tea.

And what a tea it was! There was hot buttered toast soggy with butter; there were soft fresh buttered currant buns; there were several kinds of sandwich, amongst which David recalled in particular the very thinly cut brown bread and cucumber ones; there were sumptuous cakes and buttered scones filled with thick honey.

It might have been and probably was designed to distract the attention of small boys from the impending parting and entry into a new strange world. If so, it succeeded, and David together with the other new boys temporarily ignored the future to take advantage of the present while their parents chattered above them until a bell rang somewhere within the school and there was a general move to the door.

Outside it was cold and a thin rain was falling as, suddenly filled with a hitherto unknown sensation of apprehension, David bade his parents goodbye. His mother's voice was husky and his father was unnaturally hearty. Then they were in a taxi which absorbed and removed them from him even before it disappeared up the drive.

A small forlorn figure in his tweed coat and shorts, David turned and entered his new world.

This world proved to be very different from his limited expectations, and for the first few nights his pillow was wet with tears. However, most young children are able to adapt to new circumstances quickly and David was no exception.

The headmaster, though unanswerably authoritative, was fair, while his wife was aloofly motherly, and the masters in their various ways kindly. In particular, as the term went on, Mr Deedes, the junior games master, who also taught mathematics, became very friendly and helpful. He would go round the class while David and his fellows struggled with their simple sums and sit down with them in turn explaining and encouraging. He would sit very close, smelling of tweed and tobacco, and it was very confidential and encouraging. David liked him in particular.

After about six weeks of the term had passed Mr Deedes took him aside after an afternoon session of rugby football one Wednesday and complimented him on his progress, adding that it was apparent that he showed considerable aptitude for the game, which Mr Deedes sincerely believed to be the finest game in the world. Then he went on to say that it was his aim to give all the help in his power to young aspirants who showed keenness and promise.

"From time to time," he went on, putting his hand on David's shoulder as they walked back towards the school across the playing field, "I pick out a boy I believe will benefit, and give him individual instruction. You see, there is a lot of theory involved in this remarkable game and the sooner young players with obvious talent start to get a grasp on it the more splendid their rugby prospects become. To this end I have made a collection of diagrams and photographs, which are most helpful in illustrating the finer points of the game, and I believe you deserve to have these shown and explained to you. As I have said, this is a privilege I only grant to special boys, and for that reason I must particularly ask you not to talk about it to anyone else. Will you promise me that?" And he squeezed David's shoulder in a conspiratorial manner.

David was flattered and interested. "Yes sir," he said.

"Splendid! Then we will make a start next Sunday after morning chapel. Meet me in the changing room."

"But the changing room is out of bounds then, sir."

"Not if you are with a master; and it has the advantage of privacy."

"David was much excited and proud to be singled out in this fashion and almost immediately broke his promise to Mr Deedes when he told his friend, Baker, what had passed between them, though he did so on the understanding that he told no one else.

Baker, who had been at the school for two terms already, was impressed and told David that he had heard rumours of another boy who had been similarly privileged.

The following afternoon David changed for games with a feeling of elation before going to the boot room where the boys put on their playing boots. This was a small square room with boot lockers on two opposite walls that smelt strongly of leather, floor polish and wet clothes. At the opening between this room and the adjoining changing room was a step frequently used by senior boys as a seat while putting on their boots, and at this opening David was confronted with a problem: a barrier of backs in blue and white jerseys blocked his way. There was the usual hub-hub of conversation and he was unnoticed. He stood for a while undecided what to do. He could not very well push through without appearing rude and the row of backs seemed huge, for to a child of eight boys aged twelve and thirteen are near to grown-ups. Something had to be said.

Selecting the two middle backs he spoke.

"Please make way for a fat little Sahib," he said.

Later, as he matured, he appreciated that this was a pompous and unlikely thing for a small boy to say, though at the time it seemed both friendly and polite. It was certainly a mistake.

Two severe faces turned up at him and they belonged to Jules and Rathbone, the two least sympathetic prefects in the school.

"What beastly cheek," said Jules.

"Come and see me afterwards," said Rathbone.

These ominous words and the plunge from a general feeling of content into one of shocked alarm left David speechless. What had gone wrong? Why was his most reasonable request regarded as cheek? What would happen? These questions revolved ceaselessly in his anxious mind all through the games period, through the "little tea" that followed and the evening lessons after that; for it was not until the evening free period that he could make his unwilling report to Rathbone.

He found him in the passage that led from the main entrance hall right through to the door leading to the main playing field. Although big to David, Rathbone was rather a small boy for his age and distinctly tubby. He had tow-coloured hair which tended to fall across his forehead and he wore glasses. His lips always seemed to be chapped.

"You told me to come and see you afterwards," David said diffidently.

Rathbone looked at him with evident dislike.

"You are a nasty cheeky new boy," he said, "and cheek to prefects is serious."

"But I didn't mean to be cheeky."

"If you don't know that calling a prefect a fat little slab isn't cheek you will have to learn that it is, and I intend to see that you do."

The implications of this shocking statement left David weak with dread and alarm. For a few seconds he felt an odd feeling of dizziness before he blurted out: "I didn't say that."

"It's no use lying too: Jules heard you say it as well."

"But I didn't say it," said David weakly.

"I'm going to take you to the Headmaster who will probably beat you, which is exactly what you deserve. I haven't time now. Come and see me during first break tomorrow."

He turned and went through the door into the top form classroom.

As for David, he hardly knew what he was doing for the rest of that evening and lay in bed for a long time before sleep gave temporary respite to his whirling mind.

Everyone must know what it is to wake to unresolved trouble and will therefore understand David's horrible sensation the next morning. It was not just that he was extremely frightened: no one had been caned during the six weeks he had been at the school, but other boys had told him of the experience and the red and blue bruise stripes across the buttocks observable in the bathroom afterwards: it was also the anticipated shame. And what would his parents think when they learnt that he had got into such serious trouble so early in his school career? His mother would be anxious and unhappy and his father disappointed. The more he thought about it, and he could think of nothing else, the more awful it all was. It never occurred to him that the Headmaster might not beat him: a beating seemed inevitable. At breakfast he felt slightly sick and ate little. Baker and the other boys near him at the table must have thought him strangely silent for he was normally a talkative little boy.

After the meal he found Rathbone waiting for him in the hall. David felt ghastly. The staircase up to the first floor led up from the hall and at the top was a landing from which one approached the panelled door of the Headmaster's study. In his imagination David felt himself climbing up those steps behind Rathbone, heard the knock at that door, felt himself be led into the study, listened to the prefect's report of his heinous crime and pictured the grim look on the Headmaster's face as he took a cane from some cupboard. After that there was a kind of blur involving bending over the arm of a sofa, the swishing of the cane and unimaginable pain.

Rathbone peered at him through his glasses: his chapped upper lip seemed to have no edge.

"Both Jules and I are going to take you to the Headmaster and Jules is busy at the moment; so meet us both here this evening after prep."

David's feeling of relief was rapidly followed by the appalling realisation that a whole day of fearful anticipation lay before him; and during morning lessons his trouble was accentuated by rebukes from masters over his lack of attention.

To the young the passing of time can seem interminable, and by lunch David had reached the desperate conclusion that he could not stand the wait until the evening: somehow this dreadful misery must be brought to an end before that. He decided that he must go to the Headmaster as soon as lunch was over, confess his crime for which he was truly sorry, and get the beating over.

Accordingly, he climbed the stairs with wildly beating heart and knocked on the door of the Headmaster's study. No sound came from within and after a pause he knocked more loudly. Still no response: the Headmaster was not in. After steeling himself to take this step it was a new blow and for a time he stood there, a picture of misery, wondering what to do next. After a minute or so one of the matrons, a middle-aged, kindly woman in a uniform of blue and white, which always looked most stiffly starched, passed by. She gave him a smile but said nothing, thinking no doubt that he had been told to wait outside the study for some reason. More time went by and the changing for games bell rang. It was no good: he had to give up.

During the games period he thought of telling all to Mr Deedes, but an opportunity did not occur and it was then that he decided to go to his aunt Emily for help and advice. She lived in London and had always been very kind and understanding. He was sure he could rely on her. London could not be far away since the journey by train had seemed so short, and once there someone would be able to tell him where she lived. The more he thought about it the better this solution to his trouble appeared to be. He thought he had a rough idea where the station near the school was, and from there he could follow the railway line to London.

While, in his ignorance, the journey by foot to London seemed a fairly simple matter the problem of escape from the school itself appeared a major one; yet, as things turned out, this was to prove the exact inverse of reality.

When "little tea" was over he entered one of the cubicles in the lavatories and waited for the bell to ring for evening lessons. Within a few minutes the clamour of movement to the various classrooms ceased and he ventured out into the main passage that led from the front hall where the boys' overcoats and school caps hung, communicating at the other end with a swing door leading to the back of the building.

All was very quiet in contrast to the preceding din, and the drone of the master's voices within the classrooms was all that he could hear. He seemed to have moved from one world into another.

He crept down the passage and cautiously took his overcoat off its hook: he had been long enough in England now to understand the cold of late autumn. He did not take his cap: that seemed superfluous. Then he tiptoed back up the passage to the back door, opened it gently and went through. Outside it was already getting dark, the sky being overcast, and he was glad to get into the overcoat as he hesitated a moment in the chilly early evening before crossing the gravel playground to the boundary hedge that led behind a wooden carpenter's shop and rifle range up the side of a playing field to the road. Furtively, he hurried along this hedge and at the end he stopped to look back at the school buildings, half expecting to see signs already of alarm at his disappearance; but all remained quiet and undisturbed. Lights shone through the classroom windows and it was possible to detect the heads of boys at their desks.

He scrambled through the laurels and stepped onto the pavement of the road leading into the town.

It was a melancholy evening in keeping with his circumstances. The trees were bare and their branches were dark against the grey sky: some of their leaves remained along the side of the pavement where they had fallen and not yet cleared away. No one was in sight.

David started to walk quickly towards the town and soon reached a dip where a railway bridge crossed the road. Painted upon its metal side he was able to discern the white letters "Dead Slow", large and ominous in the dim light. Why dead? he wondered, before passing under it. He saw a lamp lighter at work with his ladder lighting the street gas lamps. David eyed the man anxiously, but he did not appear to notice him at all, which gave him confidence.

The street led on towards the centre of the town and now there were a few people about. A bus went by. While the sky grew steadily darker the lamps and shop windows seemed to grow brighter. The shops were beginning to line both sides of the street and there were a few side roads. To David's great relief no one took any more notice of him than the lamp lighter; but he became aware of a new problem: he was uncertain how to find the railway station. Not unnaturally he had not attempted to remember the way six weeks before when he had first made the journey in the opposite direction with his parents. He knew that he could ask someone the way, yet he dared not, for he felt the guilt of the fugitive who fears suspicion everywhere.

When he arrived at a main crossroads he stopped. The shop windows here were larger and the buildings higher. This might be the centre of the town and there was nothing to help him decide which road to take. Time was passing and a feeling of panic began to grow in him. He crossed to the street opposite and stopped again. For the first time he began to wonder whether he had made a mistake in leaving the school. This solution had seemed such a good one during the afternoon and already it was becoming plain that the difficulties were far greater than he had assumed. But he was certain he could not give up and go back.

Then he heard the unmistakable sound of a train pulling out of a station and it came from somewhere along the street to his right. Filled with new hope he set off in that direction and soon the road began to slope down and bend to the left leading to a railway bridge with the station set back to its right.

He had found the station, but there was a new problem. In which direction was London? He had no idea.

Desperately he entered the station building.

He found himself in a shabby hall, poorly lit by a single hissing gas mantel suspended from the dirty ceiling. On one side there was a door with "Waiting Room" written above it in what had once been white letters, while on the other side was a small opening with a counter, behind which David detected a man in a dark jacket. Opposite the entrance through which he had come was an opening that led onto the platform, and over this opening was fixed a large clock which showed the time to be twenty-five minutes past five. The time surprised him for it meant that only about half an hour had passed since he had left the school: it had seemed so much longer. His spirits rose a little.

On one side of the opening to the platform there was a board fixed to the wall with what was clearly information about train arrivals and departures on printed sheets. David approached this and studied it earnestly, but however much he tried he could not work out the vital information he needed. He would have to risk an enquiry employing cunning.

David went to the counter and addressed the man behind it. He had a beaky nose and blackheads.

"Can you tell me, please, which platform the next train from London comes into?"

The man looked up to see only a small nose, two eyes and a tousled head of hair above the counter. If he was surprised he did not show it, seemingly prepared for any eventuality.

"On t'other side, sonny," he said.

He looked sideways at the clock.

"Next one'll be the six four."

More than half an hour to wait! David moved away to the notice board and pretended to study it. In this way he was able to collect his thoughts and prepare himself for the next stage of his journey; but a delay of half an hour was worrying. He stole a glance towards the ticket counter and noticed that the man had moved away; so he went to a point near the entrance with his eyes on the small bit of platform he could see through the opening opposite him and the clock above.

The minute hand of this clock moved forward in jerks and seemed dreadfully slow: each time he waited for the next jerk forward he began to wonder whether the clock had stopped before it suddenly jerked on again. He longed to get on: any action was preferable to this anxious wait. Yet, there was nothing else that he could do.

The minute hand had reached thirty-two minutes past five when a man in uniform wearing a cap came from the platform and stood at the opening. At the same time David caught the sound of an approaching train which quickly increased to a rattling roar as the great engine crossed the opening followed by carriages, their brightly lit windows flashing past to begin with and then gradually slowing as the train drew up at the near platform.

This must be a train to London before the one travelling in the opposite direction due to arrive at the other platform at four minutes past six. Now David knew his direction and there was no time to be lost. With a huge sense of relief he slipped out of the entrance and set off in the same direction as the train.

Not many people try to follow a railway line from a station in a town. It is surprisingly difficult. The first problem is to get to the line.

David retraced his steps to where the railway bridge passed over the road near the station and found his way blocked by a line of houses which ran right up to the embankment. He walked under the bridge only to find the same obstacle. It was now quite dark and getting colder.

As he walked on he looked to his left for an opening that might lead him back to the line, and after a time he came across a small side road which he turned down. The houses with their short front gardens continued on either side. Then to his concern the road began to swing

32

away to the right. He had quite lost sight of the railway line. He wondered whether he should risk entering one of the front gardens and attempt to pass between two houses, hoping to reach the line through a back garden – providing the line was there. He had almost made up his mind to try this when he reached another road off to the left, which he hastened down. It was now so dark that he could not see what lay at the end of this road and when he reached the end it was a cul-de-sac!

That settled it! He would have to cut through this barrier of houses. Selecting the darkest corner, he climbed over a low crenelated brick wall onto a flower bed, crossed a short strip of lawn and came to a close boarded fence at the side of one of the houses with a similarly boarded door with a latch. This he very gently depressed as he pushed the door, which opened quite easily, although in spite of his care its creaking sounded piercing in the pervading quiet. He waited and listened for sounds of alarm, but silence filled the night once more. It was very dark beyond the door and he could see nothing except the shapes of the house walls on either side, which towered up in dim silhouette against an only slightly less black sky that showed no stars.

He went forward very slowly towards what he hoped was the back garden thinking that if he could get across that and over the fence at the end he might come nearer the line again. He was sure it was the right direction. As he moved along the side of the house he thought he could detect space that was less dark ahead and began to tiptoe towards this a little faster. It was a mistake. His foot struck something like a step and as he brought his other foot forward to recover his balance it landed fair and square amongst what may have been empty milk bottles. The din was appalling.

Throwing caution to the winds David flung himself forward into what indeed turned out to be a garden, and ran across what may have been a flower bed and a short stretch of lawn followed by soft, newly dug soil; perhaps a vegetable garden. On the other side of this a tall black obstacle caused him to stop before he realised it was a hedge of some kind and he threw himself down beneath it to crawl amongst weeds and fallen leaves through some thick stems to a position that he hoped was safe.

Almost immediately a light glimmered from whence he had run and he heard the voices of a man and a woman. They seemed to be inspecting the havoc he had caused by the back door. He could not hear clearly what they were saying because at this point it began to rain and the rattle of the raindrops on the hedge above him interfered with the sound. He thought he heard the word burglar and something about the police. Then he heard the voices grow fainter and the couple must have gone out of the door in the board fence he had come through and left open. Possibly they assumed the interloper had fled that way. Later, the voices grew louder again and he lay very still, conscious of his pounding heart. By now the rain was falling heavily and drips of water were reaching him.

Then he heard the train. It was approaching from the direction of his head where he lay and towards him. The sound grew in intensity and as it came by him with a roar and rattle he knew that the line was on the other side of the hedge he was lying under. Quickly taking advantage of the covering noise he scrambled towards it and found himself in long wet grass on the other side of the hedge at the bottom of a low embankment; the train was passing above, its lighted windows giving him a glimpse through the glittering rain of a line of hedges and fences to his right, parallel to the embankment with long grass and weeds stretching between.

It was time to get on fast and as soon as the train had passed he struck off in the direction from which it had come.

Though his eyes quickly adjusted to the dark and he could see enough to keep in the right direction, the grass and weeds through which he struggled were tall, concealing the ground beneath and he fell several times. It was also very wet and soon he was soaked to the skin with his overcoat sodden and very heavy. Worse still he was in danger of losing the thin house shoes that he had come out in. It became obvious that it would be folly to attempt to carry on like that and he climbed the embankment to the railway lines where he was able to walk along the sleepers. Fearing that he might be run down by a train coming from behind him he walked along between the nearer pair of lines so that he might see a train approaching and have time to run to one side. As it turned out he found he could detect the approach of a train in either direction with adequate time to take avoiding action, though the awful noise, vibration and suction terrified him. To begin with he lay down by the track to escape detection, but after a time he became too tired to do more than kneel near the line while a great train roared and rattled past. The bridges worried him: there was so little room between the track and the side wall or railing, and he was afraid that he might be caught in the middle of a bridge when two trains were passing over. So, at each bridge he stopped and listened carefully before running across as fast as he could. Gradually, however, the number of trains passing became fewer and finally ceased altogether.

The rain came and went in spells, but it made little difference now, for he could not be wetter than he was.

At first his mind was occupied in ensuring that his squelching feet kept to the railway sleepers, which was not easy because there was a significant lack of coincidence between his normal step and the distance apart of the sleepers; and, of course, he had to keep alert for the sounds of an approaching train. Later, when he might have begun to reflect upon his plight, he became so tired that he could not think of anything more than keeping going.

He must have plodded on in this way until early morning for there had been no trains for a long time when a warning sound penetrated his fuddled brain and he just had time to stagger away to the side of the track before one went by again. When it had passed and its last rumble had faded into the blackness he found that he was standing near a wire fence on the other side of which stood a large dark shape, which on closer inspection proved to be a haystack. He climbed through the wire and walked round it. A part of it had been cut away to near ground level and covered with a tarpaulin, leaving the rest towering above him in the wet darkness.

He lifted a part of the tarpaulin and crept into the dry scented hay.

When he awoke he was extremely moist but beautifully warm and he lay in the prickly soft hay reluctant to start again. The patter of rain upon the tarpaulin above him had ceased and it was very quiet and snug. Yet, he knew he must not waste time. After walking so far already London could not be much further, and his stomach reminded him that he was hungry.

Cautiously lifting up the side of the tarpaulin he saw that it was daylight, the leaden daylight of an overcast English winter day. He crawled out and looked about him. The haystack stood near the corner of a field of grass. It was a big field and beyond it in the direction he was travelling and on the other side of a hawthorn hedge lay a ploughed field followed by a wood, through which the railway ran. The land was flat and he could not see what lay on the other side of the field. In the direction from which he had come there were scattered houses, as there were on the other side of the line. What could only be farm buildings relating to the land he was on stood several fields away. The only sign of life was some cows about a quarter of a mile away.

He had learnt in India not to drink from open waterways and observing a pool of rainwater lying in a hollow of the tarpaulin, he drank

35

from it. It tasted tarry.

Then he set off again. He followed the wire along the edge of the field parallel with the railway line and went through the hawthorn hedge. There was a narrow band of rough grass along the edge of the ploughed field and he was able to walk on this as far as the wire at the edge of the wood. Inside the wood the undergrowth was dense and wet, so he climbed under the wire back onto the railway line.

He had hoped to see the edge of London on the other side of the wood and was bitterly disappointed to see more fields and a small village beside the line, where, when he reached it, he found there was a small railway crossing with white gates. There he had to cross a road, and feeling very conspicuous he ran across it; but the very few people who were about took no notice of him.

In this way he walked on for several hours, always keeping near the railway lines, and becoming more and more hungry as the time went by. From time to time a train went by and once he caught a glimpse of a restaurant car with people sitting at tables, which increased his longing for food even more. He began to imagine a loaf of bread and tearing great pieces out of it with his teeth.

London was obviously much further than he had expected and he began to fear he had set off in the wrong direction. This was a dreadful possibility and he anxiously considered the information he had been given the evening before that had led him to decide upon the direction he was taking. Perhaps the station clock had been wrong and the train that had come into the station was indeed the six four from London. He should have checked this somehow. The doubt grew with his hunger and with them both a sense of despair. He wondered what he could do. He needed advice and, far more than that, he needed comfort. Oh! If only London would come into sight!

It was the rain starting again that finally decided him. It had been his firm intention not to go to any house until he reached his aunt's flat, but with his doubts, anxiety, exhaustion and hunger his spirits were very low, and the renewal of the rain just as he approached a small group of houses was too much for him. He would ask for a little bread and milk, temporary shelter and at the same time find out whether he was going in the right direction for London and how much further it was.

He walked from the railway lines to a road where it passed between the houses and choosing the first house on his left he went through a white wooden gate up a short paved path with a small lawn on one side and a flower bed on the other to a pale green front door upon which hung a large black knocker. He stood in front of it while the rain splashed round him on the doorstep and beat upon his head and shoulders. He could hear the water from the roof gutters running with a gurgling sound down the rainwater pipes. He lifted the knocker and let it drop.

The sharp bang cut across the noises of the rain and he was committed.

Quite soon, he heard footsteps on the other side of the door, which opened to reveal a small lobby and a middle aged woman in a blue woollen dress with a flowered apron standing with a hand on the door she had opened. She was inclined to shortness and plumpness, and on either side of her healthy-coloured plain face her brown hair was formed into tight rings like earphones. She stood regarding David without expression through thick-lensed glasses with gold-coloured rims.

As she said nothing David felt he should start the conversation.

"I'm very sorry to trouble you, but I wonder whether you could let me have a little bread?" He would have liked to ask for a loaf, such was his hunger, but trimmed his request for fear of appearing greedy.

There was a pause without response from the woman, so he thought that he should go on.

"You see, I haven't had anything to eat since tea time yesterday and I'm rather hungry. I'm on my way to see my aunt in London. I'm afraid I haven't got any money to pay for the bread, but I'm sure she will send you the money when I tell her."

At this point the woman's face softened and came to life.

"Gracious me," she said, "you'll catch your death out there. Come inside out of the rain."

She spoke with a burr to her voice with which David was not familiar.

"You look like you've fallen in the pond."

Gladly David followed her through into a warm kitchen where a black iron range included a grate through which the burning coal glowed cheerfully. The floor was of polished red tiles and against one wall stood a scrubbed wooden table with three cane-bottomed chairs.

"Now then," said the woman, "let's have that wet coat off and we'll dry it while I make some sandwiches and a pot of tea. Gracious me, but you're wet through to the skin. We'll have to have all your things off. Wait a minute while I find something for you to wear." So saying, she pushed a large black kettle onto a hob over the grate and left the kitchen by another door.

She was back again before David had done more than take off his soaking shoes and stockings, coat, pullover and tie; and handed him a thick pair of striped pyjamas, saying, "They're my son's and you'll find them over size, but they'll do while we dry your clothes. But before you put 'em on give yourself a good rub down with this." And she handed him a rough towel.

Happy to give way to her kindly authority, David did as he was told and was soon seated in the warm pyjamas several sizes too large for him with his feet in a mustard bath in front of the glowing grate, while the woman hung his clothes over a wooden clothes horse where they began to steam, and put his shoes on a rack above the stove after she had scrubbed the mud off into a basin with a worn scrubbing brush. By the time this was done the kettle was boiling noisily and she made tea in a round brown teapot that was warming nearby. She set out two saucers and put cups upon them, and while, as she said, the tea was "drawing", she prepared some bread and butter in thick slices and cut some ham from the larder in thin slices, made two marvellous ham sandwiches and placed them before David on a plate.

"Going to London, you said; that's a tidy way to be walking, and in such weather too! I expect you like sugar in your tea: boys usually do."

Dazed and happy at the turn of events David ate and drank, feeling warmer and better every minute. This kindly woman was providing the comfort and sustenance he so badly needed, making him feel less alone. Nevertheless, he was disturbed at the remark about London being a tidy way to go, which he took to mean a long way further. Surely that could not be right: he had walked so far.

"London is such a big place too," she continued. "Do you know where your aunt lives?"

"I don't know exactly where she lives," he replied, "but when I get there I'll ask someone to tell me."

The woman busied herself with cooking preparations by the sink.

"To be sure," she said.

"How far is it from here to London?"

"Twenty miles or more. That's to the middle of course."

Twenty miles or more! David was stunned.

The woman turned to look at him thoughtfully and observing his dismay added that his aunt probably lived on the near edge, which would not be so far, and that it was not really so far when one came to think of it: when she was his age she walked more than five miles to school and back in all weathers.

"Where's your home?" she asked, and when David told her she raised her arms in astonishment. "India! Now that is a long way away: you haven't walked from India, I'll be bound."

David felt they were getting onto dangerous ground, expecting her to ask next where he had come from; but instead she said: "Well now, I have to get Mr Tate's dinner ready, and seeing as how you've finished your sandwiches I'm going to ask you to make yourself useful while I nip round next door for a minute. I've these potatoes to peel. Here's a knife. Put the skins in this bowl and the skinned potatoes into this one.

Glad to do something in return for the woman's kindness, David set to work as she went out. He had never peeled a potato before, but he found it easy enough after a few wary trial cuts and he had finished the work before her return. With nothing else to do he stood by the sink where he found he could see through the window to the adjoining house, and as he did so he saw a youth emerge in a grey mackintosh and flat cap. He walked to a wooden shed and took from it a bicycle which he wheeled down a path to the road where he got on and pedalled off out of David's sight. Almost immediately the woman came out of the same house and started back to her own.

David returned to his chair and considered. The bicycle had given him an idea, and as soon as the woman was back in the kitchen he put it to her.

"If I could borrow a small bicycle I could bike to London."

"Well. that's an idea," she replied unhelpfully.

"Do you know anyone who would lend me a bike?"

"We'll talk to Mr Tate about it when he gets back for his dinner."

She gave a stew she had on the hob a stir and went on: "Mr Tate always gets back for his dinner punctual. Now, Ted – that's my son – can't because he works at the Gas Works and it's too far; and my daughter, Janet, is in service."

David would have liked to pursue the matter of the bike a bit further and to ask what being in service was. His uncle Dick, who was a farmer in Hampshire, had once talked in his hearing about a bull serving a cow and he could not understand the relationship. Another question in his mind was whether the woman was Mrs Tate. He thought it would be more polite to refer to her by name. However, it was not easy to interrupt the steady flow of her conversation.

"Have you any brothers and sisters?" she asked.

David shook his head.

"Families aren't generally as big nowadays," she went on. "Now, I was one of eight. There's a good family for you! We were five boys and three girls." Her expression suddenly became sad and she abruptly changed the subject. "Is it very hot in India?"

David said that it was, much hotter than in England.

"And I suppose there are lots of lions and tigers and such like?"

He told her there were plenty of tigers, though they lived in the jungle and it was only tiger skins he had seen on the floors and walls of people's houses.

"It's a good thing we don't have to worry about such creatures here," she continued, while she prepared a cabbage and put the pieces into a saucepan of water. "Sometimes we do have a bit of trouble with foxes – they go for the chickens you know – and the shepherds do have a spot of bother with dogs chasing the sheep; but that's rare. We're lucky, I suppose. I'm told they do have wolves in some places on the other side of the Channel. I wouldn't like that at all . . ." And so she talked on while she busied herself about the kitchen and David found his mind wandering, only giving half his attention to what she was saying so as to be ready to give the occasional answer when expected. He drowsily wondered how soon it would be before Mr Tate returned, and how long he would take to procure a bicycle for him, if indeed he could. With such a long journey ahead of him it was essential to get started as soon as possible: as it was, he had lost so much time and the whole enterprise was going to be much bigger that he had imagined when he had taken the decision to start upon it. And suppose Aunt Emily was not at home when he reached it? Uncle Edward might be in without her and he rather frightened David. He was very tall and dark and when he spoke his voice was extremely deep. David had a strong feeling that his uncle would not be in the least sympathetic over his problem. There was another thing: he did not know the time and wondered whether the woman would offer him a sofa to sleep on for the night before he started off again: she had talked about preparing dinner for Mr Tate, which he thought of as an evening meal, though he felt sure he had not slept in the haystack throughout most of the day, tired though he had been. He wondered how long it would take him to reach London on a bicycle: after all he had not ventured on his own bicycle beyond the compound at his home in India, and his grasp of speeds and distances was tenuous. How warm and comfortable it was in this kitchen. He knew he must go on, but he did wish it was not necessary. Oh! To be home again with thousands of miles between him and the overpowering troubles that now beset him. Memories of his time in India slipped into his thoughts. The heat of the sun, the drenching roar of the monsoon and the transformation of the landscape immediately after it started, when an overall fresh greenness replaced the dry brown aridity; the friendly servants and his kind old *ayah*; Sergeant Major Stoner – how he wished he could consult him now; his father teaching him to ride on one of his horses; a ride on a camel with the breath-taking moment when, in reluctant response to the cries and blows of its dark owner, it rose to its feet, lifting its hindquarters first so that he had to hang on desperately to avoid pitching over its head onto the stony earth. The camel became a bicycle, which David was riding through the rain along the steel line of railway. The bicycle was much too big for him and he was forced to push at each pedal as it came up for a mere part of its circle. Strangely it was not difficult to stay on the thin rail and he was making rapid progress to London when he heard the unmistakable noise of a train coming up behind him. He tried to pedal faster, but the line seemed to become greasy and the quicker the bicycle wheels went round the slower he went. The train was gaining on him and he could not turn round to see how near it was because of keeping his balance, nor could he fling himself off. The train noise became louder and louder while the bicycle went slower and slower until the roar engulfed him and he was in a haystack hiding. He peeped out from under a wet tarpaulin to see the train had stopped on the line nearby and the engine was a huge stuffed tiger with wheels at the end of its legs. On its back was Jules with a long cane and he was looking to where David hid. He slipped down off the tiger's back and walked steadily and purposefully towards the haystack.

"I know where you are hiding," he said, "and I've come to take you to see Mr Tate, who will certainly beat you, you nasty cheeky new boy."

"You've had a nice little nap," said the woman as David started back into consciousness again. "And it will do you good: you must be tired out, poor boy."

She went across the kitchen to the clothes horse and felt his clothes.

"They're dry again and you can put them on. The top coat is still a bit damp, but that won't take much longer now."

While David did as she suggested she glanced through the window and then turned towards him with a curious, almost anxious expression. He thought he heard the sound of a car drawing up in front of the house and he was going to ask whether Mr Tate had arrived when there was a loud knock on the front door and, wiping her hands on her apron, the woman went to open it, shutting the inner door to the lobby behind her.

David continued to dress, hearing a man's voice in conversation with the woman. Presumably, this was Mr Tate at last.

41

He was on the point of pulling on a stocking when the door opened again and he sat rigid with shock.

A policeman in a blue mackintosh and cap stood before him.

"Master Drummond?" he asked.

He admitted it.

"Well then, my lad, you'd better get those clothes on fast and come along with me. It's a good thing you've been found."

The woman came into the kitchen behind the policeman.

"I'm so sorry," she said, "but it really is for the best; it wouldn't do to let you try to go to your aunt's in London and everyone so worried about you."

David said nothing. The lash of experience cuts deep as it begins to drive out innocence, and this was his first experience of betrayal.

After that everything happened quickly. Dressed again in his now dry clothes he was placed beside the policeman in the front of his car and the drive back to the school increased his gloom when he observed how soon it was accomplished in relation to the time that he had taken.

David had a feeling that it was long ago that he had stood at the heavy dark panelled door and yet it was but yesterday! That time his knock had been without response: this time he heard the deep voice of the Headmaster say: "Come in."

With a curious feeling of not being himself, but another little boy he was observing, he entered.

The Headmaster was standing in a thick brown tweed suit, tall and ominous, with his hands behind his back in front of a coal fire. David wondered whether the cane that he was surely about to experience to the full was concealed there. His mouth felt dry and he wondered anxiously whether he was going to be sick.

"I was told to come to see you, Sir," he said.

"Yes, Drummond." There was a pause during which David noticed the tick of the clock on the mantelpiece and faint cries of boys in the school below: boys who were carefree and unladen with sin, and not about to experience its ignominious and painful reward.

Then the Headmaster went on and to David's astonishment his voice was kindly.

"Come and sit down: I want to have a little chat with you."

Feeling more dazed than ever David sat down on the edge of a large arm chair while the Headmaster lowered himself into another nearby. There was no cane in his hand.

"Now Drummond, I am sure you are a truthful boy and will answer

42

my questions truthfully. Where were you trying to go?"

Still the calm, gentle voice: it was unbelievable.

"To see my aunt Emily in London, Sir."

"Why?"

"I wanted to ask her what I ought to do."

"And you decided to do so after you came up to try to speak to me yesterday and found I was not here?"

"Yes. Sir."

The Headmaster's knowledge of his abortive visit was yet another mystery until David remembered being seen by the matron.

"You are new to the school, Drummond, and I want you to understand and remember that if in future you are seriously worried about anything you may without hesitation come to talk to me about it and if I am not here you may come over to Private Side. Any boy is entitled to that in similar circumstances. Is that clear?"

"Yes, Sir."

"Naturally, when it was found that you were missing I made careful enquiries, and I know what was worrying you."

Again David was astonished at the Headmaster's perspicacity, though at the same time he was dreadfully afraid he was going to burst into tears: the burden was very heavy for small shoulders.

"I want you to understand," the Headmaster continued, "that you have nothing to worry about and that you can speak freely to me. Do you understand that?"

David said that he did, struggling to keep a sob out of his voice. But the Headmaster's next question so surprised him that the tears stopped forming.

"Have you met Mr Deedes in the changing room or any other private place before?"

"No, Sir," he replied, wondering what on earth the Headmaster was talking about.

It seemed that for some reason the Headmaster was relieved by this denial, and he went on: "In that case there is nothing more to be said and you have no reason for further concern: Mr Deedes has left the school."

For several years David puzzled over this curious interview with the Headmaster. His only regret was that Mr Deedes had gone and that he had missed his private instruction on the theory of rugby football.

CHAPTER 3

*"Don't go into Mr MacGregor's garden; your father had
an accident there; he was put in a pie by Mrs MacGregor."*

BEATRIX POTTER

"This is my baby sister," said Peter.

David looked at the little girl in a white blouse, yellow skirt and
white ankle socks above sturdy brown shoes. He knew that her name was
Jill and that she was twelve. Her hair was dark like her brother's and
neatly bobbed. Her slightly pale face was rather solemn though her
expressive hazel coloured eyes were friendly.

"Hello!" he said.

"Hello!" she replied.

An advantage of moving onto a public school, shortly before his
fourteenth birthday, David had discovered, was an increase in school
friends. Peter and he had taken to each other during their first term
together and now, almost a year later, he was spending a part of his
summer holiday with Peter's family in a village close to London; so close,
in fact, that within twenty years it was to be swallowed up to become just
another suburb of that ever growing city. The house was large and at that
time the garden was extensive, including well mown lawns and
herbaceous borders dense with flowers, a rose garden, an apple orchard,
a vegetable garden and a hard tennis court. At the end of the garden a
stream ran through a thin wood.

Mr Talbot, Peter's father, was large and initially awesome as befitted a
successful business man from the City, while Mrs Talbot was slight and
charming with the same dark hair as her two children. She was warmly
welcoming and sympathetic over David's long partings from his parents.

"I can't think why they don't form English schools in India," she said.

"Not enough English people out there," said her husband. "The
sacrifices inherent in the conduct of an Empire are far more extensive
than generally understood."

"As sisters go," said Peter when he showed David round the garden, "Jill is a good egg. We've always hit it off. She has her feminine quirks of course." He pointed to a series of wired cages on a makeshift bench in the corner of the orchard they had reached.

"Her animals," he said. "She is mad about them. Has been as long as I can remember. And when one dies!" He lifted his eyes towards the sky with an expression of comical exasperation. "Which they do of course from time to time, especially hamsters. One of those popped off at Easter and we buried it ceremoniously at the edge of the veg garden. Unfortunately a fox dug it up and ate it, which added to Jill's grief no end. At present there is an overgrown species of rabbit with a kick like a mule, two guinea-pigs and several budgerigars."

David looked at the two yellow labradors accompanying them.

"Don't they keep foxes off?" he asked.

"Hansel and Gretel? They stay indoors at night."

When they reached the kitchen garden David saw a gaunt figure in ancient grey flannel trousers and an open necked shirt that was none too clean hoeing through some rows of lettuces.

"That's Ware, our gardener," explained Peter softly. "He's a bit cracked, but valuable. He lives with a sister who's a bit cracked too. In fact, the whole family has various screws missing. We refer to him as 'Earthenware' and his brother, who works in the village store, as 'Hardware', while his sister is 'Software'. She spends most of her time making weird rag dolls for poor children. She showed us them when we visited her once. My sister chooses some peculiar names for her animals, but you should have heard some of the names Ware's sister called her dolls! And when she picked up one and said: 'I call this one 'banana'' we nearly laughed out loud! Mind you, it was a sort of yellow colour and curved. You see what I mean?"

"But he understands gardening?"

"Adequately, though he does do odd things. When he first came my mother, who likes gardening herself, discovered that he puts pegs in where he has not planted bulbs or lines of seeds instead of where he has; and when she asks him to bring in a lettuce or a handful of carrots or things like that he tends to bring whole trugfulls to the kitchen as though we were a school or something."

Behind the eccentric gardener, in a corner where two boundary hedges met, was a wired enclosure about three metres square, and David asked what it was.

"There's an old well there. The sides have collapsed and the wire is there to prevent people from falling in. I suppose it ought to have been filled in long ago, but we never got round to it. There's no water in it now, just earth and stones. Jill and I looked down it once with a torch."

"Is it deep?"

"No: about fifteen feet or so."

"Have you ever tried to explore it?"

"I wanted to, but mother objected and father put it strictly out of bounds."

They walked to the wire mesh surrounding the tennis court and looked across it to a tall evergreen hedge on the other side.

"We'll play tennis tomorrow if you like. We'll get Jill to play too: she's beginning to play reasonably well. Later on during your stay, mother will probably organise a tennis party. With weather like this we must go to the lake for a swim. And there is Modern Times, the latest Charlie Chaplin film, on at The Odeon. We could all go to that one evening."

"You have a lake?"

"Yes, only about half an hour's bike ride away. Not ours of course – a public one. We have a spare bike for you to use. The Svedbergs next door have a small swimming pool, but they swim in the nude."

"In the nude!"

"Yes, they're Swedish."

At the back of the house facing south with the garden spread out before it was a verandah which reminded David of some houses in India. When the weather was good, as it was now, the family took tea on it. It was warm and peaceful with only the very occasional sound of a car on the road on the other side of the house, for in the mid-thirties there were so few about. That was why Peter and David were able to bicycle to the lake and other places of interest so easily. Frequently Jill went with them and very gradually her initial shyness thawed. One afternoon after tea David asked Jill to show him her collection of animals and they walked together down to the hutches and aviary in a corner of the orchard.

It was another glorious late August afternoon and the apples were almost ripe. Jill reached up and picked two from a branch and handed one to David.

"They're still a bit sour," she said, "but Peter and I eat them. Try one: you can throw it away if you don't like it." And she took a neat bite out of hers.

"Oh! I love them like this," he replied. "When I stay with my grandfather and grandmother they have apple trees in their garden and I start eating them before they are as ripe as these. They're very good dipped in sugar at the end of lunch and dinner."

"I'm not sure whether Mummie would approve of that: she might say it is not good for your teeth."

"I won't do it here then!"

By this time they had reached Jill's small zoo and stopped before the largest cage. In it sat a large white rabbit solemnly chewing some lettuce. He regarded them steadfastly with the one eye they could see and twitched his pink nose.

"She looks very contented and comfortable with all that straw," said David. "What's her name?"

"It's a he," said Jill seriously. "His name is Braithwaite."

"Hello! Braithwaite," said David gravely.

The rabbit showed no sign of interest.

"How old is he?"

"Four years and two months. He's the oldest of my animals."

"He looks very big and healthy: you must have looked after him well."

Jill moved to the next cage where two ginger coloured guinea pigs were basking in the warm sunlight. They seemed less stolid than Braithwaite and made quick movements when David approached.

Jill introduced them. "Tufty and Rufty," she said. "They're quite young – only ten months."

"They're very nice."

"And very tame. Would you like to hold one?"

David nodded.

She lifted a latch and opened the door with care. The guinea pigs were not alarmed and she picked up one and gave it to David who held it gently against his chest while tickling its head with a finger.

"That's Rufty," she said as she stroked the other's back.

"They both look alike to me."

"Well, you've only just met them."

After she had replaced Rufty in the cage and closed the door they went on to inspect the budgerigars, which were white and blue and chirped as they hopped from perch to perch.

"I like their colours," he said.

"My very best friend, Helen, who is coming to the tennis party tomorrow, was given a red squirrel. They're rare now and very pretty. But after a few days it turned into an ordinary grey squirrel. It had been dyed red by the salesman."

"What a cheat! I hope they got their money back."

"No; she couldn't say anything. It had been given as a present you see."

One Sunday afternoon towards the end of David's stay Peter's father and mother gave a cocktail party and because the weather continued warm and dry the party spread into the garden. Peter and David were asked to pass round plates of small sandwiches and other titbits while keeping their eyes open for people with empty glasses. Jill's friend, Helen, came with her parents and the two girls soon retired to the roof of the garden shed where they ate apples as they talked and watched the dull grown-ups performing one of their curious rites.

Mr Talbot was on the verandah with a retired Judge called Sir Louis Float and a balding little man with a white toothbrush moustache, whose name David never discovered. He proffered nuts and a plate of minute cucumber sandwiches and overheard a snatch of their conversation.

"Just as we emerge from the slump," Mr Talbot was saying as he helped himself to four of the cucumber sandwiches and dispatched them in one mouthful, "Europe seems bent upon self destruction; Spain is on the point of civil war; Mussolini brazenly flouts the League of Nations by invading Abyssinia and, most ominous of all, that upstart German corporal called Hitler reoccupies The Rhineland without a peep from the degenerate French."

"Come now, Harold," said Sir Louis, "that is hardly fair upon the French: they were bled white in the war."

"So were the Bosch," replied Mr Talbot, taking a handful of nuts. "They are full of beans again."

David moved on and after some boring people gossiping about others or servants or shopping or children or the Duke of Windsor and some woman called Mrs Simpson there was a pretty red-haired American lady in a green frock describing the making of what she called "anadama bread". This sounded more interesting and after handing round a plate of biscuits he hovered to hear more. It appeared that something called cornmeal and molasses were essential and that kneading of dough was not necessary; but the bit that intrigued him most was when the stout woman asked why it was called "anadama bread" and the red-haired woman replied: "Well, honey, I come from New England and they make it there. The story goes that there was a Bostonian whose wife's name was Anna and she was real lazy. She invented this easy way of making bread and when a guy asked him who made it he replied: 'Anna Damn 'er'! And

48

the name just stuck."

Further on down the garden he overheard a tall, ungainly woman with her mousey-coloured hair in an untidy bun say to a portly little man in a brown tweed suit, who Peter had told him was the local Member of Parliament: "If there is another war shall we all be bombed?" Another pale man in the group nodded gravely as if certain that they would, while an elderly lady, who might have experienced a Zeppelin raid during the Great War and would certainly remember its other horrors said: "Surely, we cannot have another war?"

"Do not be alarmed," said the MP in an extraordinarily deep voice. "In the unlikely event of another conflict with Germany our air defences are extensive and impenetrable. There would be powerful ante-aircraft batteries sited south of London, which would bring down any bombers crossing the coast and in the event of there being night air raids the whole region is divided into a grid of square miles with a search light at each corner. Any enemy bomber would be picked up and passed from square to square until brought down long before reaching its objective."

David, who had been reading H.G. Wells, would have liked to ask what would happen if great waves of bombers came, but did not have the temerity to do so.

His next stop was with a group, one of whom was extremely tall and thin in brown plus-fours and with very large feet making him look rather like a strange wading bird. His name, David recalled, was, rather surprisingly, Dr Little. Now retired, he was regaling his small audience with his experiences in practice in Essex.

"Frequently," said Dr Little, "when visiting patients in the countryside I would ask for urine samples, and very often these were supplied in lemonade or ginger beer bottles. It was also an agreeable habit on the part of my patients to express their gratitude for my services by giving me bottles of home made wine – elder flower, birch, oak leaf and such like – in like bottles. Unfortunately the variation in colour of the liquids was slight and the bouquet often not dissimilar with the result that I was compelled to throw all down the sink upon my return to my house!"

Wondering why on earth Dr Little asked for urine samples from patients, David moved on again and in this way fulfilled his role as a form of under butler until the party came to an end with the departure of the last guest.

About an hour later Jill discovered that Braithwaite was missing.

She had gone down the garden to give the animals their evening feed and found the door to Braithwaite's cage open and the rabbit gone.

Peter's theory was that some silly female guest had lifted the latch to have a closer look at the animal, even to stroke it, and not replaced it properly afterwards.

"However it happened," said Mr Talbot, "we have to face the fact that Jill's rabbit is missing and must be found. You three children form a search party and work over every inch of the garden in an organised way. Work in line with about three yards between you and put down sticks to mark where you have been so that you don't waste time going over the same ground twice. It is a big rabbit and white, so it should be easy to spot."

But in spite of following Mr Talbot's advice Braithwaite was not found. After supper they tried again until it grew dark and Mrs Talbot called them in.

"He might have got into a next door garden," said Jill, whose calm impressed David. He had expected floods of tears.

"I'll telephone both the Svedbergs and the Johnsons and ask them to look out for him tomorrow," said her mother.

Out of earshot of his sister, Peter said to David: "The fox will probably get him tonight. He probably hasn't had such a good meal for ages! "

The next morning at breakfast Jill looked as though she had been crying and David determined to have another search. Lying in bed that morning before getting up, the thought had come to him that when they had carried out their hunt the evening before they had not looked down the disused well in the corner of the kitchen garden. It was out of bounds to Peter and Jill, but the restriction had not been applied to him. He asked Peter if he had a torch.

"Why?" asked Peter.

"I'm going to have another look for Braithwaite."

"But it's daylight: why a torch?"

"Just an idea. Have you got one?"

Peter regarded him with that contemplative look reminiscent of his sister.

"You're not thinking of going down the well, are you?"

"It's the only place we haven't looked."

Peter went to get his torch.

"We'll not tell Jill," he said. "We mustn't get her into trouble as well and anyway we don't want to disappoint her."

"Don't you come either," said David. "There's no point in getting either of you into trouble."

"You are not going alone," said Peter firmly. "And anyway you'll need a ladder."

Outside the spell of fine weather was over. The sky was leaden and it was cooler.

The two boys carried a ladder from the garden shed behind the garage down to the well and laid it beside the wire enclosure. David took the torch and climbed through the wire.

Inside the enclosure the grass was coarse and long and mixed with docks and stinging nettles. The latter were vicious and as he crawled forward cautiously to find the concealed edge, David wished he was wearing gloves.

"Can you pass me a stick?" he asked.

With that he was able to beat down a path forward and quite quickly one hand went through the vegetation and he could feel the side of the hole. He beat down a space about two feet wide and lying on his stomach inched himself forward to peer over the edge.

It was dark and he could make out nothing. He crawled back for the torch and tried again. This time the interior of the hole was eerily revealed in shades of brown, grey and black. As Peter had explained the sides of the old well had fallen in and filled up the bottom with earth and stones. Apart from some mosses no vegetation grew there: it was too dark. The sides were rough and sloped steeply with occasional projections of rock showing pale grey in the beam of the torch. As he moved the beam down to the concave bottom something whiter came into his view; white and hunched with long ears: it was Braithwaite!

At this moment of triumph it began to rain.

They slid the ladder over the top of the wire and gently into the well.

"You won't be able to carry him," said Peter. "he's bound to struggle and kick and he's very strong. I'll get a sack."

When he returned Jill was with him in a mackintosh.

All she said was: "Pick him by his ears and support his behind with the other hand."

David dropped the sack down the well and with the torch in one hand climbed down the ladder.

The rabbit did not seem in the least pleased to see him and hopped heavily away. He rested the torch on a slab of rock and approached it very slowly before grabbing its ears and lifting it as bidden with his other hand beneath it. It was surprisingly heavy. He put it on the sack and tried to open it, whereupon the rabbit hopped back to its previous position. He needed another pair of hands. He glanced up towards the hole above where the vegetation formed a rough dark frame to a circle of comparatively bright grey sky, from which the rain was now falling heavily. Against this light he could see two heads looking down in silhouette.

"I'm coming down," said Jill, and in a few moments she was with him.

"Hold the sack open and I'll put him in," she said in a quiet firm voice.

Not for the first time David was impressed by the little girl's composure.

He did as she instructed him and almost immediately Braithwaite was in the sack.

After that it was simply a matter of climbing back up the ladder, David first with the sack and Jill after with the torch.

When Braithwaite was back in his hutch, looking as if he had never left it, the ladder was returned to its shed and all three were standing round the cage, their hair plastered to their heads and the shoulders of the two boys' coats black with wet, Peter said: "Mother's not going to be well pleased with the state we are in, and we'll get stick from father this evening when he gets home for going down the well."

And Jill said: "I don't believe he'll be cross and anyway I don't care: Braithwaite is safe." And two tears ran down her cheeks to join the raindrops already there.

Later, changed into dry clothes, David and Peter were standing together at a window looking out at the rain.

"Pity the good weather didn't last until the end of your stay," said Peter. "Next stop your uncle's farm, I suppose? I hope it picks up again for you there."

"It will be all right."

"One thing's for sure."

"What's that?"

"You've made a friend for life. My sister is like an elephant: she never forgets."

CHAPTER 4

"I paused again: a change was coming – coming – came:
I was no more a boy, the past was breaking
Before the future and like fever worked."

ROBERT BROWNING

David walked down across the grass field pimpled with mole hills to the slight hollow where he had once found the plover's eggs. They had been grouped together at the bottom of the depression in the turf and the speckled shells acted as such a good camouflage that he had nearly trodden on them. Though he glanced at the spot he knew that there would be none now on the last day of August, while overhead one of the descendants of the brood hatched from those very eggs called "Peewit! Peewit!" as it circled between him and the sky, where high fleecy clouds moved slowly, occasionally obscuring the afternoon sun and then releasing it again.

At the bottom of the grass field there was a single plank bridge over the brook quite near to the steeply banked part where he and a friend from the village had built an impressive dam during one summer holiday. Using garden spades they had spent an entire day at the work and had raised the water level upstream by about three feet before an ominous crack appeared in the middle of the gleaming clay wall, giving them only just enough warning to spring to the bank before the pent up water had hurled aside their construction with an exciting roar before quickly returning to its normal course. A few days later it had been impossible to find evidence of their toil save for the holes dug at the side of the brook to provide the material for the dam.

Beyond the bridge a rudimentary path led along one side of the brook to a gate that opened into a boggy field where care was necessary to avoid sinking into the softer ground so far that water ran into his shoes. There were areas of thin brownish reeds and sphagnum mosses, and now and then small shallow pools of clear water that were so still they reflected the sky with great accuracy until David lent over to see his face and his shadow revealed a limpid brown peaty bottom.

He never saw anyone in this field and it had become a favourite place to visit from time to time since he first discovered it years before when his ever increasing explorations round his grandparents' house carried him that far. It was long and narrow with thick woodland enclosing it on three sides. Perhaps because of this barrier it was very quiet. He would pick his way along to the very end where he could climb upon the wooden fence that separated the field from the wood and sit there looking back down a kind of rough avenue to the point where the wood stopped and fields and hedges rolled away to the whale-backed downs serenely lining the horizon. The village was hidden by the trees to the left except for the tip of the church spire.

Now school was behind him for ever he was determined to enjoy to the full this summer holiday, during which he was in limbo without any responsibility; more free, he understood well, than he ever would be again. There, on that fence, he relished the gentle comfort of being close to and at peace with nature that comes so easily to the young; so much so indeed that it is sometimes hard to contain the surge of inexpressible joy. "Whither is fled the visionary gleam? Where is it now, the glory and the dream?"

The shadow of a cloud moved slowly across the field in front of him and a white butterfly fluttered past. It would soon be time to return to the house if he wanted afternoon tea, but he would rest there a little longer in that idle reverie, perhaps not bother about tea anyway.

The silence of the place was shattered by a frightful bang close by in the wood behind him, followed by a spattering of pellets in the surrounding foliage, and a rabbit broke cover less than five paces from where he sat, cut across the corner of the field and shot into the wood again.

"Hi!" he called out. "Take care where you fire!"

There was a rustling and a scrunching of twigs and undergrowth and his great uncle Charles appeared, shot gun in hand.

"Oh, it's you, boy," he gasped. "I didn't expect to find anyone around here. Did I hit the little beggar?"

"No," said David, "but you nearly hit me!"

"No fear of that: I was firing too low."

Breaking open his gun and ejecting a spent cartridge great uncle Charles heaved himself over the fence with David's help and stood beside him while he recovered his breath.

Great uncle Charles was small and tubby like David's other great

54

uncles and his grandfather, whose brothers they were. In fact there was a marked similarity between them: they all possessed reddish complexions with fine veins clearly visible beneath the skin, hands covered with brown patches – "grave marks" great uncle Charles had once laughingly said – and clear blue eyes. In one respect great uncle Charles differed sharply from his siblings: he had retained much of his hair while the others were bald pated. This hair was quite white and slightly wavy.

They were all great talkers and the pause for breath did not take long.

"Ah well! As you are here and my quarry has made off let us return together to the house for tea. It must be approaching eight bells."

Great uncle Charles had spent his younger days in the Navy and either from early habit or as a conceit was inclined to employ nautical terms.

"You lead the way," he said. "I don't know the way except back through the wood and it's a long rough track."

"It's a bit boggy to begin with, uncle."

"In his nephew's steps he trod!" Great uncle Charles seemed in high spirits in spite of his recent failure. "Except that it's a great nephew and it was his master's steps anyway."

While they negotiated the long wet field in this manner he confined himself to humming the tune of "Good King Wenceslas" in between muttering about "that damned rabbit"; though he had obviously been brooding about David's shout of alarm because once they were side by side on the path leading to the plank he returned to the subject.

"I learnt to be careful with guns early on," he said. "It is a tradition with the British. Unlike the Yanks. Did I ever tell you about my visit to America?"

He had, frequently, as he did to everyone; but the anecdotes varied and he loved to tell them, so David shook his head.

"The ship I was serving in," said great uncle Charles, "had to go in for a bit of repair. We'd been in a big Atlantic gale and suffered some damage that we couldn't put right ourselves. Our Captain was a fellow called Romer-Bottomly – known to all as Rum and Sodomy, appropriately enough in the Navy, though hardly fair to him – and while the work was going on he very reasonably allowed his ship's officers leave in pairs for a week to go where they liked as long as they reported back on the dot. I and another young chap called Bunny Bigwither managed to get quite a long way inland and we were out walking one day when we saw a cow with a blanket hanging over its back, which struck us as odd since the weather was warm, and what was even more odd was that the blanket had COW printed on it. We couldn't make it out at all and when we got back to our hotel we asked the landlord about it. He explained without the least surprise that it was a safeguard against the city dwellers who come out for a day's shooting in the country with rifles and shoot any animal they see. Extraordinary! He knew someone who had lost a valuable horse like that. Most of the men out there own guns: the policemen too. though they call them 'Cops'. When I was in New York I was trying to find an address in 51st Street – they number their streets like that you know – and having lost my bearings without a compass I decided to ask someone for help. Now, who would you turn to in a situation like that?"

"A policeman if there was one about," said David.

"That's right – a cop – and there was one, strolling along the pavement – though they call them 'sidewalks' out there – and when he reached me I stopped in front of him and said: 'Excuse me, officer. Would you please assist me? I want to go to 51st Street.' And what do you think was his response?"

David said he had no idea.

"He was a big, heavy-jowled fellow and he looked at me under his peaked cap without any expression while his jaw worked away at a piece of chewing gum. The Yanks love chewing gum you know. Then, after quite a long time he just said: 'Then why the hell don't you go there?' and walked on. What do you think of that?"

"Perhaps," said David, "that's why the Americans think our police are so wonderful."

"And we tend to take them for granted. Our village bobby is a case in point; although he did succeed in upsetting Gregory Ogilvy once when he scolded Ogilvy for not having a lamp on his bicycle after dark."

David could remember Ogilvy, who had frightened him when he first met him, not simply because of his hunched back and his piercing eyes, but also because he would move very close when speaking directly to David, as though about to grasp him, even start eating him. Of course, David was quite young at the time and later came to regard him with others as an entertaining eccentric. His stammer had been appalling and David's aunt Emily told him that to listen to him speaking to his bookmaker, by the name of Spittal, over the telephone was an experience not to be missed.

"What happened to him? It's years since I last saw him."

"He just died in his bed one winter. The maid took him his breakfast as usual and found him dead. He came from a very good family, you know, but they broke with him – something to do with the woman he married: they considered her beneath them, though he was lucky to find anyone to take him on. And on the whole I think she made him a good wife. A pity when family differences become so serious. You get on well with your father and mother don't you?"

"Very much so; in spite of the long partings: we keep in close touch by writing letters to each other once a week."

"I am very glad to hear it. Long partings can either lead to drifting apart or the strengthening of ties. When are they due back for good?"

"My father has two more spells in India, which makes his final return due in 1945, the same year that I will be finishing my architectural studies. I think I shall go out to stay with them next summer: the long vacation gives time for it."

"An excellent idea. India is a wonderful country and you will be able to appreciate it more than when you were only a child. Remind me to tell you about some of my own experiences there; but now we are about to make landfall."

David opened the gate at the bottom of the garden and followed his great uncle up the garden path towards the great Ilex tree, under which the tea things were laid out. As they did so they passed the lawn known as the 'Lotus Lounge' owing to the propensity of all who sat there to fall asleep. It was a favourite of uncle Edward's and he was there now sprawled in a deck chair in deep slumber, an old grey felt hat tipped over his eyes. Taking no notice of him great uncle Charles advanced upon the rest of the house party, who were settling themselves round the tea table, with a gay hail, oblivious of the mood that David detected of sadness, even of mourning. David's aunt Emily was the nearest and she turned upon them with her hand raised towards her mouth.

"Hush, uncle," she admonished; "the cat is dead."

Momentarily crest fallen, great uncle Charles said: "Good Lord! You must excuse me; but the cat and I didn't know each other very well."

The cat, a nondescript tabby, had belonged to David's grandmother and had been ailing for several days. It was therefore not a surprise that its end had come, particularly as it must have been more than fifteen years old. Nevertheless, its demise had affected her quite deeply and everyone spoke in low voices as people do at the loss of a relative or close friend.

Seated on the oak garden seat behind the large Victorian silver teapot David's grandmother looked even smaller and fatter than she did when standing. Her hair was grey and white and she wore rimless pince-nez which gleamed on her round, wrinkled face.

"Where is Edward?" she asked.

"Asleep on the 'Lotus Lounge'," said great uncle Charles.

David's grandfather grunted. He did not approve of uncle Edward's proclivity to sleep.

"Be an angel and go and tell him tea is ready, David," said aunt Emily, seating herself next to his grandmother, where she looked, it seemed to him, much as his grandmother must have looked twenty years before.

When David reached his uncle Edward he found him still fast asleep, his tall body hunched in the deck chair so that his chin rested upon his chest. His arms hung down onto the grass on either side of him and his cigarette had fallen from his right hand and burnt itself out on the grass leaving a neat tube of grey ash. It seemed a pity to wake him and David stood regarding him. His complexion was swarthy to a marked degree and his white shirt, open at the neck, revealed the top of a smooth skinned chest. His compacted position exaggerated the length of his legs in grey flannel trousers so that he seemed deformed. Ever since David remembered uncle Edward was inclined to fall asleep. This habit was explained in the family as "Shellshock". "He had such a rough time on the Western Front," they would say, "and he was badly blown up." When quite young David was baffled by this explanation, wondering how a person might be so seriously afflicted. Later, he understood that sleep was uncle Edward's means of escape from aunt Emily.

After a time David put his hand lightly on his uncle's shoulder and instantly, though slowly, the man's hooded eyes opened and regarded him without expression.

"Time for tea, uncle," he said.

When uncle Edward replied his voice was very deep and he spoke slowly.

"Good of you to let me know, old boy, but I'm comfortable here. Is my presence required for any particular reason?"

"Aunt Emily asked me to tell you."

His hooded eyelids lowered.

"Ah! Then I'll come along with you." And very slowly he lifted himself out of the deck chair and extended to his full height so that his body fell into proportion again. He was a splendidly built man.

When they reached the tea party David's grandmother was remarking on the fact that they had not seen Mullen Tipping recently. Mullen

Tipping was a professional artist who lived with his wife, Violet, in a dilapidated cottage at the end of the village; and he generally paid frequent unheralded calls in order to discourse in rather wild and dogmatic fashion about matters of the moment that had caught his fancy. Possibly it was his means of escape from Violet. She had been, it was said, a "beauty" and one of his models. She was neither any longer, and it had plunged her into a state of perpetual gloom.

"He has been cocooned in his studio," said aunt Emily. "You know how he is when engaged upon an important painting."

"What is he working on now, dear?" asked David's grandmother while she poured out tea for him and his uncle Edward.

"Christ on the cross. A painting commissioned for Cowfield church. The money has been raised by subscription in memory of the town's war dead on the twenty-fifth anniversary of its beginning."

"Emily," broke in David's grandfather, "you are a mine of inaccurate information. The money was left in the Will of Lady Pagham Smythe in memory of her three sons killed during the war."

While she stood in awe of no one else, aunt Emily revered her father and a rebuke from him cut into her iron self confidence like an oxyacetylene torch, accounting for her unusually lame response.

"I knew it was something to do with the war."

"Has anyone looked at it?" asked great uncle Charles.

"Yes," she replied, recovering, "I paid him a visit the other day, which is why I know what he is up to."

"What did you think of it?"

"He wouldn't show me. He said it wasn't quite ready for inspection."

"The trouble with Mullen Tipping," said David's grandfather, "is that he is incapable of painting from imagination: he can only paint what he sees. That is why he will never be a great artist."

"He is convinced he will be recognised after his death."

"That is the balm of all unsuccessful artists."

"Speak of the devil," said uncle Edward quietly, looking towards the house, and all turned to see the artist himself coming across the lawn. He was wearing brown plus-fours with a jacket to match and a bright green bow tie. His streaky grey and brown beard was pointed in the manner of the late King George V and his eyebrows were very bushy. He advanced upon them in his usual brisk fashion. He was clearly extremely agitated.

All bade him good afternoon and someone said it was nice to see him out and about again; but he quickly brushed all this aside in his customary explosive fashion, crying out: "Have you heard the news?"

"What news?" several asked.

"The Government has pledged the country to fight Germany if she attacks Poland."

He spoke in quick sharp bursts and a high pitched voice.

"But, my dear fellow," said David's grandfather, "that was in the newspapers more than a week ago."

"What, what, what!" went on Mullen Tipping like shots from a gun. "And you sit there drinking tea as if nothing had happened! It will drag us into another war like the last one. It must be stopped, stopped, stopped!" And to emphasise this necessity he banged one fist into the palm of the other hand with each "stopped", his voice rising higher in pitch each time so that the last ended in a shriek.

"Come now, Mullen," said David's grandmother gently, pouring out a cup of tea for him. "It's no use: there is nothing any of us can do about it."

"No! No! No!" cried Mullen, this time raising his forefinger higher in the air with each word as though pointing to Heaven for corroboration, so that David began to wonder how much longer this triple reiteration was going to go on, when his grandfather rose and taking the artist by the arm steered him into a seat, saying: "Certainly the news is bad, Mullen, but Mildred is right: there is really nothing we can do about it, and when there is nothing to be done about a problem it is pointless to worry about it. Sit down, my dear chap, and join us in a cup of tea."

"It ought to be stopped," repeated Mullen Tipping in a quieter voice and took a deep draught of tea followed by a fierce bite from a cucumber sandwich.

"You should take some time off from your painting to study history," said great uncle Charles. "It is simply a matter of balance of power. Our attitude towards Europe has been hinged upon the balance of power for centuries and I trust for centuries to come. It is a policy which has maintained our freedom, independence and integrity."

"Freedom, independence and integrity!" spat out Mullen Tipping with a piece of cucumber sandwich that flew, such was the force, right across the table onto the grass the other side. "Can't you remember those terrible casualty lists? Those millions of young men lying in their untimely graves enjoy no freedom, independence and integrity."

"We cannot be sure of that," said David's grandfather. "You will have to ask the Vicar about it."

"And at what a cost in blood, wealth and suffering," went on Mullen Tipping, accepting a second cup of tea. "Chamberlain was quite right not to lead us all into war over Czechoslovakia, and now he has disappointed me. Mark my words, that warmonger Churchill is behind it all."

This remark roused uncle Edward, who having completed his tea had carefully inserted a cigarette into a small ivory cigarette holder, which he now lit with a silver lighter.

"You are quite wrong, Mullen," he said, exhaling very little smoke from a deep inhalation. "Winston Churchill is a patriot and by his exertions we may yet save our honour so gravely tarnished when your Mr Chamberlain sold Czechoslovakia down the river."

"Stuff and nonsense!" replied Mullen. "Honour is not worth such carnage. You, young man," turning to David, "it is your generation that must provide the cannon fodder. Are you content to go to your untimely grave for the sake of this chimera of freedom, independence and integrity?"

David hesitated, thinking it unfair to call him in as referee at this stage of the contest and in such a biased manner. He was not even sure of his own opinion. Modern war had become too destructive and dangerous to draw out the innate desire for heroism that lies within the breasts of most young men; and now that the German dragon had been allowed to grow again it seemed desperately late to cast down a challenge: yet, from his reading of history he had a strong feeling, even conviction, that uncle Charles had put his finger on the essential point and an attempt must be made to restore the balance of power.

His grandmother solved his problem by breaking in with: "Let us hope and pray it will not come to war. Herr Hitler knows very well what war means: I understand he fought in the trenches during the last one. Have you finished the painting, Mullen?"

Whether it was Mullen Tipping's vanity, for he was a vain man, or whether his outburst had sufficiently relieved his emotion for the time being, this remark diverted him and after speaking at great speed for several minutes about the work, he invited all down to his studio to view it the following morning after breakfast.

The early morning sun shone down brightly upon them that first of September 1939 as they walked down the village street in two small groups of three. David's grandmother, now unable to walk far, was obliged to stay behind. Uncle Edward and aunt Emily walked ahead with Mullen Tipping, who had called for them, an oddly lopsided group with the tall figure of uncle Edward on the left, the medium sized gesticulating

Mullen Tipping in the centre, leading down to the small, dumpy figure of aunt Emily on the right. David with his grandfather and great uncle Charles followed several paces behind. They walked down the road away from the church, not bothering to keep to the rudimentary pavement because the road was wide and the motor car age was in its youth, very different from the roaring, smelly flood that was to come. The cottages and occasional larger house lined the road on either side, fronting it closely and intimately. After passing Biles, the village store, whose distinct interior smell David could recall all his life – a smell compounded of the many things sold there from paint to foodstuffs combined with the lingering, pungent scent of waxed wooden flooring – they approached The Three Horseshoes public house, whose landlord was a white-haired, little man called Bob Fletcher.

David recalled how his second great uncle Jack, now dead from cirrhosis of the liver, was, hardly surprising , on very good terms with Bob Fletcher, who owned a small dog also called Fletcher. It was a nondescript mongrel, small and white with black patches and very strong views over its likes and dislikes when it came to people. For some reason it hated the vicar and used to run after him trying to bite his ankles. But it took a great liking to great uncle Jack, who used to take it for walks before his walking became limited to the stretch between his armchair and the whisky decanter in the dining room, or at the most, The Three Horseshoes.

One very hot afternoon he took Fletcher to the top of the Downs where the animal disappeared down a rabbit hole. For some time great uncle Jack sat beside the rabbit hole and waited. He could hear Fletcher barking distantly, but could not persuade him to come out. After an hour of this he decided that the wretched animal must have got its collar caught on a root, so he walked all the way down to the village to get a spade to dig it out. Then he tramped all the way back up the hill to the spot where Fletcher had disappeared only to find him sitting beside the hole.

Great uncle Jack swore that the dog was grinning at him and never felt the same about it again.

Bob Fletcher – the man, not the dog – was a mine of village stories, one of which concerned Will Langridge, who was a big, strong ploughman. He told Bob Fletcher that "he got one of them there eerywigs" in the ear and that for several days "it scrabbled and scrabbled something terrible. So" he said "I got 'old of an 'airpin and dug en out; but it was only the 'ind part; and believe me or believe me not, Bob, it were a 'ole year afore the front end came out of t'other ear!"

The same Will Langridge fell seriously ill in his sixties and seemed near to death. The women were fussing round his bed when one of them said she had a bit of brandy in her store cupboard, which she could fetch to rub on his chest in case it might do some good. When she returned with it they opened Will's shirt and began to apply the spirit; whereupon the moribund ploughman sat up and pointing to his mouth said: "Not there: down here!" and lived another ten years.

David reminded me his companions of this story as they turned a corner at the bottom of the street.

"Silly women," said great uncle Charles. "Wasting good brandy like that! Though your great grandmother would have approved. She was deeply religious and teetotal. When your great grandfather was dying the doctor advised a little brandy to ease him; but when the nurse asked your great grandmother for the key to the drink cupboard she demurred. It took us quite a long time to persuade her to relent, which she finally did with very bad grace, saying firmly: 'Very well, if you insist; but I do not approve of sending a soul intoxicated before his maker'."

"Ah, Mama, Mama," said David's grandfather. "How fortunate for her that she did not live to see the ungodly times we live in: it would have tortured her."

By this time they reached Mullen Tipping's cottage, and opening the door he ushered them along a narrow, stone-flagged passage to his studio at the back.

This studio was a room of inadequate size, though well lit by two north-facing windows. Along one wall stood a single trestle table entirely covered with battered tubes of oil paint, scores of paint brushes and palette knives, pieces of paint-stained cloth and bottles of turpentine and linseed oil, whose strong scents filled the air. Two paint-stained chairs stood in haphazard fashion and several canvasses, some painted and others untouched, were propped round the walls, and on the back of the door hung several paint-stained smocks. In one corner leaned a simple wooden cross about seven feet high and in the other stood an easel with a large canvas upon it covered with a green cloth.

"Now," said Mullen Tipping, arranging the party opposite this concealed canvas in the manner of a photographer, "stand well back and close together: it is important to get the light right. You must appreciate that this painting will be seen from much further away than where you are standing now and from a lower level. If you will move back a little, Edward, and to the left you will be able to see over Emily's head."

"Come along, Mullen," said David's grandfather impatiently, "we are here to look at the painting and you are keeping us in suspense."

"First impressions are so important," said Mullen Tipping and stepped to a position to one side of the easel. Then taking hold of the top of the green cloth he swept it off with a flourish and the work was revealed.

There was a silence while the party considered it.

"Well?" said Mullen Tipping, forever impatient. "What do you think of it?"

"No good asking me," said great uncle Charles. "I know next to nothing about art."

"Not bad, Mullen," said David's grandfather, "though I'm not sure about the face of Christ. He looks a bit fat and self-satisfied."

Mullen Tipping blew out his cheeks and knitted his brows. "He was a nice young man, a very nice young man," was all he said. He seemed put out.

"Where is he from?" asked aunt Emily. "He isn't from the village: I certainly don't recognise him."

"I was not," said David's grandfather, "suggesting your model was not anything but an agreeable young fellow: I just don't think his face looks right for a man who is suffering the torments of crucifixion."

Mullen Tipping became extremely excited. "You don't understand," he cried out. "He is nearing the end of his pilgrimage, his task on earth; he is approaching his Father and his heavenly throne!"

"Personally," came the deep slow voice of uncle Edward, who had just lit a cigarette, "I think the cross is too gimcrack: the Romans must have known how to construct sound crosses capable of bearing bodies."

David could feel the situation getting out of hand and thought that Mullen Tipping might explode, when, quite suddenly, the door which he had closed when they had entered the studio flew open and all turned their eyes in that direction.

Framed in it stood the figure of Violet, pale and distraught, her nightgown cloaked with a black and red patterned dressing gown that had seen better days. Her once auburn hair, now yellow and grey, was swept back behind her shoulders. On her feet were worn felt slippers. She stood erect and imperious for several seconds while they all regarded her in astonishment. She seemed the embodiment of an ancient sybil.

Her dark eyes swept across them all and when she spoke her voice was low and husky.

"It is war," she said. "I have just been informed by the butcher's boy."

CHAPTER 5

"Children play at being soldiers. That is sensible.
But why should soldiers play at being children?"

KRAUS

When the great truce came to its ignominious end and the revived German war machine swept to the English Channel, virtually disarming Britain, David together with many other young men reached the disagreeable conclusion that the defence of the country had become more important than their studies and volunteered to join the Army. Most of them had undergone compulsory military training at school and passed examinations leading, they were told, to automatic enrolment as officers in the armed forces in the event of their "joining up". They volunteered because they correctly thought that after the disastrous defeat in France there would be a serious shortage of junior officers. They were therefore dismayed to discover that in spite of their previous training they would be obliged to spend months in the ranks as private soldiers before spending further months in officer training establishments only to repeat what they had already learnt. Too late they understood that their zeal was misplaced. It was a first lesson concerning the inconsistency and stupidity of politicians.

By the time David realised this it was too late to draw back, so, taking the precaution to have his hair cut very short at the station barber shop, he caught the train to the place appointed for him by his new masters at the War Office.

Inside the barracks of the ancient county regiment to which he had been directed he joined about thirty other "potential officers" of his intake paraded to receive their new kit and prepare for inspection by a Sergeant. The Sergeant was not at all complimentary. He told them when he had walked down their front that they were a real shower, and a disgrace to the British Army after he had examined their backs. After that he ordered them all to parade at the Regimental barber's shop in order to avoid the discomfort of any inspecting officer treading on their hair, a circumstance

65

that caused David to reflect, as the regimental barber reduced his hair even further, how he had wasted one and six pence.

Other indignities followed.

A skinny little Corporal with a long nose took them over and said: "You will now parade for a short arm and A.H. inspection. Anyone of you 'ere know wot a short arm is?"

No one was foolhardy enough to admit it.

"That's only natural, seein' as 'ow you are ig'orant recruits," continued the Corporal. "It i'nt, as you might be thinking, a new secret weapon that is about to be revealed to you: it 'appens to be a very old weapon and every mother's son of you 'ere ought to 'ave one."

He paused, and, understanding they were expected to laugh, all giggled sheepishly.

Pleased at the success of, no doubt, this off-repeated witticism, the Corporal went on in a more amiable manner.

"I am now about to inform the MO that you are ready for inspection and in my absence you will strip down to your birthday suits and line up in two ranks at ease. When I come back with the MO I will call you to attention, and on the command 'Present short arms!' everyone of you 'ere will take 'is short arm between the thumb and forefinger of the right 'and and raise it parallel to the floor, whereupon the MO will carry out 'is inspection. You 'ave ten minutes to get ready. You!" pointing to one of their number a few years older than the rest. "What's your name?"

"Fullerton, Corporal."

"You, Fullerton, are in charge while I am away and will be responsible for the orderly behaviour of the other recruits, and for them being ready and lined up by the time I get back."

When they had broken ranks and begun to undress along the sides of the hut David found himself next to a tall, gangling young man with tow coloured hair, whose name he disclosed was Parkinson.

"I must have been mad to volunteer," said David.

"Was there no compulsion?" asked Parkinson.

"None, except that after Dunkirk I felt everyone should take an oar."

"Commendable attitude, but mistaken: no one will thank you for your sacrifice."

"But, surely you volunteered?"

"*Force majeure*. Funds ran out and my dad turned off the tap."

"That seems rather hard."

"Not really. I expended a great deal on my passion."

"Your passion?"

"The turf; the sport of kings – only I didn't have as much to play with as kings have. Hey dey!"

By this time all the party were naked, and under the fussy authority of Fullerton they formed into two ranks.

The Corporal's ten minutes extended into twenty and all were feeling distinctly chilly in the thin-walled army hut on a cold late September afternoon when the door burst open and the Corporal entered smartly. He stood to attention by the open door and shouted: "Parade! Parade shun!" And as he did so the MO came in.

"Pre-sent short arms!" yelled the Corporal; and when they had done as they had been told with varying degrees of embarrassment or concealed amusement according to their different natures, the MO, a portly Captain with a large grey moustache and very red cheeks, walked wordlessly down the lines peering at each exhibit. That done, the Corporal ordered them to drop their short arms and to touch their toes.

Now, touching one's toes is no great problem for the young and agile, and most, if not all, of them had probably done so frequently before; but on those occasions they had been clothed. It is quite another matter to take up such an inelegant, not to say vulnerable, position in public with nothing on at all; and they were undoubtedly hesitant about it.

"As you were!" shrieked the Corporal. "You're in the Army now," he continued when they had returned to attention, "and when you is ordered to move I want to see you move. Parade! Keeping your legs straight, touch your TOES!"

Afterwards, while they were lined up waiting for their injections Parkinson was immediately behind David.

"I had a distinct impression," he murmured, "that the MO was disappointed. Would it be our short arms or our A.H.s do you think? – or both?"

It was Emerson, David recalled, who pointed out that all life is an experience and that, therefore, no part of it is wasted. If he was right the tedious next few months were not in vain, and at the end of them David and his intake were dispatched to different OCTUs in batches. David and Parkinson, now known as "Punter", were sent to one on the East coast of Scotland. Fullerton, long known as "Uncle", was another in their party.

All acknowledge the beauties of the Scottish landscape and the contribution made around the world by its rugged people; but on the other hand there can be no doubt that its East coast is not an agreeable place to practise the art of soldiering during a particularly severe winter. Icy winds came in from the North Sea, there was snow and the cadets' quarters were poorly heated by ramshackle stoves which gave off choking fumes if galvanised into further effort.

Of course, there were other recollections, amongst which pride of place must be given to Sergeant Major Murdoch-Grant. He was a great, dark, hairy Highlander; the sort that David's ancestors had to face, leaping over the heather with sharp claymores in their rough hands. David and his fellows in the new intake were in his charge during the first of the three months' course and his duty was to improve their drill, as though, thought David, they were preparing to fight in Marlborough's campaigns. Their problem was his accent. He would march them down to the beach and bellow commands the various interpretations of which would reduce them to a chaos of stumbling confusion. Then, Sergeant Major Murdoch-Grant's rage and indignation was wonderful to behold and he would say such things about them that were, perhaps, better not to understand; and after the worst of his wrath was expended he would make them double up and down in the soft sand with their rifles upon their shoulders. It was a salutary way of learning a new language and they learnt it fast.

On one occasion they were given a day's exercise in the adjacent hills under the control of an elderly ex-Indian Army Major, whose name was Fellows-Poynter. He was a tall straight standing man with a clipped moustache and creased brown skin. He either found it hard or, perhaps, refused to drop words that had become second nature to him, and in the same way the exercises that he conducted were based upon his experience in forays into Afghanistan on the North West Frontier of India.

David and his comrades numbered about sixty formed into three platoons, each consisting of three sections of around six men. Every day during their time at the OCTU acting platoon commanders and NCOs were appointed from among them on a rotary basis, and on that particular day David had been appointed platoon sergeant of No 3 platoon; and it so happened that "Uncle" Fullerton was his platoon commander.

Before the exercise commenced Major Fellows-Poynter gave them a short lecture on what they were about to do.

"The Battalion," said he, "of which you form A Company is the advance guard of a Brigade in a Division that forms one of the prongs in an advance into enemy-occupied territory. For the purpose of this exercise you will be advancing from map reference . . ." and he paused while they all studied their maps to find the point, "in a Westerly direction. You will see from your maps that the start point is at the neck of a valley with a track at the bottom of it. The object will be to advance up this valley clearing away any enemy that you may encounter in order to leave the way open for the advance of the remainder of your Division and in turn the Army Corps of which you form a part. Information concerning the enemy is that they are retreating and may leave small pockets of rear guard units to delay your advance. These are to be brushed aside with speed because it is essential that the advance of the Corps is not delayed. You are expected to reach map reference . . . before 1800 hours where another Battalion in your Brigade will pass through your position and take up the role of advance guard. When carrying out an operation of this kind it is of the greatest importance to clear the hills on either side of the valley ahead of those moving up the valley itself, for it is there you are most likely to find the Wogs waiting to shoot down upon troops moving up the floor of the valley. We will start with No 1 Platoon moving along the left hand side of the valley and No 3 Platoon doing the same along the right, while No 2 Platoon with an imaginary Company Headquarters and myself as Company Commander will move up the bottom about two hundred yards behind the leading Platoons. Communication will be by runners. Enemy pockets of resistance will be represented by members of the permanent staff, who have rattles to represent small arms' fire. Any questions? Good. Off you go then and I will meet you at the start point at 0930 hours in a *nullah* that you will find there."

As they marched along the road and branched off onto a track leading to the rendezvous those of them in the two flanking platoons cursed their fate and envied No 3 Platoon, for it was clearly going to be a gruelling day scrambling about on the snowy slopes.

In some places it had drifted to as much as two feet. For some stretches the going was comparatively easy, but for the most part the ground was irregular and broken and they had to advance over it in open order with one section forward in the middle and the other two lying back on either flank in order to cover as much ground as possible. Glancing across to the line of hills on the other side of the valley from his place with the middle section David could see No 1 Platoon struggling along roughly level with them. Behind and below them in the valley the fortunate No 2 Platoon was marching along the track, occasionally sending out scouts to investigate a copse or other cover that might conceal an enemy outpost.

At the beginning they walked forward with caution, but gradually as time went by and climbing over dry stone walls, pushing through undergrowth that showered them with wet snow and plodding up inclines, tiredness and an icy wind began to numb their senses and they began to feel that the most important thing was just to keep going.

Thus, the stutter of a rattle from somewhere to their left front took them by surprise, and as David hurled himself into the snow behind a clump of gorse it crossed his mind that the war he had so blithely entered was likely to be both uncomfortable and dangerous.

Everyone else had gone to ground like him and the rattle ceased. It had come from a clump of stunted trees and undergrowth on some rising ground about two hundred yards in front of where he was lying and slightly on the valley side of the line of hills they were on.

It was a well placed enemy post with a field of fire that enabled it to fire down on the troops in the valley and at anyone, like them, advancing along the hill tops towards it.

David twisted round to look into the valley and saw No 2 Platoon continuing on its way, oblivious of the situation above: the sound of a rattle would not carry so far in this wind.

He peered cautiously round the bottom of the bush. In front of him and the rest of the platoon the ground swept gently down in untrodden whiteness and then quite steeply to the copse. On his left the hillside fell away sharply, the snow covering what may have been rugged stony ground all the way to the valley floor. On his right was an open expanse of snow in the form of a shallow dome, beyond which it was possible to see the tops of leafless trees that he assumed were part of a wood that curled round the right of the copse from which the enemy had "fired".

It was very quiet as he lay there on his belly in the snow, and it was nice to be able to rest. There was nothing for him to do. As this was an exercise 'Uncle' would not be a casualty and David would not have to take over the leadership of the platoon in his place. It was 'Uncle' who had to do the thinking and make decisions while all the rest of them could do was to wait for his orders. Poor 'Uncle': such a nice man but slow in thinking as he was in movement. It would be hell for him at first when he joined a battalion, though David had every confidence that he would quickly find a useful niche in some administrative post. How dull and lifeless the gorse bush in front of his nose looked. And yet, within three months it would be bright with colour, yellow from where he was now, but golden brown from a distance, busy with bees and other insect life. He recalled an old country saying that when the gorse is not in bloom kissing is out of fashion. Kissing! What a hope for that anyway.

There was a sound of scuffling through the snow behind him and he twisted to see one of his fellow cadets crawling towards him on his stomach.

"Uncle wants you for an 'O' group," he gasped. "He's in that dip my tracks lead to. Where's the section commander?"

David pointed him out a little way to his left and began to crawl towards Uncle's place of concealment. When he reached it he found Uncle with a worried expression on his plain, kind face below his steel helmet which he had pushed back from his forehead to reveal a little of his dark hair, damp with his exertions. Two of the other section commanders were already with him, and David told him that the third was on his way.

"This is tricky," said Uncle, and when none of the others denied it seemed comforted.

"Nice to have a rest for a moment, though," said Punter Parkinson, who was section commander of No 3 Section on the right, and he rolled over onto his back with his pack as a pillow, his long limbs spread out.

"Christ! Yes," said the other section commander present, whose name was John Bingham. He looked at his wrist watch. "And it's still only ten to twelve. Another six hours to go!"

"The gallant Major will probably pull us down into the valley when we've seen off these Wogs and let No 2 Platoon do some hill climbing," said Punter gazing into the sky.

They said nothing more until Roger Jamieson arrived from No 1 Section on the left, at which point Uncle gave his orders.

"Information about the enemy," he started in the approved fashion. "As far as I can see there is one group with a machine gun in the copse to our left front. Do you all agree that is where the sound of a rattle came from?"

They all thought so.

"Information about our own troops," went on Uncle, and then hesitated before asking "Is your section under cover, Roger?"

"Not bad." Roger was a small, wiry individual, who looked no more than sixteen.

There was silence while Uncle considered. Then he went on: "John's section was caught out in the open but managed to scramble back into some kind of cover, and Punter's is OK on the right. The object is to drive out the enemy post in the copse in order to continue the advance."

"And to protect No 2 Platoon in the valley," said Roger. "They couldn't have heard the rattle and when I last took a look they were advancing up the valley as though there was nothing above them to shoot them up."

"Oh dear!" said Uncle. "We'll have to send down a runner to warn them. When you get back to your section, Roger, will you send one off?"

"That'll leave me with only four men."

"It can't be helped."

There was a pause while Uncle collected his thoughts: the interruption had confused him.

"Method," he continued: "a pincer movement. You, Punter, will swing off into that wood on the right with your section and you should have cover to within fifty yards of the enemy. You, Roger, will be the left flank of the pincer. There ought to be cover round to the left. John's section will give covering fire in the centre. I'll come with you, Roger, to make up for the runner. You, David, will stay with John."

David did not think much of Uncle's plan, which was going to scatter their small force and might end up with two flanking sections shooting each other, but what did it matter? They were only playing anyway.

"Any questions?" asked Uncle.

"It's going to take us different times to reach our assault positions," said Punter, still on his back looking up into the sky. "How are we to know when we're both ready for the charge?"

"Oh yes," said Uncle. "We could do it by fixing a time, but it's difficult to know how long you'll both be. I'll tell you what. When you both reach your assault positions blow one blast on your whistles. The second whistle will mean that you are both ready. Start your assault immediately the second whistle blows and at the same moment John's section will give covering fire."

"So will the Wogs," said Punter.

"So will the Wogs what?"

"Know what's happening."

Uncle looked more worried than ever.

"Oh well," said Roger, "they're not real enemy and it might confuse them anyway. Let's get going: I'm getting cold."

"Good luck all," said Punter, turning over and starting to crawl back to his section. A few moments later Roger set off to the left followed by Uncle.

"Come on," said John to David. "We'll get to my Bren gunner without being spotted and tell him to rattle like hell when we hear that second whistle blow."

When they had done this David looked at his watch. It was ten minutes past twelve. They were not being particularly quick about clearing away this enemy post. Twenty minutes later he whispered to John: "I'm afraid the Major is not going to be pleased at our lack of progress."

"They must be very nearly there now."

Several minutes later there was a sound of heavy breathing and scraping in the snow behind them. It was Taffy Williams from the left hand section and he looked hot and flustered.

"Trouble!" he gasped out when he reached them. "Uncle has fallen down a bloody *nullah* and hurt his leg and arm. He may have broken something. Roger has sent him down to the valley with two blokes to help him, and as he only has Richardson and me left in his section he wonders if you could send some of yours: he doesn't think he will be of much use with only two men."

David looked at John.

"No good. If any of mine move they'll be seen. We were caught in the open and the cover is minimal."

"Oh hell!" David muttered. "I shall have to take over command. I'll come with you, Taffy. At least that will make us four for the left flank assault."

They crawled for a long way before the curve of the hill put them out of sight of anyone in the copse, after which they trotted along in a stooping posture except when they had to cross gulleys, where the snow was deeper and the stony ground beneath uncertain and they had to go more carefully. They followed the tracks of Uncle and the others, which were clearly defined in the snow. They hurried because so much time had been lost, and could feel the sweat dampening their vests and running down their backs. David wondered again what madness had caused him to leave the tranquillity of the University for this. What difference could he possibly make to the result of the war?

The shrill blast of a whistle reached them from over the hill. That meant that Punter and his section were in position and ready for the assault from the right flank. He was going to have a long wait.

When, eventually, they reached Roger and Richardson in a hollow David briefly explained that they would have to do the best they could with their tiny force and asked if they had heard the whistle.

"Yes," replied Roger. "I expect Punter is beginning to think we must be lost."

They went on together to a point where they judged the copse was to their right up the slope and started upwards, scanning the skyline

73

above them, and after a minute or two were rewarded by the sight of the top of the trees almost immediately before them. David looked at his watch. Nearly ten to one: it had taken nearly an hour to get where they were after they had been fired on! The Major would certainly not be pleased.

"Now," he said, "we'll crawl in extended line and when I stop all stop. Then I'll blow my whistle and we'll make a dash for it."

Four weary young men across forty yards of open space, uphill and in snow! He was glad they were only playing soldiers.

The sound of his whistle was piercing across the stillness of the snow-muffled hills, and as they got to their feet and stumbled forward John's rattle started up to their right, which was comforting. They could see no sign of Punter's section approaching the other side of the copse, which it was now clear was in fact a clump of woodland protruding from the main wood on the other side and joined to it by a narrow band of scrub that had been hidden from their view when the advance had been halted.

Gasping and panting they struggled towards it, surprised not to hear the crackle of the enemy rattle, until they were within a few yards of the edge. Then a familiar slow voice said: "Bang! Bang! You're dead!" and Punter stepped from behind a tree followed by the rest of his section all grinning broadly.

"Christ!" said Roger. "You might have let us know: we've still got a whole afternoon of running about to do."

"What the deuce have you been up to?" asked Punter. "We got tired of waiting for you to finish your lunch or whatever else you've been playing at, and crept here through the back to find the bird had flown. Where's Uncle?"

David glanced towards John's section, where the rattle of their mock machine gun had stopped as soon as they had straggled into the copse. He saw they had risen and were walking towards them. He was on the point of explaining before trying to get some order into a fairly chaotic situation when Roger gave him a nudge and looked meaningfully to his left. At the same moment a familiar voice said: "What the bloody hell do you think you are doing?"

It was the Commandant, who had approached unnoticed, and was plainly very angry indeed.

All turned towards him sheepishly and none replied. His words had been more of a statement than a question anyway.

He stood in his beige-coloured British Warm overcoat, his Scottish tartan cap at the usual slight angle, tapping his polished leather swagger stick against one of his tartan trews that tightly fitted his legs. When he was angry the skin on the bridge of his well shaped nose seemed tight and white, and it was very tight and white now.

"I have been watching you," he said, "for the last hour and you frighten me. You frighten me when I think that in a few weeks, if I don't send you all back to your units as totally unfit to lead men into battle, you will be responsible for the lives of British soldiers and for the success or failure of our armies. You spend a whole hour winkling out a single enemy post, which has in fact withdrawn forty minutes ago, thereby quite unnecessarily holding up the advance of an army, and then you stand about coffee housing like a bunch of bloody girl guides on a picnic. Who is in command?"

There was a short silence.

"I asked: who is in command?"

"I am, Sir," said David, stepping forward.

"Your name?"

David gave it.

"See here, Drummond, I shall be keeping my eye on you in future, and if you don't do considerably better than this you'll be back at your unit faster than shit off a shovel. Your plan was a complete dog's dinner and you have no drive or control. And, good God man! What utter stupidity to go about blowing whistles to show the enemy exactly where you are. Have you forgotten that there are such things as mortars? Mortars, man, that could have plastered the living daylights out of you. Good God! One of the Lance Corporals in my last Battalion could do better than you. Send a runner down to Major Fellows-Poynter with the message that the enemy post has withdrawn and that you are moving forward again; and add that on my express orders this Platoon is not to be relieved and will continue to work along these hills for the rest of the day."

With a last sharp tap of his stick he turned away and walked off.

"Hard lines," muttered Roger.

Punter put his hand on David's shoulder. "One has to accept," he said, "that Damon Runyon is right: all life is six to five against."

75

CHAPTER 6

"Let thy song be love: this love will undo us all.
O Cupid, Cupid, Cupid!"

SHAKESPEARE

"Roll me over in the clover, roll me over, lay me down and do it again," sang Ray lustily at David's side as they bowled along the winding road in David's ancient Riley towards Lady Dinwiddy's country house.

Ray was a most agreeable and good looking fellow officer who found life uncomplicated and happy. He had joined the army as a regular soldier shortly before the war and had survived the retreat and evacuation from Dunkirk without a scratch. His reminiscences of that period had less to do with the defeat than his successes with various beautiful girls and the glories of French cuisine. It might seem that these were about the limit of his interests, but David had discovered there was much more to him beneath the froth. A good athlete, he was well built and moved well. Together with his gaiety, dark hair and pale skin his success with women was not surprising.

"You forget," David interrupted, "that this is a real Ball, not one of your commonplace dances; and even you will not get much opportunity of rolling in the clover or for that matter in any other place."

"Don't worry, old boy," he replied, "there'll be crumpet available."

David envied his friend's confidence and would have given a great deal to possess half his talent, for his natural ardour and interest in the opposite sex was suppressed by a timidity that is difficult to understand in the sexual climate of today.

The two young officers were, as has been mentioned, in David's ancient Riley, recently bought for £30 from a friend upon his posting overseas. It had one seat beside the driver with a removable black hood and a dicky behind which could be opened up to hold luggage or to provide two more open seats. On this occasion David only had Ray in the car, the other two junior officers in the battalion going to the Ball having made other arrangements for the journey.

76

The battalion was the second of a famous regiment and David owed his posting to it to his uncle Edward, a regular soldier until his retirement in 1920 owing to ill health; it was kind of him to pull strings since it was such a select regiment, though David wondered whether his aunt Emily was the prime mover. Aunt Emily loved to organise.

It may be different now, but at that time junior officers did not have much inkling of how things come about; so David could only guess that it was Lady Dinwiddy who hatched the idea of a Ball and persuaded his CO to give his support. Lady Dinwiddy liked to organise too.

Though small, she had a formidable personality from high society, and would certainly have considered it her duty to enliven the dullness and depression of 1941 in her part of East Anglia. The presence near her country house of so many officers when the county was so denuded of young men must have seemed to her a heaven-sent opportunity.

The Adjutant had issued precise instructions, and from these it was apparent that the Ball was to be the old-fashioned kind where everyone was given a notepad and pencil and during the first stage of the evening before the dancing commenced the men were obliged without fail to book all the dances with ladies, taking care not to do so more than twice with any one of them. This neatly avoided the deplorable sight of wallflowers sitting out dances while groups of men clustered round the bar. On this occasion, since few of the officers and ladies had met before, introductions were permissible and it was necessary to accompany names with short descriptive notes in order to remember who to look for at the end of each dance. Thus, David might have something like the following in his notepad by the time dancing started: (1) Miss Jane Plummer – auburn – pale green – P.20; (2) Mrs Rudgewick – big – brown – blue and white – U.40; (3) Miss Elizabeth Boughton-Jones – tall horsey – brown – white and yellow – 25.

And so on. No doubt everyone had their own personal form of shorthand or cypher: in David's case he put the colour of the hair after the name, followed by the colour of the dress and the letters B. for beautiful, P. for pretty, and U for ugly, adding sometimes a word indicating the size or some other distinguishing feature. The last number was always his estimate of the lady's age. He would have given much to see what was written down about him in the ladies' notepads.

Owing to the limit of two dances per lady the trick was to book as soon as possible the girl of one's choice for the last dance before the interval, giving the opportunity to be with her throughout the half hour set aside for the cold table and drinks.

Mary was the girl David wanted to find as quickly as he could for this important position on his list. He had met her at a sherry party a few weeks before and had been enchanted by her. She was lovely and just nineteen.

His thoughts were upon her when Ray started a new song to the tune of "Home! Home! On the range."

It went like this:

"Oh! Give me a home where the women all roam as naked and willing as Eve.

Where brothers have gone and of fathers there're none as well as no mothers to grieve.

Home! Home! In this heaven with nothing to stand in the way

Of copulation all night till the dawn breaketh bright, and to roll in the hay all the day."

"Ray," said David, "you are a philistine with a one-tracked mind. Keep quiet for a moment and absorb the loveliness of this summer evening."

In this David was not wrong. It was one of those evenings in England when one felt good to be alive. Warm and windless with the air full of summer scents and sounds, it touched David's heart. Above them the great sky of East Anglia was the palest blue with a few cottony clouds lit by the light from the sinking sun which approached the flat horizon in a blaze of red and gold.

"Right oh!" said Ray good naturedly. "Absorb away."

David drove through the entrance of Lady Dinwiddy's estate with its handsome iron gates turned back upon red brick piers capped with stone eagles, and up the gravel drive between closely mown lawns to the front of the big brick house with clematis, wisteria and honeysuckle against its walls.

Inside they were announced by a butler.

"Lieutenant Stein and Second-Lieutenant Drummond!"

They moved forward to join a short queue of other arrivals to be greeted by Sir Nigel and Lady Dinwiddy. She was wearing a grey dress with some diaphanous material over it, her snow-white hair crowned with a jewelled diadem. Beside her Sir Nigel looked very shrunken and old in his tail suit.

After they had shaken hands and exchanged a few useless words David and Ray passed on into the big hall that was already quite full.

From this hall a fine oak staircase swept up to a gallery at first floor level. On one side double doors were thrown back to give access to a big room with a waxed board floor which had been cleared for dancing. On the other side of the hall a door led into a room with tables laden with a magnificent display of food ready for the interval.

They took champagne from a tray handed to them by a servant and set about the task of completing their programmes.

David was delayed in getting to Mary, whom he found at last in a group, looking cool and refreshing in a high-necked dress of pale blue with short sleeves that revealed her elegant young arms. Her face was happy and full of life as she enjoyed the attention paid to her. When David approached, the Adjutant himself was in the act of arranging two dances with her. His heart sank. What chance had he to be in the running?

"Hello, David," Mary said brightly as she completed the note she was writing. "I was beginning to think you might be on duty or something."

"It's been difficult to reach you: you have so many admirers. Is there any chance of my having two dances with you?"

Her long eyelashes fluttered down as she inspected her programme. It looked, as far as he could see, very full. At the same time he admired her soft brown hair and how pretty her hands were.

"Yes, I have dances Numbers 5, 9, 16 and 18 free. Which two would you like?"

"No hope for Number 10, I suppose?" Number 10 was the last dance before the interval.

"I'm sorry, that one's already taken."

Inwardly David cursed his slowness and lack of initiative. Ray would have fixed it before the night of the Ball. But now there was nothing to do except take two of the remaining numbers, and he was only just in time because a Lieutenant from another Company booked the last two immediately after him.

He walked away to get on with the business of completing his programme, which he had up to that moment kept nearly empty to allow for the probability that Mary's card would not give much scope for manoeuvre. That at least had been prudent.

By the time that he had almost filled up his card he still had no one booked for dance Number 10: either whoever he asked already had that one booked or they were not his choice for half an hour during the interval. He was beginning to grow anxious about this when he passed his Company Commander in conversation with two ladies he had not seen before. As he did so his Company Commander took his arm and turned him towards them.

"Hello there! David," he said. "Allow me to present one of my Platoon Commanders, David Drummond. David, here are two ladies who have suffered a mishap with their car on the way here and it has made them late."

He indicated the elder, a tall woman with greying black hair tied at the back in a not very tidy bun.

"Miss Bowers."

"Alice Bowers," corrected the tall lady in a deep, resonant voice. "How d'ye do."

David observed that she was wearing a satiny kind of dress in black and grey that seemed very taut over her heavy figure. Her eyebrows were black and deep and she allowed a slight dark moustache to grow over the sides of her upper lip.

"My car, I'm afraid," she went on. "Something's gone amiss inside. By great good fortune it happened only half a mile up the road, so we walked it. This is my niece, June – Mrs June Sharde."

David turned to the other and looked into a pair of deep blue eyes that held in them both humour and sadness. Her golden hair was long for the period, almost reaching her bare shoulders above her plain white dress. David thought her not especially beautiful and rather old, being perhaps about thirty; but there was an indefinable aura about her: she glowed.

His Company Commander was speaking again.

"Because of this car problem neither Miss Bowers nor Mrs Sharde have been able to fill their programmes. I'm sure that you will be delighted to have the opportunity to give them two dances each."

"Come, that is rather hard," boomed Miss Bowers. "Perhaps the young man has already made all his arrangements."

David hastened to explain that he still had vacancies in his programme and that he hoped they would both do him the honour of booking dances with him, carefully ensuring that the tenth dance would be with Mrs Sharde.

And so the matter was arranged before he and his Company Commander took them on to make further introductions; while David, his card now full, was able to give his full attention to other matters.

Not long after the band struck up and there was a general movement onto the dance floor.

"Damnable things, motor cars," said Miss Bowers as she waltzed heavily round the floor with David. "Horses were much more reliable."

David asked what make of car she possessed.

"Alfa Romeo," she replied surprisingly. "A good car really, though getting long in the tooth – like me, ha! Trouble is that those Ities crossed the floor into the other camp and it is impossible to get spare parts."

David steered her round a corner, narrowly missing Ray and a pretty dark-haired woman as they executed an elegant twist. His right arm was beginning to ache. Some women respond like feathers when dancing. Some don't. Miss Bowers didn't. She was not unlike a ship under weigh and David had to plan changes in direction well in advance, applying strong pressure to her firm waist and back before much apparent response. The concentration required made sensible conversation difficult.

"I have an old Riley," said David.

"Indeed! I shall put Frolicker onto mine tomorrow morning: he is bound to know what the trouble is. Do you know Frolicker?"

David had to admit he didn't.

"Oh! If you have any trouble with your car go to Frolicker. He has a garage between here and North Walsham. I've been to him for years and he has a real gift with cars. It's hard luck on poor June though."

David wondered how the estimable Frolicker's ability with cars could be unfortunate for Miss Bower's niece, but was too busy working at their next change of direction to put the question into words.

His partner solved the problem with her next words.

"Her husband is so often away these days and I am sure she was looking forward to a carefree evening out; and then see what happens."

'If you are worrying over getting home," said David, wondering what Ray would have to say about it, "I can easily take you both back, that is if one of you doesn't mind sitting in the dicky."

"Now that's very civil of you and I shall certainly take you up on it if necessary; but I have a number of friends here this evening and have little doubt that someone who is going our way will have room for us. There now; I enjoyed that dance very much and I shall look forward to our next after the interval. Number 20, I think. The last waltz!" She raised one eyebrow, humorously provocative.

Easing his wrist behind his back David turned to look for Mary.

She was easy to find, youthful and glittering, a little flushed from the last dance and clearly enjoying her success, for which David was half glad and half grudging. They danced a fox-trot and the contrast with his previous dance was profound.

He told her about Miss Bowers and her niece, adding, suddenly bold,

"I wish it was your car: then I might have taken you home."

She laughed merrily.

"I don't expect Mummy or Daddy would have welcomed a ride in an open dicky!"

"Perhaps that would have persuaded them to go with someone else and I could have had you to myself."

"Another pretty compliment," she said. "The officers of your regiment certainly know how to pay them."

David's heart sank: he was just one of a crowd.

At the end of that dance he turned despondently to find Mrs Sharde close by in the act of thanking the Battalion Second-in-Command. When she had done so she walked away with the obvious intention of finding her bag in order to see who was her next partner. In no hurry himself, David wandered to the edge of the room. He felt depressed, and it would in any case give her the opportunity to recall his name. He kept his eyes upon her and as soon as she had replaced the programme he walked over to her.

"Mrs Sharde: I believe I have the pleasure of the next dance?"

Then something extraordinary happened. She just glided into his arms and they started to dance. She danced exquisitely. She moulded her body to his and they might have been one. David was an indifferent dancer, but with her he felt that it was the most natural thing in the world. He had never known anything like it. Her golden hair very near to his face had a delicate scent and her hand in his was cool and firm. They did not speak: conversation seemed superfluous. He was finding it difficult to control himself: never before had he experienced a woman's body so pressed to his. He was reminded of Ray's advice.

"Always wear a jock strap at a dance, old boy: it lets the girl know that you're interested without giving you a red face when the dance is over."

When the band stopped playing she moved away from him gently and they turned with the others to go into the room with refreshments. He felt he should say something at last, but could think of nothing better than "Thank you: you dance wonderfully well."

She looked up at him and he saw there were tiny laughter lines at the sides of her eyes.

"It's wonderful to dance with a man with a good figure. My previous partner had a pot and then you meet in the wrong places."

"Major Parsons. Yes, I can imagine."

He looked round anxiously in case they were within earshot and was relieved to see the Major conducting Lady Dinwiddy to the white cloth-covered refreshment table well in advance of them.

"He perspires too." She really had a most amusing outspoken way about her.

"How did you get on with my aunt?" she asked as he handed her a glass of champagne. "She doesn't like dances, poor dear, and only came to give me an evening out."

"Yes, she told me. I'm sorry your husband is away so much: it must be very dull all on your own these days."

A shadow crossed her face and she started to ask David questions about himself.

With filled plates and glasses in hand they found two chairs in a corner where they talked as fluently as they had been silent during their dance; and as time went on David realised that she was prettier than he had at first thought, as a result, perhaps, of the animation and character in her face when she spoke and when she listened. He began to like her more and more. He might have missed the boat with Mary, but had not done so badly after all; and when the interval came to an end and he was obliged to leave her to find his next partner he was quite sorry.

"Until dance number 17, Mrs Sharde."

"June, for heaven's sake!"

"June."

At the end of several dances as he started to look for his next partner he felt a strong hand on his arm and there was Miss Bowers again.

"It will hardly be a disappointment for you to learn that I shall be unable to join you in the last waltz after all."

She raised a hand as David started to protest.

"No. No. I am well aware of my deficiencies. Mr and Mrs Shuttlington are leaving early and have most kindly invited me to travel in their car. Their house is not far from mine. Since June would clearly wish to stay to the end, may I, on her behalf, take you up on your kind offer of a lift and carry her to her home?"

"Why, of course; I should be delighted."

"Splendid! Then that's settled. I'll leave her in your safe hands. Her house is only twenty minutes drive from here. I'm sorry though about our last waltz! Now you must look for your next partner. Good night, young man."

David had to acquaint Ray with the turn of events and towards the end of the next dance he saw him coming in from the garden with the pretty little dark woman. Ray was looking like a cat with a plate of cream and she was rather flushed. She went upstairs immediately and he stood by the door waiting for the dance to end. When it did David went over to him.

"Ray," he said, "I have arranged to take someone home when the Ball is over."

"You're coming on, old boy. Which one?"

"The blonde lady in the white dress; a Mrs June Sharde."

Ray whistled quietly. "You are coming on! Never mind about me: it will give me a first class excuse to ask my particular girl for the evening to carry me back to our billets. She sports a baby Austin and I've never kissed a girl in one before."

David smiled. "If you can't arrange it there's no reason why you should not come along with us in the dicky: June Sharde's house is only twenty minutes away."

"Playing gooseberry is absolute anathema to me, and anyway I'm sure of my girl. I wish you every success." He bowed in a theatrical manner.

When David approached June Sharde for their second dance her aunt had told her of their arrangement and she thanked him prettily as she slipped against him in the same disturbing manner as she had done before.

When they had danced like this for a while she murmured near his shoulder: "Now you are left without a dancing partner for the last dance. Shall I cut mine and dance with you instead?"

"There is nothing I'd like better," said David, "but we have very strict instructions not to dance with anyone more than twice."

"Don't you ever break a rule?"

"For an exceptional reason like that, yes; but as a new and junior officer in this battalion it would be very unwise. Who is your partner anyway?"

"Someone called Lieutenant-Colonel Masters," she said innocently.

"Good Lord! That's my Commanding Officer. I might as well resign my commission on the spot!"

She gave a low laugh and her soft hair brushed David's cheek as she turned her head.

"I won't ask you to do that," she said.

When the last waltz started David wandered into the refreshment room to see if there was any champagne left and as he did so he noticed Sir Nigel Dinwiddy dozing in a chair near the Adam-style chimney piece, a balloon glass of brandy beside him on a small table. He looked so old and wizened that it seemed it was only his starched shirt front and stiff collar held him upright. His heavily lined face was the colour of parchment.

Unwilling to disturb the old gentleman, David walked softly over to the table, where there was indeed an open bottle of champagne standing amidst the shattered remains of cakes and sandwiches; but in pouring himself a glass he clinked it against a plate and Sir Nigel opened his eyes.

"What, not dancing, young fella?" he said. His voice was old and cracked.

David explained the early departure of his proposed partner.

"Ah! Then have a glass of brandy with me. It's a thirty-year-old Hennessey and you won't get many opportunities of tasting the like again. You'll find another glass in the cupboard over there, together with the bottle. Bring them over here."

He poured a liberal measure and set the bottle on the table beside him.

"Not thirty years in the wood, you understand, but fifteen all the same. It came from my father's cellar. They do say it does not improve in the bottle, but I'm not so sure of that. Nectar, don't you think?"

"It is indeed, Sir."

"So, Alice Bowers has jilted you. Well, she was never cut out for this sort of thing; any more than I am now: though, mark you, I danced with the best of 'em when I was your age. I daresay you find that hard to believe and you'll have to take my word for it."

David said he was sure of it.

"She always was a rum sort of a girl."

David assumed he had returned to the subject of Miss Bowers.

"Her sister was the best of the bunch. She married a fella called Bill Sharde, who fagged for me at Harrow. Went into the Army and did very well in the Boer War. Collected an MC. Then the Bosch got him at first Ypres – during the last contest yer know. Pity. He might have gone far."

"I suppose Mrs Sharde must be a relation of his," said David. "I've promised to take her home in my car this evening."

"Ah! Have you? Yes, she would be that pretty little fair girl that Bill Sharde's second son married. I never could understand why a girl like that should throw herself away on such a bounder. But girls will do that sort of thing. Funny how some children turn out so badly when they spring from good stock. He got himself into some kind of reserved occupation, to keep out of the services I shouldn't wonder. There seem to be a lot of men about like that this time. Not a bit like the last show when nearly

85

everyone that was fit volunteered – some of the unfit ones too. I tried, but they would insist I was too old. A lot of nonsense, but there was nothing to be done about it: I wasn't in a position to falsify my date of birth as many did."

He brooded for a while and David remained sitting beside him savouring the really excellent brandy.

Sir Nigel continued: "It is nice to see you young fellas enjoyin' yourselves; but it is a bit too much for me at my time of life. It was Lady Dinwiddy's idea: such things give her great pleasure. But then, she is a lot younger than I am."

At this point he seemed to fall asleep for a few minutes and David got up to help himself to a sandwich. The brandy on top of several glasses of champagne was making him feel light-headed. Through the doors the sound of music and sliding feet came quite strongly; one, two, three, one, two, three. He wondered how the Colonel would react to June's melting style of dancing. He, at any rate, retained a good figure and they "would meet in the right places". He smiled to himself at the recollection of her words. On the other hand the Colonel seemed so remote and lacking in common emotions that David felt that he would not experience the kind of problem that he himself had.

"And now I'm too old even for the Home Guard." His nap over, Sir Nigel was able to take up the thread of his last remarks in a manner David admired. "Old age is the very devil, yer know. Make the best of it while you're young: you'll find the time flies past and before you know where you are you'll be sitting like I am now looking forward to getting to bed, where you won't sleep well anyway, and wishing that all the business of undressing wasn't necessary. Have another drop of brandy."

He poured out some more into each glass as the music stopped in the ballroom and there was the sound of clapping. It was really time for David to go to look for June Sharde, but he did not like to interrupt the old gentleman, for whom he was beginning to feel a strong friendship; and it was such good brandy!

"But we were talking about Alice Bowers," continued Sir Nigel. "She ought to have married when she was a girl. She wanted to and was all but engaged to a nice young man from quite a good family; but he was an actor and her father, old Bowers, wouldn't countenance it at any price. When he asked old Bowers for his consent he told him that it wasn't him he disapproved of; it was his profession: and in those days young girls usually did what their fathers told them. Anyway, Alice did. It was a pity though; the stage world might have suited her and she never married. He did well too. I saw him in a play on tour once and thought he was very good. She never looked at another man, though he got married I believe. Now, what the devil was his name? You'd be bound to know it if I told you. I believe he's playing in some London show now." He smacked his wrinkled forehead lightly with a bony almost transparent hand. "That's another thing you'll discover as time goes on: one forgets, one forgets."

A strong sensation of kindly sympathy swept over David and he wanted to comfort Sir Nigel, but his mind was working slowly and he could not find what to say that might be suitable. Two events occurred to resolve this problem while creating another. The first was that Sir Nigel shut his eyes and appeared to be taking another nap. The other was the appearance of June Sharde in the doorway.

David rose to his feet a little unsteadily. "Mrs Sharde – I mean June, I do apologise: I have been talking to Sir Nigel Dinwiddy and failed to watch the time."

She glanced at Sir Nigel, apparently in deep slumber, and raised an eyebrow a fraction.

She already had her light short coat over her shoulders, obviously ready to leave and David hastened to accompany her into the hall where they thanked Lady Dinwiddy, busy saying farewell to her guests, and went out into the night and David's Riley.

The moon was shining brightly from a clear, starry sky, throwing deep shadows as he drove the car along the narrow country roads following the directions given to him quietly by June Sharde, who sat back in her seat well away from him. Apart from these occasional instructions she said nothing and since David was concentrating hard upon driving carefully – the inner part of his mind well aware of the effect that the brandy and champagne was having upon him – it was a quiet journey. At the same time he was very much aware of her presence. Her delicate scent overcame the old leathery smell of the car and the glow he had noticed when he first met her surrounded her even in the dark beneath the black canvas hood.

Her house was at the end of a short drive with the front door at the side where the gravel opened out to form a forecourt. A garage projected from the side of the house beyond the front door and tall trees at the side of the turning space threw a deep shadow across it.

As they entered the drive June spoke: "You must come in and have a drink," she said.

The idea appealed to David and instead of driving straight to the front door as he had first intended he turned the car round so that it stood at the side of the gravel beneath the trees and they walked across to the door.

Inside, the house was pleasantly furnished with thick carpets and David realised that Mr Sharde was a wealthy man.

The night was so warm that he wore no overcoat, and after June had thrown down her coat onto a hall chair they went straight through into the living room where she immediately opened a cocktail cabinet against one wall.

"Whisky and soda I should think, wouldn't you?"

David hesitated: he knew he had already drunk more than he had ever done before and whisky on top of champagne and brandy sounded perilous. Then he thought, what the hell! before answering: "That would be very nice, but not too strong: I'm feeling mellow enough as it is."

She said, "I prefer mellow men! And who was it wrote that an Englishman is several drinks under par before he starts anyway. Come take this." And she handed him a large glass of a very dark-looking liquid."

She held her own up in the air and said: "Down with Hitler!"

"I'll drink to that," said David with feeling.

"You don't like the war?"

"Not one little bit. I'm not cut out for soldiering anyway."

"You're not a regular then?"

"No, I was studying to be an architect."

"That's a very different profession; but there will be plenty for you to do when the war is over; so take heart."

"If I survive."

"That's not being mellow; it's being maudlin."

"Yes, I really don't know why: I'm sorry."

"Oh, don't apologise. It's a thought that must lie dormant at the back of every man in the services only to pop out at unguarded moments."

"I must admit I feel very unguarded now."

"Do you? How nice. Let's play some mood music."

She went to a radiogram in a corner and put on a record, remaining standing with her glass of whisky in her hand while the sickly sweet music poured into the room:

> "And in the evening by the firelight's glow
> I'll hold you close and never let you go,
> And you will tell me all I want to know
> When you come home again."

"You missed the last dance," she said. "Why not make up for it now?"

David took her into his arms but they did not dance. One of his hands was around her waist and the other behind her shoulders where it pressed against her smooth skin. Her supple body shaped itself to his as during the dancing, but now her mouth was against his and her lips opened to allow her tongue to feel delicately for his while one of her hands pressed his head downwards.

So they remained for a timeless period. David had never experienced anything remotely like it before and felt oddly dizzy when she released herself and said as she took his hand: "Come on." She led him in a kind of dream out of the room and up the stairs to a landing where there was a corridor and through a door into a large bedroom with blue and white wallpaper, a fluffy white carpet and a double bed. Here she turned to him and they kissed again until she pushed him away and said: "The trouble with uniform is the coat buttons. Why not take your coat off?"

Obediently, still in a haze, David did so and hung it over the end of the dressing room table chair before taking her into his arms once more. Greatly daring, he slid his hand that was against her shoulder to the dress strap which passed over her upper arm and began to pull it down, when she pushed herself away and said: "Undressing each other is too complicated and awkward. I'll tell you what: let's have baths and meet here again in twenty minutes. I have a bathroom through there." She indicated a door not far from the head of the bed. "And you go along to the one at the end of the passage. You'll find a towel there."

The interruption brought David sharply to his senses.

"But what about your husband?"

"Oh, for heaven's sake don't talk about him now. He's away for a few days anyway."

The curious sensation that he was moving in another world and observing his actions from afar returned to him as he went out into the passage, walked along it to the bathroom, took off the rest of his clothes while he ran the bath and lay in the warm water. The feeling persisted as he dried himself and put on a dark silk dressing gown which he found hanging on a hook and walked back to the bedroom slipperless.

When there was no reply to his gentle knock he looked round the door and saw that the room was empty. From the bathroom came the sound of bathwater running away. He passed further into the room and looked at the bed. June had pulled back the coverlet, revealing a blue-and white-flowered eiderdown over matching blue blankets and the pure white sheets and pillow cases. She had turned down one corner of the top sheet invitingly. So this was to be the stage for his first encounter with that wonder which had tugged at his body and imagination for the last five years; whose ancient enchantment he had rehearsed in unsatisfying solitude; whose mystery, instinct and intelligence informed him must be reciprocal to achieve its true magic. And this experienced and attractive woman was to be the partner to guide him along the unknown path. He stood amazed at his good fortune. How could he have expected such a woman in such a setting? It has to be admitted that all thoughts of Mary had left his mind.

While he stood there the bathroom door opened and he looked up to see June standing in the opening. She was completely naked.

Until this moment David's only experience of unclothed women was through statuary and paintings by the masters, where fluttering drapery or oddly situated pieces of foliage guard against what was regarded as immodest.

Though June stood in silhouette with the bright bathroom light behind her the bedhead light threw her frontal form into shadowed detail from the top of her fair hair thrown back from amused face to a point just above her knees where detail disappeared in the shadow cast by the bedside table. It was remarkably effective. As David had concluded from her clothed form and the feel of her body against his she had a very good figure. It was true that her breasts hung lower than the sculptors and painters had led him to expect, but their full shapeliness left him with no feeling of disappointment, while the unexpected richness of golden hair between her thighs served to stimulate his already deeply stirred senses. She could have hardly composed herself better and stood thus for several seconds, clearly enjoying the obvious effect she was having upon him. Then her right hand fluttered up to the bathroom light switch and clicked it off, leaving the only remaining light to expose her body in still more detail.

As David remained where he was in rapt contemplation, she moved further into the room and said: "You're not playing fair, David; you're wearing a dressing gown."

And as he slid it off to lie at his feet, she said: "That's better – and most encouraging too! But first let me open the window to give us more air on such a lovely night."

She lent across the bed to switch off the light and for a moment he saw her in sideways leaning view before all disappeared in complete darkness. He sensed her fragrant body pass close by him as she went to the window and he heard the curtains drawn and the blackout blind released to reveal her once again in silhouette, this time against the starry moonlit sky.

The dreamlike quality of all that was happening remained with him as she came into his arms and he felt himself shivering slightly with excitement as he felt her nakedness. He remained in the dream as they kissed and as she half turned to lead him towards the bed so that one of his hands passed over her breasts: and it was still a dream as she drew him down onto the bed with her.

Which was when the nightmare started.

They were not speaking and the only noise was the sound of the bed giving under their weight as in partial embrace they descended upon it when, cutting through the quiet there was the unmistakable harsh sound of tyres on the gravel outside. They lay quite still while the sound increased as the car approached and stopped outside the front of the house; the engine noise ceased abruptly and there was the sound of a car door being opened and slammed shut.

"Who can it be?" whispered David.

"My husband: he's come back early."

"But you said he was away for several days."

"Yes, and I tell you, he's come back early."

She did not seemed alarmed: merely irritated.

David was so appalled that he lay where he was, stupidly, his mind refusing to work.

She sat up.

"It was a mistake wasting time having baths," she said.

There was the sound of footsteps on gravel and suddenly David was able to think properly again.

"I must get away," he said.

"How?" He could see her face turned towards him in the pale light. Was there an expression of amusement on it? He thought there was.

He leapt off the bed, his brain racing feverishly now. His service jacket was across the back of a chair, but all his other clothes were in the bathroom down the passage and the passage was in full view from the hall. The chances of getting to the bathroom and back with them without being observed were too slim. There was only one way open to him. He ran to the window and looked out. Yes, there was a flat roof beneath it. He grabbed his jacket and put it on.

"Hide my clothes," he whispered and scrambled over the window sill.

As he turned to let himself down onto the roof below he caught his last sight of June sitting up on the bed with her weight taken on one arm, motionless, watching him.

As he landed on what felt like leadwork beneath his bare feet it crossed his mind that John Churchill, later the great Duke of Marlborough, had been obliged to flee the bed of the beautiful Barbara Villiers in similar fashion at the approach of King Charles II. The thought gave little comfort.

Beyond the roof he stood on lay what must have been the back garden, and David could see the roof of the garage to his left. If he could slip round behind the garage he would be able to approach his car under cover of the shadow of trees that lined the drive, and if, as seemed probable, June's husband had entered the house he should have time to start the car and get away before he came out again. He would detect the flight but might not discover the fugitive. Much would depend on June. David had an uneasy feeling that his behaviour was cowardly.

He dropped onto the lawn and crept round behind the garage feeling the absurdity of his naked nether quarters in the moonlight. It felt better when he reached the shade of the trees and he made his way stealthily through them, flitting from tree trunk to tree trunk. He could see the dark shape of his car in the shadows and beyond it another lit by the moonlight where it stood in front of the house. It looked large and expensive. The front door of the house was shut, so David concluded Mr Sharde had gone in. He hoped that he might be helping himself to a drink in the living room, which would give June time to cover his tracks, though he had to admit it was a very remote hope since her husband could not have failed to see his car and wondered at it.

When David reached a point where his car was between him and the house he turned towards it, opening the button of his right hand jacket pocket where he kept the ignition key, which he took into his hand. Bending low he left the cover of the trees and crept to the door beside the driving seat. All remained quiet. His hope of getting away increased. On a warm night like this after the recent run the engine would start easily, and then it would only be a matter of straight off and away. Possibly Mr Sharde would come out of the house at the sound and that would give June time to conceal his clothes, which she would be able to convey to him later.

Very gently he turned the door handle and opened the door, keeping his head well down, and succeeded in doing so with hardly a sound. So far so good. He slid into the driving seat as he reached out to put the key into its familiar place in the dashboard, and it was as he did this he became aware of a presence in the other seat.

"Good evening," said a deep cold voice.

In all his life David had never received a greater shock.

A hand reached out in the darkness and took the key from his before he recovered.

"I don't know who you may be," continued the voice, "but it is apparent that you have some explaining to do; and as at the same time it would suit me to take a look at you we will now go into my house."

There was absolutely nothing David could do but comply.

As he followed his captor across the drive to the front door it was apparent that he was a big man and it was with a terrible feeling of confusion and dismay that he knew that it must be Mr Sharde.

The loose gravel of the drive pricked the underside of David's feet as he walked in this way to the front door, after which Mr Sharde led him into the living room where he turned his back to the brick fireplace and, putting his hands behind his back, slowly looked David up and down. While he did this David had the opportunity to study him.

He was, as David had observed in the moonlight as he walked before him, a big man, with broad shoulders and a short thick neck. He could now see that his complexion was swarthy and his hair was black. His whole face was broad and his nose rather wide. Beneath this nose a little black moustache accentuated his small mouth which protruded slightly. His eyes were a little too close together in relation to the width of his cheeks, above which his forehead narrowed towards his hair. Years later David was to be disagreeably reminded of him by photographs of the Egyptian, Colonel Abdul Gammel Nasser.

His eyes were filled with ominous hostility as he completed his leisurely inspection.

"God Almighty!" he said at last. "It's only a little boy!"

As David made no reply at this unpropitious start to their interview Mr Sharde continued with a question: "Have you nothing to say?"

Aware that his position was hopeless David's instinct was to tell the exact truth and be done with it, but at the same time he felt the need to do all that he could to protect June, and so for the moment prevaricated.

"Am I right in believing that you are Mr Sharde?"

"Who the hell do you think I am; the local plumber?"

There was another deadly silence, broken at last by Mr Sharde.

"Don't just stand there looking like the principal boy in some bloody pantomime: it's late and I'm waiting for your story."

David took a deep breath.

"It seems," he said, "that you are under a misapprehension . . ."

"Indeed!" interrupted Mr Sharde sarcastically.

"I brought your wife back home from the Ball at Lady Dinwiddy's this evening because your aunt, Miss Bowers, who had taken her to it, was unable to do so owing to the breakdown of her car."

"Go on," said Mr Sharde grimly.

"During the drive we talked and I happened to mention that a disadvantage of the war time army is the lack of bathing facilities, and your wife kindly offered to let me have a bath here before returning to my billet. When I was drying I heard your car, and realising that my position might compromise your wife I lost my head and tried to bolt."

"Leaving through my wife's bedroom window with nothing on but your jacket."

"It was the only way I could find without coming down the stairs."

"You appear to know your way about my house very well. On how many other occasions have you 'bathed' here at night?"

The sarcasm in his voice was biting.

"This is the first time I have been here."

"It will be most interesting to see what a judge has to say when you recount such a cock and bull story in Court."

"In Court?"

This was a new twist to an already appalling situation.

"Yes, in Court. You don't suppose, now that I have caught you red handed, I shall let the matter rest there. I have known for some time what has been going on, though I did not for one moment imagine that my wife would stoop so low as to take a promiscuous youth for a lover, and I shall take immediate steps to obtain a divorce, naming you as co-respondent."

"You are quite wrong," said David stoutly. "I give you my word of honour that I have never slept with your wife."

"I never suggested you slept with her. I am stating that you fucked her."

The crudity and implications of this remark left David speechless.

"In order to save time," continued Mr Sharde, "what is your name? It is of no use attempting to withhold it: I can easily find out."

"I have no intention of concealing it and would have given it to you before if you had given me the opportunity. You are making a terrible mistake."

"It is you, not I, that have made a mistake, you randy rabbit."

David struggled to restrain his increasing anger. He was at Mr Sharde's mercy and it was plain that he was relishing it.

94

"You are insulting," he said.

"Insulting!" spat out Mr Sharde. "Insulting! It is impossible to insult such a little shit. Rather it is you that insults the regiment to which you belong. Again I ask, what is your name?"

David gave it and asked whether he could now recover his clothes and have the key of his car back.

"No," replied Mr Sharde. "I shall hold both your clothes and car as evidence in case you attempt to deny your presence here."

"But my billet is more than ten miles away from here!"

"That is your business, not mine."

David wondered what June was doing. Was there any hope that she might come to his rescue? There was no noise at all from upstairs.

He tried another approach.

"Mr Sharde," he said, "it is very late and we are both tired. Would it not be better if we meet tomorrow in order to discuss the situation rationally?"

It was a forlorn hope and it failed.

Mr Sharde glared at David for a time, his small eyes bright with hate, and then walked past him to the door, which he opened and said: "Get out!"

David stood his ground.

"This is absurd," he said. "You cannot expect me to walk ten miles without shoes and wearing only my service jacket."

"What you do when you leave my house does not interest me. If you choose to wander about without your shoes and trousers it is your affair."

It was clear to David that short of trying force, which would in the circumstances be foolish in the extreme, there was no hope at all of altering his tormentor's attitude. On the other hand he had no intention of walking back as he was. There was only one thing to do. He walked across the room to the telephone that stood upon a table by a window and picked up the receiver. To his relief, Mr Sharde did not attempt to hinder him and remained standing by the doorway watching while he asked the operator to give him his battalion headquarters. When the duty officer answered he explained that he was stranded, gave his position and asked for a vehicle to pick him up. Then he walked past Mr Sharde without another word, through the front door and once more across the drive to his car where he got in and sat down to wait. Behind him the front door closed.

When confronted by the extraordinary the British soldier can be wonderfully tactful, and the driver who arrived about an hour later gave no sign of interest or surprise at having to go out in the small hours to pick up one of his officers naked from the hips down as well as shoeless.

Neither was David surprised when he received a summons two days later to go to the Adjutant's office at battalion headquarters.

He was distinctly stiff.

"The Commanding Officer wishes to see you," was all that was said.

David knocked on the CO's door and heard the familiar voice say: "Come in!"

He marched smartly up to the front of the CO's desk and saluted. As he was not told to stand at ease he remained stiffly to attention.

"Mr Drummond," the CO's voice was grim and formal. "I have had a telephone conversation with a Mr Sharde."

He paused as though he expected a reply, so David, attempting to conceal the anxiety within him from his voice, said: "Yes, Sir."

"He alleges that he found you trying to escape from his house early in the morning two days ago without your clothes having been in bed with his wife. What have you to say?"

The army had taught David not to waste words at times like this.

"The first part is correct, Sir: the second part is not."

"Explain yourself."

David then gave the facts without embellishment, and when he had finished there was a silence between them as they looked steadily at one another, the CO behind his desk and David standing stiffly to attention before him. When his CO spoke again David thought he could detect less steel in his voice, though what he had to say was unpleasant enough.

"You will perfectly understand, Mr Drummond, that as Commanding Officer of this battalion in time of war I have no time to spare over young officers who allow their physical needs to overcome their judgement, and that, furthermore, it is my duty to guard against the name of the Regiment being smeared by scandal. Fortuitously, I received a request during the week from Division to put forward the name of a junior officer for posting to the staff of a Home Guard training school in quite another part of the British Isles, and I have submitted your name. As it may take some time for the War Office to confirm your posting, if indeed it does so, I am sending you back to the Regimental Depot forthwith. By taking this action and in view of your age I think it is possible that Mr Sharde may not pursue the matter further. The Adjutant will give you your movement orders."

It was obvious to David that his CO regarded it to be the end of the interview, and he was well aware that he should now salute and depart.

Nevertheless, he remained standing stiffly before him, shaken and unbelieving. To be returned to Depot after only a few months in this splendid battalion! And to be sent to a Home Guard training school to instruct old men to fight a modern war. The disgrace of it! And the disappointment! Also, how would he be able to explain it to his friends and family? And what would uncle Edward think of it after the trouble he had taken? These thoughts passed rapidly through David's mind before he burst out with: "But surely, Sir, is it not probable that Mrs Sharde's corroboration of what I have told you will persuade her husband to drop his charge without my dismissal from the battalion?"

"Doubtless," replied the CO dryly; "but, if the action I am taking is not successful, your problem, Mr Drummond, will be that Mrs Sharde confirms that you had sexual intercourse with her."

CHAPTER 7

"If a thing can go wrong it will."

MURPHY'S LAW

"It is good news you are not a regular," said Captain Baker. "We thought you might be when we heard that the powers that be were posting another officer here. Now that the school is a going concern and doing good work we expect the Army to alter its attitude towards us. So far we have been grudgingly accepted with some suspicion and amusement: now that our success is established there are indications that the top brass believes the Army should take us under its wing and correct our unorthodox approach: regular soldiers hate the unorthodox. The appointment of a new Commandant and Adjutant were the first indication and we thought you might be another. As it is the Army will not have had time to cast you in its standard mould."

David asked how the school had started.

"Alec Payne, the journalist and author – you may have read some of his work – had the idea and pulled the necessary strings to get it off the ground. Then he gathered in a few of his friends from the civil war in Spain, all with first hand experience of fighting a trained and well armed enemy with scratch troops facing modern weapons, which is of course exactly the same condition as the Home Guard will find itself in.

"Is he here now?"

"No, he left in disgust when the War House appointed the new Commandant. He's back in civvy street. The rest of us, the originals, being less mettlesome, hung on. And, after all, the school was not our brain-child: it was Alec's. We'll be pushed out in due course, but meanwhile we are doing a very useful job at a crucial time when our approach is most needed. Later, when the Army moves in and sets about trying to make the Home Guard a sort of branch field unit it won't matter. Either the Germans will have invaded and the contest decided or they won't invade at all."

The two of them were strolling through the park-like grounds that surrounded the great house that had been taken over to house the Home Guard Training School, and they had reached a point where a long, narrow, mown grass terrace ran for about a hundred yards straight to a wooden seat placed at the end. On one side was a wood of ash and young beech, while on the other there was a magnificent view of the valley and the hills beyond. It was late September and the leaves on the trees had taken on the warm colours of autumn. They had begun to fall and here and there lay upon the grass, mute tokens of the approaching end of another year. At the end of the terrace, behind the wooden seat, a clump of laurels formed a stop. The still warm sun was low in a cloudless sky and the air held that indefinable sense of ripe richness and gentle melancholy which accompany autumn in England.

David was rather more than medium height, but his companion stood well above him, walking erect and broad-shouldered in his immaculately tailored battle dress. He was, David supposed, round about thirty-five years of age.

On his arrival that afternoon David had reported to the Adjutant who had sent him into the Commandant's office for a short, stiff interview which left him with an impression of a small sharp-eyed man with a pointed moustache who found young officers a nuisance; after which he had been directed to his sleeping quarters and into the hands of Captain Baker for a general introduction into the working of the school. As it was a Sunday the school was empty, the previous week's course having left that morning and the next one not due in for another couple of hours.

"Apart from the Commandant and the Adjutant, there are four instructors here and you will make a fifth. I'll introduce you to them later. There is Tubby Maddox, an explosive expert; Jake Donovan, who loves bombs and all funny weapons; Ceddie Roussel, an artist who instructs on camouflage and fieldcraft; and myself. I deal with tactics and theory. You will find our approach pragmatic: after all, we learnt how to fight in the International Brigades in Spain. Did you take much interest in the Spanish Civil War?"

David replied truthfully that he had followed it in the newspapers, though he had found it intensely confusing and ultimately boring.

"All war is boring for most of the time and confusing all of the time. The bits that are not boring are the most confusing of all. Still, I know what you mean: it was exceptionally confusing, particularly on ours, the Republican side."

They reached the wooden seat and Captain Baker sat down upon it, patting the space beside him as he did so.

"Coming from a regular battalion you will find a free and easy atmosphere here," he continued. "With the exceptions of the Commandant and the Adjutant we are all on Christian name terms and we are hoping to break down the Adjutant before long. What is yours?"

David told him.

"Mine is Timothy, or Tim as everyone seems to prefer."

He paused to collect his thoughts and as he did so passed his hand down the back of his head in a characteristic gesture.

"Home Guard units in this part of the country send selected officers and NCOs to us for courses lasting a week. We take ninety at a time and divide them up into three groups or classes. I expect the Commandant will agree to your spending your first three weeks here attending the lectures and exercises as though you were one of the students. After that you will be able to stand in for any one of us. You'll find the Home Guard very keen and willing to learn in spite of the inclination of many of them to fall asleep during lectures, especially after lunch. Our real problem is the acute shortage of weapons; but we are getting round that in various ways as you will find out. Members of the Home Guard may be elderly and for the most part out of condition, but they have the advantage of being entirely defensive, fighting in prepared positions on their own well known ground. The key to their role is that every hamlet, village and town in Great Britain will be an obstacle for the invading forces, which will slow them down and tire them, giving our commanders time to decide when to counter attack with what small field forces remain after Dunkirk. Your training will help you to understand how town fighting favours the defenders and how vulnerable tanks are at short range in narrow streets where they cannot manoeuvre or support each other easily. I keep on hammering in the rule that every built-up area must be turned into a defensive 'hedgehog'."

He fell silent again, gazing pensively out across the valley to the grey blue hills beyond. A yellow leaf fluttered slowly down from above and landed on David's knee where he let it rest. There was a great quietness behind the gentle bird song.

"It is difficult to imagine all this as a battlefield," he said.

Tim Baker nodded. "And when the noise and smell and mess of war arrives it is difficult to believe it can ever be like this again. Make the most of it: whatever comes next, the world is going to be a very different place."

"No doubt we shall see the end of great houses like this one and other changes in our lives as well; but whatever happens lovely autumn afternoons like this will be with us."

Tim looked at David keenly.

"So much depends upon the way we look at beauty. You know the great chorus in 'Fidelio' when the prisoners are permitted for a short time to leave their cells and venture into the sunlight? Their vision is a very different one from the free men and women outside."

"Are you so convinced we are going to lose this war?"

"Not convinced, though we deserve to, and I think it likely."

Later when David got to know him well Ceddie Roussel told him: "You must forgive Tim's bouts of depression: he took our failure in the Spanish Civil War very hard." And when David asked whether Tim was a Communist Ceddie said: "No: he believes the Anarchists had a better solution." And seeing that David had not the slightest idea what those aims might be explained how the Anarchists expected at the end of the violent period of the revolution that not only private property would be abolished, but also the State itself, each locality being responsible for its own social mechanism.

"But surely that is in essence, Communism?"

"No: Communism envisages an intermediary period where the State is the principal authority. It is true that Communism envisages the State withering away, but Tim and the Anarchists fear that the state will not do so and merely become just another form of oppression."

"How did the Anarchists and Communists get on together?"

"They didn't in the long run. In point of fact one of the causes of the failure of the Republican side was its hopeless division into several groups, while on the other side General Franco was successful in unifying the Nationalists in spite of the disparity between Fascism, absolute Monarchism and Catholic youth: quite an achievement in Spain. It is one of the ironies of this world that the idealists always fall out while the oppressors have a fixed unity of purpose that weighs the scales heavily on their side."

"And Tim is an idealist?"

"He was. Now he has grown pessimistic. As I said, he was very upset about our failure in Spain. Also, he had many friends there on the Republican side. Frederico Lorca was one of them and he has the greatest admiration for his poetry. The Nationalists shot him for no apparent reason early in the war, you remember."

David didn't, but shook his head sadly.

"Then, his wife left him recently, and he is beginning to drink too much."

101

At the end of their walk in the grounds of the great house Tim Baker and David mounted the flight of steps leading to the colonnaded front entrance and entered the splendid hall, which rose to the level of the ceiling of the first floor. The white and beige coloured marble floor still gleamed in spite of neglect where it was not protected from military hobnailed boots by matting. On the far side a wide stone staircase swept up to the first floor landing, its dark mahogany handrail supported on an elaborate wrought iron balustrade.

From this hall the large panelled doors were framed with elaborately carved surrounds. Between two niches in one wall there was a standard type military notice board made of cork sheet in an incongruously simple wood frame, and on it were pinned standing orders and other notices for the benefit of the incoming courses. One sheet of paper caught David's eye and he stopped to read it.

"Saluting
(1)   A salute is the military way of saying 'Hello'.
(2)   A salute is the quickest way for a soldier to say to an officer: 'What are your orders?'
(3)   A salute is not undemocratic: two officers of equal rank, when meeting on business, salute each other.
(4)   A salute is a sign that a comrade who has been an egocentric individual in private life has adjusted himself to the collective way of getting things done.
(5)   A salute is a proof that the Home Guard is on its way from being a collection of well-meaning amateurs to a steel precision instrument for eliminating Fascists.

"Taken word for word from the 15th International Brigade's weekly paper *Our Fight,*" said Tim Baker, who had watched David quietly while he was reading.

"But surely the Home Guard don't need to be told why to salute? They are all old soldiers from the Great War."

"Not so. You may be surprised to find out how many are too young for that. Also, quite a number come from the ranks of reserved occupations. And again, there are many who have reached high positions in civil life who now find themselves in subordinate positions in the Home Guard."

"You were with the International Brigade?"

"After the battle round Brunette near Madrid until the end of the

Aragon offensive."

"Where did you go then?"

"I was wounded."

"Badly?"

"In the balls."

"Oh hell!"

"Yes," he said.

The ante-room set aside for the instructors attached to the school was a small one in the basement lit by a window high in one wall which faced a sunken area. When they entered it after their walk they found Tubby Maddox and Jake Donovan playing chess. Tim Baker introduced them.

Tubby Maddox was an exceedingly thin, tall man with white hair that stood out in disorder above his pallid lean face. His expression was vague and he might have been taken for an elderly don from one of our universities had he not been in battle dress, which hung round his bony frame as though he had shrunk since he first bought it. He waved a long white hand in a gesture of greeting and returned to the matter of his next move. David learnt later that he had been a scientist before the war in the Research Establishment at Farnborough.

Jake Donovan was nearly bald and behind a pair of metal-rimmed glasses his eyes were watery. When young he may have been quite good looking, but now, in late middle age, his skin had taken on a pouchy look and his nose was distinctly red with that touch of blue that sometimes denotes a heart problem. His posture in his easy chair was curiously crouched and this was explained when he stood up to go to a cupboard where he filled a glass with whisky and water before returning to the game. One of his legs was shorter than the other with the result that his body was thrown out of line and compensated for by the opposite shoulder being raised higher than normal.

"Jake has been blown up so many times that a surgeon would find difficulty in locating parts of his interior," Ceddie Roussel once said.

"It'll be fine to have some young blood about," said Jake. His voice had the faintest Irish lilt about it. "And what is more, there will be somebody I might be able to beat at chess: playing against Tubby is like competing with a mechanical calculator."

Tubby Maddox's lectures were concise and his demonstrations dramatic: he certainly knew exactly how to use explosives. Ceddie Roussel taught the arts of camouflage and fieldcraft with wit and skill. Tim Baker was most convincing as he expounded his views of the role of the Home Guard, and gave lectures on street fighting, clearly based upon his personal experiences in Spain. But Jake Donovan was the most startling and entertaining.

Putting down a sawn off shotgun, Jake picked up a Mills bomb "This," he said, "is a lovely little bomb and very handy in close quarter fighting." He tossed it from hand to hand as if to illustrate its handiness. "All you have to do is to pull out this little wire," and as he said this he withdrew the safety pin; "and when you throw it, off flies the handle and down goes the plunger and five seconds later off she goes!" And he placed the bomb upon the table, releasing the arm so that it did indeed fly off with a clatter onto the floor. There was a rapid scraping of chairs as some of the audience began to take cover, while the little Corporal at David's side disappeared through the door like a hare from a trap.

"– If the bomb had been armed with a fuse," went on Jake as though nothing had happened, "which this one hasn't. Now, don't go being ashamed of the fact that some of you shied when I did that: this little fellow is not to be underestimated, small though it looks. When one of them goes off the high explosive inside distributes the metal outer casing at very high speed all around and I wouldn't want to be without cover inside a hundred yards of it."

Later, Jake took up a bottle little larger than a ginger beer bottle, filled with what appeared to be two liquids, orange coloured at the bottom and clear at the top.

"Here we have a cocktail," he said, holding it up for all to see. "A cocktail – for the benefit of those amongst you that are teetotallers – is a mixture of lively ingredients, and this one is called a 'Molotov Cocktail'. Some bright spark dreamed it up during the late war in Spain, where you may recall the unfortunate Republicans had no tanks at the start until the kind Russians sent them some, and no anti-tank guns, so they had to contend with the tanks provided for the Nationalists by the Nasties and the Ities. It's just a standard bottle filled with petrol, water and phosphorous. Looks innocuous enough, doesn't it? But those of you who know a little about chemistry know that when phosphorous is exposed to the air there is spontaneous combustion, so that when you lob one of these onto an enemy tank, preferably over the driver's vision slits, the bottle breaks against the steel, the phosphorous catches fire, which sets off the petrol and whoopee! All you have to do is to pot the buggers as they bale out. If they are silly enough to drive in amongst your houses you can just drop them on them from the windows. However, you'll be wanting to reach a little further than you can throw from time to time and a clever Mr Northover has designed a simple cheap projector, which most of you should have by now in your units."

He put the bottle down and turned to a five foot length of standard steel pipe fixed to a stubby tripod, one leg of which was longer than the others and had an elementary seat welded to it.

"With this neat little fellow all you have to do is to find a concealed position near the road the Nasties are coming along, and sitting on this little seat you open this simple breach block and pop in a 'Cocktail' with the neck of the bottle going in first. Behind the bottle you put in this cylindrical charge with the sponge rubber pad first to cushion the bottle from the big shove the charge will give it when you pull the trigger here. Don't go making the mistake whatever you do of putting the charge in the wrong way round with the rubber pad at the back because if you do it won't go off, and there you'll be sitting like a spare prick at a wedding and only able to wave as the tank goes by. This Northover projector, as it is called after the good Mr Northover, will, if your aim is good, put a 'Cocktail' onto a tank up to seventy-five yards away. And, what is more, if it's the enemy infantry that are moving up on you, you can pop in a Mills bomb with the pin out instead of the bottle and put that among them. When the charge sends the bomb upon its way and it comes out of the end of the barrel, off flies the arm and down goes the plunger inside to set the fuse burning. Five seconds later, just as the bomb arrives amongst the bastards, off she goes to their considerable detriment. Aiming the projector high like a howitzer you should be able to put a bomb a good two hundred yards away."

At this point the door beside David opened quietly, and glancing round in expectation of seeing the frightened little corporal returning, he found one of the Orderly Room staff with a slip of paper. He handed it over, saluted and slid away closing the door gently behind him. It was a message. The first words David read were: "PUSH OFF," and for an unpleasant half-second he thought the Commandant had already decided to dispense with his services and that he would be on his way back to the Depot once more. Then common-sense and experience corrected him and he knew it must be a code word, so beloved of the Army. He saw also that the message was addressed to "All Instructors" and marked "Urgent". He had not the smallest idea what it meant though the solution was simple: he rose to his feet and walked up the hut to where Jake was now going into detail over the Northover Projector and handed it to him.

Jake read it and turned to the class.

"There now," he said in the same quiet conversational manner he habitually used. "It seems we're all going to have a chance of giving Hitler a black eye at any moment now. This message that I have in my hand informs us that the invasion is imminent and all forces are being alerted. Mr Drummond and I have to go to the Commandant to get our orders. Meanwhile, the senior officer among you will organise you into three equal sections and take command as though you are a platoon. As soon as possible the arms available will be distributed among you and you will be given further orders. The other classes will be doing the same. Come," he said to David, "we'll be off to see the Commandant."

Outside the hut David expressed his surprise at not having been given the code word for this eventuality.

"Sure, that was an oversight on the part of the Adjutant; though I wouldn't be saying anything about it if I were you. We had a plan all worked out before the new Commandant and Adjutant arrived, which I believe the Commandant has scrapped and has been working on a new one that he hasn't divulged yet. We'll be learning all about it now."

The tall, thin figure of Tubby Maddox emerged from behind another hut on the other side of a wide lawn as he headed in the same direction. They joined him and after a few words reached the HQ hut where they found Tim Baker and Ceddie Roussel waiting for them with the Adjutant. Chairs had been arranged before the Commandant's desk and all sat down before him.

"Gentlemen," said the Commandant portentously, passing a forefinger along the underside of his silky moustache in two rapid movements, "the balloon is about to go up. I received a message from Southern Command twenty minutes ago informing me and all other Commanders in the Command that the German invasion of these islands is imminent, which is why I issued the code word and called you here for this 'O' Group. What have you all done with your classes?"

"That will do for the present," said the Commandant after they had relayed their orders, "but I intend that each platoon will be commanded by an officer instructor. Captain Baker will command No 1 Platoon; Captain Donovan will command No 2; and Captain Roussel No 3. Captain Maddox will take command of a small section of permanent staff, whose names are on this list," handing a piece of paper over to Tubby, "and will prepare remotely controlled charges at these points." He took up a billiard cue and pointed to four points on the map of the house and its grounds on the wall behind him. "Mr Drummond will take command of the remainder of the permanent staff with the following duties: (1) Post two sentries on the roof to be relieved at two hourly intervals. Their task will be to keep a look out for enemy parachutists and to report any sighting

106

immediately. (2) All available weapons are to be stacked in groups in the hall of the house ready for distribution under my supervision at 1645 hours. (3) Arrange for the arming of a hundred Mills bombs. (4) When all these matters have been attended to report back to me for further orders. You will have Sergeant Pendry to assist you.

"As the duties of Captain Maddox and Mr Drummond are the most urgent you will both set about them immediately while I brief the other officers on their roles. Carry on."

When David had set all these things in motion he did a round to see that all was well. The cook and an assistant were on the huge flat roof, pleased to have a change and enjoying the sunshine in spite of the chilly late autumn air. The possibility of early and sanguine conflict seemed to have made no impression upon them. The NCOs appointed to supervise the weapon collection had everything under control and he climbed up some stairs to the room where he had left Sergeant Pendry and Corporal Onions setting about the arming of the Mills bombs. He found Sergeant Pendry working on his own, swiftly and with practised fingers; already there were three boxes of twenty bombs primed and ready in the adjoining room.

David asked what had happened to Corporal Onions and learnt that he had been ordered to report to the Commandant. Stifling his irritation at this manner of taking men away from his small command without a word to him, David said he would give the Sergeant a helping hand until the Corporal came back and sat down beside him.

Sergeant Pendry was a short, broad man of about thirty five years with dark hair and a small moustache. He came from the Midlands and it was rumoured ran two wives, one in the south and the other in the north of England. If true, the complications did not appear to give him concern, for he was one of those fortunate persons blessed with a sunny temperament who ride through life on springs that absorb the inevitable shocks and bumps to a degree well above the average.

"If the enemy try and push through this place they're likely to take a knock," he said as he worked away. "Do you think they will, Sir?"

"That depends where they land and where they head for. If one of their thrusts comes through these hills and the army stops them in the valley they might well try to get round by this hill."

"It's steep and there are only two roads," said Sergeant Pendry. "It's hard luck we haven't been issued with one or two of those Blacker bombards."

Sergeant Pendry had recently returned from a course on the Blacker

107

bombard and was full of praise for its efficacy as an anti-tank weapon. He had explained to David that it was small and low, fired from a prone position, discharging a heavy explosive missile with a hollow charge up to a range of about seventy five yards with devastating effect.

"Yes, it may be they are on the way to the Home Guard just too late," said David.

"We're experts at that, aren't we, Sir?"

"What?"

"Too little and too late."

"We always seem to muddle through."

"Anyhow, I'm glad it's them and not us that 'as to do the Channel crossing."

Sergeant Pendry's aitches were a little uncertain.

"Seasickness?" asked David.

"That's too mild a word for it. Put me in a boat, be it ever so calm, and I'm *horse de combat*."

"I expect you'd be all right after a bit. You would get what is called your sea legs. Admiral Nelson used to be seasick every time he went to sea."

"Ah! That's just what my family say; but I know it's too bad for that. I'd die if it was rough. That's why I didn't go into the Navy in the family tradition you might say. We come from the west country you see. My father fought at the battle of Jutland and my grandfather used to talk about the days when the ships were painted black and yellow. He was a Petty Officer at the finish. My brother's serving in the Dorsetshire, what finished off the *Bismark*. There was a great to-do I can tell you when I didn't follow them."

Such an extreme example of a not altogether unusual weakness struck David as a serious misfortune, and he wondered what the Sergeant would do if posted overseas, to the Middle East theatre of war for instance, or even India, the former being at that time a very real possibility.

"You missed going out with the B.E.F. in '36?" David asked.

"Yes, thank Gawd. I was an instructor at our Depot. They was just going to send me out when 'Itler kicked us out."

In this way they passed the time while working on the bombs until only a dozen remained to be armed, at which point David said he should make another round of inspection and left the Sergeant to complete the work.

On the roof again he found the two sentries alert, though beginning to feel the chill in spite of their greatcoats. The sun was sinking into a bank of grey-purple cloud that had formed over the western horizon and the cold wind was building up. They had seen nothing of interest.

Down in the great hall David found the collection of weapons nearly complete and sent two soldiers up to Sergeant Pendry to help him bring down the boxes of Mills bombs. All would be ready before the time set by the Commandant. He was going to have a problem over the distribution of the inadequate number of weapons. Presumably, all Home Guards without any other form of weapon would be issued with a couple of Mills bombs each: it would be better than nothing at all.

An orderly room Lance-corporal came in through the entrance doorway and, seeing David, came across to him as quickly as his steel-studded boots permitted without slipping on the marble floor. He came to attention noisily and saluted.

"Commandant's orders, Sir," he said. "Sentries to stand down and all further preparations to be stopped. Please report to the Adjutant, Sir."

On the way David met Tim Baker. "Just another balls up," said Tim, "Southern Command appear to have failed to inform the Adjutant that the message was to do with an army exercise and that it should not have been sent to us in any case. We'll have to start unscrambling the eggs."

Curiously, everyone seemed disappointed.

David was reminded of his conversation with Sergeant Pendry the following April. He was in the ante room half reading *The Times* and half listening to an argument between Tubby and Jake. When not playing chess they frequently held amicable arguments. This time it was about Communism. Tubby, like many highly intelligent men of the period, was an ardent believer, spending much of his time among the staff spreading the creed in a quiet, studious way. Jake, on the other hand, had a lively disrespect for all ideologies.

"The Russians have always been meddlers," Jake was saying. "Whatever they profess to believe in at any one moment in history their desire for expansion runs like a red thread. You and I went to Spain because we were outraged by Fascism and the excesses perpetrated by the Nationalists: Stalin only sent supplies of arms to the Republicans because he wanted to see Communism installed in Spain as a part of his hegemony."

"Stalin wishes to see Communism everywhere," replied Tubby, "because he knows that therein lies hope for the future of mankind and the disappearance of the oppressors and the oppressed; but his aim in Spain was to counter the Germans and Italians who were breaking their word and sending arms and even soldiers and airmen to help Franco. He was able to see with his usual clarity of mind that the feeble policy of non-intervention pursued by Britain, France and the USA was leading to the breakdown of European order once more, which indeed it did."

"You've a brilliant mind but starry eyes, Tubby. We'll not go into the rights and wrongs of Communism all over again: only time will show you the extent of your foolishness in that respect; but are you not able to comprehend the value to the Russians of exploiting dissension in Europe?"

At this Tubby lifted the forefinger of a bony hand and pointed it at Jake.

"There you are wrong once more: the Russians were most anxious to avoid another explosion in Europe, fearing they would become involved and needing time for the great experiment to work. These gigantic steps forward in the history of man cannot be accomplished in a short time: a long period of peace is essential. Stalin could see clearly how dangerous Hitler was becoming, as was proved in March of 1938 when he proposed a grand alliance within the League of Nations against Hitler, which I do not need to remind you was rejected by Chamberlain, an act so incomprehensible that –"

But Tubby's flow was interrupted by the entrance of Tim Baker, who with a quick apology told them he had just been with the Commandant, who had given him instructions which he was to pass on without delay.

"It seems," he said, "that the powers that be are worried that the Home Guard in Northern Ireland are becoming dispirited and think they are forgotten. So, it has been decided on high that we should mount a display near Belfast to be attended by a multitude of Irish Home Guards, local bigwigs and even a General. We are to demonstrate the weapons available to the Home Guard, in particular the new Blacker bombard which is beginning to reach units out there."

"Are we all to go?" asked Jake.

"Not you, I'm afraid. It is to be Tubby, David, Sergeant Pendry and me."

"Now isn't that just like the army!" said Jake. "Here am I with the blood of old Ireland running in my veins and I'm the one that is to be left!" And he threw his twisted body back into the depth of his chair with an expression of deep disgust. "

"We'll miss you, Jake, but orders is orders," said Tim, taking a chair himself and proceeding to outline the operation.

The demonstration was set for one week hence on a Saturday afternoon, and he, Sergeant Pendry and David were to set off for Stranraer in Scotland by train early Wednesday morning in order to catch the ferry to Larne on Friday, which would give them time to prepare for the show. Tubby was to leave the following morning so that he would have enough time to make a preliminary reconnaissance and with the aid of the local Home Guard lay one of his remotely controlled tank ambushes at some suitable point.

"Oh bother!" said Tubby, who never used bad language. "That leaves me no time to deal with several outstanding matters of some importance."

"And not enough time the other end, I fear," said Tim. "Though if anyone can do it you will. In point of fact it is cutting it mighty fine for all of us: I daresay the order was given several weeks ago and has been filtering through the 'usual channels' ever since."

He went on to explain that the general idea was that he would give a talk over a loudspeaker system to the audience and would then paint a verbal picture of an enemy column of tanks approaching a village. The first shot would be Sergeant Pendry's with a Blacker bombard, followed by David using a Northover projector with "Molotov Cocktails" and a Mills bomb to discourage imaginary enemy supporting infantry. It would then be assumed that the column disposed of David's post and moved on to be engulfed in Tubby's fire ambush, a dramatic finale caused by firing barrels of diesel fuel from a concealed position by means of explosive charges.

"Would you arrange for a couple of targets to be put up, representing tanks, when you get there," said Tim to Tubby, "so that David and Sergeant Pendry can show the accuracy of their weapons as well as their effect?" I leave you to select the assumed line of advance to the enemy column since it must end at a sunken place for your fireworks. Has anyone any questions that can't wait until we are on our way? There will be plenty of time for the three of us going together both on the train and the boat."

It was then that David remembered Sergeant Pendry's allergy.

"It's not really a question," he said. "It's just that I happen to know that Sergeant Pendry can't take boats: they make him very ill."

"A lot of people are seasick," replied Tim. "As a matter of fact, I am myself. The answer is whisky and dry biscuits, mostly whisky."

David shook his head dubiously. "I gather it is much more serious in his case."

"He'll have to put up with it: he can't expect to spend the whole of the war in this country; and anyway, it's not a long crossing and he will have an afternoon and a night to recover in."

As it turned out Sergeant Pendry took the news of his forthcoming ordeal rather well and the three of them reached Stranraer late on Thursday afternoon without mention of the sea crossing ahead; for, as has been said, the Sergeant was not easily discomfited. Certainly, he looked a trifle pale, but so were Tim and David after the slow and tedious journey in wartime trains, whose awfulness had to be experienced to measure.

When they reached the hotel in which they were to sleep that night Tim insisted at the end of an indifferent meal that they should all three go to the bar for a drink before going to bed. They stood at the dingy little bar with two large whiskies for Tim and David and a pint of thin wartime beer for Sergeant Pendry.

"No spirits for me, Sir," he said. "I'm a beer drinker, thanking you just the same."

"It will be whisky and dry biscuits for you tomorrow, Sergeant," said Tim. "A sovereign remedy for those of us who find the sea unsettling." And without giving him time for any reply he turned to the barman to ask his opinion for the weather the following day.

They were the only people in the bar that evening and they had the whole attention of the craggy Scot, whose broad accent and rippling rs recalled to David his time a little over a year before at the Scottish OCTU on the opposite coast. His bony face was deeply lined and tufts of fair hair grew beneath his cheekbones. He dried a glass with immense deliberation as he replied: "It has been verra variable fur a time ye ken. Today it's bin raining off and on and a wee bit of wind is getting up that could get worse during the night. You'll be catching the Larne ferry tomorrow?"

Tim nodded, and David stole a glance at Sergeant Pendry who remained staring into his by now half full pint of beer, his face a mask.

"Was there a Captain in the hotel the night before last?" Tim went on. "An elderly man with white hair."

"Verra thin and a wee bit wild-looking?"

"That would be him."

"There were a fair number in here that evening, but I couldn'a have mistaken him. He didn'a rest long and went off to his bed early. He was away on the Larne ferry the next morning."

"Well that's fine," said Tim, turning to the other two. "Tubby will be busy preparing the ground for us." He finished his whisky and asked for another, pointing to his and David's glasses. David shook his head: he wanted to be fresh for the following morning. He left them to it and went to bed.

He woke to the sound of a strong and gusty wind that hurled rain against the window pane of the bedroom Tim and he were sharing; and later when they reached the ferry they learnt there was to be no sailing for at least twenty-four hours: a German submarine had been reported in the neighbourhood and until the Navy was satisfied that it had been seen off or sunk no merchant ships were allowed out of harbour.

They gazed out at the grey and choppy sea beneath low scurrying clouds and swore at their bad luck. At least David and Tim did: Sergeant Pendry was clearly delighted.

"I'll get through to Tubby by telephone," said Tim. "It may be possible to postpone the demonstration until Sunday, in which case if we cross tomorrow there will be no difference for us: arriving just before the start is cutting it too fine."

But when he got through to the Headquarters where Tubby was based in Belfast he was informed that Captain Maddox was out on the demonstration site and that it was out of the question that there should be any postponement: the whole operation had gone too far. If necessary Captain Maddox would have to do the best he could with assistance from the local Home Guard. A message would be sent to him to prepare him for that possibility.

While Tim and David looked at one another grimly at this unwelcome news Sergeant Pendry was elated.

"The Navy will have a bit of a job getting rid of that submarine," he stated with evident satisfaction. "My father what was in the Navy and my brother that is in a cruiser now, both say it's always a tricky business with subs."

He became rather tight that evening, putting away seven or eight pints of beer, and led on by Tim confessed that he did indeed run two homes.

"For the duration, you understand, Sir," He did not disclose whether he was married to both the ladies.

"Pendry's private life is no business of ours," said Tim later as they prepared for bed, "but I suspect his wishful thinking will lead him into trouble before he's finished. Just as he is likely to be disappointed tomorrow morning when the ferry does sail, so he is going to be in serious difficulties at the end of the war with two wives, if wives they be, on his hands. Wartime gives latitude that peacetime denies."

"My impression of him," said David, "is that he is the kind of man who will bounce through trouble like a rubber ball."

"Bully for him then: such people are very fortunate. I have known a few. An Englishman I knew during the war in Spain was blessed with the same advantage. No setback got him down. He was also able to think quickly, which I suspect Pendry cannot. I remember this man telling me after the quarrels between the Anarchists and the Communists in Barcelona had blown up into street fighting – he was working with Barcelona Radio at the time – two heavily armed types flung open the door and shouted: 'Whose side are you on?' 'Yours,' he said and the men went away. A pity we won't have him with us tomorrow."

"You believe we'll sail then?"

"Oh yes: these submarine scares are frequent. The Navy has to play very safe with such a soft target on this run. It'll be the very devil: we shall have no time for proper preparation and mighty little time for discussion with Tubby. I don't like it at all."

Tim was right and they did sail the next morning and Sergeant Pendry was right when he had told David that he suffered from acute seasickness. In fact, David had never seen anyone so ill. When he had emptied his stomach completely he just lay on the deck covered with a couple of blankets procured from a sailor, sweating and retching and white to the lips. There was nothing they could do to comfort him. It was a rough crossing and he was by no means the only soldier sick – the ship's rails were lined with the unfortunates – though nothing could compare with his illness. David was usually all right provided he kept in the open air and stayed warm. Tim carried out his own remedy and produced a few dry biscuits and a bottle of whisky he had managed to procure which was full when they started and empty when they reached Larne.

"Come," he said thickly, "we'll have to carry Pendry off."

And that was what they did, or David did because Tim was showing difficulty in walking himself. Poor Pendry did his best, but his legs seemed to be made of rubber and the journey down the gang plank was a nightmare, not improved by the broad grins of the several sailors who watched their progress.

They were met by a sleek staff officer in a large, khaki-painted saloon car, who was flustered and not at all in the mood for sympathy. They managed to get Pendry into the front seat beside the driver and the three officers packed into the back where an aroma of whisky soon made itself evident.

"I hope you have had something to eat during the voyage," said the staff officer with stunning tactlessness, "because there is no time now for lunch: we must go straight to the demonstration ground: there is only half an hour to go before the scheduled start and the General is a stickler for punctuality."

"Bugger the General!" said Tim, causing the staff officer to start in horrified disbelief. "We can't be held responsible for German submarines and even if there had been food available on the boat, which you should know there isn't, it isn't exactly the weather for eating at sea. You can see the state our Sergeant is in."

There was an awkward silence while they drove out of Larne into a green area of fields and hedgerows and Tim fell asleep. It seemed to David it was up to him to ease the atmosphere, but for the life of him could not think of anything not banal. Finally he asked whether Captain Maddox would be on the site waiting for them.

"Naturally," said the staff officer curtly, and David tried nothing more.

They drove on in frigid silence, leaving the fields behind and climbing steadily up into open moorland beneath a leaden sky.

The final approach to the demonstration area was along a narrow road in a state of considerable disrepair and open on both sides to the surrounding moor. It ended at what may have been a small brickworks, long abandoned, windows broken and doors missing. Stinging nettles and other weeds grew against its damp walls. At the near end stood a tall chimney, gaunt and singular in such an open landscape which stretched away to where the ground fell out of sight. A muddy parking area had been formed in front of this building and four buses were neatly lined up next to it. To their left as they drove along the last hundred yards of road there was a gully with a track at the bottom. To their right the ground fell away gently and David could see two white tapes laid out in the form of an inverted S that ended in the gully. On the two bends stout wooden targets had been erected approximating to the size of tanks. About fifty yards from the first target a Northover projector had been placed, looking like a toy, while a Blacker bombard had been positioned rather further from the other target, squat and even more insignificant in appearance than the projector. By both weapons lay boxes of ammunition. Their audience was drawn up in two ranks in a long line beyond the brickworks: there must have been more than a thousand of them, all in battledress.

Their driver stopped the car alongside the first bus and as the three in the back got out they were greeted by Tubby Maddox. There was no time to waste and he quickly explained that he had laid out the tapes to represent a road along which the imaginary enemy column would advance. As the first tank approached the first target Sergeant Pendry would fire two shots from the Blacker bombard and destroy it. He would have the help of a Home Guard as loader. It would then be assumed that the enemy would overcome this first ambush and continue along the road to the point where stood the second target, at which David would fire two "Molotov Cocktails" and set it on fire. At this setback imaginary enemy infantry would form up in a slight hollow preparatory to attacking David's post and he would fire two or three Mills bombs amongst them. In spite of this the enemy column would fight their way through to the gully where Tubby had prepared one of his fire ambushes.

"I found some disused brick recesses at the side of the gully," said Tubby. "Well concealed by undergrowth, which are admirable for my purpose. In them I have had three barrels of fuel placed with the usual charges and when I press the button they will blow out in the form of a fan filling a good hundred yards of the gully with flame. It will be a convincing climax. I had a bit of trouble with a couple of natives while the preparations were in progress: they were extraordinarily agitated, and I had to speak most severely to them before they gave up and departed. What's the matter with Sergeant Pendry?"

He had only just observed that the Sergeant was still in his seat in the car.

Tim explained breezily, adding that there was nothing to worry about, given a few minutes on his feet in the open air.

"How long have we got?" he asked.

"Ten minutes," said the staff officer sharply. "So you better get cracking. The General will expect you to start as soon as he arrives. He has to leave for an important conference immediately the demonstration is over."

They got Sergeant Pendry out of the car and stood him up; Tubby went into the brickworks where he had set up his post; Tim set off for his place in front of the audience where a microphone had been placed, and David and Sergeant Pendry walked towards their weapons while David told him what was expected of him. He still looked very ill and staggered like a drunken man. He listened obediently with glazed eyes, only an ingrained sense of discipline keeping him going. It seemed wise to lead him all the way to the Blacker bombard and leave him there with his Home Guard loader. As David walked back to his Northover projector two civilian cars followed by a military one flying a pennant drove along the road to the brickworks and stopped. The General had arrived with, presumably, the mayor and other functionaries. It was a relief the General had not been there to see Sergeant Pendry's progress: he might suspect that Tim was drunk, but he would have been sure that Sergeant Pendry was; and Generals do not as a rule give opportunities for complicated explanations.

David inspected the Northover projector. It was brand new and all seemed to be in order. He turned his attention to the ammunition lying in a metal box to one side. There were six bottles containing the "cocktails" with their charges and two Mills bombs, which he hoped had been properly armed: there was no time to check now. Even as he put them beside him in a convenient position and sat down upon the seat of the projector he saw out of the corner of his eye the General stalking across the car park with an ADC slightly behind him. He was tall and slim and the red round his cap and on the lapels of his immaculate service dress stood out in the surrounding sombre colours. At such a distance it was not possible to make out his features clearly, though a military moustache was evident. As David turned to look more carefully he was struck by the General's ADC. He seemed vaguely familiar. But there was no time to think about that and he prepared the projector for the first shot, sitting upon the rudimentary seat with legs stretched out on either side of the central tripod. When he was satisfied that he had done all he could he looked over to where Sergeant Pendry and the Home Guard were lying behind the Blacker bombard. He could see the big missile in position on the protruding spigot of the weapon. Tubby would be in the brickworks ready with his plunger and Tim was behind the microphone. By the narrowest of margins they were ready.

The loudspeaker crackled and Tim's voice came over loud and clear.

"Welcome to this exhibition of firepower now available to you in the Home Guard. I'm sorry it has not been possible to arrange a better day for you, but the demonstration we have prepared will not take long and you will soon be able to return to your firesides and warming cups of tea."

A low murmur from the audience indicated agreement.

After describing the weapons to be demonstrated and their capabilities he went on to paint an imaginary picture, carried on by his author's imagination and the whisky he had imbibed on the ferry.

"I am asking you to imagine that we are not out in the open moor as we are here, but in the outskirts of a village. Around us stand the houses, and the chimney you see to your right is the spire of your village church. The main street is along that gully, whose sides are the fronts of the houses and shops along that street. As you all know, or should know, your essential role is to defend your villages and towns as strong points, taking advantage of the excellent cover they provide and denying them to the enemy for as long as you can, thus delaying him and causing him serious casualties before our regular forces strike back. In the example you see before you this afternoon a series of ambushes have been prepared along the road leading to the village. The white ribbons you see represent the road and towards the end of the ribbons you will observe a Blacker bombard. I ask you to imagine that this Blacker bombard is sited in the back garden of a house with a field of fire upon the road and defended by a section of Home Guard with rifles and grenades in the house and out-houses around. Further into the village another ambush has been prepared, this time built round a Northover projector; and in case the enemy is determined and presses home his attack in spite of his losses to reach the main street, a fire ambush has been set up to engulf them.

Imagine then an enemy column of tanks and supporting infantry racing down the road towards Belfast. It reaches this outlying village with the usual motorcycle sidecars the Bosch favour as scouts out in front. The Home Guard unit is well trained and allows the motorcycles to go past without firing a shot. Then there is the grinding roar of approaching tanks and the first one comes round the corner into the sights of the Home Guard behind the concealed Blacker bombard, who puts two high explosive missiles into it –"

He paused expectantly, waiting for Sergeant Pendry's shots. Nothing happened. David could see the Home Guard loader saying something to the Sergeant, whose head came up as though he had been asleep. Lord! David thought anxiously: what happens now? However, Tim was equal to the situation.

"Aha!" he said. "We have a canny man at this weapon. He has allowed that first tank to go by, waiting for the next one, which –"

He got no further. Sergeant Pendry had at last become aware that he was expected to fire and there was the sharp report of the bombard as he pulled the trigger and the heavy dumbbell-shaped missile hurtled ponderously towards the target.

Sergeant Pendry was a practised and accurate shot with the bombard, which was not in fact the easiest of weapons to aim. Alas, on this occasion either the effects of his seasickness or the sudden reminder from his loader destroyed his skill and the missile flew over the top of the target, striking the turf fifty yards beyond it and sliding away for a further

118

hundred yards before coming to rest. Without a hard strike against a solid object it did not detonate and lay there in full view like a stranded whale.

The communal sensation of ante-climax was almost tangible. Yet, there was still some hope: the loader had slid on a second missile even before the first had come to rest and Sergeant Pendry fired again. This time his elevation was correct but his aim was wrong and the second missile flew past the side of the inviolate target to join its unexploded comrade beyond.

The painful hush that followed the second misfortune was broken by a murmuring from the audience that was not complimentary either to the Blacker bombard or the team of experts sent from the mainland.

David cast a furtive look at the General seated upon a shooting stick not far from where Tim was standing with the microphone in his hand. He was like the Sphinx.

"There," said Tim valiantly, "you have an example of how the best laid schemes can go wrong in war, which emphasises the importance of further points of defence. We must regard that post as wiped out and look to the next to do better. Over-confident that the resistance is feeble, the enemy tanks come on fast, and now the first one is opposite our second ambush."

The Northover projector, unlike the Blacker bombard, was not a difficult weapon to use with fair accuracy at short range and by now David had plenty of practice: so that in his heart of hearts he had no doubt he would hit the target fare and square with his first shot. Nevertheless, isolated as he was with so much depending on him, he felt his heart pounding and the adrenalin flowing in his veins. How deeply do such small matters affect the ordinary mortal! With what extreme care did he aim the barrel and how gently did he squeeze the trigger! The most careful and experienced instructor could hardly have done it better.

There was a roaring noise and out of the barrel shot a tongue of flame which fell to the ground in front of the projector forming a line of smokily burning chemicals leading straight to him. He knew exactly what had happened: it was an accident he had heard of and never experienced before: the bottle had burst inside the barrel of the projector. Instantly he opened the breach, inserted another bottle and charge and fired again. Exactly the same thing happened. Frenziedly he tried once more with the same result. By this time he was engulfed in choking fumes and felt like picking up the infernal weapon and hurling it at the target. He heard Tim's voice over the loudspeakers.

"There's something the matter with our damned guns today, General:

there goes another of our posts! However, the tanks do not waste time with it: they roll on towards the centre of the village, leaving their infantry to pinch out the pocket of resistance. It is reported to our gunner that some of them are forming up in the hollow you can see a couple of hundred yards beyond the projector, so he slips in a Mills bomb and fires it amongst them."

Feeling really desperate David opened the breach once more and removing the safety pin of a Mills bomb he slipped it in with a charge behind it. He swung the projector round and aiming it high to give the bomb sufficient trajectory to carry to the hollow he squeezed the trigger for the fourth time. At least a Mills bomb could not burst in the barrel and if it did he felt it would be a merciful release for him. It did not burst in the barrel. Instead, the whole projector gave a kind of convulsive belch with a big recoil and the bomb was lobbed a few feet in front of him to lie upon the turf, looking as innocent as a child's ball. But this was no child's ball! It was encapsulated death and he was in deadly danger. Scrambling off the seat in a kind of backwards somersault he lay as flat as he could wishing he was wearing a steel helmet instead of exposing the unprotected top of his head towards the forthcoming blast. Even the beret that had flown from his head would have given more comfort than nothing. Never before had David clung so closely to the earth that was his mother. In the position he was now in with his head turned sideways with one cheek flat upon the coarse wet turf he could see with his top eye, the other being below the grass level, his audience going down too.

Time is a curious phenomenon. Five seconds can be as nothing to us and a whole week may pass as though it were a mere breath. Those five seconds seemed to pass so slowly that David began to wonder whether the bomb had been armed: the series of failures had been so consistent that yet another would be no surprise, this time saving his life. He was on the point of lifting his head to look at the bomb when it went off. There was the familiar sharp explosion accompanied by a fierce whizzing sound of small and lethal pieces of metal, some of which struck the projector with loud clanks, and David knew he was untouched. Rising to his feet he saw the General, Tim and the rest doing the same, and quickly Tim's voice came over the loudspeakers once more.

"Alas for our second post: the Bosch were too quick for it and it has been eliminated; but they are moving with more care now, appreciating that the village is defended, keeping fairly close to one another in order to give each other support."

Whether it was the whisky or his natural *sang-froid*, Tim was making a magnificent best of an appalling situation and David was lost in admiration.

"The leading tank is entering the High Street, its turret moving this way and that, prepared to shoot at any sign of resistance. The second follows and the third. They are nearing the church and it is time to fire our ambush. Fire!"

From where David was standing he could not see into the gully which lay beyond the cars and buses, but the audience would be able to have a clear view down it and all heads were turned in that direction. As Tubby pushed down the plunger concealed within the brickworks building, the charges previously laid would hurl the barrels of flaming fuel across the gully turning it into a sea of flame and black smoke. David knew this because he had watched similar demonstrations from the hands of Tubby each week at the Home Guard school.

What in fact happened was altogether more remarkable. As Tim's command "Fire!" faded away the whole ground at the edge of the car park including a length of the approach road lifted into the air. For a second the ground bulged upwards before it broke into fragments and a great cloud of flame and smoke shot into the sky with a thunderous roar and a shuddering of the ground beneath David's feet. The two civilian cars which had arrived with the General's disappeared, while the latter described an elegant curve before landing heavily on its roof between where David was standing and the catastrophic explosion. As a mushroom shaped cloud formed in the air over the dreadful scene lumps of rock, brick and earth rained down from above, and while he continued to watch dumbfounded the brickworks chimney began to keel over very slowly before gathering speed as it broke into several parts and crashed with a prolonged and hideous sound onto the line of buses.

As David watched this new disaster Tubby staggered out of a doorway covered with dust and rubble.

Very slowly the dust settled and the air cleared to display a large crater, at the bottom of which the remains of the fuel and two cars burned smokily. It was indeed, to use Tubby's words, "quite a convincing climax."

David was unable to recollect very clearly what happened after that, such was the confusion, except for the General's rage which was very terrible. The one piece of good fortune was that, apart from some bruises, there were no casualties with the single exception of the Town Clerk, who being a very stout man had not found it easy to hurl himself to the ground when David's Mills bomb fell out of the end of the projector and instead had bent down while turning his back to it with his ample posterior acting as a shield. By a quirk of fate, and there can be no doubt that fate was in an intensely mischievous mood that afternoon, a single sliver of steel from the bomb pierced his left buttock.

Later in the ante-room of the mess, to which they had been allotted, Tim, David and Tubby sat disconsolately round a small table before dinner. The mess waiter had placed the drinks they had ordered upon this table, half a pint of beer for David and double whiskies for his companions, before much was said.

"I am quite unable to account for it," said Tubby, referring to the great explosion that had dwarfed the other calamities. "The charges I placed personally behind the fuel barrels were the normal ones. The explosion that took place involved several hundredweight of explosive."

"Perhaps," said Tim, "you were supplied with barrels of nitro-glycerine instead of fuel."

"Impossible," said Tubby, who was not in the mood for facetious remarks.

"Well, whatever may have been the cause we are in for the chop," said Tim. "The whole affair could have been made to measure to suit the powers that be: it is just what they have been waiting for. You and I, Tubby, will be on our way back to civvy street with the speed of light; and the world being what it is, David, I'm afraid you'll be on your way back to your Depot: the blood of as many scapegoats as possible will flow."

"I'm beginning to feel like a yo-yo attached to my Depot," said David.

"I have little doubt that Tim is right in so far as he and I are concerned," said Tubby kindly, "but I am confident that you will not be caught up in the avalanche."

"Let's drink to that hope, anyway," said Tim, lifting his glass high in the air. "And we'll couple the toast with one to old Oirland and its little people; for between them they've done for two of us for sure!"

The mess waiter approached them.

"Excuse me, Sirs," he said, "but is one of you gentlemen named Mr Drummond?"

David owned to the name.

"You're wanted on the telephone, Sir."

"If it's the gallant General tell him to take one enormous running jump at himself," said Tim, ordering another double whisky.

122

Puzzled to receive a telephone call at all where he was, David followed the mess waiter to where the telephone stood in a kind of cupboard.

"Hullo?" he asked.

"Is your second name Jonah?" The slow voice was familiar.

Playing for time to allow his mind to work, for he was tired, hungry and depressed, David said he certainly felt as that unfortunate must have felt when inside the whale.

"Calamity seems to be your shadow, my dear David, though, perhaps, only when I am in attendance – probably something to do with our stars."

Then it came to him: it was Punter Parkinson whom he had not seen since their OCTU days; it was he whom David had seen and half remembered with the General after getting out of his car.

"Punter!" he exclaimed with pleasure. "How good to hear your voice. Where are you?"

"Hush! The enemy has ears everywhere. At HQ actually, not more than a quarter of a mile from you: I'm on duty tonight. I recognised you in the arena when I arrived with my General. I hoped to be able to have a word with you at the end of your act, but, as you might imagine, I became fairly occupied trying to arrange transport for His Nibs, who could hardly be expected to walk to Belfast in his advanced state of seniority. Generals get out of the habit of route marches you know, What a simply splendid shambles! I wouldn't have missed a second of it. And what a finale! Four cars and four buses written off at a stroke and a Town Clerk bagged to boot. It may seem churlish to offer a note of criticism, but you should not have included the General's car: alas, the great man is deficient in a sense of humour and is really very cross."

"You may have enjoyed it all: I didn't. Are you one of the General's staff?"

"An ADC, though not I suspect for long."

"Congratulations."

"It is an experience. It puts me in a position to be able to tip you off that he is sending a stinker of a report about your circus."

"We thought that inevitable."

"Such a pity; but we are all worms, as Winston once said. How long are you staying in this damp country?"

"We leave tomorrow morning."

"I don't blame you, though it's very disappointing. I was about to propose that we should have dinner together tomorrow evening: we have so much to tell one another."

All they could do was to agree to keep in touch by letter and exchanged addresses.

"I will do my best to arrange for the church bells to be tolled when you leave tomorrow," ended Punter. "In the circumstances a band might be thought inappropriate. Don't take life too seriously."

The rapidity with which Tubby, Tim and Sergeant Pendry left the school surprised David, and Jake was swept away on the same tide. They were replaced, as Tim had foreseen, by officers "cast in the standard mould". Tim had been right, too, when he had foreseen how the army would turn the Home Guard into a kind of branch field corps, for which they were totally unsuited. Within a month of his departure the new "Battle Drill" was being instilled in the school courses. He was wrong, though, about David, who was kept on. Ceddie Roussel was the last of the founders to go, leaving to become Chief Instructor at a school of camouflage. It was all very dull and pointless and when July came round David decided it was time for him to go. There was no difficulty: the Commandant had hinted broadly several times that young officers were too badly needed in the field to be lecturers in such establishments.

A few days before David left he received a letter from Punter. At first he twitted David because he had not abided by their agreement to correspond, and went on to give an account of his own, on the whole tedious existence, "though the occasional bouts of frenzied activity helped the time to move along; as for example, during a recent five-day exercise when we were successful in driving a largely imaginary enemy force back across the border using a largely imaginary army to accomplish the feat. We were rather pleased with this exploit in spite of a superior General over my General, who came over to judge and comment afterwards. He slated my man over certain aspects. Fascinating to observe how even Generals have other Generals upon their backs to bite 'em! Who, one asks oneself, bites the top General of all? Worth remembering when next receiving a rocket – to use the peculiar jargon current in the army – from a superior; for one can spend the time while he lashes you with his tongue thinking that he too is subject to such indignities."

Punter seemed disappointed by Northern Ireland, "where even the famed beauty of the colleens is grossly exaggerated: though it may be that the true Irish of the south provide the genuine article." By informing David that he hoped he would reply quickly since he might be changing his location shortly he let him know he was on the verge of posting elsewhere. He ended: "I wonder where you are now? It seems possible that your lively display here in the spring turned you against the Home

124

Guard, or even – perish the thought – turned the Home Guard against you; and that you are now serving the King in another sphere. You will have heard, no doubt, that the trouble with the extraordinary drainpipe affair you were trying to use with such disastrous results had a bent end? The Irish are inclined to be clumsy. Were you also informed about the findings of the Court of Enquiry into the simply magnificent finale to your show? In case you were not, and the army's lines of communication do not always extend as far as those of us who are most concerned, it will interest you to know that your explosives johnny inadvertently selected a spot for his demo, precisely where a large cache of stolen gelignite had been tucked away by the IRA. Hence the big bang. Your man should be given a medal really."

CHAPTER 8

"Tut, Tut; good enough to toss; food for powder,
food for powder; they'll fill a pit as well as better:
tush, man, mortal men, mortal men."

SHAKESPEARE

Amongst the miseries of major modern warfare is the loss of affiliation: men live and train together in tightly knit units and no sooner has close relationship and understanding of each other's strengths and weaknesses been formed than it is undone by postings elsewhere, casualties or disbandment of whole units. Generals wielding divisions, army corps and armies do not have the time nor the power to prevent this baneful effect upon the inherent strength of small corporate teams: yet the consequence is that fighting efficiency at the edge of the sword is blunted, which is why the swords soon turn into bludgeons and skilled cut and thrust degenerates into clumsy battering.

After leaving the Home Guard training school David joined an infantry battalion, which in due course was selected amongst others to form the nucleus of a Beach Group. These were complicated and remarkable bodies of different skills designed to land upon open beaches immediately behind assault forces in order to form open harbours for landing reinforcements and nourishing the forces fighting their way inland. They were to carry out this role until the artificial port at Arromanches became fully operational and the port of Cherbourg captured. David had, perhaps naively, assumed that when the Beach Group he was in had completed its task on the beach the battalion would shed the specialist units and be sent forward to the front as a whole. Vain belief! The severe casualties sustained by front line battalions in the savage fighting in the close countryside between the river Orne and beyond Bayeux demanded piecemeal replacements, and the battalion melted away, beginning with junior officers, that favourite dish of Mars, followed by NCOs, more senior officers and the remainder. That was depressing enough in itself; but heralded for David a covey of troubles in the closely grouped form, long remarked as a phenomenon, which gives

126

encouragement to astrologers and a sense of helplessness to all.

Now the last officer remaining in "B" Company, itself a mere handful of other ranks, he sat upon the edge of the slit trench he had slept in with a warm morning sun on his back and the silver sea just visible beyond the mangled fields and hedgerows that divided his position from the beach. Everywhere there was enormous activity as reinforcements of men, lorries, tanks, guns and supplies poured in from the sea and headed inland, the constant noise increased by the roar of aircraft landing and taking off from air strips behind him. Stacks of supplies stood amongst the gaunt, still witnesses of the assault a month before; here the skeleton of a tree stripped of leaves by high explosive, there two burnt-out tanks by a ruined house, and everywhere the general detritus of war.

Other duties over for the time being David turned his attention to the latest Army Bulletin of Current Affairs pamphlet – issued monthly to all units throughout the war with the laudable intention of keeping the rank-and-file up to date with current affairs and to instil knowledge by means of wider ranging articles. Officers were instructed to impart the contents to their men, usually accomplished in monthly lectures when practicable. When first experienced early in the war they seemed innocuous, on the whole aiming to keep up morale when nothing seemed to go right, some of the more recondite articles even interesting; but as the war drew towards its end it began to dawn upon David that an increasingly powerful, though subtle, campaign was being conducted with the intention of ensuring that the majority of the armed forces would vote for the Labour Party in the first post war election, a campaign, as it turned out, conducted with considerable success. David wondered where the editor and his team operated and who was responsible for their appointments. Clearly, it was a magnificent vehicle for left wing intellectuals and it seemed odd that the attention of the Conservative members of the Coalition Government had not been drawn to it. Probably they were far too busy trying to win the war.

The pamphlet he had in his hand that sunny morning contained a gentle eulogy on the anticipated benefits from nationalisation, then an untried theory much admired by Socialist thinkers, the implication indicating that such a step forward would only be accomplished under a Labour administration. Brought up on the tenets of Adam Smith, David was unable to grasp how the writer could possibly believe in such a drastic removal of the impelling laws of supply and demand, and gave it to his batman asking for his comments.

His name was Rowe and he seemed mildly enthusiastic.

127

"It stands t'reason," he said, pushing his steel helmet to its customary position on the back of his head. "Working people will always work better and 'appier when they know it's for their mates and not for the rich bosses."

"Isn't there the danger that once you have huge monopolies, which after all is what nationalisation involves, their power in the land will be so great they might hold the country to ransom?"

"'Ow d'yer mean?"

"Well, for example, the railway men could threaten to close down the railways, or the miners could stop digging coal, or the dockers refuse to run the docks, unless given all they asked for."

"They can do that any 'ow. What this 'ere bloke is saying is there'll be less trouble when big industries like them belong to the people instead of the bosses."

"There will have to be management – what you call the bosses – and don't you think the men will feel the same about them as they do about the private enterprise management now?"

"Sorry, Sir; I think you're prejudiced. Working men'll never let their mates down."

"We are all prejudiced in one way or another, Rowe, but now I'm looking for an answer that makes sense and I'm not so confident that your railway man looking for more pay and shorter working hours is going to care tuppence for his fellow workers who have to use the trains."

Rowe's round rubicund face went blank as it always did when he was disinclined to pursue a matter further – what David's mother would have called a "boot face" – and he turned his attention once more to the cleaning of David's equipment, sitting on a stone found in the hedge at an earlier date and rolled out to form a simple seat. There was no point in trying to lead the discussion further. After two years together David knew him pretty well, as no doubt Rowe knew David; a mutual understanding between officer and servant that is a considerable boon, especially in wartime.

It had not been so at the beginning. Though carrying out his duties as well as any average English conscripted soldier, there was a withdrawn sullenness about Rowe that David thought would be impossible to accept for long. It may have been the class barrier that had become increasingly frictional as the war progressed, or trouble at home, or a way of concealing shyness; possibly a mixture of all these ingredients. However, after about two months of this, two events took place that cut through his reserve.

The first of these occurred when David had driven the Company van with Rowe to a field-firing range in the New Forest in an attempt to further his constant struggle to arrange for soldiers to learn to shoot with some degree of accuracy, an aspect of their training which left most senior officers surprisingly indifferent. On their way back David noticed that their road carried them to a point not far from the farm rented by his uncle George where he had spent many happy holidays during his schooldays. Uncle George had married his mother's elder sister. He was a big man with a rich Hampshire accent. The son of a grocer in a nearby small town, his education had been basic, but he extended his knowledge by extensive reading during the long winter evenings and he always had something sensible to say. His aunt Anne was plain and motherly, and having no children of her own had directed her loving nature towards him, doing a great deal to make up for the long absences of his mother.

"I have an aunt and uncle who rent a farm near here," David explained to Rowe. "We will pay them a visit and they will give us tea." And he turned the van down the familiar track which led to the brick and tiled farmhouse.

David did not know what Rowe expected, but the genuine warmth of the reception that encompassed them both followed by the farm tea which was in reality a supper of boiled eggs, bread and butter and homemade jam with a huge brown pot of tea and milk fresh from the cows quickly broke down Rowe's restraint and he began to talk in a way that David had never heard before.

"Good to get your feet under the table," he said afterwards. "It don't 'appen so often down 'ere in the south: not a bit like it is up north."

Shortly after Rowe went absent without leave for three days and David covered up for him. He returned just before he could do so no longer. Though depressed he was very grateful not to have to face a military problem in addition to the one he had at his home where his young wife was associating with an older man.

"This war don't give a bloke a chance," he said morosely. "There's this geezer with lots of lolly in a reserved occupation and plenty of time. She's fallen for it good and proper, the silly kid, and there don't seem to be anything to do."

After these events Rowe and David felt comfortable together.

There came a call from beyond the hedge that the post had arrived.

"I'll go 'ave a looksee," said Rowe and went down the side of the field to where a gate had been, his broad body carried on slightly bandy legs and steel helmet well back.

When he returned he had a letter for David from a friend serving in Burma, with whom he kept up an occasional correspondence. It informed him that the friend had been posted from his battalion to a job at Divisional HQ, which he was finding most congenial after the extreme rigour and danger in the front line. Tucked away in the heart of the letter was a sentence which brought David up sharply: "Did you know that Punter Parkinson bought it a few weeks ago?"

As a war goes on one becomes hardened to the sudden extinction of individuals who have circled for a time within one's orbit, even totally unexpected disappearances like that of Mullen Tipping, killed while sketching on the South Downs by a bomb dropped from a fleeing Heinkel bomber during the Battle of Britain; but occasionally such abrupt departures from the stage of life catch one off guard as was David's case now. Punter had seemed indestructible. As David thought about him a clear picture came into his mind of Punter's tall slim figure standing in the snow on the edge of a Scottish wood as he struggled with two fellow cadets up the slope towards him, saying; "Bang! Bang! You're dead." Now somewhere where snow was unknown he was dead. David wondered as his mind worked to adjust to this new turn of life's kaleidoscope how it had happened. Probably he would never know. He hoped that it had been quick and not one of those nasty "died of wounds" cases. He recalled a recent letter from Punter after leave from the front line of his fascination for the "stupendous crookedness of racing in India," going on to tell how he had found a girl, "a delectable WAAF with breasts like ripe peaches and with whom I am happy to be able to throw into the scales the arts of love to balance my enforced practice of war, though thoughtless Fate provides so little time for the former and so much time for the latter. Would that one could be exchanged for t'other!" One moment there he was, the humorously iconoclastic good friend, and the next, oblivion. Hell and damnation; what a ghastly waste it all was.

"Sir!" said a voice, and David looked up to find a soldier standing before him, his right hand descending from a salute. Sergeant Major's compliments and the CO wants to see you, Sir."

David shook himself slightly and stood up.

"Tell him I'm on my way."

Battalion HQ was in a farmhouse, miraculously undamaged by the fury of the initial bombardment and assault. He walked across the by now familiar yard, once no doubt sprinkled with chickens and guarded by a chained dog, with cows in their byres at night and possibly a pig or two. Now there remained no indication of animal life and military impedimenta replaced beasts. Recognising David the sentry on duty at the front door saluted smartly and let him past. The Adjutant's office was at the top of the ancient and worn staircase and adjoining the CO's own, both previous bedrooms.

David had hardly considered what the purpose of this summons might be: his mind was too full of Punter's death. It could be something to do with necessary reorganisation due to the rapidly shrinking battalion or even instructions concerning his own posting, likely at any moment. But when he greeted Dick Bidell, the Adjutant, it was apparent there was something amiss: his manner was unusually constrained and stiff as he immediately reported David's presence to the CO.

"Something wrong?" asked David.

"The CO will tell you."

The CO, rather a dull, industrious regular soldier, bad at communication, was likeable as one got to know him and David admired his dedication to the Army that he loved. Now there was an ominously grim look on his pale face, and as so often at such moments David searched his conscience anxiously endeavouring to recall some error or failure on his part.

"I have bad news for you, David."

The use of his Christian name made it evident that this was not a matter of fault. Perhaps circumstances, ever present in the army, made it necessary for him to be reduced from the rank of captain to lieutenant, sending him forward as a platoon commander once more; bad news indeed, though hardly warranting such serious treatment.

"Your parents have been murdered."

The shock was severe, and the CO, observing it, indicated a chair saying: "Sit down," before continuing.

"It appears that a fanatical young Indian approached them while they were seated upon the verandah of their bungalow and shot them. I need not tell you how sorry I am. I daresay you will receive official notification shortly and I thought it best to let you have the news personally first."

Sadly, there are young people upon whom the death of parents makes little impact. Unfortunately for David at that moment he dearly loved and admired his, and this sudden and unexpected information shook him to his core. He slowly took the offered chair and wondered what he could say. He had gone very white and the CO himself seemed lost for further words. Finally David lamely said: "I was very fond of them."

It seemed curious to him how quickly their real presence had already

131

evaporated from his mind and how he automatically used the past tense. Even at the moment when the mind is numbed with shock the brain continues to classify information and store it in revised form.

"In the circumstances you will need to be occupied," said the CO "Lack of occupation permits brooding and that never did anyone any good; so I have instructed the Adjutant to send you forward with the next draft, due to leave tomorrow. He will give you details."

He stood up and extended a hand.

"I'm sorry we have to part on such a sad note. Good luck!"

On David's return to the next office Dick Bidell was at ease once more and expounded freely upon the theme that "our crackpot liberal thinkers" were largely responsible for such outrages, encouraging a minute proportion of educated Indians, thirsting for the power which independence would provide.

"The chimera of independence means nothing to ninety-nine point nine percent of the population," he continued, "which will regret it and suffer for it and die for it. Have you a good batman?"

Such a sudden change of course was characteristic of the Adjutant.

"Yes, very," replied David.

"Then I'll put him down for the draft you will take with you tomorrow. What's his name?"

"Rowe E.M."

Early the next morning Rowe and David were in a lorry filled with other soldiers destined to join front line units. They joined the constant flow of lorries, tank transporters and other vehicles which filled the worn out tracks and roads and climbed up onto the low ridge behind the coast. At the top David looked about with interest, seeing the country inland for the first time, an interest tempered with anxiety in case a sneak enemy aircraft got through the allied air cover: these dense lines of vehicles were such a target moving slowly in daylight over open ground. That they were free to be so concentrated was an amazing proof of their air superiority without which the whole operation would have been doomed from the start. David felt better when they were down off the ridge into broken wooded country, beyond which there was less sensation of standing out like flies on a window pane, and the column began to thin out. Here they were in the true *bocage* and he understood why the allied advance had not been quicker: it was ideal defensive country. Fields were small and

132

surrounded with barbed wire in thick hedges. Small woods abounded and the land was broken up by a series of little hills and valleys, frequently with streams at their bottoms. The road they were taking was narrow, winding and severely rutted and their progress was slow and very bumpy. David kept looking towards the west in the hope of catching a glimpse of the twin spires of Bayeux cathedral, though without success. They crossed the main Bayeux Caen road near a battery of medium artillery and twisted towards the village of Christot to the east of the fiercely contested ground round Tilly where they began to see evidence of the battles in the form of groups of wrecked and burnt out vehicles of various kinds; armoured cars, tanks and lorries. One tank had its turret torn completely off, lying absurdly several yards away on a bush that it had flattened. Such scenes of desolation and destruction would appear in clusters wherever engagements had been fought out, divided by areas of calm and beauty that accentuated the horror. Here and there they passed temporary graves with rifles or posts set up above them crowned with the helmets of the pathetic occupants, mutely sorrowful testimonies of tragedy. There were more British than German, and a grim feeling of apprehension began to overlay David's earlier sense of stimulation.

Dismounting at the Divisional HQ which was their goal, Rowe and David were quickly dispatched to the battalion they were to join. The CO was at Brigade and David spoke briefly with the Adjutant before going on again to "C" Company where he was to be Second-in-Command. He found Peter Darking, the Company Commander, dealing with some paper work in what must have been the kitchen of a cottage on the outskirts of a small village which had been badly damaged. The table was littered with papers and maps, and a half full bottle of red wine stood in the middle.

"Have a glass," he said. "It's rough but heartening. Or, if you prefer, there is some very fair cider in the larder. You must be thirsty after your drive. Lunch is just about due and I'll put you in the picture while we have it. After that I'll introduce you to the Sergeant Major and we'll go round the platoons. Just now we are still one officer short and No 2 Platoon is commanded by its Sergeant."

Peter Darking was tall, good looking and very tired. It was soon made clear to David that the battalion had just been relieved after a stiff engagement with a tough German armoured division which had been carrying out a series of counter attacks since the capture of Tilly, and that "C" Company had been lucky to get off with twenty casualties when compared with the other three, which had been badly knocked about.

"Your predecessor was unlucky," said Peter, munching a bite of bully beef sandwich while pressing thumb and forefinger round the bridge of his nose as though to drive weariness from his eyes.

"He had the misfortune to step on a shoe mine. Hence your presence. Still, he might have done worse, only losing a foot: some of the villages are plastered with booby traps. Watch out for odd articles lying about: we lost a man the other day when he picked up a piss pot wired to a grenade. German humour. Monty keeps up the pressure, but it is very much a matter of nibbling away. You must have observed the country on your way here: bags of cover for the Bosch. It seems a big new drive is in the offing and our Div is holding the fort while preparations are afoot. I must admit it will be nice to take a back number for a while: it has been definitely hectic this last week. In any event, we should now have a few days quiet."

He was wrong. That very evening orders arrived that they were to move forward to relieve the remnants of an infantry unit of an armoured division in the direction of Villers-Bocage, and they marched off as the sun was setting over the western wooded countryside, beyond which the rumble of gunfire increased as it turned to dusk.

"That'll be the Yanks," said the Sergeant Major as he marched alongside David in front of Rowe and Peter's batman at the end of the column. They use up ammunition like chewing gum."

To their front, apart from some sporadic machine gun fire away towards Caen there was no sound. They might have been marching on an exercise on a peaceful summer evening, until the well loved scents of the woods and fields at such a time of year were overlaid by a sweet, sickly smell and they passed a field of dead cows, their bellies bloated with gases of decay to give them the appearance of bladders filled with water, the legs protruding like sticks. A little further on it was possible to make out the dusky outlines of two stricken tanks before they entered a wood and it became too dark to see much. Later they left the wood and marched in the dark under the stars and a pale slip of a moon.

They climbed a low rise and descended through another wood to a small village standing at a crossroads, and there they went through the usual procedure of taking over from the unit that they found there.

Its very young major in command had grown a surprisingly bushy ginger moustache below a large nose and exhausted eyes. His HQ was in a blacked out living room of the local *notaire*, not surprisingly absent. It was lit by a Tilly lamp.

"I gather," said Peter, "your attack went well at the start and then

134

ground to a halt here."

"You gather right," said the major. "We really began to think we were onto a breakthrough at last and just as we were all thinking of the long awaited swan towards the Rhine and the end of the bloody war we ran full tilt into strong opposition just beyond this village and it stopped us dead – rather a lot of dead in fact."

He pulled across a map case with a map behind a piece of transparent talc and, taking up a red chinagraph pencil, marked out points as he talked.

"The road you came down goes straight from this village up to and through a wood. About eighty yards before it enters the wood there is this lane going off to the right, running parallel to the face of the wood, with the odd farm building along it."

His pencil followed the line of the lane on the map.

"This road through the wood was our main axis of advance and tomorrow you will see that there is an isolated house just before the edge of the wood, and since it is important I shall call it 'House X'"

He drew a ring round a small black mark on the map denoting the house in question.

"The remaining villagers we talked to told us that the Bosch had passed through fast several hours earlier, so our armour set off again at a rate of knots. Just as the lead tank reached 'House X' a bloody Bosch put a Panzerfaust into it from one of the lower windows and all hell was let loose. An eighty-eight opened up from the left hand of the wood and brewed up a couple more before our artillery got going and quietened it down. I put one platoon up the road to keep the Bosch in 'House X' occupied while the other two worked their way round the right among the buildings along the lane. I then called down another stonk from our artillery to disturb any Bosch at the edge of the wood and told the two platoons to move in when it was over, which was where it all went wrong. The stonk came down short amongst our blokes and when that was over what we had left started across the open ground towards the wood only to be moved down by a spandau from - you've guessed it - bloody 'House X'

I tell you, it was a bloody shambles: we lost two officers and forty-five other ranks in less than five minutes."

He stopped, his face haggard.

Peter broke an awkward silence: "When was this?"

"Day before yesterday. It was raining, you remember, so we couldn't call up the Typhoons; but we fairly plastered the wood with our mediums and in the evening our patrols found that the Bosch had scarpered."

"So, where do we stand now?" asked Peter.

"We moved up through the wood, which, as you can see from the map, is roughly the shape of a dumb-bell – the first and smaller part being joined to a much bigger one by a narrow neck of trees on the other side. What I have done is to place a standing patrol at the neck of the wood and another in 'House X'."

He went on to point out the dispositions of the remaining remnants of his force.

"No hope of a squadron of your Churchills for support?" asked Peter without conviction.

"None whatever, I'm afraid, mate; the whole Div is being pulled back to lick its wounds and prepare for something bigger, I believe."

Once the process of relief was accomplished and the last of their predecessors had disappeared into the darkness up the road by which Peter's company had come, he turned to David and said: "I'm not happy about that furthest standing patrol and I haven't replaced it: it doesn't do to get too scattered. Tomorrow I'll get the CO on the blower and ask him what he thinks of the whole battalion moving forward a bit, say to the end of the wood."

David was asleep in his "fleabag", made by Rowe for him by sewing two grey army blankets together, when the noise woke him: heavy firing and explosions from the direction of "House X". Peter was up and away immediately with a quick call to David to hold the fort. It was just growing light and David watched him running up the village street, sten gun in hand, his map case flapping at his hip, past one of the burnt out tanks and up the hill. David picked up the field telephone and spoke to the Adjutant, reporting that there was some trouble and that he would be back to him again immediately he knew more.

There was nothing to do but wait. The noise up the road continued and then diminished before breaking out again, reaching a crescendo and stopping abruptly.

"Sounds as though we've beaten the buggers off," said the Sergeant Major. "Probably tried to bounce us at dawn."

As he spoke the figure of one of the company came limping down the road without his rifle and his arm held across his body.

"What you done with your rifle, Quilton?" demanded the Sergeant Major.

"They came at us all of a sudden," gasped the soldier, who they could now see was ashen-faced and bleeding from both his arm and leg.

"That's no excuse for leaving your rifle," said the Sergeant Major sternly.

"They took the 'ouse."

This was serious news and the matter of the missing rifle took second place.

"Where is Major Darking?" David asked.

"Fixing up a counter attack when I left. Can I sit down, Sir?"

Instructing the Sergeant Major to take Quilton inside their HQ building and to call up stretcher bearers, David set off with Rowe to see the situation for himself. Disposed round Company HQ was No 2 Platoon and David made a point of speaking to Sergeant Jeffs, its commander, warning him to have his platoon ready to move if necessary, an unnecessary precaution since he was already doing so. A small cockney with a snub nose, his attitude impressed David.

Following instructions learnt from Tim Baker and transmitted to the Home Guard during his time as an instructor David avoided the open street and led Rowe round the back of the houses on the right of the road, scrambling over walls and fences, each covering the other as they did so. In this manner they quickly reached the lane leading away to the right as described to them on their arrival and hurried across it. Two buildings further on they found a section of No 1 Platoon occupying the ground floor.

"Keep your 'eads down," said a Lance Corporal. "They've just been firing through the winder."

David asked for the Platoon Commander and when told that he was upstairs, climbed up to a small landing where an open doorway displayed a disordered bedroom containing the officer he was looking for with three more of his platoon. They had met briefly the day before and David knew that his name was Bird, inevitably called Dicky. He was small, freckled and tubby and. according to Peter, reliable. At the moment he looked worried. He quickly explained that the Germans had crept up through the wood during the night and surprised the standing patrol in "House X" and were now occupying it. No 3 Platoon Commander and his Sergeant were missing and the remaining section which had been in the adjoining building was now under the command of Dicky Bird. Peter Darking had organised a hasty counter attack as soon as he had reached the scene, which had failed with more casualties, including Peter himself, killed outright. They were in point of fact back where their predecessors had been three days before.

Standing well back in the room David inspected "House X", the next house up the road from the cottage they were in. It was quite a large house in comparison with the others in the village and built in stone. Round it there was a hedge about four feet high enclosing a garden. Between it and the cottage they were in the road ran straight between post and wire fences without any cover for about forty yards. In the road, just in front of the house, stood the lead tank which had been knocked out when the advance of the armoured division had been stopped. Beyond that the road ran into and was swallowed up by the wood.

David quickly saw how the open space between his force and the enemy put him in a strong position should they attempt to press forward. On the other hand, a frontal attack upon them in daylight would be suicidal. Any attempt on the left, as the moustachioed Major had pointed out, was equally hopeless. It was easy to see why he had elected to try the right flank, which at least gave a means of approach along the buildings on the lane, though there was still the ground between them and the face of the wood to cross. Unfortunately, all this would be just as apparent to the enemy who understood the business of warfare so well. He would have to go and have a look.

Borrowing two men from Dicky Bird's platoon, they scuttled along behind the buildings on the lane without mishap until they reached the end one, which they cautiously entered and peered out of a ground floor window, eyes level with the sill.

Opposite was the wood, looking quite harmless in the warm light of the rising sun. Between it and the backyards of the buildings along that side of the lane a weed-filled ploughed field stretched from the garden of "House X" to the end of the wood and on beyond to embrace the wood on another side, becoming very big and reaching the outbuildings of a farmhouse about a quarter of a mile away to their right front.

David looked at "House X" once more, now about two hundred yards to his left. Its windows glared back like malevolent eyes. Behind any there could be guns ready to sweep the open space between him and the wood, itself capable of concealing any number of enemy. Even had he not heard the story of the last debacle, the hazards were very plain to see. It was a cleverly chosen place for defence, typical of their experienced and astute enemy. No wonder he had come back for a repeat performance of his last success.

David pondered the problem.

The best solution would be to wait for darkness, and if the CO would not agree to that, smoke was a poor alternative. There was hardly any wind and if one of the platoon mortars put several smoke bombs down on this side of the wretched "House X" to mask it they might rush the assumed defences in the wood without being caught in the flank from the house. After that it should be possible to drive through the wood to isolate the force in the house before making another attempt to take it.

Leaving the two men in the house with instructions to watch for any enemy movement David returned to Dicky Bird's position.

"How many smoke bombs has your mortar man?" he asked.

"None; only HE"

"And No 3 Platoon?"

"Missing."

"Do you know whether Sergeant Jeffs' platoon has any?"

"I doubt it."

David and Rowe returned to Company HQ the same way they had come, ordering Jeffs up on the way, David's heart sinking when the absence of smoke bombs was confirmed.

"A couple of carriers are being sent up for the wounded," said the Sergeant Major. "The Commanding Officer wants to speak to the Major. He don't seem to be in the best of tempers."

"The Major is dead, I'm afraid, Sergeant Major, and I have taken over command."

When David got through to Battalion HQ he was put straight through to the CO

"Who is that?" The CO's voice was sharp.

"Captain Drummond, Sir."

"Who the hell are you?"

There was the sound of another voice in the background and the CO spoke again.

"Put me on to Major Darking."

"He's dead, Sir."

After a slight pause the CO's crisp voice came on the line once more: "I see. What are you doing about that enemy pocket?"

"I have made a reconnaissance and in my opinion it is a strong position and it would be best to wait until dark and then use more force than I have available."

"How do you know it's a strong force?"

"I cannot be sure about the strength of the force, but it is a naturally strong defensive position and the enemy has already used it with

139

considerable success against the armoured division we relieved yesterday evening."

"That was a prepared position and was cleared out. This is probably just a patrol. It is out of the question to wait until dark. Get at them and knock them out before they have time to consolidate."

"I find we have no smoke, Sir. Can some two inch mortar bombs be sent up with the carriers that are coming up for the wounded?"

"They've left and there isn't time. Don't be so windy, man. Get in there using your fire power and guts. Every moment counts."

One of the many difficulties experienced by junior commanders on the battlefield is their lack of comprehension concerning what is going on higher up the chain of command: the point of the rapier is hardly in a position to understand the movements of the hand that controls it. That is why soldiers are taught discipline and obedience; for argument and discussion in the heat of action would render any force incompetent. On the other hand, the man on the spot must know more about the local situation than his commanders further back; the age-old conflict between not seeing the wood for the trees and not seeing the trees for the wood, a delicate point now exaggerated by the fact that neither the CO nor David knew each other, indeed had not even met. It seemed to David that the CO should come forward immediately to assess the situation for himself; but at the same time he was aware that the CO might have other pressing matters to attend to, genuinely believing all that was needed was sharp stimulation. There is something to be said for drive and aggression. Of course, David did not think all this out during his brief conversation with his faceless CO: it was all a part of the background of his mind, instilled during years of training.

So he said: "Yes, Sir," and returned to his little front line.

No 1 Platoon's Bren gun had gone in the surprise attack at dawn, leaving only two. The greatest danger lay from "House X" since its occupants could rake any advance to the wood over the ploughed field from the flank. David decided that Sergeant Jeffs' platoon, so far unaffected by the morning's events, would have to be the one to carry out the attack into the wood and that both remaining Bren guns should be placed in upper rooms of buildings along the lane with instructions to fire at every opening and possible point of cover around "House X" from the moment that the attack started. He left the six men remaining from No 3 Platoon in the last house before "House X" as a stop in case of any attempt at further advance by the enemy, telling them to start firing their rifles as fast as they could at the edge of the wood until Sergeant Jeffs' platoon got near to it to give as much impression of strength as possible, besides trying to keep enemy heads down, if any, in the wood. The survivors of Dicky Bird's No 1 Platoon were to be the reserve, giving covering fire as found to be necessary, later assaulting "House X" once Sergeant Jeffs had cut it off and could fire upon it from the wood.

Glancing at his watch as David joined one of the Bren gunners in an upstairs room of a cottage with the faithful Rowe beside him he saw there were still five minutes to go before zero hour. Sergeant Jeffs' good sense and quick thinking had helped to get all ready in good time.

It was a humble bedroom with an enormous double bed pushed aside against one wall, a hideously carved and equally over sized wardrobe facing it. Sitting on the edge of the bed with his Bren gun ready sat a very young soldier, whom David immediately recognised as one of his company in the Beach Group.

"Hello Wilde!" said David. "This is a pleasant surprise. We have at least three of the old team anyway."

Wilde smiled wanly: David recalled that he had always been shy and unassuming. Probably eighteen, he had only joined the Beach Group two months before "D Day". Though not strong his all-round reliability and his accurate shooting had earned him the relatively important role of Bren gunner, which position he had obviously retained.

"It would be wise to keep well back in the room while you fire," said David. "That way you are less likely to be spotted. Can we lay our hands upon a piece of furniture to put on the bed to give you a rest for your gun?"

"There's a chest of drawers in the passage," said Rowe, and in a few moments they had it on its side on the bed with Wilde behind it.

"We'll fix 'em between us," said David.

Then they heard Sergeant Jeffs' whistle and all hell was let loose as the Bren guns and rifles opened up, the noise in their small room deafening. Methodically as he had been told, Wilde fired bursts into the windows of "House X" while Rowe banged away with his rifle from the right hand corner of the window.

David watched and listened as best he could for any enemy response as, looking sideways past Rowe, he saw the left hand section of No 2 Platoon scrambling through the backyards and out into the open plough, the remainder out of his sight. They were nearly half way across before his rising hopes were dashed. From the end of the wood a Spandau opened up with its crackling hail of bullets, while, in spite of their own fire another Spandau fired from the vicinity of "House X". Miserably he watched the men on the left of No 2 Platoon go down before he turned to try to see where the Spandau near "House X" was located.

"I seen it!" shouted Rowe. "In the shed there between the 'ouse and the 'edge." And he began to fire his rifle in the direction he had indicated.

David moved behind Wilde to direct his fire at the shed when something hit him like a sledge hammer and he was sitting against a wall with his steel helmet pushed down over his face and Wilde lying across his thighs with blood pumping out of his throat in great crimson spurts.

CHAPTER 9

"Sometimes, in a woman's brow
Beneath the shadow of her hair,
The lover, gazing as I gaze now,
Suddenly finds perfection there;
Sees in her eyes the fire
That burned a city for one man's want,
And made Leander in desire
For Hero swim the Hellespont."

RICHARD CHURCH

"When are you going to stop these dreadful flying bombs, dear? It's getting as bad as the blitz; worse really because they are so unpredictable. Then, the warning sirens used to give you a chance to take cover or at any rate be prepared for what might come. Now, there is no warning except for that horrid buzz that gets louder and louder and just when you are hoping it will go past it doesn't, the buzz stops and you know the thing is on its way down and the best place for you is under the stairs or the table, and it is no longer at all easy for me to do that."

Sybil Duval was speaking to David from the armchair she filled, one fat and heavily beringed finger grasping her drink. David could understand her problem: it would indeed be difficult for her to take any kind of evasive action with anything approaching alacrity. How difficult it is for the young to imagine such ruins of womanhood as once fresh and desirable! Yet, according to his aunt Emily, this same loose mass of fat and flesh had been a "beauty" with numerous adventures under her belt, even having enjoyed an affair with Basil Boone, often described by his aunt as a "matinee idol" in the post first Great War period. He was present, too, in another part of the room, still retaining the vestiges of the once splendid figure and melodious voice which had plucked the heart strings of so many women.

It is always difficult to carry on an intelligible conversation with someone sitting below you at a party, particularly when that person is inclined to deafness and the noise level rising appreciably. Aunt Emily believed in serving what she called "zonkers" in the early stages of her parties, adding that, "it was the secret of such events." This brew of indeterminate mix, slightly orange in colour and smelling of rum, served from large glass jugs with plenty of ice was having its usual effect.

So David simply replied that he thought they would stop soon.

"They would have done already if only that bomb had killed Hitler," said Lucienne Fawcett-Brown, standing nearby. "But life is a series of 'if onlys', isn't it?"

News of the tragically abortive attempt upon Hitler's life had come through very recently and was the subject of much speculation.

Lucienne Fawcett-Brown was another old friend of aunt Emily, whose female friends seemed innumerable, though younger and better preserved than Sybil Duval, in fact quite different in appearance. She was slim and neat with dyed fair hair done in the wavy style of the period. Certainly she used too much make-up, but it was well done and the quantity probably necessary. According to aunt Emily she came from a titled family of ancient lineage which had come down in the world and she was now separated from her husband.

Feeling his duty done with Sybil Duval, David turned his attention to Lucienne and soon discovered that she worked as a secretary in ABCA, whose official pamphlets issued to the forces has already been mentioned. Still more interesting, she referred to her immediate boss as an expert in explosives, this coming about with reference to the comments in connection with the bomb that had failed to destroy Hitler.

"He is an ex-Farnborough aircraft establishment scientist and a dear – really the traditional professor type."

"What does he look like?" asked David, interested.

"Thin and tall with wild white hair. Why? Do you know him?"

"Is his nickname Tubby?"

"Absurdly, yes; though his proper name is William Maddox."

So that was where Tubby had arrived after his ejection from the Home Guard Training School! He would be happy there taking part in the subtle dissemination of left wing doctrine David had noticed in recent issues before wounded and returned to England. Doubtless some of his left wing intellectual cronies had gladly arranged for his addition to the staff.

Quickly explaining their past association David asked for his telephone number: there would probably be time for him to arrange a meeting during his stay with his aunt in London before leaving for the remainder of his sick leave at the farm in the New Forest where he had taken Rowe before "D Day".

"What are you talking about?" asked Sybil. "I'm afraid my hearing is not what it was."

"We find that we have a mutual friend," shouted David.

"What a small world it is!" said Lucienne.

"David darling, you must make sure that everyone's glass is full: I can see several that are nearly empty."

Aunt Emily had approached them from behind on a round of inspection to ensure that the men under her command were fulfilling their duty.

Turning, David could see over her head uncle Edward, no doubt similarly reminded, making his way to the table near the door where the jugs and spare glasses were placed.

It was earlier explained that aunt Emily was short and plump like David's grandmother, now staying in an hotel in Taunton with his grandfather, their house having been taken over for the duration of the war by a small girls' school evacuated from the south coast and their London flat damaged during the Blitz. Then, aunt Emily's dumpy body had given an impression of softness: now, tightly enclosed in dark blue Red Cross uniform, it seemed solid. A handsome woman, her black hair was only tinged with grey and her skin, though palid, comparatively unlined. One of those independent, dominating women, from whose ranks our Florence Nightingales and Mrs Pankhursts spring, she had volunteered at the start of the first world war to join the Scottish Women's Ambulance Brigade as a driver. How she obtained the position David never understood, being utterly unmechanical, unable to drive and her only connection with Scotland being an unsuitable engagement to be married to a Scottish Presbyterian minister, fortunately broken off immediately after she spent several days in his gloomy manse with his no less gloomy mother. Possibly, it was managed through one of her already growing number of female friends, some quite influential. In any event, she learnt how to drive the primitive ambulances of those days and set off with the Brigade for Russia to take part in the confused aftermath of Tannenburg. After many adventures, which she was always happy to recount, she had a disagreement with the austere leader of the Brigade, who, according to aunt Emily, "did not appear to need to obey the calls of nature and did not expect anyone else under her command to do so either," causing much discomfort and even the occasional "accident", and set off with another ambulance to escape the subsequent debacle through

145

Romania, her formidable leader deciding to take the Archangel route with the remainder of the Brigade.

After her safe return to England aunt Emily went to France, where she drove ambulances until 1917 when she married the twice wounded uncle Edward. Now she was back as a Red Cross driver working from a local headquarters. Since she had not driven anything more than a bicycle in the interval it was fortunate that the exigencies of wartime had so reduced the quantity of traffic in the London streets.

Though not very full of people, about ten present at that moment, this living room of her London flat was so full of furniture that a journey across it was not easily accomplished. Bulky armchairs and a sofa covered with faded mauve- and cream-flowered material stood scattered about, mingling with gilt pseudo rococo chairs and several mahogany occasional tables. If closely inspected all would be discovered to be broken or damaged in one way or another, roughly repaired if essential for stability, but otherwise blemishes remaining.

David picked his way carefully towards the folding dining table already mentioned with a view to collecting one of the glass jugs of drink and taking it round. As he did so his arm was taken by Dr Sparkinge, interrupting a conversation with Herbert Davis, an unusually spruce looking unsuccessful actor now teaching at the Royal Academy of Dramatic Art.

"How are you feeling, old fellow?" asked the doctor. "Your aunt tells me you have made an excellent recovery from your wound."

He was a wealthy Harley Street doctor, who had looked after the health of aunt Emily and uncle Edward for many years, charging very reduced fees for reasons of friendship or altruism. He was a small portly man with a round red face, pince-nez and hardly any hair. All bald men give the impression that their scalps have been polished, but Dr Sparkinge's looked as if it had received special treatment. Not altogether surprisingly, he was known to his intimates as "Plugs".

Confirming his aunt's favourable report and explaining his immediate mission, David continued to the table and began to work his way round the room jug in hand. When he reached great uncle Charles he found him happily exchanging anecdotes with Basil Boone.

Immensely good looking, tall and masculine, Basil Boone must have been on the verge of sixty. Accepting the liquid that David poured into his glass with a nod of thanks he continued some tale of a fashionable actor, famous for his success with women, who, it appeared, was moving forward towards his latest conquest unclothed when she made some reference to the magnificence of his erection.

"Henry," continued Basil Boone, "was not in the mood to dilly dally and cut her short, saying in that splendid voice of his: 'Madame, I come to bury Caesar, not to praise him!' "

Then, drawing David into the conversation with the utmost charm of manner he talked of Beerbohm Tree.

"Now," he said, "there was a great actor with a lively sense of humour; a wicked sense of humour. When young I was one of his company and my earliest recollection of this attribute of his is when we entered a Post Office together to buy a penny stamp for a letter which he wished to post. He was made impatient by the sluggishness of the clerk dispensing postage stamps: there was, I think, a delay over some matter to do with a parcel presented by a lady before us. When, finally, he obtained the clerk's attention he gravely asked for one penny stamp. The clerk, after the manner of his kind, spread out a large sheet of stamps of that particular denomination with a view to tearing one off, whereupon Tree raised his hand. 'One moment, if you please,' says he, 'it is that one I require.' And he points to a stamp in the very middle of the sheet."

"Ho, ho. ho!" laughed great uncle Charles. "He sounds like Willy Bilson, a shipmate of mine many years ago: he could never resist practical jokes. Got him into hot water sometimes."

But they were not to hear about Bilson's exploits: Basil Boone once centre stage liked to remain there, and swept on sonorously.

"He had a sense of humour that could be cruel too. I remember a young actor joining our company who proved to be insufferably conceited. One day he was travelling between towns where we had engagements, in the same railway compartment as Tree and four of the rest of us. The others had gone on ahead or were following – I forget which – and Tree held all our six tickets. Noises nearby indicated the approach of the inspector, and Tree turned to this young fellow and said: 'Quick! Get under the seat: we will humbug the inspector.' Pleased to be given a principal role, he obediently scrambled under the seat, though not without difficulty, the seat being near the dirty floor and he being a large young man; but by the time the inspector opened our door he was quite out of sight. 'Tickets please,' says the inspector in that blank way they have, and Tree hands him all six tickets. The inspector takes them, clips five and looks up with a puzzled expression. His eyes move round the five of us sitting expressionless. 'Has the other party gone down the corridor?' he asks. 'No,' replies Tree. 'But,' says the inspector, 'you have given me six tickets when there are only five of you travelling.' 'Certainly,' says Tree in the most casual way you can imagine, 'the other is under the seat: he prefers to travel that way.'"

"I never had the good fortune to see Tree act," said great uncle Charles; "but I did see Irving play Richard II: he was most impressive."

"A very fine actor in the more solemn Shakespearean roles and in melodrama, and one of the greatest actor-managers, full of ideas and innovations. He did much for The Stage. Many thought him too proud and lacking a sense of humour, but it was he that told me of the second rate theatrical company with an engagement at a provincial theatre. Several of the cast had imbibed too heavily prior to the curtain going up, and Horatio – they were playing Hamlet – got the bird from the audience. Towards the end of Act I Scene I, during which the ghost was obliged to sit down briefly on a battlement, the noise grew so great that the players could hardly be heard. Horatio stopped in the middle of his lines and staggered to the footlights. 'If you think I'm drunk,' says he thickly, 'just wait until Hamlet comes on!'"

"Ho, ho, ho!" laughed great uncle Charles. "Just the sort of thing that my brother Jack might have done had he been on the stage. You remember Jack, Basil?"

"Indeed I do, very well; a delightful companion at all times, even when drunk," replied Basil Boone, continuing to command the conversation. "The Stage has had its fair share of heavy drinkers. George Cooke was probably the most spectacular. He died early last century, surprising all that he could live so long drunk. He was an actor much admired by his colleagues. After his death Kean stole one of his toe bones when his grave was shifted, keeping it as a relic of one that he called: 'The greatest of actors' until to his displeasure Mrs Kean threw it away. One wonders what happened to his skull, which he bequeathed to an American friend, a Dr Francis, who gave it to a troupe of players for the graveyard scene in Hamlet. I daresay it is still being so used. Perhaps one day it will appear in a film. One that can be fairly called a steady trouper, George Cooke."

Further reminiscences by Basil Boone were interrupted by uncle Edward proffering salted nuts, the approach of aunt Emily with Pearl White and the sound of the telephone ringing in the adjoining hallway.

"That may be Algy to let us know why he is late," said aunt Emily. "Go and answer it, Teddie."

She turned to the rest of them and went on: "He has to work so hard at the War Office and has been unable to get away before I expect."

She referred to Brigadier Algernon Tuck, DSO, whom David had not

148

met, though his aunt had described him as a remarkable soldier who had planned "D Day": an all embracing feat that would have indeed placed him in an astoundingly brilliant category.

"Come along, Basil, you have not yet talked to Lucienne." And David was left with great uncle Charles and Pearl White.

The latter was the actress wife of Herbert Davis, still chatting with Plugs where David had passed them. More successful than her husband, she had nevertheless failed to go as far as her ambition and looks had promised.

"Everyone agrees she is a good actress," aunt Emily would say, "but she just doesn't come across."

Once genuinely and now artificially fair, on close inspection the lines on her still fine features recorded the passing years. She had a vague manner which David found peculiar. Great uncle Charles asked her about her work and she replied that she was "resting" after a tour with ENSA, playing in "Dear Octopus", a play, thought David, that must have utterly baffled innumerable other ranks. While she talked David was able to consider his great uncle.

There was no doubt that the years of war had taken their toll. He was much worn and bent since the time in the summer of 1939 when he had narrowly missed David with a wild shot at a rabbit at the edge of a Sussex wood. His white hair was distinctly thinner and the fine blue veins under his ruddy skin more pronounced. Also, as indicated by his comparative subjection by Basil Boone, he had lost some of his lively spirit, though by no means all, as when Pearl had finished her description of her recent activities and the conversation flagged for a moment, he lifted one of the salted nuts from the plate left behind by uncle Edward and said: "Did I ever tell you, Pearly – these nuts remind me of it – or you David, of the conversation overheard by my lamented brother Jack in the 'Three Horseshoes' one evening? Two villagers were talking over their pints of mild, and one of them – it was old Tom Langridge I think – was describing some salted herrings his wife had presented to him for his supper. It appeared that they were over salted or, perhaps, she had not soaked them long enough in fresh water. 'Saalt!' said Tom – Jack was so good at imitating the incomparable Sussex accent, you remember. 'Saalt! Oi've never 'ad saalt 'errings like 'un. Why, I tell yer, they was as saalt as Lot's wife's arse!'"

Aunt Emily's voice broke through the noise of conversation. "He says he will be a little late, as I suspected; but we are to carry on with supper without him. He is bringing one of his staff and a girl friend with him.

149

David darling, will you come and help me bring in the food."

The food consisted of steaming bowls of aunt Emily's current version of borsch, depending upon the ingredients available during the period of severe food rationing, and white bread followed by stewed plums of her own bottling. The distribution and consumption of these required skill and care in such a cluttered room and by the time the necessary organisation had been accomplished Brigadier Tuck and his party arrived.

David was at the other end of the room when uncle Edward ushered them in. The Brigadier entered first, resplendent in khaki uniform with red tabs. He looked very short beside uncle Edward. His face was round and pink and his hair ginger. He grew a closely cut military moustache. Behind him came a girl of about nineteen with dark hair, wearing a pretty red and white summer frock, closely followed by a slim naval Lieutenant in his late twenties. David took them all in as a whole and then concentrated upon the girl. There was no doubt in his mind that he knew her.

While general introductions were taking place at the other end of the room David searched his memory. Of course, he had it! It was Jill; and a flood of happy memories came back to him. She was the younger sister of a school friend at whose home he had spent several periods during school holidays. Then she had been small for her age and it was her present medium height that had delayed his recognition of her; that and the dramatic change that takes place between a girl in her early teens and fresh young womanhood. They had always got on well together, her brother bringing her into many of their activities. A host of happy recollections pleased David as they came back like slides projected rapidly: tobogganing one winter when there had been quite thick snowfall, heavily wrapped up against the damp and cold though hot with exercise and laughter; tennis parties on hot summer afternoons, Jill neat and serious as she competed admirably with others older and stronger than herself; swimming in the nearby lake; family picnics in the hills. How good it was to see her again! David excused himself to those near him and, leaving his plate and glass upon the mantelpiece, crossed the room.

She spotted him as he negotiated people and furniture while she stood listening politely to those around her and he felt chastened that she clearly recognised him immediately when he had hesitated, though his heart was warmed at the expression of pleasure that so quickly followed one of surprise.

"Jill!"

"David!"

Her eyes, as he recalled now were hazel and the kindest he knew.

She asked: "What are you doing here? I thought you were in France."

She coloured as she understood how she had given away that she had been following his progress, probably through her brother, now fighting in Italy.

"I am on sick leave and this is my uncle and aunt's flat."

There was a subtle, fresh scent about her and her hair was glossy.

"Why sick?"

Her lips were delicately tinged with colour and looked soft and warm.

"A bullet in the shoulder: not a bad wound. It had spent much of its force passing through a soldier in front of me, poor fellow. My batman was splendid, looking after me and getting me back to our MO in a very short time in the circumstances."

"Good for him; but what a beastly experience: tell me more about it."

They were interrupted by aunt Emily introducing David to Brigadier Tuck.

"My nephew – you remember, Algy, I told you – wounded at the head of his troops."

She had always over-dramatised and it still made David cringe inwardly.

"Well done! Well done! The slogging match should soon be over and we'll have the Hun on the run to finish the war in Europe by Christmas."

The Brigadier's voice was surprisingly high pitched.

He introduced David and his aunt to the naval lieutenant.

"John Rylands, a most valuable member of my staff. He had a date with this young lady – er –"

"Jill Talbot," put in Rylands in a pleasantly modulated voice.

"Yes, Miss Jill Talbot; and because I kept him working late he kept her waiting; so I thought the least I could do was to give them a lift in my staff car and get them a drink before they go on to have dinner together somewhere."

As he finished uncle Edward arrived with full glasses for all and started a conversation with Rylands, while aunt Emily led the Brigadier off to meet the others, leaving David free to talk with Jill once more.

Her hand that held her glass was elegant and the nails only lightly tinted.

"Must you leave so soon? It's so long since we last saw each other and there is so much to say."

"We can meet again: I'm working in the War Office."

David's visit to the New Forest was immediately postponed.

"What about tomorrow evening?"

She hesitated: then; "Yes. I finish at six."

"We'll go to Rules, a very good place to eat and talk; unless you prefer Quaglino's or The Hungaria where one can dance."

"Rules sounds fine: I've never been there."

"We can go to Quag's and The Hungaria on the following two evenings."

"We'll see; but tell me more about your wounding. How did it happen?"

"It was in a thoroughly messy affair, though we muddled through in the end, thanks largely to a Sergeant Jeffs, who got a DCM for his part in it; but I'll tell you all about it tomorrow. Where shall we meet?"

"In front of Swan and Edgar's?"

"I'll be there at six and wait until you arrive."

Rylands turned to them.

"I think we ought to be going, Jill," he said.

It was the last thing anyone said in the room for a time.

The closed windows and heavy curtains with the noise level in the room had prevented them hearing the unmistakable spluttering drone of the flying bomb which must have cut out close overhead. It struck nearby, only a few buildings away along the street and the explosion was deafening. At the same time the floor heaved, there was a splintering crash of shattered glass and the lights went out.

How they were there David could not remember, but he was lying with Jill behind the sofa, his body partly over hers. She felt warm and soft. Some plaster from the ceiling fell on his back and disintegrated.

The silence, accentuated after so much noise, was broken by uncle Edward's deep voice.

"Is anyone hurt?"

There was a murmur of surprised "No's" and the sound of movement in the pitch black darkness.

"Stay where you are while I check the black-out and light some candles."

Jill made no move to slip from under David, even seeming to relax there a little.

She simply said: "There's nothing like war for bringing people together."

For the remainder of his leave David spent every moment that he could with Jill, grudging every moment he could not. Unfortunately the latter were greater than the former because of her work at the War Office where she worked a six-day week, and having time on his hands he telephoned Tubby Maddox and arranged to meet him for lunch. Fearful that Tubby might elect to lunch at one of the awful British Restaurants set up by the Ministry of Food, David insisted that he would be host and that they would go to any little restaurant of Tubby's liking in Soho. Tubby agreed and proposed a small and unpretentious one called La Palerma in Greek Street. In his vague way he seemed quite pleased at the prospect of their meeting.

After several wonderful evenings with Jill and an invitation from her to spend the weekend at her home so that he might meet her parents again, David began to feel that his life had suddenly become very full and his projected long visit to the farm shrank into a weekend.

He found La Palerma without difficulty in spite of the increased destruction since his last visit to London in May. It was, as Tubby had described, both unpretentious and small, occupying the ground floor of a down-at-heel brick block about four storeys high. Just inside the cerise-coloured entrance door there was a small space divided from the dining area by a worn patterned screen where a few chairs and small tables indicated waiting while taking a drink. To one side there was a recess with hooks for coats on the wall. All the paintwork was in need of at least a clean.

At one of the tables sat a stout, middle-aged man in airforce uniform with a girl, and a glance behind the screen showed that three of eight white cloth-covered dining tables were already occupied.

David sat down at the spare small table which had a green glass ash tray on it. His arrival had been noted and a very thin, ill looking waiter came round the screen and asked him if he would like an aperitif. He spoke with a foreign accent. Confirming that a table would be reserved, David ordered a gin and orange and settled down to wait.

In such close proximity it was impossible not to overhear the conversation between the couple at the other table, the man being, David now observed, a Flight Lieutenant in the RAF Regiment with a large black moustache. The girl wore a brown skirt and white woollen pullover fitting close to her neck and showing her well-shaped breasts to advantage. She was young and not bad looking. The Flight Lieutenant did most of the talking, for the most part concerned with his experiences in the Western Desert where he painted an important role for himself. After a few minutes of this he said it was about time to go in to lunch, though, with a guffaw, he would not advise an inspection of the basement kitchen. With this blend of good and bad news he guided the girl by her arm past the screen and at the same moment the entrance door opened and Tubby came in with another man.

"Hello! Hello!" said Tubby. "I'm truly sorry we are late: you haven't been waiting long I hope?"

He had not altered, his long, lean face as pale as ever, white hair sticking out in disorder, and the brown tweed jacket and grey trousers replacing the battle dress hung round his tall angular body in the same way, as if fitted before a serious illness had caused considerable loss of weight.

"This," he continued, "is Anthony Bell, a friend of mine. I asked him to come along too; though on the clear understanding that I pay for the lunch."

He brushed aside David's not very ardent protest, not sure that he was carrying enough money to cover three lunches, and David shook the newcomer's hand. It was small, soft and cold.

"A trifle pale and older, but not much change in your appearance," said Tubby, giving David a quick look over, and began to explain that while he himself had plenty of time his friend was in a hurry and it would therefore be necessary to go straight in to lunch.

While he spoke David made a quick inspection of Bell. About forty years old, he had one of those clear pink complexions that questions whether shaving is necessary. His head was slightly large for his small body and he had tried to conceal baldness by carrying a few strands of long hair that remained from one side to the other as some bald men do, thus accentuating their loss. He was wearing a smart beige suit of lightweight material and an apricot-coloured tie.

David was a little put out by his presence since he had hoped to be able to talk freely with Tubby and to enquire about associates at the old Home Guard training establishment. However, there would be time for that if Bell left early as seemed probable.

They took their seats at a table in a corner. The fairly clean table cloth had a cigarette burn in it.

"I have explained to Anthony that you were in the 'D Day' landings and that you are at present on sick leave," said Tubby; and David was relieved that he left the matter there, tired of explaining the circumstances of his wound.

"When do you think you are likely to go back?"

"In three or four weeks time, I think: it depends upon the result of my next medical board due in three weeks."

"It appears that the British and American armies are on the point of breaking out of the bridgehead at last, so perhaps you will join in the advance to the Rhine, where, metaphorically speaking you will be able to shake hands with our gallant Russian allies."

"You believe they will advance so far?"

"Undoubtedly. Ah! Here is Frederick with the menu."

Menus at this time in the war were bleak affairs and this one was no exception. They selected their dishes from the limited range quickly and decided to drink water, wines being scarce and expensive and beer of poor quality.

Tubby continued, addressing Bell: "A most satisfactory line of demarcation, don't you agree, Anthony?"

"Indeed," replied Bell in a cultured voice. "Germany will at last be crossed off as a world menace and the benefits of Communism will rapidly become patently obvious to the remainder of Europe."

"The dream of a united and peaceful Europe fulfilled at long last," said Tubby.

Already one bond that united these two was apparent.

The soup arrived and they started upon it.

"What is the morale of our troops like?" asked Tubby.

"Well," replied David, "the initial excitement has worn off and the harsh realities of fighting are having their effect: I am sure all will be glad when it is over."

"Not all, not all: there are many who enjoy it and others who enjoy the fruits. Can you put your hand on your heart and say that Generals Montgomery, Patton and company are unhappy men; or that the armament manufacturers and black market profiteers are dissatisfied? Capitalism feeds on war while the working man pays for it."

Tubby had not changed a bit, and feeling that they were getting onto awkward ground David turned to Bell.

"When training the Home Guard together there was a splendid Irishman called Jake Donovan who loved to argue this particular theme with Tubby; partly, I suspect, because he was Irish and argument was meat and drink to him." Then back to Tubby: "What has happened to Jake?"

"Back in Ireland I believe: we have lost touch. Tell me, are the ABCA publications widely read?"

"On the whole I would say yes when conditions are suitable."

155

"How do you mean conditions are suitable?"

"When out of action and not busy, which, as you know from your own experience, Tubby, is a large proportion of the time."

"Would you say it has much influence?"

"Not 'much', but some. To what extent do you contribute?"

"Oh, a little here and there; sometimes giving advice upon certain scientific matters; sometimes assisting with the odd article upon current affairs; we work as a team."

"Are you one of the team?" David asked Bell politely.

"Oh no," replied Tubby for him. "Anthony moves in a far more important sphere."

David looked enquiringly at Bell, but he did not enlarge, merely wiping his mouth delicately with his table napkin while the main course was distributed, a concoction of chicken in a white sauce, probably with rabbit, possibly even cat; and his work remained an enigma.

"You gave the impression at the school that your sympathies were with Socialism," said Tubby. "Where do you stand now?"

David hesitated while the babble of conversation rippled about them from the other tables, now nearly all occupied. Opposite he could see the Flight Lieutenant still talking. Then, cowardly, he prevaricated.

"I once heard it quoted that there was something wrong with any young man below the age of twenty-five who was not a Socialist."

"Socialism is protean: you must make up your mind, David."

There was a certain tenseness in the atmosphere which David did not like. The meeting was not turning out as he had hoped and expected, and he felt sure that the taciturn Bell was the cause of it.

They ate in silence for a while until David felt that he might make another attempt to alter course.

"I heard about the Court of Enquiry in Belfast," he said to Tubby. "I hope you were completely exonerated?"

"Of course not: the Establishment wanted a scapegoat, as it usually does, and the Army was not going to admit incompetence; but that's all past history. What do you intend to do when the war is over? Not back to your architectural studies I presume when there are so many other fields for your talents and much time passed."

"I don't believe in changing horses in mid stream."

"The stream has washed your first horse away."

"I still feel it is my vocation."

"You will find a student's life fairly spartan after five years as an officer and a gentleman."

"You would not know that my father and mother were murdered in India."

Tubby pursed his lips and shook his head sadly and David continued: "A very serious personal loss, but it does mean that I shall have a small income at my disposal, my father having saved some capital over the years."

"Ah! Privileged: that does make a difference;" and Tubby looked across at Bell meaningfully.

Shortly afterwards Bell said that he must go and bade David goodbye, his face expressionless. David had a distinct impression that he had been tested and found wanting.

His departure altered Tubby's attitude and he became more free and friendly, chatting of this and that.

David asked him if he had any news of Ceddie Roussel.

"He was running a school of camouflage when I last heard about him. He may well have moved to France by now."

"And Tim Baker?"

"Ah! Didn't you know? No, you would have missed it. He shot himself, poor fellow."

"That old black magic has me in its spell;
That old black magic that I know so well.
Those icy fingers up and down my spine;
That same old witchcraft when your eyes meet mine."

The seductive tune with the emotive words carried Jill and David round the small dance floor of Quaglino's restaurant. They did not speak, relishing the music and their closeness to one another. David had received his orders and was due to leave for France in one day's time. British and American forces had broken out of their bridgehead and were racing towards the Rhine while in the east the Russians were driving on again so that there was much hope that the war might be over by Christmas.

The contrast between the last month for David and its predecessors was immeasurable. He and Jill had spent nearly every particle of her free time together and they were deeply in love.

When they returned to their table David said: "I can't get over the good fortune of your coming to that party at my aunt's flat, a happening

157

of extraordinary importance, even marked by a Wagnerian accompaniment."

"Preferably without the carnage nearby that might so easily have included us."

"Curious how after a time in war one becomes accustomed to the sudden destruction of unknown people."

"A form of shield develops. Without it many would go mad."

Inadvertently David had led her thoughts in the wrong direction and she was suddenly downcast. He hastened to direct them to a new path and, as so often in similar circumstances, spoke carelessly.

"You never did get your dinner with John Rylands: I do feel a bit guilty about cutting him out in the way I have."

Her expressive eyes turned mischievous.

"You are only around for a short time: he'll have months to make up for it."

David was sure she was teasing, but the remark gave him food for thought, and the following day he went to see his bank manager, followed by a visit to Bond Street where he spent some time with an understanding jeweller.

Jill and he spent that evening together again, dining and dancing, without David mentioning the small cardboard box which lay in his bedroom in aunt Emily's battered flat.

Jill had promised to come to Waterloo station to see David off the next morning, granted a half day by her superiors at the War Office.

Waterloo station, that stage for so many tragic partings; the very name so suitable for the two such sanguinary wars of the century. How many men had left those grey platforms, leaving wives, sweethearts and mothers never to return! The spectre of such sorrow and heartbreak still lingered around the ugly, dirty interior after the second war had come to an end until some enlightened authority carried out the brighter, cheerful refurbishment that we see today.

The great concourse was thick with people, quite a number in uniform, moving as always like a disturbed ants' nest. It was less restless on the platform where David drew Jill aside behind a boxlike waiting room.

"Look Jill," he said, pulling a narrow diamond ring from his pocket, "this is a gage that I would like you to wear for me. If I do not come back or if I return crippled you are to regard it as a memento of a precious time that has meant more to me than I can explain. If, on the other hand, I get back in one piece I shall be asking you to turn it into an engagement ring if you are prepared to work that magic."

Jill stayed silent for a moment. Then, "Put it on for me," she said huskily, giving him her hand, her eyes glistening with tears.

"It may not fit without adjustment."

"Try."

It slipped on easily.

"It will need a slight tightening. Easier than enlarging," he said.

Her arms went round his neck.

"My darling," she said, "what a wonderful way to propose. The magic is swift and we are engaged from the moment you put it on."

If David had wanted to protest that that was not exactly his intention it would have been impossible for her sweet mouth was against his. His arms went round her waist holding her supple body close against his and they stood in a private world in which all around them was inexistant.

Thus it was that David and Jill tied a knot in the intricate cobweb of time.

CHAPTER 10

"Oh it's Tommy this, an' Tommy that,
an' Tommy, go away;
But it's 'Thank you, Mister Atkins',
when the band begins to play."

RUDYARD KIPLING

The war over with, a little to his surprise, David alive, he was obliged to concentrate upon picking up the threads of his interrupted studies, marriage and a home.

The last was the problem: London University was back in London and it was in that battered city that Jill and he would have to live for at least the next four years before he could qualify and look for a job.

The second-in-command of the battalion he was serving with in the occupation forces in Germany, Major Henry Postgate, was a Londoner, so David asked him for his advice.

"You will find it very difficult," said the Major, "unless you can say you were resident in London before the war."

"As you know, my home was in India, though I did stay with relatives in London from time to time during school holidays."

"Mm. That might provide a small lever. How much can you afford in the way of rent?"

"I understand I shall get a grant as a married man of £300 p.a. during my time at the university. Jill will work as a secretary to bring in a bit more. I suppose we could stretch to about two pounds a week."

"That's very tight. Why create these difficulties by getting married?"

"I found the right girl."

"Too hasty, my dear fellow: there are plenty of right girls about."

Henry was a bachelor.

He mused; then said: "I suggest you write to the Clerk of the Borough in which those relatives live explaining your situation and asking him if he can help."

David's letter to the Clerk of the Borough Council brought a formal reply enclosing a form to be completed, the nub of which, as the Major had foreseen, was a clause requesting full details of David's previous residence in the Borough. To this he appended an asterisk and a statement repeating what he had already written concerning his unusual situation. The Clerk replied briefly that it was not possible to consider applications from anyone not previously resident in the Borough. David wrote again, asking how he could possibly claim residence anywhere in the United Kingdom, pointing out that one had to start somewhere; and added that his Council's attitude towards returning members of the armed forces was shabby.

He wrote too warmly. Supplicants are never in a position to allow feelings of displeasure to become apparent.

The Clerk's riposte was cold, succinct and final.

"Dear Sir," he wrote, "I have to acknowledge your letter of the 15th Ult.

"As made clear in previous correspondence, my Council's decision with reference to applications for Council tenancies in the Borough is only those who are able to substantiate their requests by showing that they have been residents in the Borough for a reasonable period of time are eligible for consideration as future tenants.

"Since your case does not fall within these confines your application must be refused.

"In confutation of your proposition that, as a member of HM Armed Forces, you expect to receive special treatment, I am driven to remind you that in the late war all were in the front line.

"Yours faithfully."

"Officialdom never likes special cases," said the Major; "preferring everything to run along comfortably in regular channels: exceptions cause problems and additional work. It was worth trying, though, as I feared, it turns out that you will have to forego hopes of hearth and home until the housing situation in England eases. I would gladly have you in my flat for a trifling stipend but for the fact that the spare bedroom is only adequate for one." He shook his head sadly, murmuring: "Too hasty, too hasty."

The mess waiter came over to them and told David that Colour Sergeant Pollock was asking for him. David found him outside. He was a dark little man with a very smooth brown skin.

"Beg pardon, Sir," he said as he saluted, "might I make a request?"

This surprised David because there had never been any accord between them, it being his conclusion that the Colour Sergeant disliked him.

David asked him what he could do for him.

"It's like this, Sir; I understand you are going on leave at the end of the week, and I was wondering whether you would be in London at all?"

"Very probably."

"Well, Sir, it's like this: I 'ave a particular girl that lives in a flat near Euston station and she 'appens to be extremely partial to chocolates. It also 'appens that I 'ave obtained a box of Swiss chocolates which I am anxious to get to 'er. You might say I should post them to 'er, but I do not trust the army postal service, which I 'ave observed does not treat parcels with proper respect. You see, Sir, they are soft chocolates, which are 'er favourites. You might ask why I don't take them myself, and the reason is that I am not due for leave for three months and in this warm weather they are likely to deteriorate."

He paused while David waited, wondering how on earth he had managed to get hold of a box of Swiss chocolates, an amazing luxury at that time.

"Well, Sir," he went on, "I was thinking you might be kind enough, if you are likely to be near Euston station and I was to give you 'er address, to drop them off on 'er?"

Later he brought David the box, carefully wrapped in stout brown paper and neatly tied with string, and with it a sealed envelope addressed to Miss Amy Muncer, Ardbeg Road, Euston, London.

On their way to an agreeable hotel run by friends, David and Jill spent a night with his aunt and uncle before catching a train from Euston station the following day, an arrangement which would give them time to find the flat occupied by Colour Sergeant Pollock's girl friend and deliver the box of chocolates. It gave aunt Emily an excuse to have a party.

The flat in Earls Court inhabited by aunt Emily and uncle Edward had not altered at all from the dramatic evening when David and Jill had met again and a flying bomb had exploded nearby as if to mark the momentous occasion. Even the hole in the ceiling of the living room remained. Indeed, as David stood, glass in hand, listening to the general murmur of conversation, with several of those present who had attended that previous party, he had a curious sensation of time slip, almost feeling that at the end of his leave he would be returning to the battle raging in Europe instead of to a comfortable station in northern Germany.

Diligent death, unappeased by the rich harvest of the last five years, had culled two of the original band, Sybil Duval and, more surprisingly, Herbert Davis; while Basil Boone was touring with ENSA, playing Elyot in Noel Coward's "Private Lives". Replacements took the form of a suave and good looking musician called Julius Caesar, a Mary McClune, an old crony of aunt Emily newly returned from Eire where she had taken refuge for the duration of the war, and Katushka. The first two David had met before, Julius Caesar paying him great attention while in his early teens, an interest later explained when aunt Emily mentioned, "Darling Julius – they say he has tendencies, but he is such a dear man and plays the piano divinely. Anyway, what people do in private is their own business." Katushka, David had only heard about, his aunt "adoring" her, though uncle Edward in an aside remarked that she was "a pain in the arse." It seemed that she was a ballet dancer from Eastern Europe, whether Russia or Poland never made clear, now much reduced in circumstances scratching a living giving dancing lessons.

David was with Lucienne Fawcett-Brown, Brigadier Tuck and uncle Edward when the conversation turned to the recent abrupt end to the war with Japan.

Lucienne said: "When I heard of the atom bomb dropped on Hiroshima I felt physically sick."

"All warfare is sickening," said the brigadier, "particularly modern warfare."

"You are in danger, my dear Lucienne," said uncle Edward, "of falling into the common trap and finding yourself shocked by the effects of war when highlighted by a dramatic event such as the bombs on Hiroshima and Nagasaki. I have no doubt at all that Algy here could confirm that the slaughter would have been hideously worse if the allies had been driven to end the war by invasion of the Japanese mainland."

"Indeed," said the Brigadier, "it was known that the defences were formidable and that the Japanese would defend their soil with the same suicidal determination shown by their kamikaze pilots."

He turned to David.

"What does our front line soldier think?"

David was explaining how his approach to this awful problem was hardly objective because the Division in which he was serving had been given the "honour" of representing Britain for the first assault upon the Japanese beaches, and to a man the atomic bomb had come as an unqualified relief, when his aunt came and asked him to talk to darling Katushka.

He turned to see her standing by herself in the attitude of a dancer in repose, one foot placed at an angle in front of the other, left hand turned a little outwards near her thigh; she was looking dreamily into the half filled glass in her right hand with head slightly turned to one side, giving the impression that an inner tension was developing within her, possibly leading to a solemn dance round her upheld glass. His enquiry as to whether she would like her glass replenished arrested any such extravagance, remarkable at even one of aunt Emily's parties.

She turned her hollow eyes to his without altering her introspective expression and shook her bronze red hair slowly from side to side murmuring, "I am quite drunk, thank you."

This unusual admission was expressed in a cracked voice, the accent so extraordinary as to be almost unintelligible; and, indeed, for the first few minutes of their subsequent conversation David hardly understood a word she said, doing his best, as one does in such circumstances, happily unusual, to respond with nods and smiles at what seemed appropriate moments. After a while he gathered that she was talking of his recent marriage, concluding with an unmistakable question: "Arre you goot in bed?"

Most would agree that it is a difficult enquiry to answer, better directed to recipient rather than practitioner, and David fell back upon a diplomatic "I hope so."

At this Katushka became agitated.

"It is not goot onlee to 'ope," she said. "It is much important; verry much important. When I first marry I am not goot in bed." She made a broad gesture of dismay, even horror, and looked tragic.

David expressed confidence that the imperfection was soon overcome.

"Neverr! Neverr!" she exclaimed, taking another dramatic attitude and spilling some of her drink upon the carpet. "We arre gettink too leedle money."

Momentarily baffled, not grasping any obvious relationship between poverty and sexual prowess, David shook his head sadly.

"My hubsan haff bits of forniteers that 'e ees gettink from 'is mudda, but 'e ees gettink no bed. We are sleepink on der floor."

Rapidly adjusting his thoughts David expressed regret at such an unfortunate deficiency, going on to explain that as he and Jill had not yet found anywhere to live the matter of furniture had not arisen, though when the time came he would certainly follow her counsel.

She went on rapidly about her "hubsan", whose disappearance David failed to understand and then asked another direct question.

"Arre you likink Danzink?"

"In point of fact," he explained, "the Russians have Danzig in their zone of occupation: the British zone being to the west of the Elbe."

"No! No! danzink, danzink!" She appeared exasperated at his lack of comprehension.

"I think, David," said Dr Sparkinge, coming up behind David and to his rescue, "you are under a misapprehension. Katushka is talking about dancing."

"Yees. Danzink! Danzink! What else you tinkink?" She flung her thin arms wide distributing the remains of her drink in a glittering arc.

The opportunity to escape was too good to miss and taking her glass with the assurance of a refill David rather unkindly left Dr Sparkinge, his bald head as polished as ever, to fill his place.

"Phew!" he said as he joined Jill and great uncle Charles. "I begin to understand what uncle Edward meant. My aunt does pick some curious friends."

"She always has, dear boy," said great uncle Charles. "When confronted with Katushka, fortunately a rare event, I sail behind a smokescreen of deafness. It works like a charm. Of course at your age it would not be appropriate."

David was sorry to see that great uncle Charles was looking older and more shrunken than when last seen at the flying bomb party: the war had wasted him considerably, as it had done to many elderly people of his acquaintance. Nevertheless, he retained his engaging loquacity and continued: "Your beautiful wife and I were discussing the difficulty you are experiencing in finding a mooring after your forthcoming release from His Majesty's Forces. I am very sorry. The little hotel in Bloomsbury where I am anchored might be able to find a space for you if I spoke to the manager, with whom I have a happy relationship, but I understand that the cost would be beyond your means even for the few months it might take you to find what you are looking for.

"Your predicament reminds me of a young shipmate of mine towards the end of the last century – that dates me, does it not? His name was Plunket, though always known by his intimates as Bonzo, a nickname I can only ascribe to the fact that he had a large brown birthmark under one eye. He married a pretty little thing and finding some difficulty in the time available before we cast anchor in finding a berth he installed her in a gypsy caravan just outside Pompey – Portsmouth you know – which was our main base in those days. I can't recall how he got hold of it, if

165

ever I knew; but he made it very snug, being a handy sort of chap, and whenever we got back from a trip he would join her there. There was enough land round the caravan to make a little garden, and Mrs Plunket – I forget her Christian name: Edith, was it? Or perhaps Edna? I cannot recall: my memory fails me a great deal these days – made a nice flower garden, trim and colourful. They invited me to tea one afternoon and I was impressed. They seemed very happy together. Which was why it was such a great surprise the next time we got home and Bonzo arrived back at the ship looking most put out. What do you think had happened?"

They said they were quite unable to guess.

"No caravan and no wife."

"Where had she gone?" asked Jill.

"He never did find out. Both had vanished into thin air. All that remained was long grass and weeds where the flowers had been. Poor old Bonzo: he was dreadfully cut up about it."

"Thanks for the warning, uncle," said David. "No caravans!"

Later, the party over and the last guest departed, aunt Emily rebuked David for attempting to pull Katushka's leg. "She is so sweet," she said, "but does not share our Anglo-Saxon sense of humour."

David denied any such venture.

"Well," said his aunt, "she asked me whether your wound had been a head one and if the damage was permanent."

David and Jill found the house indicated by Colour Sergeant Pollock without much difficulty. It was in the middle of a terrace of brick and stucco, one end in ruins and the exposed party wall shored up with heavy baulks of timber. The front door was at the top of a flight of steps bridging a basement area and the bell push caused four bell-like notes within.

A wispy little woman of about fifty years opened the door. She wore a brown woollen dress and felt slippers. She looked at them timidly through glasses which tended to slip down her very small nose and seemed displeased when they asked for Miss Muncer. It appeared that Miss Muncer had left her flat three weeks before and not paid the rent due soon after her departure.

"She told me," said the wispy little woman, plainly the landlady, "that she was going to spend a weekend with her parents in Nottingham. I thought at the time it was a bit funny her taking so much luggage; but she has been a good tenant for more than two years, always paying her monthly rent regular, and I didn't think about it much. Now I'm beginning to wonder."

David explained who they were and their errand, and she softened a little, giving her name as Miss Tingle, though still keeping them on the doorstep.

David asked if she had the address of Miss Muncer's parents.

"No, and I didn't think to ask, not expecting any trouble really."

David told her that he might be able to find out something from Colour Sergeant Pollock and she asked him who that was.

David said: "A friend of hers in my battalion, the same one that asked me to bring this box of chocolates. He must have been here. Don't you remember him?"

"No," she replied, "there's been no soldier here."

"He may come in civilian clothes. He is a dark-haired man of about thirty."

Miss Tingle put her head on one side and looked puzzled.

"Her brother comes to stay with her sometimes. He is dark and not much taller than me; but he's called Mr Muncer and not Sergeant – who did you say?"

"Pollock."

"No, not Pollock."

"Did you ever hear his Christian name?"

Miss Tingle considered, pushing her glasses up her nose with one finger. Then she said: "Yes, she called him Les."

Aside to Jill David said: "I don't know Pollock's initials, but I can check when I am back in Germany. I should think it's him all right." Then to Miss Tingle: "This is all very odd. Do you mind if we come inside?"

"Oh, I'm so sorry," she said. "Please come in. I'm afraid I'm a bit confused."

She led them through a small hall with a staircase leading up and another one leading down to a sitting room filled with heavy Victorian furniture and they all sat down in upright upholstered chairs before an ugly marble fireplace with an oil painting of a lion and a lamb lying down together before a haloed figure pointing upwards.

"You have a nice house," said David, "and it seems you were lucky to escape the Blitz."

"Yes, it was very bad round here and the end of the terrace was hit. I expect you noticed."

She pushed her glasses up and blinked at them.

"Is Miss Muncer your only lodger?" asked Jill.

167

"No. There's Miss Clamp on the top floor. She's a school mistress. And they aren't lodgers. The house is divided into my part on the ground floor and basement and two flats on the first and second floors. When my father passed on, the house was too big for me alone and I had it divided up. It worked very nicely till this happened."

"I expect there's a simple explanation," said David. "Perhaps Miss Muncer has been obliged to stay with her parents because one of them is ill or something like that."

"Then why hasn't she written and why hasn't she paid the rent and why did she take all her things with her?"

"Have you looked in her flat?"

"Yes: I have the spare key and when she didn't come back I went in to see whether she had left a note or anything. It was then I found she had taken all her things – all her clothes and bits and pieces. I wasn't prying you understand, just looking for an explanation. It was Miss Clamp – she was with me – that looked in the cupboard in the bedroom and found it empty."

"I can well understand your concern," said David. It is very strange. I'll tell you what I'll do. I'll ask Colour Sergeant Pollock to find out what is going on immediately I get back to my battalion in a week's time and then I'll write to you. He is bound to know because Miss Muncer is a friend of his. Meanwhile I'd better hold onto this present, leaving you my address and telephone number in England so that you can let me know if Miss Muncer turns up."

"That's ever so nice of you. I've been really worried about what to do. I'm on my own, you see. There's Miss Clamp of course and Nancy next door, but it's not quite the same as having a man to help." She got up from her chair and pushing her glasses up she asked: "Have you got time for a cup of tea?"

David looked at Jill, who said: "That would be lovely, Miss Tingle."

"The kitchen is just downstairs," said Miss Tingle. "I'll only be a moment."

"I'll come and help," said Jill.

Left alone, David wondered at Jill's decision to take tea with Miss Tingle, not in his opinion a desirable way of spending even a small part of their time together before he returned to Germany. He went over to the window and looked through the net curtains. It had stopped raining and a watery sunlight made the wet pavements glisten. There was little traffic about so soon after the war and the clicking steps of a woman walking past in a red raincoat were distinct. Quite soon noises of cups being placed on saucers and the murmur of voices came up faintly from below. Obviously, the kitchen was directly beneath the sitting room.

He wondered idly about Miss Muncer and Colour Sergeant Pollock. Plainly he had no intimation of her flight, if that was what it was, when he made his request. Could it be a modern version of great uncle Charles' tale of Bonzo Plunkett and his wife with no solution ever found? In the meantime what was he to do about the box of chocolates? If Miss Muncer did not reappear before the end of his leave should he take it back to the Colour Sergeant or leave it with Jill? Instead of sympathy he felt irritation: it was an unnecessary intrusion into his leave.

A small dog of mixed extraction trotted purposefully along the opposite pavement. Do dogs plan their movements or do they act on the spot upon some scheme that enters their minds? Certainly, this one knew exactly where it was going. Or might it be returning from some business? If so, it was successful: the animal was decidedly jaunty. It brought to David's mind another little dog owned by an elderly spinster called Miss Jelph who lived not far from Jill's family. It was curiously called Busby, and Miss Jelph was devoted to him. She was a sharp-nosed, angular woman who gave the impression that she continually detected an unpleasant smell in her neighbourhood, alleged to be so prudish that on the rare occasions that married relations had stayed with her she had placed them in separate bedrooms. This characteristic must have made Busby's conduct a torture to her; for he was a randy little dog. Indeed, it could be fairly stated that he was a canine Don Juan. His search for an outlet to his phenomenal sexual drive took him far afield and Miss Jelph was constantly calling upon the local police to assist in recovering him. All who knew Miss Jelph and Busby assisted in reporting his whereabouts when he was seen trotting to or from his latest conquest, ears and short curly tail erect, the picture of confidence and contentment. Few had the heart to interrupt his busy progress and conduct him to his home. The difficulty was that as time went on more and more sightings of Busby were reported as his progeny increased, for some reason exactly similar in appearance to their insatiable parent, possibly inheriting his remarkable prowess, thus multiplying Busbys by compound interest. The memory made David smile and reminded him that he must ask Jill what had happened to Miss Jelph and the original Busby and how the Busby progeny had been absorbed in the region. At the same time Jill and Miss Tingle brought in the tea.

Later, in the train, Jill told David that Miss Muncer's flat consisted of a sitting room, a dining kitchen and a bedroom large enough for two. The rent was two pounds a week inclusive of rates.

"You found out a lot in a short time," said David.

"We got on very well." Jill sounded rather smug.

It was almost immediately after their return from the hotel to Jill's parents that the two policemen called. They wished to talk to David though expressing no objection to doing so in front of Jill and her mother. The round-faced one with a ginger moustache did most of the talking, his thin colleague listening and watchful. After general preliminaries David was invited to tell all he knew about Colour Sergeant Pollock and Miss Muncer. It was little and did not take long.

"We understand, Sir," continued the round-faced one, "that you have in your possession a parcel handed to you by Sergeant Pollock and that he requested you to give that parcel to Miss Muncer."

David confirmed it.

"May we inspect it?"

David got the parcel and handed it over.

"It's a box of chocolates," he said.

The round-faced policeman proceeded to undo the string and take off the brown wrapping paper, revealing an unmistakable chocolate box flamboyantly decorated, the top held on with a red ribbon, which he deliberately untied.

"One moment, officer," said David. "Have we the right to open it in this way without the knowledge of Colour Sergeant Pollock?"

"We have, Sir," he replied. "Would you like to see the warrant?" And he pulled from his breast pocket an official looking document.

Startled, David waved it aside, and the officer took off the lid. Inside were a splendid assortment of gleaming chocolates arranged in frilly paper cups. Jill, her mother and David gazed with wonder at such a display, not seen since the first year of the war.

The officer placed the upturned lid on a small table nearby and proceeded to transfer the chocolates to it one by one with the utmost precision, revealing the usual chocolate-coloured, ribbed paper designed to divide the top layer from the bottom. The last chocolate from the top layer slotted into the lid, he took hold of a corner of the dividing paper between his forefinger and thumb and drew it back. Underneath were revealed layers of English bank notes. While David and Jill's wonder changed to astonishment, the two police officers exchanged looks of satisfaction.

"You see, Sir," said the round-faced officer, "you have been employed as a go-between."

170

"Is it stolen money?" gasped Jill's mother.

"Not exactly stolen, Ma'am; money obtained through the black market in Europe. As you well know, Sir," turning to David, "members of the armed forces serving in Europe are not permitted to transfer more than fifty pounds each leave to this country, that being a safeguard against criminal activities. It has come to our notice that this soldier has been illicitly transferring funds raised from his activities for some time, employing Muncer as his contact in the United Kingdom. We have had the latter person under surveillance for several months and a warrant for her arrest was issued a few days ago. Unfortunately, she must have become suspicious and scarpered, if you'll excuse the expression, Ma'am; as you and your good wife discovered, Sir, when you visited the house in which she had been living."

"So that accounts for her disappearance," said David.

"Yes, Sir. At present she is at large. When we entered the premises with a view to making a search of her rooms we were informed by the landlady of your visit and its purpose. Fortunately, you had left your address with her and we were therefore able to trace you without difficulty."

"And what about Colour Sergeant Pollock?" asked David.

"We have been in communication with the Military Police and he will be apprehended and brought back to this country. In due course you must expect to be called as a witness to give evidence."

"What will happen then?"

"With an open and shut case such as this they'll do a stretch – some time in prison, Ma'am."

When they had left, taking Colour Sergeant Pollock's present with them, David turned to Jill, an idea forming in his mind.

"Do you think," he said, "that we could take over the lease of Miss Muncer's flat?"

"Yes," said Jill. "It's all arranged. I discussed the possibility with Miss Tingle when I was helping her with the tea and she jumped at it. I'll telephone her now to tell her what had happened and that it's on."

Which shows, thought David, why I am now sure that Colour Sergeant Pollock dislikes me as well as another facet of Jill's worth.

CHAPTER 11

"– Only these skulls
ring emptily and need no requiem,
Being at peace. Lie easy now, poor bones."

PAUL DEHN.

There was nothing unusual about the "Black Dog" public house on the edge of the City of London save for the fact that the tenant landlord owned such a large animal. David discovered this for the first time when inspecting the house from top to bottom in connection with a Party Wall Award. The firm of architects in which he was now a partner had been commissioned to build a new office block on a bomb shattered site to one side of the pub and behind it; and when building against existing property The London Building Acts contain comprehensive requirements involving the preparation of such mutual agreements.

The "Black Dog" was and probably still is a narrow public house with its main entrance from a street that runs down towards the river Thames over what was once the river Fleet, now ignominiously transformed into a sewer. At the back there was another door leading out from a passage, at the side of which were the lavatories for the use of clients. This door opened onto the bombed site.

The first and second floors were set back at the rear with a flat roof which provided a balcony for the use of the landlord, his wife and, as it turned out, his appropriate black dog.

"Hang on a mo'," said the landlord, who was with David on his tour. "I'll just secure Jason; he's inclined to be a bit suspicious of strangers," and he took a stout lead from a peg and went out onto the balcony alone. When he came in again he had an enormous animal at the end of the lead. David supposed it was part Alsatian and part wolfhound, though its size indicated some other larger breed in its ancestry, possibly Cerberus. It regarded David with malevolence and growled in the most intimidating manner showing yellow teeth.

"He's a guard dog," said the landlord unnecessarily, a big man with yellow teeth himself. "Because he's a bit uncertain with strangers, as I say, we keep him out on the balcony when the weather is OK and in the house upstairs when it isn't. I let him have his exercise at the back where he can't come to any harm."

"Once the contractor starts on the site I'm afraid he'll have to be kept off it," said David.

"Never fear; I'll only let him out after work and at weekends. You'll be keeping an area open at the back, no doubt."

"Yes, essential for your rear access."

"Just let me know the times for work: we don't want him to take a nip at any of the builder's men."

Certain that such a dog must be utterly incapable of delivering anything so minor as a nip, probably removing a pound of flesh at each bite, David assured the landlord that he would be given this information and went out onto the balcony.

From that vantage point the site of the proposed new building was completely displayed, the ruins largely cleared away. On the far side St Bride's Street climbed up the slope at an angle, its near side supported by the original brick arches that were once the retaining wall for the vanished old office basements and now open to the light, giving the impression of an ancient bridge now bricked in five or six feet behind the face of its arches. On the left a narrow walkway ran down the side of the pub to join Farringdon Street, and on the right the building adjoining its other side returned in the form of an L to complete the enclosure. The floor of the open site itself was strewn with bits of brickwork and the stumps of old foundations mantled with the ubiquitous Rose-bay Willow-herb of bombed London. The railing of the balcony was faced with wire mesh, doubtless to prevent Jason from leaping through and devouring tramps unwisely dossing down below.

After the usual delays obtaining the various consents that are a part of building in London, in this case aggravated by the need to satisfy two powerful authorities, The London County Council and The City of London, tenders were invited from contractors and a contract signed with one of them.

A good foreman, or site agent in the stilted modern vernacular, is exceedingly important both for the success of a building job and the peace of mind of its architect; and David went to the first site meeting with anxious interest. An access ramp had been formed from St Bride's Street at its lowest end and there were now two wooden huts. He entered the one with the words SITE AGENT painted on the door and found two

173

men bending over a bench which ran along one wall and covered with drawings. They straightened up at his entry. One was a director of the appointed firm of contractors and the other was David's old batman, Rowe.

David stood astonished.

Rowe was in grey flannel trousers with a brown sports coat instead of uniform, but he had hardly altered at all since last seen at the Field Dressing Station in France before David was placed in an ambulance and carried back to a hospital. They had lost touch for the simple reason that letter writing was not one of Rowe's strengths. David did not even know whether he had survived the remainder of the campaign; and here he was, a huge smile on his round face, probably expecting David since he would have been given his name.

"Good morning, Mr Drummond," said the director. "May I introduce you to our site agent for this job, or do you already know each other as Mr Rowe thought likely?"

Recovering from his surprise David grasped Rowe's hand and shook it heartily.

"A real turn up for the book," said Rowe.

"And what a happy one," said David.

Little more that was personal could be discussed between them then because the Engineer and his assistant arrived and preliminary matters concerning the foundations of the new building had to be considered; but when that was done David and Rowe were left on their own and it being midday David proposed that they should go into "The Black Dog" for a pint.

"As long as we don't meet that bloody great hound," said Rowe pointing to the balcony.

"It hasn't caused any trouble, I hope?"

"It's stopped now, but when we were putting up the 'uts you should 'ave 'eard it bark! Foaming at the mouth it was."

"Then it will have a fit and die when the work really starts."

"I 'ope so; it gets on your nerves."

David took the opportunity to introduce Rowe to the landlord and they then retreated to a corner with their beer and sandwiches to bring each other up-to-date with their lives since parting.

Rowe had not continued as a batman after David's removal, electing to return to a platoon where he was quickly promoted Lance-Corporal and then worked his way up to Sergeant before demobilisation. After the events that brought about David's wound the battalion had been

174

withdrawn for a thorough rest and training with the large number of replacements necessary after the heavy casualties it had endured and saw no more action until a rather unpleasant crossing of the Meuse Escaut canal just before the Dutch border, not far it seemed from where David had been involved to a smaller degree in another battalion which he had joined after his return to the front. After that they had without knowing it shared the miserable winter of 1944/45 along the river Maas, the fighting through the Reischwald Forest, the Rhine crossing and the advance to Bremen.

"What happened to the battalion CO I never met?" David asked.

"He was promoted Brigadier and we never saw 'im again."

"And Sergeant Jeffs and Mr Bird?"

"Sergeant Jeffs was taken back like you because 'e got wounded too. Don't know what 'appened to 'im after that. Mr Bird got killed in that Reischwald."

Diffidently David asked about his home life.

"All in order," Rowe replied. "My Missus and me came together again when I was demobbed. It turned out the bloke she had been with was married with three kids and never told 'er. She learnt a lesson and I agreed to let bygones be bygones. After all, between you and me, what I didn't tell 'er was that I 'ad some fun myself after that no fraternisation lark, and what's good for the goose is good for the gander. We've two nippers now; both boys."

"I married just after the war in Europe was over and we have a couple too, except that they are a girl and a boy."

"A pigeon pair: that's great."

The landlord of "The Black Dog" served excellent sandwiches, his beer was good and as David had other work in the area he decided to make it a luncheon place whenever it suited his movements.

About a week after his visit with Rowe he called in and stood at the bar while he waited to attract the attention of the barmaid to give his order. "The Black Dog" was usually very full and that day was no exception.

"Splendid pub this: have yer tried it before?" said the man who stood next to him. He was middle-aged, of medium height and large belly, with eyes which protruded like a fish on either side of a very purple nose. He wore a tweed suit of a reddish brown tint matching the colour of his sparse, well oiled hair brushed flat to his narrow head, neatly parted in the middle. At his throat was a green bow tie with white spots.

"For the first time a week ago."

"I didn't spot yer. Have this one on me: what are yer drinkin'?"

David noticed that he had a pint of bitter in his hand and said: "That's kind of you: the same as yours."

The man rapped the bar top with a coin in an authoritative manner.

"Come along now, Daisy my love: a pint of bitter for this thirsty young man."

And in a moment the pint was before him.

"There's a good girl!" He turned to David again. "They know me well here," he said. "Major Withers T.D." He was obviously particular about the T.D. "May I ask yer name?"

David told him.

"Work nearby?"

David explained.

"Ah! An architect." He pronounced it arch-itect. "Any chance to get abroad in yer work?"

"Not so far."

"You should try. There is so much of interest abroad. Take my son: he's always travellin'." And Major Withers was away. He was inordinately proud of his son, apparently an only child, whose work was never explained. He seemed to have been everywhere, even spending several months in Russia, his travels explained in the greatest detail while they alternately ordered new pints of beer and David ate his sandwiches, the Major declining to eat anything. Eventually, as he was on the point of ordering another round David snatched an opportunity to look at his watch and explain that he had an appointment and must leave.

"What, already?" The Major seemed horrified. "You should allow more time for yer midday break, if you'll forgive me for sayin' so. Yer work will be all the better for it. Take the advice of an older man not without a little experience. Hard work is to be applauded, but it must be interlarded with relaxation if you are to give of yer best. My son has had the good fortune to become acquainted with many great and successful men around the world, and I know he would back me to the hilt over this. All, he would acknowledge without hesitation, should spend part of their days recharging their batteries. You see, my dear chap, the human body is not unlike an electric motor: run it for too long without recharge and it will become weak and inefficient. Ah! I see you insist in spite of what I say. Well, good day to yer and I look forward to resumin' our little conversation when you come here again, not before long I trust."

By this time David was half way to the door, grinning and nodding desperately, and when outside in the roar and bustle of Farringdon Street he took a large gulp of polluted air before walking up to Fleet Street to catch a bus back to his office.

The next time he entered "The Black Dog" he did so with infinite precaution. Yes, there was Major Withers with another victim beside him and David was able to order his beer and sandwiches further down the bar without catching his attention. Relieved, he carried them to a small table against the back wall where there happened to be a spare seat next to a small man with large, horn-rimmed glasses who looked rather like a frog.

"Free?" asked David indicating the seat.

"Certainly," said the frog-faced man; "and you need not worry: I will not regale you with an endless tale of a son." His eyes twinkled behind the thick lenses of his glasses.

"You spotted me in the clutches of Major Withers the other day then?"

"Oh yes. My heart bled for you and there was nothing I could do to help. Everyone has to undergo their baptism of fire. He is a thundering bore. Have you ever been in here in the evening?"

"No; I like to get home as soon as I finish work."

"Should you do so you will observe that the gallant Major passes through three phases: the first, as you have discovered, is an extravaganza on his peripatetic son. This lasts through the midday session when he sticks to beer. In the evening he builds a group around him and funny stories are exchanged, the balance of stories being heavily on his side. He will now be drinking pink gins, beer apparently keeping him up a lot at night. His stories are not at all bad; the trouble is that they never change. That is phase two. At about nine-thirty he will be very drunk though still lucid and something will start him off on his wartime experiences, all in the British Islands and extremely dull."

"Is this every day?"

"I think so. I am not here regularly, preferring to keep changing pubs, but I understand so."

"One wonders at the state of his liver."

"Yes, it is not only money he is expending. He is plainly a man who knows he is a failure and like the Ancient Mariner must expunge his misery repeatedly. He is one of the regulars here, a rarity in this particular pub, which has a large variable clientele. There is another of the regulars over there sitting on his own smoking a pipe: he is as quiet as the Major is voluble. He comes in every midday, buys two rounds of sandwiches

177

and a pint of Guinness. I have never observed him talking to anyone. Not far behind you is a tired looking little old woman, who is an office cleaner. She drinks Ruby Port. She has two young children and they have to let themselves into their Council flat when they get back from school and shift for themselves during their holidays until the return from work of herself and husband. 'Latch key kids they're called, I believe. I was not surprised when she confided in me one evening that one of them had 'got into a bit of trouble'. What can you expect in such circumstances?"

"You seem very interested in people."

"Part of my job."

"Which is?"

"Journalism."

They exchanged names, the journalist's being Guy Sadler, and chatting on David found him to be an agreeable companion.

It was a few days after these encounters that Rowe telephoned David from the site.

"We've a spot of bother, Mr Drummond."

"What's the problem?"

"You remember that we've got round to the excavations near St Bride's Street: well, we've run across a lot of bones."

"Bones?"

"Yes; skulls and bits of skeletons: there's a great big 'eap of them, 'undreds I should say, all mixed up together. I was going to 'ave them sent off in the tip, only one of the lads talked and we've got a Bobby 'ere. Do you think you could get down?"

"Undoubtedly a plague pit," said David's senior partner. "They abound round the edge of the City. The river Fleet would have been one of the boundaries and the death carts just carried the bodies over the bridges and deposited them in pits on the other side. You'd better go along and sort matters out."

When David arrived at the site Rowe was with a stolid looking policeman and two of his labourers, one with a pick and the other with a spade. Nearby was a dirty wheelbarrow. Other labourers were digging at the side of "The Black Dog" some way off. Jason, usually giving a background disharmony of baying barks at any sign of activity, was quiet, possibly owing to a sore throat.

Rowe introduced him to the policeman and pointed to the wheelbarrow, full of skulls and bones; and then led him to the excavations where there were many more covering an area of about fifty feet. Skulls and bones lay higgledy-piggledy mixed up with yellow clay in

178

a grisly cluster. In spite of their brownish-yellow colour they looked surprisingly fresh and it crossed David's mind that three hundred years is not after all such a long time, about twelve generations. It brought home to him the misery and fear of that dreadful period of plague immediately before the Great Fire of London in a way that written history cannot do.

"This must have been an old plague pit from 1665," he said.

The policeman looked more stolid than ever.

"That's as may be," he said in a dogged manner. "But we 'ave 'ere 'uman remains, as I am sure you will agree, Sir; and the matter 'as to be investigated in the proper manner."

"But surely, Constable, we don't have to do anything special in such a clear case as this. Look at the bones: they've obviously been here a long time."

"That will 'ave to be something for the Coroner to decide in accordance with usual procedure."

Behind the policeman Rowe raised his eyebrows heavenwards as he envisaged delay in the building programme with all that that entailed.

David tried a new tack: "I am sure you will understand, Officer, that building contracts such as this depend upon keeping to the programme. Otherwise a great deal of money is wasted. If we are obliged to wait for a Coroner's clearance before proceeding it will be very serious for my client."

The policeman considered this aspect gravely for a while; then, flexing his knees slightly, almost as if he were playing a part in "The Pirates of Penzance" he made a proposal.

"We can't 'ave that now. What you need to do is to 'ave the remains stored in a temporary sepulchre as decently as possible, leaving the ground clear for the work."

"A sepulchre?" repeated David stupidly.

"A temporary sepulchre," said the policeman.

Rowe came to the rescue.

"What about one of them arches?" he said, pointing to the brick supporting arches along St Bride's Street.

Again the policeman pondered. He was not a man whose mind worked swiftly and they waited anxiously for his decision.

Then he said: "Very suitable, I should say. Now I better note down some details." And he brought his notebook from behind his back.

And so the pathetic remains were transported in wheelbarrows to form a tangled heap under one of the arches and the Coroner was informed.

"They didn't need dentists," remarked one of the labourers pointing to several skulls when David viewed the macabre pile in its new position. It was true that all the skulls showed fine sets of teeth.

"I expect they were mostly young people," he said. "Life expectancy was short in those days even without the plague."

"I should think you were relieved it wasn't a Roman temple or something of that sort," said Guy Sadler when David told him what had happened soon afterwards. They were in "The Black Dog" where David had called in on his way home after a late session with a client in the City, Jill and the children being with her parents for the night.

Major Withers had several cronies round him at the bar where he was telling a story. His barking voice could be heard quite clearly above the general hum of conversation.

"'Him Big Chief Sitting Bull. Him mighty warrior!'" he was saying in a deepened voice, his arms folded over his chest. Then altering his voice in imitation of a female American tourist: "'Say! Has he fought in any battles?'" Again the arms folded and standing very upright: "'Him Big Chief Sitting Bull. Him mighty warrior. Him fight in many battles!'" The arms came down and it was the tourist once more: "'Say! Has he killed anyone?'" Again the Red Indian guide: "'Him Big Chief Sitting Bull. Him mighty warrior. Him fight in many battles. Him kill forty-five braves!'" 'Say! Is he married?' 'Him Big Chief Sitting Bull. Him mighty warrior. Him fight in many battles. Him kill forty-five braves. Him twenty-one wives!' 'Gee! Is he hostile?'" The Major drew himself up even further as he indicated the climax: "'Him Big Chief Sitting Bull. Him mighty warrior. Him fight in many battles. Him kill forty-five braves. Him twenty-one wives. Hoss style, dog style, monkey style, any old style, him fuck 'em all!'"

"He's reached his Red Indian stories," said Guy, idly turning over the pages of an evening paper on the table in front of them. "He'll soon be into the third phase."

A paragraph in the paper caught David's eye.

"Just a minute," he said, interrupting Guy's progress, and read more closely.

It was an announcement of the death of William B Maddox MP and went on to give a short summary of his career. Though David knew that Tubby had stood for Parliament after the war and caught the tide of Socialism to give him a seat in Atlee's administration he had not noticed that he had kept it when the Conservative Party returned to power.

He explained his interest to Guy with a description of the disastrous demonstration to the Home Guard in Northern Ireland and the unresolved mystery of the presence of Anthony Bell at the luncheon in Soho towards the end of the war.

Guy's eyes flickered behind the thick lenses of his glasses and seemed suddenly interested.

"I know little of Maddox," he said, "but tell me more about Bell."

"There is little to say," said David, surprised. "He took such a small part in the conversation and left early: he just seemed odd."

"Tell me exactly what he did say."

"He was obviously devoted to Communism, like Tubby Maddox, but did not work with him in the ABCA set up. I got the impression that he was sizing me up for some reason or other."

"Very interesting. I wonder why he was considering drawing an architect into his network?"

"Network?"

"Yes, Bell was and is a recruiting agent for the Russians."

"That's ridiculous: Tubby would never have thought of me as a potential Russian spy."

"Oh! No question of that. I don't suppose your friend Maddox ever got near the inner circle. No, Bell is one of those responsible for building up teams of trouble makers, chiefly in industry; the aim being to damage industrial relations in this country leading eventually to the collapse of the economy, so making way for a Communist takeover: classical Marxist stuff. The atomic bomb put paid to Stalin's plans to take over all Europe without stopping the momentum of the Red Army as it smashed through Germany, but there's more than one way to skin a cat."

"If you are right that would certainly account for the way in which Bell lost interest in me when I made it clear that I was able to continue my studies after the war and intended to do so."

"Ah! Then he was not interested in you as an architect. You had me puzzled for a moment."

"But how do you know all this?"

"I have been working at it for a long time. When I am ready the whole thing will be exposed by my paper if I can get the editor to publish it; or I may turn it into a book."

"Tell me more. What do these trouble makers do?"

They move from firm to firm, easy in a time of full employment, and foment grievances among the workers. The more intelligent ones are instructed to work their way into positions of influence such as shop stewards or even into more potent positions within the TUC. It is a long term plan."

Guy was deadly serious and David found it rather frightening.

In the background he could hear Major Withers' voice clear and strident. "Now listen to me; it is purely a question of treating the men properly. This is something that I know from experience. When I was in command of a base I always made sure that the paper work got done in double quick time and that left me with plenty of opportunity to get among the men." He must have moved into Guy's phase three.

"Surely," David said, "you should alert the police as soon as possible."

"Not interested: not their job."

"MI5 then."

"No, I think my way is better. I have to build up the evidence. 'Softly, softly catchee monkey!'"

David wanted to learn more about this previously unknown aspect of Guy, but there was a sudden cry from near the back entrance followed by a dramatic silence. He looked up to see everyone present looking with horror towards the opening. Following their united gaze he beheld Jason standing there, black, huge and glaring, and in his massive jaws he held a yellow human thigh bone.

There was a slithering crash and the sound of broken glass; Major Withers had fainted.

CHAPTER 12

"Power is so apt to be insolent, and liberty to be saucy, that they are very seldom on good terms."

George Savile Marquis of Halifax

If we are happy to receive the benefits of civilisation we must accept the drawbacks of bureaucracy: so far in the history of mankind the two go together. Sometimes, however, harried by bureaucratic interference, after guiding a commission through the perilous period of gestation, an architect may need to discharge his pent-up frustration, not unlike the phenomenon of an accumulation of static electricity that can lead to a stroke of lightning. To do so gives temporary comfort and is usually unwise.

So it was with David when, after a surfeit of disappointments, he won through to an interesting building contract on the south bank of the River Thames beyond Greenwich where that wonderful architect and engineer Christopher Wren, who in his time had his disappointments too, has left one of his marvels.

Not that David's work was in any way comparable, being an extension of a factory, albeit on a site approaching the magnificence of Wren's extension to form Greenwich Hospital.

At this point the river and the sky dominate the scenery to such an extent that the ugliness of man's work on both banks is subordinated. Thus, by night and by day the scene is always beautiful, the light and shadow being in constant change. To add to the attraction there is interest: to the west the City alters from the clarity of a Canaletto to a variety of fascinating silhouettes; and above all, there are so many boats, some of them quite large: the water is never still.

The water! Someone once told David that the water there was so polluted that if a man fell in a stomach pump had to be applied before artificial respiration. He thought this an exaggeration, though he would not have chosen to experiment: the water did not look inviting and close inspection showed a peculiar greyness and an unpleasant smell. All this was before the amazing success of The Thames Water Authority (with its own bureaucracy) that has made it possible for salmon to start moving up river once more.

David had this tale of the stomach pump in mind when the sanitation and drainage officer of the local authority directed that the roof rainwater from the proposed new building should be discharged into the river: he was concerned about his already overloaded sewers.

This seemed to David a thoroughly sound idea. There could hardly be objection to a dilution of that foul brew: the proposal could only be applauded.

How often in life do the simplest undertakings disclose all kinds of unexpected complications that, had they been foreseen, would deter all but the foolhardy! Of course, past experience should have taught him that nothing to do with building in or near London is simple.

The Port of London Authority seemed unenthusiastic. Its first reaction took the form of a long document headed: "Regulations with respect to applications for accommodations (other than moorings) in the River Thames." It began by stating: "Every application for permission to carry out works (whether permanent or temporary) upon the banks, or in, under or over the foreshore or bed of the river or adjoining creeks, should be made to the Chief Harbour Master, Port of London Authority, upon printed forms obtainable on request and be accompanied by drawings of the proposed works." Numerous regulations followed and three sets of four drawings were required with the form of application.

David dispatched these things and waited.

Three weeks later they all came back: the drawings were on paper and should have been on linen; the colours were wrong; and another submission should be made in the proper fashion.

The Flood Prevention Department of London County Council was less demanding: it only asked for one set of drawings and its main concern was that the flood water might escape from the river via the proposed rainwater pipe, though how the water could possibly mount the pipe to escape at roof level fifteen feet above the tow path was for David a mystery.

Unfortunately, before he was able to satisfy this authority the negotiations were bedevilled by the discovery that his clients' flood board was missing.

At this point an explanation is necessary. Along that stretch of the river the tow path was barely high enough to hold back the highest tides and in certain circumstances it was possible for the tide to flow over it.

184

There was, therefore, a second line of defence in the form of a low wall at the back of the tow path. Above this barrier were the boundary fences to the riverside properties, and where the barrier was interrupted by access gates anti-flood boards were compulsory. At regular intervals flood prevention officers journeyed up and down the river with binoculars checking every board.

David's clients possessed just such an access gate and just such an anti-flood board, and someone had removed it. It may have been the contractor, who did not know any more than David did about anti-flood boards: it might have helped to light a brazier when the weather was bleak. Possibly it had just fallen to pieces: it was extremely old. But whatever its fate it had gone, the Flood Prevention Department was exceedingly grumpy about it, and thereafter there was a marked lack of goodwill in negotiations and a considerable delay in obtaining a consent.

It was at this point that David learnt that a very high voltage main cable lay two feet below the tow path. That was a serious snag; it did not give sufficient space to bury the large rainwater pipe above it and tunnelling beneath it threatened hideous costs. Happily, some gingerly exploration proved the records false, the main cable lying three feet deep, permitting sufficient depth for the pipe above.

David felt he was winning through when a curt note reached his office from the Local Authority to enquire why a licence had not been applied for to take a pipe under or across or over the tow path. He was dumbfounded. But, he explained, it was all being done at their own request. That, came the reply was the affair of another department: a licence was necessary and an annual rental too.

Gloomily he added this to the annual rental to the Port of London Authority and did his best to explain it to his clients while he decided never to put rainwater into the Thames again, clearly a river to be left alone and admired from a distance.

All this in conjunction with other trials at that period led to a release of pent up emotion mentioned already.

In those days, before *The Times* became an ordinary newspaper, a frequently entertaining article used to be published on the Court Page; and David turned to this safety valve of free expression for respite. Rather to his surprise, satisfaction and concern his light description of the experience was published under the heading "Red Tape on the River." While the surprise and satisfaction were long-lasting the concern was justified, for though the Court Page articles were always anonymous, outraged authority is quick to put two and two together. Only two days after the publication David was with the Site Agent, a shrewd Irishman named McGahany, when they observed through the window of the Agent's hut the approach of a dapper little man wearing an Anthony Eden hat and carrying an immaculately folded umbrella and a black brief case. His car with chauffeur moved on to turn and park off the approach track beyond the future factory car park in process of preparation.

"Now, what can this little fellow be wanting?" mused McGahany, familiar with all sorts of visitation. "He looks like a bit of trouble."

After stopping for an instant to ask the way from a passing labourer the unexpected visitor came to the hut and knocked sharply upon the door.

"Come in," said McGahany, and in he came.

Closer inspection showed the first impression of spruceness to be justified: the newcomer was neatly dressed in pin stripe trousers and black coat with white, starched collar and grey tie, his stiff white cuffs showing half an inch beyond his coat sleeves. His shoes were black and gleaming.

"Good morning," he said in an unfriendly way. "My name is Prewitt and I represent The Port of London Authority." He spoke with a London suburban accent.

Removing his hat to reveal a crop of short stiff grey hair which seemed to stand on end he placed it with his umbrella on a pile of drawings at the end of the work bench. He had a square, palid face with a shortly clipped tooth brush moustache the same colour as his hair. His eyes were small and sharp, giving the impression of short-sightedness though he wore no glasses.

"Before going any further may I enquire who you are?" he continued still holding his brief case at his side.

They introduced themselves.

"Ah! Excellent," he said. "I hardly hoped that I would catch the architect at my first visit." He unzipped the brief case with a swift movement and pulled out a copy of *The Times* opened at the Court Page. This he placed on the bench in front of them and put a small neatly manicured finger upon the article which David saw was his own. The heading "Red Tape on the River" looked very large.

"Is either of you responsible for that?"

McGahany, who knew nothing about it since David had told no one, was expressionless and began to read it.

One should always think before speaking, particularly in a delicate situation, and David said nothing.

Though visibly impatient Mr Prewitt allowed him to read without

186

interruption. After a while a smile came over the Site Agent's face followed by a chuckle. This was too much for Mr Prewitt tapped the article twice with his finger and repeated: "Is either of you responsible for that?"

McGahany shook his head slowly, still reading with obvious amusement.

"And you?" said Mr Prewitt facing David.

"Yes, I wrote it."

"Aha! So the architect is responsible. Very unwise, Mr – Mr – ah?"

"Drummond."

"Very unwise, Mr Drummer, very unwise indeed." And Mr Prewitt took a pair of spectacles from a box in his brief case. He placed these carefully upon his small nose and began to write in a neat little leather bound note book which he produced from a waistcoat pocket with a silver pencil.

There was another chuckle from McGahany as he continued to read.

A purple tinge began to suffuse Mr Prewitt's cheeks and he puffed himself up.

"I have been sent down here by my superiors," he said, "to discover who perpetrated this scurrilous rubbish and to report the information back to them. What action they will take I cannot at this stage say –"

Another chuckle from McGahany was too much for Mr Prewitt, who turned to him and said: "Your merriment is very much misplaced, Mr – ah?"

"McGahany."

"Very misplaced, Mr McGuy, very misplaced indeed." And he wrote again in his note book.

Ignoring Mr Prewitt, the Site Agent spoke to David. "Very neatly put, Mr Drummond. "And but for this little chap here I might never have seen it which is something I'd be sorry to have missed."

Mr Prewitt's colour turned a deeper shade of purple as he snatched the copy of *The Times* from the worktop and thrust it back into his brief case as though afraid that McGahany might make copies of the article and distribute them as pamphlets.

"I deplore your attitude," he said addressing them both. "It is very improper, very improper indeed. As I was saying when so rudely interrupted, I cannot say at this stage what action my superiors will take. Unfortunately, consents cannot be withdrawn, but there are other ways of punishing impertinence and you may rest assured they will be applied."

"May I say a word?" asked David.

"There is no point," said Mr Prewitt, putting away his spectacles. "I have acquired the information that I came for and I give you due warning that we will be watching you in future. Good day to you." And he picked up his hat and umbrella, opened the door and left.

"A man," said David, "without, I fear, a sense of humour. He must find the going rough in life."

"Now there's just a chance he's going to be needing that sense of humour he's missing," said McGahany looking steadily out of the window at the rapidly receding figure of Mr Prewitt. "If so, it'll be worth the little bit of trouble."

David followed his gaze.

As previously mentioned, Mr Prewitt's chauffeur drove on after dropping him in order to turn and park beyond the future factory car park. This car park was to be surfaced with concrete slabs about five feet square, the concrete being poured in situ. Nearly all these slabs had been laid and had hardened, but there was one that had been poured a short time before Mr Prewitt's whirlwind visit and it lay directly between him and his car. Usually it is not difficult to remark the difference between concrete that has set and concrete that is still fluid, but on this occasion there had been a heavy shower of rain earlier in the day, leaving the hardened concrete wet and dark grey very much the same as the new square. Also, Mr Prewitt's rage, briskness and possible short-sightedness must be taken into account. It was really his briskness that caused the scale of his misfortune. To step into eight inches of freshly laid concrete is disagreeable, but to do so at speed is disastrous. The first foot sinks in followed by the second and momentum does the rest.

It was all over in a couple of seconds and Mr Prewitt, so neat and dapper and pompous one moment, lay flat on his face in wet clinging concrete, his brief case to his left, his hat several feet in front and his umbrella pointing out of the churned up surface as if to mark his ignominy.

CHAPTER 13

"For one and all, or high or low,
Will lead you where you wish to go;
And one and all go night and day
Over the hills and far away!"
ROBERT LOUIS STEVENSON

France being a civilised country, and there are many who have argued that it is the most civilised country of all, has its share of bureaucracy, and David began to run into one of its tangled nets the same year the unfortunate Mr Prewitt immersed himself in wet concrete.

He and Jill, their two children now old enough, decided to start taking their summer holidays in France. They could not afford hotels and the package holiday business had not taken off, so they bought a caravan after some experience of caravanning in England with one lent by a kind friend.

They wanted to take their caravan right down to the Mediterranean, but in the 1950s annual holidays were for two weeks and there were no motorways which does not give time to haul a caravan all that way, spend an adequate time in the south and then haul it all the way back again.

It was Ray Stein who proposed a solution.

David ran into him by chance at Lords Cricket Ground during a Test Match. They had not seen one another since soon after Lady Dinwiddy's Ball when David bade him goodbye before leaving the battalion for the Home Guard Training School. Twenty years had altered them both; yet they recognised each other immediately.

"David, by all that's holy!"

"Ray! What are you doing here?"

"Playing tiddlywinks: what do you think!"

Debased by professionalism, as all great games ultimately are, first class cricket retained its fascination for the initiated who filled the ground and they would not have met in this way but for the fact that they were both members of the MCC and were watching from the pavilion. They were both standing in the Long Room watching the game through the big plate glass windows before moving out into the sunlit white benches of the lower terrace. One of the attractions of cricket is that it is a leisurely game: the moments of high drama being brief and well spaced. This means that it is possible to watch with concentration and talk at intervals as well. For this reason David and Ray during the course of the afternoon were able to give each other outline histories of their progress through life since their parting.

Ray had remained with the battalion until the end of 1943 when he had been posted with the rank of Captain owing to his fair knowledge of the language as a liaison officer with the Free French where he served until the end of the war in Europe and soon after obtained a plum job as commandant of a hotel in Chamonix where allied officers were able to take leave.

"Dear boy," he said; "that was a time to remember: good food, good wine and plentiful crumpet: I was really sorry to be demobbed."

"Lucky sod," said David. "And there was I stuck as a regimental officer in a particularly dull bit of Germany."

Ray was distinctly stouter than when last seen and his dark hair was receding in the middle, while the remembered pallor of his complexion had altered towards a ruddier tinge. He was married with two boys and was very rich.

"Father," he explained, "was an Estate Agent before the war and did fairly well, but it was the war that made him. He became a firewatcher during the Blitz and watched over the City in more ways than one. During the fiery nights he did his duty and took steps to buy the pick of the smashed-up sites during the days. After the war he turned developer and made a mint. Alas, the strain of day and night relentless toil had taken its toll and he died suddenly last year of a heart attack. Mother had died several years before and I, the only son, reaped the harvest, a not unsatisfactory one even after our greedy and spendthrift governments had clawed out what they consider their share, a share large enough to decide us to emigrate to the south of France where taxes are not so extortionate and we shall be able to pass on our fortune to our young without further slices removed as fines for dying."

David explained his simpler plan to visit the same region made impossible by distance and time.

"Why not," suggested Ray, "leave your caravan with us at the end of your hols? Then you will be able to drive straight back unencumbered, which should save you three days."

This idea pleased David and he said so.

"No problem for us: we have plenty of room and Esther likes people. You must arrive in time to stay with us for at least a couple of nights. It will give us a chance to introduce our wives and children and provide you with some comfort after the rigours of camping. I don't know what the French regulations are about leaving caravans about their country: you should look into that one. Never underestimate the French when it comes to regulations. They, themselves, take little notice of them, but it is generally unwise for foreigners to take the same tack. There might even be something in the Code Civil about it: Napoleon thought of most things in between winning battles."

David asked him when they were going to leave.

"Next week. Otherwise an earlier meeting would be on the tapis."

At home David found Jill dubious either owing to feminine intuition or the equally feminine matter of what clothes she might have to add to her wardrobe, previously comparatively unimportant. Nevertheless, David made the enquiries advised by Ray and received a document which stated: "In order to encourage tourists, the French Customs permit caravans to be retained in France beyond the period normally allowed to temporarily import a vehicle providing that the caravan is placed under seal for not less than six months in each year . . ." Fascinated by this somewhat mystical method of overcoming their own regulations, they read on to discover that the process required the services of a Customs Agent and, of course, documentation.

The documentation took the form of an impressive booklet called a *Carnet de Passages* with many colourfully printed pages. It explained, amongst other things, that upon arrival in France the first sheet would be removed by a Customs Officer and that they should post the remainder to the Agent near the place where the caravan would be sealed for the minimum statutory six months. At the same time they had to give a precise address, date and time for the sealing ceremony.

All went according to plan and they reached Ray's villa on the day arranged under the blazing summer sun of the south.

The villa was magnificent with a view across the top of the town to the sea and a large garden, grey and green with Mediterranean shrubs round grass kept fresh by water sprinklers turned on every evening during dry weather. Several tall, thin "Italian Cypress" punctuated the scene, seeming black in the intense light. At the side of the terrace that lay between the villa and this garden a venerable "Umbrella Pine" spread its branches against the rich cobalt of the sky. A flight of gleaming, pale marble steps led up to the big front door and at the sides of these were placed large terracotta plant pots filled with white and pink petunias which had grown so strongly that they now tumbled over the pot edges onto the marble. The house was painted white and the shutters a cool pale blue. On the south side a wide-paved terrace divided the lawn from the living and dining rooms. At the back the gravel drive curled round to what were probably once stables, now used as garages and outhouses.

"That," said Ray, as soon as introductions were over, "is where you can leave your van. Place it close to the house where it will be in shade for most of the day."

While the villa and garden were beyond David's expectations, Ray's wife, was a surprising disappointment. With his remembered taste for and success with pretty women David had prepared himself and Jill for someone quite out of the ordinary as his final choice. Esther, however, was rather plain and dumpy. Her presumably dark brown hair, judged by the colour appearing near the roots, was dyed blonde. She wore a white dress, which looked cool and smart, while emphasising her poor figure. It was not David's only experience of a voluptuary who selects a homespun wife. On the other hand she was warm and welcoming and David soon began to respect Ray's good sense, previously over the matter of women not apparent to any marked degree.

Their two boys were well mannered and, after initial shyness, all four children took to one another. Ray seemed delighted with Jill, who naturally blossomed under the rays of his admiration, and all seemed set for a very successful end to the holiday.

It was Esther who struck the first discordant note.

"But, David," she said towards the end of an excellent dinner, "you do not really expect anyone to come tomorrow? This is the Midi."

True Anglo-Saxons, Jill and David had not considered this possibility, having great confidence in the efficiency of Customs Officers.

"Of course," David replied, suddenly doubtful. "All has been arranged in writing."

"He'll find out," said Ray with a wink to Jill.

The next morning everyone else drove down to the beach, leaving David to keep tryst with the Customs Agent and to witness the sealing.

It was very hot and he lay in a deck chair in the shade of the "Umbrella Pine" while he waited. Eleven o'clock had been the time selected by him for the event. He wondered idly what form the ceremony would take and how long it would last; how many officials would attend and just how the actual sealing would be accomplished. Would, for example, old fashioned sealing-wax be employed or some modern device? Would there be some special seal? Whatever the method it must clearly avoid damage to the caravan. Perhaps it would be a ribbon, red, white and blue no doubt, thus allowing the Agent to unseal it in a ribbon cutting ceremony, so pleasing to authority.

At half past eleven he got up and collected a book. Shortly after midday the fat little woman with hideous bronze hair, who acted as cook and housekeeper while her husband tended the garden, came out and asked him if he would like an aperitif before lunch. The Pernod and water in a tall glass with ice floating in its milky coolness did him good, as did the light lunch prepared for him on Esther's instruction, taken with a delicious half bottle of Chablis Premier Cru left for him by Ray. He took his coffee on the terrace under the shade of a blue and white canvas awning before returning to his deck chair where he dozed until the sun moved round to beat upon him so that he longed to be with the others in or at the edge of the sea.

At three o'clock he collected his sketching apparatus and set to work upon a preliminary water colour. At four o'clock he admitted defeat and went down to the beach to join the others, where Esther's expression reminded him of the Mona Lisa.

"They won't come tomorrow either," said Ray. "Don't worry: I'll deal with them when they do turn up and let you know what happens."

Five weeks later David received a letter from Ray making good his promise. In it he wrote: "One man came from the customs several days ago – unusual out here, officials preferring to make an outing of it in pairs or more. It is not impossible that he started out with a chum and lost him on the way, being pretty tight himself. His name, by the way, was Lepetit; suitable as he was only five feet high. He gazed at your van for a long time and then said he would like to look inside. I didn't think you would mind, so I let him in and he showed great interest, almost as though he was contemplating purchase, admiring some aspects and criticising others. After that I rashly offered him a drink and he stayed for quite a while in a very chatty mood, though a bit difficult to follow at times. Finally he rose unsteadily to his feet and gravely pointed out that the van had no engine. To this I had to agree. 'In that case,' he said, 'there is no need to seal it!' I wonder if he got back to his office safely? He weaved off in his Deux Chevaux in a hair raising fashion. I think you may safely forget the whole nonsense now."

Four months later David received a bill for sealing the caravan and other contingent expenses.

That was interesting. It seemed to him that he could do one of two things. Either he could refuse to pay for a sealing that never took place, or he could pay without question. He and Jill mulled it over for a while and then decided on the latter course, reasoning that Customs officials in the south were probably less hide-bound than the stuffy regulators in Paris; and that if David played ball with them they would play ball with David. In any event, if the caravan remained without a seal it would not be necessary, in fact impossible, to unseal it. They wondered, too, how long they might have to wait for an unsealing if it took so long to seal.

Two years later they discovered their mistake.

It appeared that one of the principal Customs Inspectors on the Riviera had visited Ray's villa with the express purpose of inspecting the caravan, only to find it missing – hardly surprising as it was by that time standing on a farm a hundred miles west. "It is a curious fact," wrote Ray, "that nearly all Frenchmen are small while a few are very tall, like De Gaulle. This man was one of the tall. And like Le General he was tiresomely stiff and humourless. He arrived without warning and demanded to see your van. I explained that you had taken it elsewhere. He wanted to know where and I told him I did not know. I offered him a drink and he refused. I fear that you may hear more."

They did. A cross letter came through their motoring association from their agent on the spot, informing them that since the caravan was under French Customs Seal it was strictly forbidden to remove it and that they had committed a serious offence. Penalties were not mentioned but a heavy fine was implied. David was to submit his defence.

"The trouble is," he said to Jill, "while they do not know where it is in France they might in due course find out and we cannot now bring it back to England: we would be picked up at the port of exit. I don't suppose the Inspector would accept our excuse that Monsieur Lepetit said that sealing was unnecessary even if he is still in the service, which seems unlikely. I fear we may have to pay the fine whatever it is."

David's Practice had suffered a bad year. A large Income Tax demand based upon previous good years had to be paid and he had just paid a pair of school fees. A further payment was depressing.

"Why not," suggested Jill, "write to Ray and ask him if he has any advice: he knows much more than we do about the French and their ways."

"I don't like to bother him about our problems."

"Not much bother to write a letter, and I think he would like it."

Ray answered by letter without delay.

"No problem," he wrote. "I have devised a scheme. On no account inform them of the whereabouts of the van, but let me know its exact position. Write to the farmer authorising him to allow me to tow it away, adding that I will pay the rental on your behalf. Meanwhile, I will have a further number plate made up giving the number of my car and apply to take 'my' van on holiday to England, suddenly, though briefly I assure you, interested in camping. We shall then tow it to Calais, cross the Channel with it and bring it to your house, where we will remove my number plate and reapply your own. We have been thinking of making a visit to England anyway and this will give the trip a bit of spice. In due course the English Customs may get as excited as the French when the 'imported' van is discovered to be in England still, but it is hardly likely that extradition proceedings will be instituted for either of us over such a minor affair. You will be able to point out that you have your van in England and ignore any further correspondence while I shall similarly put all letters from the English Customs straight into a wastepaper basket. Monumental indifference must be the order of the day. We shall wear them out in the end: no official likes to make extra work for himself. I shall give you the exact dates when I have them."

When Ray and his family rolled up to David's front door with the sunbeaten caravan safely in tow Jill had prepared a feast for them and she and David were loud in their praise and thanks.

"If they want to play 'silly buggers' so can we," said Ray.

CHAPTER 14

"By no endeavour can magnet ever
attract a silver churn."

W.S. GILBERT

Decisions marking major changes in direction in life are the product of previous incidents of one kind or another. David and Jill could think of three that led to their buying a cottage in France before such ventures became popular. One was the difficulties they had experienced over leaving a caravan in that country, the second was a remark made by Ray Stein and the third was David's cousin Clare.

The brush with authority over their caravan, happily concluded without financial loss, has been described. Ray's remark, made while watching cricket with David at Lord's, referred to the very low prices then being asked for small farmsteads in the southern half of France owing to the steady depopulation of rural areas, considerable repair and improvement being necessary, but extraordinary value none the less. As for Clare; she was the grand-daughter of David's great uncle Charles who died shortly after the war. She was gorgeous. A redhead with sea blue eyes she was willowy and elegant, intelligent and amusing. David always said he could have fallen in love with her himself as many men did; alas, in vain; for marrying well at nineteen she learnt rather bizarrely that she was Lesbian.

"It seems such a frightful waste," remarked David. "How can such a thing be?"

"I haven't the faintest idea," Jill replied. "Not, as you ought to know by now, having any tendency in that direction. Perhaps it is Dame Nature settling her long overdue account with mankind. Eventually when all women are Lesbian and all men homosexual man will become extinct like the dinosaur. They overreached themselves. I wonder whether their comparatively rapid disappearance was because they turned Lesbian and homosexual? We ought to write to the Royal Geographical Society propounding a theory."

At the time I am writing about, Clare was thirty-five and living only a few miles distant from David and his family in a flat with a friend, a beefy girl called Billy, who had played hockey for England. Clare's part in their initiative took the form of a reference to an advertisement she had noticed in the agony column of *The Times*: it described a house for sale in the Dordogne region of France.

"It could do no harm to write," said Jill.

After a considerable lapse of time, not unusual in business correspondence with the French, the advertiser replied in the most affable manner, letting them know that it was with the utmost pain that he was obliged to inform them that the house in question was in process of being sold, but that if they would be so good as to communicate again giving details describing the kind of property they were looking for he would undoubtedly be able to find something for them. He gave his name as Monsieur Malfoix, which they hoped was not a bad omen.

Their immediate response drew another letter from Monsieur Malfoix two months later, informing them with regret that he had decided to retire, but that if they would be so good as to communicate with his partner, Monsieur Bill Carter, now in the Tarn et Garonne region, he would be certain to help: and Monsieur Bill Carter did indeed, sending them a list of possibilities and suggesting that they take the first opportunity to travel down to his area so that he might conduct them on a round of inspection.

"Go on; have a go!" urged Clare. "You could both do with a short holiday anyway after your coughs and sneezes of the winter. Billy and I will look after the children."

So, taking a week from his annual holiday, David drove south with Jill.

The department of the Tarn et Garonne lies to the south of the Dordogne, the Lot et Garonne and the Lot. Across its middle the river Aveyron enters the river Tarn, which in turn flows into the river Garonne on its way west to Bordeaux and the Atlantic ocean. To the south the great Toulousian plain sweeps south-west towards the Mediterranean, while to the north the landscape is sharply undulating, the lines of bumpy hills broken by many streams to form sinuous valleys. This area is less densely wooded than the Dordogne and the soil is poorer, as are the innumerable farmers with their tiny farms. The southern part is studded with buildings built with Albigeois brick – not the prosaic brick of northern France, but a deep red, glowing narrow brick such as the Romans used – the two ancient towns of Montauban and Moissac marking the rim of this brick region. The northern area of hills and valleys possesses buildings built with creamy-white limestone which contrasts delightfully with the big, curved, soft red tiles and overhanging eaves that throw deep shadows on the walls below under a high midday sun.

That was the part of France covered by Carter at that time, and once there David and Jill no longer regretted the Dordogne.

The first rendezvous with Bill Carter was arranged at a cafe in a certain townlet perched upon a steep hill as are so many in that part of France where much warfare over many centuries made defensive settlements essential. It was a glorious day in late May and the sun warmed Jill and David through and through after a damp and chilly spring in England as they sat side by side at a little metal table sipping Pernods through chunks of ice and keeping a watch for the arrival of the man that was Bill Carter, quite unaware what he might look like. Half an hour after the time set they wondered whether some mistake had been made and began to talk of going to the address to which they had written, when a smart, bright red sports car ripped into the square and swung into a parking space in the middle. A large, dark-haired man of about forty leapt out and approached them with long strides. He was dressed in dark green trousers, an open-necked, yellow shirt and his shoes were of brown suede. This they knew must be Bill Carter.

Neither had he any doubt who they were, coming straight to their table and extending a large hand to Jill.

"Bill Carter," he proclaimed in a loud and friendly voice. "I apologise for keeping you waiting: I was kept by another client whose vexatiousness it is impossible to exaggerate. If you run into a Mrs McKenzie steer clear. How are you finding it down here and are you comfortable in your hotel? Allow me to buy you another drink; no, I insist: *garçon, trois pernods tout de suite.*"

By this time he had shaken hands with them both, taken a third chair and mopped his high forehead with a silk handkerchief pulled from a breast pocket in his shirt.

"You have chosen a good time of year to come," he continued, not permitting time for replies to his questions. "It is not too hot and the French have not started their absurdly concentrated annual holidays. How many days have you got to look round?"

David explained that they could manage four or five.

"Enough," said Bill Carter. "We'll start this very afternoon and continue thereafter until you have found what you are looking for, only leaving time to clinch a deal verbally and sign a *Sous Seing Privé*. Hah! I see you do not know what a *Sous Seing Privé* is. Why should you? Such

198

practical matters are not touched upon by our uninspired French teachers in England even supposing their knowledge extends so far. I'll explain."

At this point in his rapid flow of words the garçon arrived with the Pernods and Bill Carter stopped while they were put before them, allowing an opportunity to consider his appearance. His complexion was ruddy, his nose overlong and his chin cleft. His eyes were good, set well apart, giving a reassuring sense of honesty, the wrinkles at the sides indicating humour. He was on the whole a good looking, big man.

"Here's to the successful outcome of your trip!" he said, raising his glass and taking a large mouthful. "Hah! That's exactly what I needed after a morning with Mrs McKenzie. Yes, about the procedure for buying property out here: the actual final legal transfer is made with an *Acte de Vente*, but the mutual agreement to buy and sell is sealed by a binding contract called the *Sous Seing Privé*, when the buyer puts down ten percent of the agreed price. Both are done before a *Notaire*, who is something like an English Solicitor, though not so highly qualified and wide ranging. He hangs onto the deposit until the formal signing of the *Acte de Vente* takes place, usually a few months after the *Sous Seing Privé*. The considerable advantage of the French system over the English one is that it cuts out Dutch auctions. You see, it is not only the buyer who stands to lose his deposit if he backs out at the deal: the vendor has to pay ten per cent if he changes his mind."

"Something after the Scottish procedure," said David.

"The Scots and the French have many links."

"How do we find a good *Notaire*?"

"You'll find them in every town, even quite small ones. They work on their own without partners and generally start up by buying their practices from other *Notaires* when they retire, die or get struck off, a not unusual occurrence in rural France. But you have no need to concern yourselves about that: I know an excellent *Notaire* in this very town, with whom I deal almost exclusively; Maître Prat. He is also the Mayor. I'll make a point of introducing you at the first opportunity."

"Pratt?" David asked, astonished. "But that's an English name."

"Spelt with one T; though you may well be right since there were plenty of English around during the Hundred Years War. The French would naturally drop the second T as time passed by. Anyway, five hundred years have removed all trace of Englishness and you will find him French through and through."

David and Jill thought themselves very fortunate to have Bill Carter to help them through the hoops and asked him how he came to be working in this way in France.

"I was born under a wandering star," he said; "and I like people. I went to America after leaving Harrow and worked in various jobs; then to Australia, where after a spell on a sheep farm, I wrote for the Australian Broadcasting Corporation. Tired of that, I came to the Dordogne, where I met Monsieur Malfoix and suggested that he should have an English partner to help with the English who were beginning to take an interest in property away from the spoilt Riviera. He agreed and I worked with him for a bit until he suddenly decided to go in for building. A bit later I came down here: *et voilà*"

He tossed down the last of his Pernod, inspected the slip of paper left by the garçon and put down some coins.

"Come!" he said. "Let us be off. We'll work our way round the possibilities. I'll lead the way."

"So began three days of search that led at last to the Valley of Honey and Beynac Haut.

The pattern of each day was the same, though the properties and their occupants varied considerably. David and Jill followed the bright red sports car, winding up and down steep hills and along the valleys where the soil was richer and the small field filled with new growth, the variety surprising them. There was tobacco, maize and melon; fresh wheat and barley; sunflower plants, grey green plants of globe artichokes and sorgum; grassland with cattle and orchards of apple, cherry, peach and plum. Here and there along the valley streams tall poplars stood in serried ranks as though on parade. Scattered everywhere between the villages were white stone and red-tiled farmsteads. It was when they began to leave the valleys that they saw the vineyards, for the most part grown for the sweet white Chasselas eating grape of the region, though most farmers kept a field of suitable grapes for their own rough purple wine. All were bright green so early in the year, strictly pruned and trained on post and wire lines. Further up the narrow winding roads they passed through woods of false acacia, their racemes of white, scented flowers already showing, followed by stunted oaks before they reached the thin soil plateaux on the highest ground where grey and coarse plants grew, before plunging down into yet another valley.

The last visit on their first day will serve to indicate one of their inspections.

The road suddenly straightened and they drove down an avenue of great plane trees, hideously mutilated by inexpert pruning to look like mottled columns sprouting greenery on top, a frequent introduction to a village. This was a hamlet clustered round a large church attached to the houses by the usual network of electric and telephone wires as though a giant spider had passed over. Beyond this hamlet they crossed an ancient stone bridge with a flat-hatted man fishing drowsily in the late afternoon sun. For a time their road ran close by the stream and then turned sharply to climb up a subsidiary valley. After passing through a cluster of farm buildings which straddled the road, carefully avoiding chickens and ducks, they turned up a stony white track where Bill drew up on a grassy verge covered with wild flowers and came back to them. Taking his weight on his right arm with his hand grasping the rim of her door where it joined the roof he leant in towards Jill and said: "You are bound to like this one: it's a gem. I wouldn't mind buying it myself. It's going for fifteen thousand francs – a bit over a thousand pounds – and has roughly three hectaires of land going with it. Like all these country houses you are seeing it requires a fair amount of work, but then the prices reflect the fact. But I warn you the old bird who owns it is a miserable old hag. She's been widowed recently and is going to the local old people's home. Her name is Madame Villeneuve."

The track wound between rough hedges of hawthorn, broom and blackthorn to end in front of a two-storied stone house on a ledge of ground set into the hillside. Some forty yards beyond the house on the same plateau was a large barn, its roof indicating imminent collapse. The steep slope behind was covered with coarse grass studded with spiky juniper bushes. To their right the valley shimmered in the bright sunlight beyond a small field of potato plants thick with weeds.

They drew up their cars between the house and the barn near a well with a steaming heap of manure stacked behind it.

"Gives the water flavour, I suppose," remarked Jill as they got out to join Bill while an enormous Alsatian dog leapt and barked gratingly at the end of a rusty chain attached to the barn wall.

"*Couche!* You bloody Cerberus," yelled Bill, driving the enraged animal into a frenzy of bounds, each one threatening to break its neck, or, more serious for them, its chain.

"So many French dogs are kept prisoner like this one," shouted Bill. The wretched beasts become bitter and anti-social, which is of course the idea. They have one job and that is to guard."

"I hope the chain holds," said David as the animal gave one particularly savage leap.

"If it breaks the thing to do is to get down onto all fours and face it," said Bill.

201

"Who on earth told you that?"

"An Australian I met. He insisted that it is infallible, though initially nerve-racking while it sniffs your tail."

"Is one obliged to return the sniff?"

"Happily no: apparently, disappointed, it moves off and you crawl to cover in an off-hand way."

By this time they were near the door of the house and met Madame Villeneuve standing in the opening. Bill had been right about her: she was small, skinny and very ugly. The black dress she wore was stained and above the tattered felt slippers her naked ankles looked dirty. She did not smile when Bill introduced them, peering at them with suspicious little eyes beneath sparse grey hair that hung lankly round her ears; and when David took her hand it felt cold and bony.

The inside of the house was even more dilapidated than the exterior, and the scent of wood smoke mingled with other less agreeable smells. The room they had entered was the kitchen, dining and living room and on either side were small bedrooms from which a worn staircase led up to a disused granary now filled with a dusty assortment of broken furniture, empty sacks, cardboard boxes and rusty agricultural implements. All the creaking, grey floorboards were reaching the end of their time with openings between the joints. In the main room an old earthenware sink emptied straight out over a projecting hollowed stone onto a weedy, cobbled yard between the house and the rough slope up to the trees. At the side of this yard stood an earth closet, whose decaying door was closed with a deeply rusted latch. After they had looked at the buildings, the barn beyond repair, the old crone asked if they would like to look round the land; but discouraged by what he had seen David declined.

Would they take something?

Politeness demanded that they should.

She sat them round a small table next to the kitchen sink on a variety of wooden chairs. The table was covered with a tattered plastic cloth crudely patterned with once vivid colours at the red end of the spectrum, and upon this she set out three glasses. Then she opened a yellow painted cupboard by the fireplace and took out a dusty bottle containing a little murky liquid. Pulling out the projecting cork, which might have fulfilled its function in many a previous bottle, so brown and stained it was, she divided the contents, happily only two or three mouthfuls each, between them. It was at least a change from the green plum in *eau de vie* to which they had become accustomed.

"You do not drink yourself, Madame?" said David.

She shook her head grimly and crossed her wizened hands before her, remaining standing. She might have been a witch anticipating the result of a potion.

David inspected the drink more closely. It had the appearance of a yellowed white wine thick with lees. After some desultory conversation there seemed nothing for it and David lifted his glass with a spoken wish for Madame Villeneuve's good health and a silent one for theirs. It looked horrible as it got nearer and had a curious stench. Alerted by the last, he took a very small sip and looked anxiously at Jill. Significantly, Bill left his untouched.

Afterwards in their car Jill said that they ought to have taken their cue from Bill.

"Yet it was Bill who told us we must drink with the natives: it's the custom."

"With is the operative word: presumably if they don't it lets one out."

"One lives and learns."

"One learns and hopes to live."

They laughed together anxiously.

An hour later, no ill effects apparent, they sat down to their dinner in the dining room of their hotel.

The English abroad generally avoid their own nationals, and but for the overturned bottle of wine David and Jill would never have made friends with the Gumbles. They were dining at an adjoining table, an older couple, possibly in their late sixties. He was small and square with a round face like a well matured Cox's Orange Pippin topped with grey hair tightly brushed and combed with a neat parting in the middle. She was taller and slim with snow white hair drawn back from her clear forehead. Finely formed features indicated past beauty and she carried herself elegantly in a simple, light grey dress.

The two couples exchanged nods and smiles; then, true to tradition, paid no more attention to each other.

It came about like this. David and Jill had completed nearly all their main course when, finding he had no paper on him and reluctant to draw upon the tablecloth, David endeavoured to illustrate for Jill's information how one might improve upon one of the houses seen, employing gestures, action generally frowned upon in England though perfectly acceptable, indeed routine in France. They had held back a quarter of their bottle of red wine to be enjoyed with the cheese due to follow, and an imaginary bathroom struck it with sufficient force to turn it across the middle of their table.

It is astonishing what a mess a single glass of red wine makes: a quarter of a bottle has an appalling result. Plates were full of it, the bread supplied in a wicker basket absorbed it and there was enough left over to turn most of the tablecloth scarlet.

But the French take such catastrophes in their stride, and while David made helpless noises indicating regret, horror and apology, their waitress moved the impedimenta on the table, swept away the ghastly products of his clumsiness, spread a sparkling clean cloth and set all in order once more in little more time than it took to say: "These things happen," and "There we are!"

It was then, as David steadied himself and Jill comforted him with some remark about the absurd instability of wine bottles, that he observed their adjoining fellow countrymen instructing the waitress, who quickly brought them another bottle of wine. As she did so the small man leant across and said: "An old tradition in France, you know."

They were all four soon sitting at the same table.

Mr Gumble was a retired solicitor and had recently bought a house in the area with the help of Bill Carter.

"A most helpful young man, if a bit too full of himself," said Mr Gumble. "He appears to have two problems. One is that he cannot settle down to anything for long, and the other is women. Take care!" And he raised a stubby finger at Jill. "He will make a pass at you."

"He will have to move fast," said Jill with laughter in her eyes. "We leave after three more days."

"But you will be back and he is a fast worker!" His sharp little eyes twinkled as he went on: "He is at present living with the wife of a *Juge d'Instruction*, while I understand that his Australian wife is chasing after him. On the side he seduces female clients or their daughters. Failing with Margaret," nodding towards his wife who shook her head amusedly, "he made an attempt at our daughter who happened to be with us at the time."

"He was, I think, a little put out by that failure," said Mrs Gumble in her soft, agreeable voice.

"Hardly at all," said her husband. "He follows Sir Francis Bacon's maxim that a wise man will make more opportunities than he finds. Nevertheless, as I have said, he will help you in many ways over the vagaries of property purchase in France. We found it useful to listen to him on that score."

The following morning David and Jill were taken by Bill to meet the *Notaire*, Maître Prat.

His house looked less dilapidated and more spacious than the others in the narrow street. Beside the ancient open door, varnished long ago, a black panel was secured to the wall. Inscribed were the golden words: "*Me. Pierre Prat. Licencie en droit. Notaire.*"

Bill led them straight through and along a dark passage to a waiting room containing a few wooden chairs and a bench. The walls were hideously covered in a brown and red paper resembling the tartan of some unknown Scottish clan, and upon them were hung faded brown photographs depicting parts of the town early in the century. The boarded floor was worn and grey. From the yellow ceiling hung a single electric light bulb, unlit in spite of the pervading gloom, the only window facing another building across a narrow alley. A second door, painted a livid green, led into the Maître's office.

On the bench sat two middle-aged men in rough country clothes and flat hats, while one chair was occupied by an enormously fat woman of uncertain age in black with a mauve and yellow scarf over her head. All were engaged in noisy conversation.

"Accurately timed appointments are unknown in this part of France," said Bill, setting one of the chairs for Jill. "I arranged this time with Maître Prat, but we shall have to wait our turn. How long it will be is anybody's guess: time is of little importance. When you come to live here you should remember that: expressions of impatience only surprise and hurt the natives. 'Why agitate yourself?' they will say. 'There is plenty of time and while waiting there are so many things to discuss; your health and the health of your wife, my health and the health of my wife; the state of the crops and the weather; and, of course, politics.'"

"Can you understand what these folk are saying?" asked Jill.

"Not a word: they are speaking in Patois. All the people down here use it as their first language. Mind you, even when they speak French even a Frenchman from the north would not understand them."

The door to the office opened and a man and a woman came out, the man indicating that the Maître was ready for the next, whereupon the two men on the bench got up and went in together.

"Two down and one to go," said Bill. "We may be in luck."

The enormously fat woman fell silent, probably shy in the presence of foreigners, until another man entered wearing an ancient hat of brown felt, with whom, after the usual polite exchanges all round, she started a new conversation.

David told Bill of their meeting with the Gumbles the previous evening.

"Charming people," said Bill. "You will like their house; they have spent a great deal of money on improving it. He was a big shot in a well known firm of Solicitors in the City dealing with Company Law. He got all his money out to Switzerland just before the clamp down, being in a position to know it was in the offing."

"Any children?" asked Jill.

"Three," said Bill "and several grandchildren. The youngest daughter came out with them when they were looking for a house. Rather a tragedy; she lost her husband in a road accident. An attractive girl, too."

There was another interruption as another man entered and civilities were exchanged.

"I think our best plan," continued Bill, "when we have finished here will be to sit in the sun over an aperitif before having lunch at a little restaurant I can recommend before going on to visit other houses I have in mind for you," and he went on to talk about them until the office door opened once more and the fat woman waddled in to replace the two men with flat hats.

David asked how if they decided to buy a house they should deal with the financial side of the transaction apart from the deposit paid to the *Notaire* as stakeholder.

"You will have to send the money to the *Notaire* before the day of the signing of the *Acte de Vente*, when the vendor and the buyer have to be present, though it is permitted that another accredited person may stand in for the buyer if for some reason the latter cannot be present as does happen with people from far away such as yourselves. I have done that for several English clients and could do the same for you if you wish. It is a long way to come just to sign a document. Do not be surprised when that time comes at the behaviour of the *Notaire*. At a certain stage he will ask for your assurance that you will pay his percentage fee based upon the agreed price of the property. To that question you will of course say: '*Bien sûr, Maître.*' He will then tell you that he is leaving the room while in fact remaining seated before you. He will then hand over the purchase money to the vendor and say that he is now returning. After that he will complete the necessary forms giving a price for the property amounting to half of what you have paid. That puzzles you? I will explain.

The State charges a tax on the sale of property which is a fixed percentage of the recorded sale price. Needless to say, the people did not like the introduction of this tax one bit and sought means of avoidance. French rural communities are closely knit, the various functionaries being in close relationship with the rest, frequently related. It did not take long, therefore, for a buyer and a seller to get together with their *Notaire* and agree that the official price should be half the actual one, thus reducing the tax. Naturally, the *Notaire* would not accept the idea unless he received an assurance that his fee would be based upon the full price paid and that in theory he should not be a party to the business. Hence the little pantomime I have described. The idea spread like wildfire and is now a standard procedure. Now, you may say: 'As an honest Englishman I shall have nothing to do with such deviation from rectitude,' and refuse to agree with the arrangement. In that case both the *Notaire* and the vendor will be astonished and without objection since it is you who will pay the tax in question. Should you decide upon that course, as one of my English clients did, you will be making a mistake, for it did not take long before the French taxation authority learned what was going on and doubled the tax to rectify matters. Therefore, you would in fact be paying twice the tax required."

"How dotty," said Jill.

"Hah! But supremely French, don't you agree?"

That led them on to discuss differences in the French and English characters until their time came to enter Maître Prat's office.

It was a small, dark room and the overall impression was one of dust and greyness. The worn unpolished floor boards were light grey; the worn piece of carpet in the centre of the room was a darker grey, though probably light when new; the walls were distempered grey and the paintwork grey. Although the *Notaire's* solid desk was of varnished dark wood with florid carved ornamentation, thick dust on all projections made it seem grey too. Behind this desk sat Maître Prat, his trousers, his sweater and even his complexion grey. The effect of all this greyness caused the blue beret on his round little head to stand out as if in sudden revolt. He was never seen without this beret, Bill later remarking that he probably wore it in bed. Similarly they were never to see him without a short stub of cigarette apparently rooted in the right hand corner of his small mouth in his moon-like face with eyebrows so curved that they gave an impression of permanent interrogation, as if he viewed the world around him in a state of continuous astonishment. Before him his desk was strewn with papers, a cavernous brown china ashtray, a heavy table lamp and a telephone of ancient design, perhaps one of the earliest made.

Following the initial shaking of hands all round and introductions, Bill explained their short courtesy call prior, they hoped, to finding a house that suited them, in which case they would have the pleasure of asking Maître Prat to handle the transaction as he had done so smoothly in the past with other English clients.

Maître Prat studied them all in turn through his small grey eyes without expression, a thin trail of smoke curling upwards from his cigarette stub. After a long pause David felt it was perhaps up to him to attempt some conversation.

"By a remarkable coincidence, Maître," he said, "my first platoon sergeant in the British Army during the late war was called Pratt; he was an excellent man."

Did a light flicker in those eyes? It was hard to say in the poor light. Then the Maître replied: "All Prats are excellent." It was the only occasion David and Jill detected a sense of humour, if humour it was, in the little man during their several encounters with him.

Again there was a pause, broken by the piercing ring of the ancient telephone on the Maître's right and he lifted the receiver to answer. As he did so the cigarette stub rolled mysteriously from the right hand corner of his mouth to the left, where it remained for the duration of a rapid and unintelligible conversation, at the end of which the stub rolled back as mysteriously to the right once more. That achieved, he asked David what houses he was considering and Bill told him, whereupon the Maître, speaking in a high pitched voice so accented and rapid that neither David nor Jill were able to understand him, warned them, as Bill explained afterwards, that one of the two houses which they were due to view that afternoon was about to have a small metalworks constructed opposite.

"Which rules that one out," said David. We are aiming at peace and quiet. But it was thoughtful of Maître Prat to warn us of it."

"The Maître is a good friend of mine," said Bill, "and I bring him a fair amount of business; but to be realistic he would not have given you the warning unless he had some grudge against the vendor, probably aware that he did not vote for him at the last election."

"But that's terrible," said Jill, "I'm not sure we want a legal man so lacking in integrity."

"You forget where you are, my dear: this is deepest rural France. Why, the other day I heard of another Mayor who when elected said during his election address: 'I know who voted against me and it will be the worse for them!'"

"Surely someone reported him?"

"Certainly. He was hauled in front of a tribunal at Toulouse where he was carpeted, but remained the Mayor just the same. Anyhow, it's no skin off your nose. I am only sorry we have to cut down the possibilities by a quarter for this visit at least. The next house is the traditional three room stone cottage with a barn and about five hectares of land. It is offered for rather more than the others, twenty thousand francs. The owners, Monsieur et Madame Jaubert, are forced to sell because to buy the house he borrowed most of the money from his brother, who has since died, and he has to pay the money back to the legatees."

"Poor people," said Jill. "What will they do?"

"Oh! He'll find a job somewhere with accommodation to go with it or they will go to relatives. He's a very practical old fellow, a retired merchant seaman. He makes a very good wine from his own grapes. Drink some if he offers it."

"Unlike our last experience."

"Hah! That old bag. On other occasions she produced a very hard little prune in water which had a little *eau de vie* passed over it. Did you feel any after effects?"

"None so far, but some bacteria take their time to get going."

"In that case you will be back in merry England again with all the resources of the National Health Service to put you right."

"If they are capable of isolating whatever it is!"

"My dear Jill," said Bill, resting his hand lightly on her thigh, "you look marvellous and I refuse to believe you can be sickening for anything."

He was carrying them as before in his red sports car along a valley to a pinnacled bastide, turning right below it up a winding narrow road which took them up onto the line of hills that so typically separated them from the next valley. At the top was a crossroads where he drove straight on, leaving tarmac to follow a lane surfaced with white stones. It looked very pretty, dappled with blue shadows from the stunted oaks and rough hedge shrubs which lined it as they bumped along over its uneven surface. They passed an abandoned stone quarry on their left, now used as a communal rubbish dump, which Bill pointed out as very useful in country areas where there is no organised refuse collection. Further on as they rounded a bend and the trees to their right came to an end, they looked down a beautiful valley with an abandoned Quercy church at its bottom. It was a gem, built in creamy-white limestone with an apsidal east end and roofed with the big curved tiles of the region. At the far west end there rose a stone wall high above the roof and pierced to contain a bell. Beside the church ran a small stream which sprang from the upper end of the valley, whose sides were terraced and planted with plum trees along the upper steepest levels ending in green meadows with cows round the church. Above and behind the church stood a squarely built stone house whose roof had fallen in, proclaiming the passing of the last curé responsible for a vanished congregation.

Continuing along the side of the valley they passed through more oakwood and a clump of sumach with the lane turning gently leftwards and upwards until it ran out in front of a stone cottage and barn. The latter faced them directly with its great doors under a bonnet ended roof, while the cottage stood to their left with a central entrance door and windows headed by gently curved brick arches. Through the gap between the cottage and barn they could see a grassy terrace with chickens and another glorious view beyond. Behind the cottage the field swept up to the usual crown of oakwood.

As they climbed out of the car the door of the cottage opened and two dogs shot out barking loudly with wagging tails and friendly eyes. On a low wall a small ginger cat regarded them with alert interest. The dogs were followed by a small, wiry man dressed in blue trousers and open-necked shirt. His face was wrinkled and brown and he wore a blue beret. This was Monsieur Jaubert.

He walked briskly to them and shook hands all round while the dogs sniffed their legs and were delighted to have their heads patted. Another cat, white this time, popped out of a hole cut through the barn door near the ground and strolled past in the stately manner of cats to the undergrowth beneath two high oaks while the first one began to wash deliberately.

Introductions over, Monsieur Jaubert ushered them into the cottage where they met Madame in the central kitchen, dining, living room. An ample woman, taller than her husband, she gave an immediate impression of motherly warmth. Her round, ruddy face indicated a once pretty country girl. Now her hair was white and her hands rough and worn. Over her clean brown dress she wore a sleeveless smock-frock of faded green and yellow flower pattern.

They sat round the table and chatted while Madame Jaubert prepared coffee. They found the accent of these two different and much less demanding than that of the previous owners encountered.

The room was dominated by the fireplace in the middle of the back wall. It was a very high and wide fireplace, the mantel shelf being at David's shoulder level. Along this shelf a thick brown material, perhaps a piece of old carpet, had been nailed, hanging a good foot and blackened on the lower middle edge by heat from fires. Obviously it had been hung to lower the opening in a futile attempt to stop fires smoking. On the mantel piece were ranged a variety of articles including a fully rigged sailing ship in a bottle. On the smoke-stained yellow wall above hung a cheaply framed and faded photograph of a group of sailors, probably the ship's company of one of the ships Monsieur Jaubert had served in. On one side of the fireplace a glass-fronted cupboard had been inserted and china cups and plates were ranged within. The ceiling was of boarding above heavy oak beams roughly cut and holed by beetle. The floor was cement. In the middle of both side walls were worn plank doors painted yellow, giving access to the two bedrooms, and at the other end of the front wall a window provided more light. Under it stood a work table, and on the return wall next to it was a shallow brown sink supported on unplastered standard French hollow bricks. There were no taps, water being brought from the well in buckets, one of which stood below the sink in the space between the hollow brick walls. An iron pipe ran from the sink waste to pass through the front wall to eject waste water straight onto the ground outside. Between the window and the entrance door a range of pots and pans, all spotlessly clean were suspended from hooks screwed into a plank fixed to the wall.

The coffee was strong and good and Monsieur Jaubert insisted upon adding rum, without which he insisted coffee was a wishy washy drink.

Afterwards, he took them on a tour of inspection. The house was built with its back dug into the hillside and the rear roof slope ran to form a covered area in which it was plain he made his wine. Close beside the opening into this stood the stone well with a single pitched roof and a wired, wooden-framed guard at the opening. Inside a rusty chain encircled a stout wooden spindle with four projecting levers at one side to lower and raise the chain with bucket attached. They looked down the well and saw the glint of water at the bottom.

On this side of the house they were on the terrace of rough grass they had glimpsed as they arrived and it gave the best view they had yet found, marred only by a tall concrete pillar erected in the foreground, from which a wire ran over the terrace to the eaves of the house. Other similar pillars poked out of orchards, fields and vineyards below them carrying wire to another line in the valley. This was the electric supply.

The barn was huge and handsome with enormous oak trusses supporting the heavy tiled roof. In front of it and directly opposite the front door were two stone sheds, one a wood store and the other the earth closet. They obscured another fine view.

David asked whether he might inspect the interior of the roof and Monsieur Jaubert brought a ladder, opened a heavy hatch in the ceiling of the central room and helped him up. There was light enough up there, the strong sunlight beating through the innumerable crevices between the tiles and reflected up from the newspapers spread thickly across the boarding to act as a cheap insulation. Dust and spiders' webs were profuse in this quiet limbo world between the ceilings of the busy rooms beneath and the colourful curved tiles of the roof above that knew the heat of the summer sun and the cold of winter nights. Satisfied that the solid oak structure was sound enough David climbed down dusty but content. This, he was sure, was the house for them and knew without asking that Jill was with him.

They explained to Bill that because of David's work, while they would be able to sign the *Sous Seing Privé* the next day and hand over the deposit to Maître Prat, they would not be able to attend the signing of the *Acte de Vente* when the balance of the costs reached him. That being so, they asked Bill to act for them as he had explained he could. He was most pressing that Jill should come out on her own and seemed put out when she refused.

Nevertheless, he was pleased to have earned a quick fee, just as Maître Prat beneath his dusty exterior was plainly glad to look forward to his percentage. As for the Jauberts, they made no attempt to conceal their joy, gratitude and relief after no doubt expecting some hard bargaining ending in a reduced price. In turn Jill and David were delighted to have found even more than they had looked for.

In fact all seemed "as happy as the marriage bell," as Aunt Emily was fond of saying, and they gleefully boasted of their good fortune to their friends and relations.

A lesson life teaches that takes time to learn is never to be cock-a-hoop about anything: the Fates, whatever they may be, take pleasure in placing banana skins round corners to bring low the exultant.

The first indication that all was not well dawned upon David and Jill when several weeks elapsed after the expected signing of the *Acte de Vente* without their hearing from Bill that all had been satisfactorily accomplished. David wrote to him twice without reply. He telephoned Maître Prat's office with great difficulty only to be told he was away. He checked with his bank manager that the money had been transferred and was assured it had. They began to become very anxious, for in those days two and a half thousand pounds was a large sum to lose, not to speak of what they had come to regard as a Shangri-La. Finally, David wrote to James Gumble, and he was quick to reply.

"I very much regret to report," he wrote, "that there is every indication that you may have been the victims of deceit. I have made enquiries on your behalf and discover that ex Maître Prat has been forced to relinquish his position as a *notaire* – 'struck off' would be the expression employed in the United Kingdom – while Mr Carter has disappeared. With regard to the former, I understand that there was some spurious use of public funds – you will recall that Prat held the post of Mayor. With regard to the latter, nothing is known, save that the lady with whom he was living is broken-hearted and is likely to return to her husband. I am out of my depth when it comes to the vagaries of French law and can only advise you to instruct a London firm of solicitors with French connections. My heart bleeds for you. Pray let me know if there is anything that you think we may be able to do to assist further."

"I wonder," said Jill, "where the poor Jauberts stand in all this?"

"Probably pocketed our deposit and sold the property to someone else," replied David, made unkind by his disappointment and concern. "Is it the French who call us *Perfidious Albion?*"

"No, the Jauberts were much too genuine to do any such thing. Anyway, Maître Prat held all the money. I expect they are even more worried and disappointed than we are. Should we write to them?"

"I don't see what good it could possibly do: we are not in a position to pay the same money all over again."

"What about James Gumble's suggestion?"

"To find an English solicitor with knowledge of French law. We know none. I suppose we could try the Law Society."

"What about the British Consulate in Bordeaux?"

"That's an idea! But time is passing and with it our hope for that house."

"We shall have to give up that dream, simply concentrating upon getting our money back or as much of it as possible."

Reluctantly David had to agree. It was a bitter disappointment.

When he telephoned the British Consulate in Bordeaux the next day all that the official he spoke with proposed was that he would send a list of suitable French Solicitors in that city.

The Law Society gave the names of two London firms with French connections and after some delay the one David telephoned informed him that in the event of default by a *Notaire* the matter should be taken up with *Le Conseil Supercou de Notaviat*.

At that stage David had to make a journey north relating to some work for which his office was responsible and was away for several days.

Before he left he said to Jill: "While I am away I'll make a draft of a letter to this Conseil for you to vet when I get back before we send it off. What a bind it all is."

His trip was not improved by troubles on the site and a difficult Local Building Surveyor, so that he returned home in a sombre mood.

Jill's welcome was more than usually warm and her smile happier.

"Good news!" she said. "All is well: the house is ours!"

David gaped.

"Bill Carter has been here, bringing the signed *Acte de Vente* with him. All is in order and there is nothing to worry about."

"When was he here?"

"Last night. He arrived during the afternoon and left this morning."

"He stayed the night?"

"Yes. I had to give him dinner and a bed, bringing such marvellous news."

"Yes, but whose bed? You alarm me."

A mischievous look glinted in Jill's eyes.

"Well," she said, "one must do one's best for a bearer of such good tidings, and he had taken a lot of trouble on our behalf."

"Jill," said David, "you are not telling me . . ."

The telephone cut through his words and he picked up the receiver.

"What's the matter?" asked Clare's agreeable voice. "You sound angry when you should be celebrating."

"So you've heard about the house. I'm sorry but it seems there is bad news with the good and I've only just learnt about it. What can I do for you?"

"Nothing. I'm only ringing to thank Jill for such an amusing evening."

"What evening?"

"Hasn't she told you about last night? She invited me to dinner to meet your friend Bill Carter and to stay the night. It was such fun!"

Feeling dazed, David passed her on to Jill.

Jill said: "Not a bit: it was so good of you to come at such notice . . . Yes, he is amusing isn't he? . . . Oh, he did seem a bit disgruntled when he left – a shame really since he had been so kind and helpful . . . That's true, but all the same . . . Not at all; it is for me to thank you for helping me out . . . Yes . . . Yes . . . He's only just got back and I haven't had time to tell him everything . . . Goodbye."

"Darling," said David, "I'm tired and my mind is working slowly. Will you please explain what you have been up to in my absence."

"Did you really believe I had given my all to Bill?"

"It sounded like it."

214

"And it worried you badly: how nice!" The mischievous look was still on her face.

David said: "I understand the good news. Now please tell me in simple terms what you and Clare have been doing."

"Of course: I was going to when you began to go off the deep end. You see, when Bill arrived like that without warning I was a bit thrown, especially when it became apparent he knew you were away."

"How?"

"I have no idea; but he knew all right. He had a plan, and conceited though it may seem of me, I could see it."

"Not in the least conceited: the man has good taste."

"I simply had to ask him to dinner and stay the night after hearing his good news, though I could foresee what I might be letting myself in for. Then I had a brilliant idea. While Bill was getting his things our of his car – yes, he had come prepared – I tell you he had a plan – I rang Clare and asked her to join us for dinner and to stay the night. Mercifully, she was free and could."

"What if she couldn't?"

"Why then; I might have had a lot of fun." Her eyes were twinkling again.

"Jill! Jill! I have never understood why women seem unable to resist men's advances without support."

"You don't understand women; and Bill is a very attractive man."

David shook his head in sorrow.

Jill continued: "He said he has suddenly decided to give up working in France and was on his way to another part of the world, carefully not saying where."

"Probably trying to escape the women after him."

That thought crossed my mind, too. I asked him why and he just said he needed a change. But before departing he had completed our transaction and handed me the stamped *Acte de Vente* to prove it. I asked him whether he knew anything about the unseating of Maître Prat and he said no, seeming genuinely sorry to hear about it."

"A likely story!"

"I don't know: I think you may be rather hard on him. After all, he has turned up trumps over our transaction."

"What was Bill's reaction to Clare?"

"He was put out."

"I bet he was."

"But when Clare arrived looking stunning he was most impressed.

After that it was absolutely fascinating to observe him gradually transfer his courtship from me to Clare; and she played him along beautifully."

"How unfair."

"Don't be inconsistent, darling: you can't have it both ways."

"How did he take Clare's inevitable rejection?"

"He didn't know much about it until this morning. You see, he had brought along bottles of gin and Grand Marnier to oil the wheels of seduction. I dropped out of the running early, but by then he was clearly aiming for Clare, and you know how strong her head is. She literally drank him under the table. We had to put him to bed. It was terribly funny. He kept on making ineffectual amorous advances while we were taking his clothes off, mumbling: 'Hah, an orgy!' and the like. We left him sleeping like a log, and when I took him a cup of tea this morning he had a dreadful hangover, poor lamb. At breakfast he only ate a bit of toast and was terribly sheepish."

"You shouldn't have teased him so."

"You wouldn't have said that just before Clare rang! Anyway, Lotharios shouldn't attempt landings on Lesbos."

CHAPTER 15

". . . and there Sir Breuse Suance Pite overthrew
Sir Gawaine, and then he rode over him . . ."

SIR THOMAS MALORY

Invariably short of money herself, aunt Emily contrived throughout her long life to mix with the wealthy, often invited to accompany them abroad or to spend periods in their great houses as a member of a house party, frequently and inexplicably without uncle Edward. Judging by the quantity of stories she recounted, culled from her experiences, anyone without knowledge of her proclivity to exaggeration would be excused for assuming that she had spent the greater part of her life in such exalted circles.

One concerned an extremely prosperous stockbroker with extensive interests in the USA. Finding herself sitting next to him in 1932 at a dinner party in some enormous house in Scotland, and never one to show diffidence under any circumstances, save before her father, she expressed her commiseration over the recent Wall Street crash.

"Do not allow it to worry you, my dear young lady," he replied; "I am still very, very rich."

This anecdote came to David's mind when he thought of Prince Verkhovenski. He, too, was very, very rich. To illustrate the magnitude of his riches David told how he had heard that on some occasion an inexperienced member of a well known London firm of Estate Agents acting in connection with a lease the Prince was negotiating asked him for a letter of recommendation from his bank. The Prince smiled kindly and said: "My dear young man, I own the bank."

Prince Verkhovenski owned many things, including a magnificent château on the Loire, a house in Arizona designed by Neutra and a charming villa in Switzerland; but his base for his extensive business operations was an apartment in Paris not far from Les Invalides and the tomb of Napoleon.

David met him through the Prince's fourth wife, a spoilt American with a fortune of her own. To elude boredom she was in the habit of buying *pieds à terre* around the world, driving architects, interior decorators and builders mad with her constantly changing ideas and demands, tribulations compounded by the unusual hours she kept, sleeping between four a.m. and midday and assuming that all in her employ did the same. Most clients fancy their architects to be exclusively engaged upon their projects, but to be awakened at two in the morning to discuss at length and in detail the position of a power point or the colour of the ceiling of a boudoir requires mental agility and good temper of a high order. David learnt all about this when he acted for her over a London *pied à terre*, as he also learnt, on completion of the work, that she did not like to pay professional fees. Though quite proper and agreed before hand she disputed David's and was incensed when he insisted, even obliged to threaten legal proceedings, before they were wrested from her.

It was, therefore, with surprise, even astonishment, that he received a telephone call from the Prince's secretary in Paris instructing him to fly out there to discuss a project of importance. Nevertheless, an architect does not question opportunities, however mysterious, when presented by men of the calibre of Prince Verkhovenski and the following morning he reported to the Air France counter at Heathrow airport where his return ticket awaited him.

When he opened the envelope he found he was booked to travel first class.

Wealth undoubtedly provides agreeable advantages. On the other hand, it carries with it one serious disadvantage: the rich cannot relish the enthralling pleasure of treats normally beyond their means, a circumstance long understood but brought home to the unprivileged from time to time; as on the occasion when David and Jill scraped together enough money to lunch at a famous French restaurant. For them it was an experience of extraordinary interest and excitement, details lodged in their memories for the remainder of their lives. Yet, while they floated through those three hours as if in a wondrous dream, a couple arrived in a Rolls Royce and rushed through a hurried meal, clearly unimpressed by the culinary marvels, even leaving on departure an unfinished bottle of the most expensive wine on the wine list, noted by David to be £80 a bottle.

Thus, this unique experience on a sunny day in spring was as remarkable for him as it seemed commonplace to his five fellow first class travellers.

Two were smartly dressed French business men, one very small and the other very tall. They talked incessantly with much gesticulation and no smiles. Two were an elderly couple, the man with a stout little body and long legs that reminded David of humpty-dumpty; the woman in a mink coat and blue hair. The fifth was a young man in a dark suit apparently suffering acutely from some illness, haggard and pale, moving as though in a dream.

They were kept apart from the humble group of second class passengers, even climbing a separate mobile staircase to their position at the front of the aircraft, where they sat in great comfort in a spacious cabin attended by a white-coated steward, a man of grave mien and humorous eyes. Immediately they became airborne this steward moved round with a selection of newspapers, both English and French, asking if they would take champagne. With the exception of the ill young man they all did, and while sipping that nectar, caviar on toast and other delicacies were served. Accepting a second glass, David regarded the ill young man with sympathy, feeling certain he would be better for at least a few mouthfuls. The young man lay back in his chair with closed eyes looking so ghastly that David wondered if he might die during the journey and how the efficient steward would deal with such an eventuality, not, he supposed, unprecedented. The steward certainly knew how to look after the living, refilling David's glass immediately it was empty. He began to feel very well. As they crossed the French coast Havana cigars were proffered and he threw himself back in his chair, blowing out clouds of fragrant smoke with a sense of glorious abandon. This, he thought, gazing round at his fellows in Elysium, was the life, and wondered at their lack of appreciation. The ill young man could be excused, but why were the two business men so desperately serious and the elderly couple so sour? Of them all the attentive steward pleased him and he slipped him a handsome tip before descending the steps to the tarmac with particular caution.

How good it was to enter Paris from an airport on a fine May morning lifted by champagne and in the front of a chauffeur-driven Citroen! It was the sacred period between midday and two p.m. when the French turn their attention to the serious matter of luncheon and the traffic was less intense than at other times of the day, giving David the opportunity to observe familiar splendid buildings, streets and squares with unusual placidity. The sunshine brightened ancient stonework and cast deep shadows from carved cornices, columns and other features, warming his heart as well as the crowds along the pavements and sitting at the little cafe tables in the open air. The latter reminded David that the food provided in the air had been no more than an appetiser, that his breakfast had consisted of one piece of toast and marmalade and that he was hungry. How ironic to be in this Mecca of wonderful cooking with no time to stop either for lunch or, his return ticket being for the late afternoon flight, for dinner! Possibly the Prince had arranged for something to have been kept for him: a delicate *hors-d'oeuvre* followed by cold chicken and camembert, washed down with a white wine from the Loire?

The car slid quietly to a standstill outside a magnificent eighteenth century building and the chauffeur indicated the front door at the top of a flight of steps. Clutching his slim brief case David mounted these and pressed a bell push. Almost immediately there came a crackle from a polished brass panel let into the stonework of the door recess and a male voice enquired who it was. When David had given his name and mission the voice bade him wait a minute and when he turned to look about him he noticed that the car had slipped away. The street was a short one joining two busy thoroughfares and lined with other fine old stone buildings, whose well painted shutters indicated prosperous ownership. Some cars were parked along it, all big and highly polished and it was comparatively quiet between the hum and roar of the streets at each end. David was reflecting upon the run of luck Paris had enjoyed over the centuries, saving so much of its glorious past from despoliation and the destruction of war, when the great door opened and a major-domo in blue and gold uniform invited him in. He passed from the sunlight into a hall floored with white and grey marble, from which a stone staircase swept up two floors, its black and gold wrought iron balustrade of intricate design lit from a skylight high above.

Instead of leading him up this staircase the major-domo took him to an opening in a side wall where lift doors stood open, and ushering him in with extreme respect turned and pressed a button which caused the door to close and the lift to ascend. He wore immaculate white gloves.

Arriving at the first floor he preceded David along a thickly carpeted corridor to an ante-room where he indicated an easy chair by an elegant mahogany table with newspapers and magazines neatly ranged upon its highly polished surface. When David was seated the major-domo enquired whether he would take a cup of coffee and a liqueur, an invitation that destroyed his dream of luncheon. He accepted the coffee and when the major-domo returned with it upon a silver salver he informed him that the Prince would be able to see him in a quarter of an hour. Meanwhile, if there was anything he wanted he should ring the bell set upon the table. The bell reminded David of the Princess, who amongst other unusual conceits insisted upon having one installed within reach of anywhere she might be seated. They had to match the furniture or wall, with wiring concealed even if that meant drilling holes through priceless furniture, the wiring running down the back of supporting legs to reach the floor and beneath floorboards of parquetry with all the problems involved. He wondered whether she was in the house and if he would meet her once more, not looking forward to such an encounter after their recent contest.

Half an hour later one of the gilt and white double doors facing him opened and the Prince beckoned him into the adjoining room, where he shook him by the hand before seating him opposite a huge desk covered with folders and elegant silver in the form of a huge ash tray, a cigarette box, an ink stand, a paper knife shaped like a duelling sabre and a magnifying glass.

David placed his brief case on this desk before him and waited for the Prince to speak.

He was a big man, about sixty years old, with broad shoulders and heavy jowls. His hair, surprisingly abundant, was grey and white, and his rather flat square face was florid with eyes behind large metal rimmed glasses that were small and sharp. He looked a clever and a determined man whose anger might be terrible. Now he was quite genial.

He asked David if he had enjoyed a comfortable flight and said he was glad it was such a fine day for his visit, Paris being at its best in spring. These preliminaries over, he asked whether David knew Algeria. Before a reply was possible there was a discrete knock on the door to the passage and the appearance in the opening of the white-gloved major-domo, who stood as though awaiting some instruction.

"Your brief case," said the Prince to David, "is on the bell," and waved the major-domo away.

David had forgotten the multiplicity of bell pushes associated with the household and was embarrassed. The Prince, on the other hand, seemed pleased at his discomfiture as he went on to explain in flawless English what he wanted of him.

It appeared that the Algerian Government, newly wealthy owing to huge oil and gas finds within their borders, had ambitious plans for development, and amongst these was a very large scheme for the transformation of an oasis in the desert south of the Saharan Atlas mountains into a vast tourist centre with hotels, a sports stadium, and olympic-size swimming pool, an airport and ancillary accommodation. To give the project publicity it had been decided to put the scheme out to international tender, inviting consortia to compete, ideas and estimates to be submitted in outline before the selection of a short list for the final detailed competition. The Prince, whose activities embraced large scale development, was inclined to participate, and as a first step David was to go to Algeria with an Engineer of his choosing to make a reconnaissance and prepare sketch plans and a report prior to the preparation of a first stage submission. He took a folder and handed it to David.

"You will find," he said, "the requirements set out by the Algerians with other information in this. You will make a point of meeting all the officials and ministers you can, explaining that you are acting for a consortium with my backing. Take drawings and photographs of your work and convince them that your office is suited to carry out the design work. Leave it to me to satisfy them that I shall select the very best contractors and that finance is no problem. If, when you have studied this dossier, you have any questions, either telephone me here or come out again for a discussion. In any event, you must act quickly. How soon can you go?"

David considered. His office was very busy and he could ill afford two or three weeks away in Africa. On the other hand, such an opportunity could not be allowed to pass, both because of the project itself and the possibilities that might be opened up in the future with such a man as the Prince.

"I would like to consult my partners," he said; "but it should be possible to leave within three weeks."

"Too long: you must go in not less than two weeks. As to the matter of your fees; I shall pay your reasonable expenses and nothing more unless the consortium in which you will play your part obtains the contract."

That was harsh and David had to say so, pointing out that with all the Prince's experience he must know the enormous amount of work involved and in this case carried out at speed. When he had finished the Prince looked at him steadily for a minute or more, gently tapping a gold pencil on the blotter before him. Then he asked: "Do you want this work?"

"Very much; but we cannot afford it on the terms you propose. There is also the Consulting Engineer's time and later that of a Quantity Surveyor to take into account."

"You are not prepared to gamble a little for such a prize?"

"I am prepared to discuss it with my partners, a Consulting Engineer and Quantity Surveyors; but I have to tell you that I think it improbable that all will consent."

"You are not so witless to be unaware that if you were to please me with your work there might be other opportunities?"

"The suggestion gives me satisfaction, but even so I must stand by what I have explained."

"And what do you think I am doing? Do you suggest that my time is not valuable also? In the event of my consortium failing to win this competition no one will pay me for my time."

David patiently explained what the Prince knew very well already, that there would be a very great disparity between his workload and theirs, and the negotiation continued. But for the fact that the Prince was prepared to argue the matter at length, he would have assumed that there could only be one conclusion and his journey pointless.

Then, quite suddenly, the Prince said: "I will pay you five thousand pounds. to cover your work and the work of your Engineers and Quantity Surveyors for the second stage of the competition in the event and only in the event that the consortium is selected to participate. That is my last word."

The offer was mean, but the stakes were high and David accepted.

The Prince stood up.

"Come," he said, "let us join the Princess for tea."

She was seated in a sumptuous room decorated in a soft blue, white and gold. Her dress was superb and her hair, immaculate as always, was dyed ash blond. Her smile as David greeted her held no hint of rancour and he felt a sense of relief.

She pressed a button fitted to the table beside her chair and very soon the major-domo entered bearing a Sevres tea service set out upon a lace cloth over a silver salver, which he set down deferentially within her reach. He was followed by a pretty little maid carrying another much larger silver salver covered with a mouth-watering selection of neatly cut sandwiches and a gleaming chocolate cake. By this time David was very hungry indeed and wondered how many sandwiches he might consume without passing the bounds of good behaviour, only one slice of cake probable.

When the maid withdrew the Princess poured the tea and before following the maid the major-domo placed a cup before David and another before the Prince.

There followed some conversation without mention of the purpose of David's visit and the Prince and he took second cups of tea. Time passed and David wondered how he might draw attention to the sandwiches, perhaps passing some compliment on their splendour. His ambition to devour five or six before a slice of cake dwindled to two. But how to do so? Good manners presented a serious obstacle. How, for example, to interject any reference to the succulent display that lay almost within his reach when the Prince was discussing the absurdity of past disapproval of the Heptameron written by the gifted sister of Francis I, Marguerite de Navarre? Or a brisk conversation around General de Gaulle's recent resignation? David glanced at his watch and saw that the time for his departure was growing near. The matter was becoming urgent. It was then that the Princess began a criticism of a play currently running at the Comédie Française and pressed the bell as she did so.

The major-domo entered.

She said: "We have finished, Jean. You may take everything away."

David watched in shock and sorrow as the great silver salver with its delectable load was swept away as pristine as it had been when brought in. There was nothing to be done and he rose to leave.

David invited Ian Pargeter to go with him to Algeria. He was a partner in a large firm of structural engineers, a man of wide experience and a friend. He was extremely tall and thin, nicknamed at school "The Stork", and walked with a slight limp owing to a war injury. His gaunt frame and pale complexion belied his love of good food and wine.

When David first put the proposition to him he reminded David of a recent international competition his firm had been involved in. It was for an extensive development of a large site not far from Vienna and a multitude of heavyweight consortia had submitted detailed schemes in accordance with the terms of the competition, which also stated that the winner of the first prize would be appointed to act over its realisation. In the event the Austrian judges declared that since none of the entries deserved the first prize two second prizes would be given.

"In point of fact," went on Ian, "several of the schemes were brilliant: it was just that the cunning buggers wanted all the charisma of an international competition and ideas for their own architects and engineers. I see no reason why the Algerians won't apply the same skulduggery. Still, as you point out, this Prince is someone to get in with and probably has a lot of pull to boot. I'm prepared to have a go if you are. If nothing else we might eat and drink well. Surely some of the art of French cooking must have rubbed off on the Algerians and I cannot believe that wine we suffered during the war was anything more than stuff they cast off."

The Prince's secretary sent them their air tickets with the information that they had been booked in at the King George Hotel in Algiers. The only thing they now lacked were copies of the brochure they had hastily put together illustrating work their two firms had carried out, an important card in the hand they had to play in order to convince the Algerian ministers and officials of their experience and ability. One of the strikes, so prevalent in the United Kingdom at that time, had delayed the printing and they were forced to be content with their postage by air to await collection at Algiers airport.

When they reached Algiers after a delay in Nice where they changed flights it was late and dark. The aircraft descended through thick clouds into a drenching downpour. By the time they had passed through controls and had their passports stamped it was eleven o'clock. Hardly able to see further than ten yards because of the pitchy darkness and the heavy rain they found a taxi and told the driver to take them to the King George Hotel as quickly as he could. The prospect of baths and comfortable beds occupied their minds. The airport is quite a long way from the centre of Algiers and they had to pass through an area of rebuilding on the way where huge sheets of water had collected on the roads, shining dirty brown in the taxi's headlights and dimpled with raindrops. On either side holes and gaunt silhouettes of structures and machinery were dimly discernible. It was nearing midnight when their taxi climbed the hill and drew up before the hotel. For some reason, not immediately apparent, the taxi driver insisted upon coming with them as they hurried through the rain into a reception hall.

Behind a heavy wooden counter stood a wooden looking young Algerian in a blue suit.

They put down their suitcases and with sighs of relief gave him their names. His expression remained impassive. Nonplussed, they went onto explain that a room had been booked for them. At this he shook his head.

"The hotel is full," he said.

"But that cannot be so," said David, "the Prince Verkhovenski's private secretary booked the room a week ago. See," he went on, extracting a letter from his brief-case, "this is his confirmation."

The Algerian allowed his dark eyes to flit over the letter David held out to him.

"The hotel is full," he repeated.

David looked with desperation at Ian, who asked whether they might talk with the manager.

No, he was asleep and in any case it would be of no use: the hotel was full. It was not that the Algerian was unfriendly: he was utterly indifferent.

Finally, they gave up and asked if he could recommend another hotel in Algiers, even telephone for them?

No, he knew of no hotel which had a free room.

At this point the taxi driver took the cue, for which he must have been waiting. He knew of an hotel where there was almost certainly a room. He would take them there.

There seemed nothing else to do but comply.

Outside it was still raining hard and David looked back through the glass door to see the clerk take a cigarette from a packet and light it. They might have been beetles trodden on and immediately forgotten.

After driving for half an hour the buildings began to melt away and they could discern trees and open ground.

David asked how far the hotel was.

"Not very far: just a few kilometres further. It is a fine new tourist hotel beside the sea. You will be very comfortable there."

"We're trapped," said David to Ian. "If we had known it was so far we would have insisted on telephoning from the King George. If it is full too he will probably suggest another further along the coast. The whole thing may be a ploy to run up an enormous fare: as it is I am not sure we are going to have enough ready money to pay the blighter."

"I expect," said Ian, "he is taking us to an hotel run by one of his relations, constantly keeping him supplied with suckers like us."

Half an hour later the taxi turned through a gateway after a short approach drive, and drew up before a large building dimly visible through the darkness and rain by the light of several spherical lights on posts.

Inside it was immediately apparent that the taxi driver, accompanying them as before, had spoken the truth: it was a modern hotel in the international style, very newly finished. Behind a long reception desk of polished wood and white marble an encouragingly large number of bedroom keys hung in rows. The click-clack of their steps on the marble floor woke the receptionist dozing in a chair concealed from them, his head resting against the wall beneath the keys. He stood up slowly, eyes full of slumber, and regarded them with perhaps a little less indifference than the one at the King George. Like him he wore a blue suit.

Yes, a room was available for as long as they wished. What was more, it was a room with a bath and WC en suite.

That problem solved, they turned to their taxi driver and asked him how much they owed him. It was as David had feared, more than they carried in cash. Without hope they asked the receptionist whether he could change a traveller's cheque. No, that was not possible. The driver interrupted genially to say that it was of no importance. They would require a taxi the following day to take them into Algiers and he would be delighted to undertake that duty. In Algiers he would take them to a bank where they could cash travellers' cheques and settle up with him. Indeed, he would be most willing to act as their means of transport throughout their stay.

"Possibly," said Ian when they were alone in the bedroom, "he is a relation of the sour type we encountered at the King George and they split the profits. Not a bad scheme when you come to think of it."

"He won't be happy when we arrange to hire a car tomorrow."

"We will pay him off and lose him at the bank: he may take us to a car hire firm run by another relative."

Ian seemed obsessed by eastern family associations.

The next day the storm had passed and they were able to see their surroundings. In spite of a bright sun shining hotly from a practically cloudless sky all looked drab with the exceptions of the glittering sea beyond a rocky beach and the line of mountains to the south. On the way to Algiers the land on either side of the road seemed unkempt and the occasional farmhouse in a state of considerable dilapidation. Algiers itself, remembered only from old photographs in a family album taken before the second Great War, was a considerable disappointment. Instead of handsome tree-lined boulevards and clean white buildings all appeared run down, grey and dirty.

Following the advice of a tourist office they found a car hire firm down a murky street and after much form filling and the payment of a large deposit they were shown an aged and battered Renault saloon coloured a vivid rose madder. David had just signed a document in which it was certified that the car they were hiring was in good condition and hastened to draw attention to the various dents and a missing inner rear door handle. Such defects, they were assured, were of no importance and anyway there was no other car available. They returned to the office and pointed to the clause stating their agreement that the car was as good as new. It was, they were assured, merely a matter of form and of no account. They made a list of all that they could see wrong and handed over a copy, which was accepted with tolerant amusement and put aside, on its way, no doubt, to a waste paper basket. All this took time and they had to hurry to keep an appointment with an official in the British Consulate, a Mr Oldacre, who, their brief informed them, would assist them in their task.

Owing to the name David had expected an elderly diplomat deeply versed in the intricacies of Algerian officialdom, and was therefore taken aback when they entered a well lit but bleak office to be greeted by a very young, slight man with fair hair and tooth brush moustache over a wide mouth turned up at the ends to give an impression of a continuous smile.

When seated they explained their errand and asked for all the advice that could be given, suggesting that it might be a good approach if Oldacre could make an appointment for them with Monsieur Abdesslam, the minister concerned with the project that was the subject of their visit.

"Difficult," said Oldacre. "You are not the only people who have been to see me about this, and I can tell you now that the minister is almost certain to be unavailable. I'll try, of course, but I can almost guarantee that you will be fobbed off with a side kick, one Monsieur Zahaf."

He picked up the telephone of the simple wood desk in front of him and asked the exchange to get him a number.

"There is little else I can do for you," he continued, replacing the receiver, unless, of course, you get into difficulties." His smile increased and he waved a hand to one side as though emphasising the absurdity of such a proposition.

"I suppose," said David, "discretion prevents you from telling us who we have in the opposition?"

Oldacre's increased smile indicated confirmation and apology.

"All that I can say, which you probably know already, is that many consortia from all over Western Europe are sniffing about."

"It is to be expected: the project being so big and success so full of credit."

"Reputation-wise undoubtedly: money-wise . . .!" Oldacre's upturned lip ends turned down for the first time and he raised a hand slightly in a gesture of doubt. "It is very difficult, you know, to get money out of these African countries; almost as bad as from behind the iron curtain." The telephone rang and Oldacre put the receiver to his ear. He talked in French to what seemed to be several people in succession.

"As I warned you," he said when finished, "Abdesslam cannot see you, but Zahaf will if you go to his office at eleven o'clock the day after tomorrow. Have you a map of Algiers?"

They produced one.

"He works in an organisation called Sonatrek – all the government organisations are Sona this and that out here – you will find it on the way to the airport, just here." He made a small ring round a block on the map.

"What do you think of Algiers?" he asked.

"Dirty and disappointing."

Oldacre nodded. "My predecessor," he said, "told me it was a wonderful place before the French were booted out. I arrived too late to see it. Since I arrived it seems to be going down hill all the time. The Algerians swarmed into the fine town houses left by the French and used the cellars as receptacles for rubbish and worse. It got so bad and the rats so dangerous that an edict was issued that all the cellars were to be cleared by a certain day and the filth piled outside on the pavements, where it would be collected by a fleet of lorries and taken away. Unfortunately, it rained like the devil the night before the collection and all the stuff was swept down into the lower part of the town, where all the shops and banks are. Lord, that was a todo!"

Ian said he was amazed that cholera was not raging.

"It's there all right, but kept dark," said Oldacre. "Just don't drink tap water in Algiers. Where are you staying?"

They told him of their experience the night before.

"Not at all unusual," said Oldacre. "Algeria is very left wing socialist orientated and all the hotels are owned by the government, managers and staff being in the State employ. Thus, there is no incentive: indeed, it is my personal belief that many managers deliberately keep a number of rooms empty to reduce work, possibly working a fiddle after the manner of Gogol's 'Dead Souls'. You will observe as you go about that your Algerian is not at all keen on work, preferring to store his energies for his night exercise with one of his wives. The birth rate is phenomenal: seventy-five per cent of the population is under the age of fourteen. Unemployment is already rife, though cushioned by the vast revenue pouring in from oil and natural gas. At present the state of affairs suits them down to the ground. The Algerian has none of our hang up over humiliation when out of work and all that clap trap. As long as he is paid he prefers it. As I see it, the trouble will come when the natural resources run out and a vast population of young people have neither work nor money. It's dynamite; and explosions of that order have a way of spreading outside a country's boundaries."

"Hence," said David, "these great projects?"

"Oh! They hardly touch the central problem. Only sudden power gone to the head. Most of the equipment and skilled labour will have to be supplied from outside the country: it just isn't available here."

"I hope," said Ian after they left Oldacre, "the Prince knows what he is doing."

When they got back to their hotel they found a telegram from David's office informing him that several copies of the brochure had been sent off in a parcel by airmail to await collection at the airport.

"With luck," said David, "we will be there before we meet Zahaf. We'll try for it tomorrow afternoon and if that fails, again the next morning before our appointment."

They had a lot to learn.

The parcel office was in a separate structure from the main airport building and far less solidly built, giving the impression of an afterthought, as though the idea of a parcel service was not considered when the airport was designed. An entrance door led straight into the office where a counter separated them from a young Algerian, whose pale skin indicated mixed parentage. He treated them with the indifference they were becoming used to and when he understood their mission he retired into a room behind, in which, before the door closed, they were able to discern filing cabinets, a typist at work and an older man behind a desk.

They waited.

On the counter lay a telephone with several telephone books, various printed sheets, an ashtray full of cigarette stubs, a writing block and a pen. Behind, on either side of the door to the office, wooden shelves were fixed to the concrete block wall, filled with tattered files, papers and several oranges. It was hot and stuffy and the air was full of flies. Somewhere outside there was the roar of an aircraft taking off.

They waited.

"Experience of Africa," said Ian, "will soon teach you to be patient. It is too hot and useless to be otherwise. Do you play chess?"

"Indifferently."

Ian pulled a miniature chess set from his brief-case, the tiny "men" coloured white and red fitted into small holes in the squares.

"With this historic piece," said Ian "we will turn you into a good player before this expedition is through."

"Why historic?"

"It accompanied me from England to Egypt and from Alamein to

230

within sight of Carthage, at which point you will recall the lorry I was travelling in encountered a mine. Otherwise it would have seen Sicily and Italy as well."

They placed the little board on the counter and began to play. They had completed several preliminary moves when the young Algerian returned. There was no information available about the parcel. He would make enquiries and if they returned tomorrow he would perhaps have some information for them.

They asked whether it was not possible to find out immediately. No, he would have to make enquiries and the office was very busy at the moment. They explained that they required it for a meeting the next day. It was no use: he spread his hands. It was necessary for them to wait. There was nothing else they could do.

Back in their hotel they found a group of new arrivals, all white males of different nationalities and all very disgruntled. It turned out that they had been given notice to leave an hotel in Algiers that morning to make room for a party of African notables.

"Told us to pack our bags and leave, just like that, without the slightest warning," said a small red-headed member of the unfortunates. "And I was booked in for another week." His red cheeks coloured more deeply with pent up indignation. He had a pointed beard with streaks of white amongst the red and spoke with the faintest touch of a Scottish accent. He joined them later for a whisky before dinner and they learnt that his name was Donald McLeod. He was an agent from a large British firm of building contractors sent out to investigate the possibilities for work.

"There's plenty of scope," he told us; "but the red tape, man, the red tape! It's like moving through cotton wool."

They told him of their mission.

"Ah!" said he. "That'll be the big scheme for that place in the desert south of Bousaada. I have to get down there to take a look at the place before I go back. We've not been approached by anyone about it you'll understand, but it's always best to be ready."

"Why not come with us?" David suggested. "We intend to drive down after two more days in Algiers and spend several days looking over the sight, basing ourselves in an hotel in Bousaada, which to our surprise appears to have rooms available, or so they told us over the telephone. It will save using two cars and you will be able to give us your opinion from a contractor's angle."

"Laddie," he replied, "that's a grand idea," and went off to book a

231

room in the Bousaada hotel for himself.

David and Ian breakfasted early the next morning to give themselves time to get to the airport and back for their appointment with Zahaf.

Behind the counter in the parcel office was a new face.

Once again they explained the matter of their parcel, and their meeting with his colleague the day before. The new man told them that would be Monsieur Djourai. He was not in this morning. It would be best for them to speak to him. They asked when Monsieur Djourai would be back. He would be there that afternoon. They explained that that would be too late: they had an important meeting with a high official in Sonatrek and it was important that they had the parcel with them. Would he kindly find out whether it had arrived. No, Monsieur Djourai was dealing with it and there was nothing else his colleague could do. Could he not enquire himself? Yes, but it would be best for Monsieur Djourai to handle the matter since he was *au courant*. Why must it be Monsieur Djourai – surely the record of the parcel's arrival was available to all in the parcel office? The office was very busy at the moment and it would be best for them to return later. How much later? That afternoon when Monsieur Djourai would undoubtedly help them. But they would be at the offices of Sonatrek that afternoon. He spread his hands. Then it would be best for them to come back tomorrow. Would Monsieur Djourai be there in the morning? Probably, but if not he would be there later in the day.

As David felt fury building up in him, Ian took him by an arm.

"Remember what I told you yesterday," he said quietly. "We shall have to come back. We shall get no further now."

They found the offices of Sonatrek in a shabby quarter. They consisted of a group of huts round a rough piece of ground with brown, cracked depressions where the water from the storm on their night of arrival had collected. Enquiries led them to a hut where they were shown into a small room with four cane chairs, one occupied by a pale man holding a brief-case and a roll of drawings. After a standard greeting he took some notes from the brief-case and read without another word. After ten minutes he was called into an adjoining office where they could indistinctly hear a conversation.

"A rival," said Ian, and they spent the next half-hour running through the presentation of their case.

Monsieur Zahaf turned out to be a fat little man of middle age dressed in a smart grey suit with a red tie. The faint smile he presented as they introduced themselves was the only time he allowed any emotion during the whole of their discussion, if it could be called a discussion when David and Ian were the only ones to say more than a dozen words. It seemed to them that they might have been talking to a stuffed dummy. They explained, in case he did not know already, the strength of their backing, it being hard to imagine a consortium with more power and financial strength than that gathered together by the Prince Verkhovenski. They went on to describe their own extensive experience and showed him drawings produced in their offices. They expressed their great regret that the brochure containing photographs of their work and other information had not arrived and promised to return with several copies after their return from their impending visit to the site of the project. When they finally dried up Monsieur Zahaf regarded them silently for a minute and then bade them *au revoir*.

"I wouldn't care to play poker with that one," said Ian as they made their way to their car.

They both felt subdued.

Donald McLeod rallied them as they dined together that evening.

"You'll get used to the Algies," he said. "They're most of them like that. It may be they're just canny, though it's my personal view they enjoy their power after so many years of playing second fiddle to the white man. You'll find the same thing all over Africa. Look at the way they hoofed me out of my hotel in Algiers to make way for a bunch of blacks. I'm informed it is not at all uncommon."

"Let's hope the bunch doesn't arrive in Bousaada while we're there," said Ian.

The first part of their drive to Bousaada was dull and saddening: so much of what must have been well kept farmland and vineyards had degenerated and the villages they passed through were dirty and dilapidated. Algerian men of all ages sat about in the sun while the swarms of children running loose were a source of anxiety.

"They must lose a few," said Ian as David braked sharply to miss two that suddenly scampered from behind a parked lorry.

It was a relief when they began to climb up into the mountains leaving the villages behind. Here the road twisted and turned through woods and forests, occasional gaps giving superb views north over a brown and green landscape to the blue line of the Mediterranean beyond. From up there Algiers shone white and clean.

"I'll tell you now," said Donald, "that good though this road is it'll be a site too small if yon great development comes off."

233

"I was thinking the same," said Ian, "and have you noticed how even this is beginning to deteriorate through lack of proper maintenance? A point for our report."

Once through the broken middle of the mountains they descended circuitously through thinning forest, catching glimpses of the rocky desert on the southern side which stretched away as far as the eye could see. At the bottom they stopped for a picnic lunch of cold chicken, bread, butter and cheese. They had to be content with beer to drink, wine being hard to buy in Algeria since the French departed.

Ian was indignant about this. "The stuff wasn't all that bad during the war," he said, "and I assumed they kept the best for themselves."

"It's their religion, I think," said David. "Islam considers wine to be evil."

"Then, how do you account for old Khayam, and why do they drink this filthy beer?"

"It's more likely that for the present they're against anything that smacks of the French," suggested Donald.

"More likely," said Ian, "that they find the tending of the vine too much like hard work."

Their picnic over, they drove down to the desert on a road that stretched straight and flat for mile after mile beneath a burning sun. The colours were marvellous, a symphony in various yellows and browns with clumps of red below a vivid blue sky streaked with high clouds. Some hardy green plants could be seen in patches, but always very low, and not a tree anywhere. Otherwise there was no sign of life. It had taken them three hours to cross the mountains, but now they were able to move fast and the sun was still high and hot when they reached Bousaada.

They were amazed at the quality of the hotel, recently built and admirably designed. It stood little higher than the surrounding single- and two-storey houses and shops. Grass lawns, shrubs and palm trees round a pool in a central courtyard were a wonderful contrast from the dusty roads around where men in flowing robes squatted and talked or dozed in doorways while animals and children moved about them.

Inside the hotel it was cool, clean and inviting, and very great was their relief when they learnt that their bookings were recorded and they were able to relax over glasses of tea in a central room divided into intimate squares of cushioned seats by low mosaic clad walls and circular marble columns supporting arched ceilings coloured blue and gold.

"Observe," said Donald, "that there are still skilled craftsmen about, though I'm prepared to wager you a double whisky that the technical aspects don't match up," a statement born out later when David and Ian discovered in their bedroom that one of the bedhead lights would not light even after a new bulb had been provided, and to flush the WC in the en suite bathroom it was necessary to remove the top of the cistern and open a valve by hand.

The site they had to inspect lay four hours south by car and they arranged their time table so that they rose while it was still dark to be on the road to drive through the magnificence of dawn over the desert, the changing lights and colours beautiful beyond words. Donald went with them on the first day and remained at Bousaada afterwards, writing up his report and, as he put it, "to repel boarders." "For," he continued, "the hotel may be nearly empty now, but you never know in this capricious country. You might return to find it full of cannibal kings attending a cookery course or a witch doctor jamboree."

For David and Ian the work was hard. Arriving at the site at about ten in the morning they would park their car at the side of the small village of adobe-built dwellings clustered round the oasis, upon which all depended, and walk over the area until the torrid heat of the middle of the day drove them back for shade, where, surrounded by curious children with gentle dark eyes, they ate their frugal meals, took photographs and wrote notes. The occasional camel ignored them with proud disdain. Later, as the heat became less intense, they would continue walking, only leaving to get back to the hotel in time for a cold meal left for them before blessed baths and a short sleep before the next day's work. For some unexplained reason none of their competitors made their appearance during the four days they were in Bousaada, though one afternoon a small plane flew to and fro over the site probably for the purpose of aerial photography.

At the end of the fourth day they arrived back to find Donald in a state of some excitement.

"There's something afoot," he said as he sat with them at their meal. "Some toughs have been casing the joint. There were four of them and they went over the place with a toothcomb, even through our rooms. They did have the decency to ask me if I minded and I must say they carried out their work without making any mess, as I hope you'll find when you inspect your things. It would be politic, I think, if you did not complain to the management, who, by the way, won't let on what it is all about."

David asked whether the toughs were still in the hotel.

"Yes, they're somewhere about. They booked in."

When they had finished the waiter told them that the hotel manager wished to speak with them.

"I told you," said Donald, "they'll be wanting our rooms for the cannibal kings."

"As long as," said Ian, "we are not to be one of the courses."

The manager was a sad looking little man wearing a red fez. He shook them all by the hand and looked apologetic.

"It has been a pleasure to house you in this hotel," he said, "and I was hoping that you would be able to stay for some time to come. Unfortunately, I have received orders from higher authority that all guests are to leave by tomorrow midday." He spread his hands. "I have, therefore, the most unwelcome duty to inform you of this. I have no choice, you understand? Perhaps you will return?"

It might have been worse: they had done enough to stimulate their imaginations, and Donald was anxious to return to England.

On their way back they stopped from time to time to take photographs, aiming to eat their picnic lunch in the shade of the trees when they reached the mountains. The last of these stops was within a mile of the foothills where a clump of huge red stones protruding from the plain about two hundred yards from the road were so lit up by the sunlight against the green backdrop of the mountain chain that they made an inviting composition. They parked the car at the side of the road and took photographs. It then occurred to David that by climbing the stones he would obtain a vantage point for a wide angle picture. So, slinging his camera and spare lens cases over his shoulder, he left his companions sitting in the shade behind the back of the car and walked across to the stones. They were rounded by wind and sand and not easy to climb. He was about half way up, about twenty feet, when he heard the sound of vehicles droning through the silence. The noise came from the road ahead of them and as he looked in that direction he saw a column of large cars travelling fast with a group of motorcyclists in advance. Half a mile from Ian and Donald with the car the column stopped except for the motorcyclists, which came on and surrounded them. By that time Ian and Donald were on their feet and David watched in amazement as they raised their hands in the air under the muzzles of submachine guns. The next moment the once familiar cracks of bullets passing over his head made David leap for cover behind the boulder he was on. Good God! They were shooting at him!

The mind works with extraordinary speed in emergencies and as David landed he understood their predicament. Someone of great importance was on his way to Bousaada where he and his entourage were to stay in the hotel he and his companions had vacated.

This was a country which had recently endured a cruel war when ambushes were commonplace. A solitary car by the roadside, at first sight abandoned, and his figure festooned with leather cases moving where a group of armed men could be concealed had raised suspicions. It was not surprising that the bigwig's escort was taking no chances. All this passed through David's mind as he leapt off the stone and landed on his knees behind it in a recess. Immediately he was given something else to think about. A few feet from his nose a snake lay curled. Probably it was as surprised as he was.

There are people who understand snakes, some even spending nights and days in their company in order to beat records. David was not one of these. In fact he probably broke the record for the shortest time anyone has spent with a snake. As the creature drew back its flat head with a hiss he was back on the stone he had so quickly left facing the guns with hands stretched as high in the air as he could reach.

He could now see how the situation was unfolding. Ian and Donald were in the road being interrogated by someone looking like an officer; their car was being closely examined and their suit cases were being pulled out of the boot; and three men with submachine guns were running towards him in open order. One of them shouted at him to come down and he obeyed, necessarily climbing part of the way with his back towards them. It is not a reassuring way to approach three armed men. By the time he reached the flat ground they were close and one of them took charge of him while the others climbed the rock cluster inspecting every possible piece of cover. The snake was having an unusually turbulent morning. David's guard ordered him to walk back to the car with his hands still raised, while he followed several paces behind. Once there, his photographic apparatus was taken from him and examined. He noticed that the officer had all their passports in his hands. By this time the inspection of the car and their luggage was over and he sensed a sharp drop in the tension. One of the occupants of the car which had driven up to theirs spoke over a radio and the halted convoy began to move again, and as it passed they noticed a pennant flying from the bonnet of the middle and most magnificent car. Later at the hotel they learnt that President Boumeddian had gone to Bousaada to open a school.

While David and Ian took the affair quite calmly, Donald was visibly shaken.

"Laddie," he said to David, "I thought you'd had your chips when you went down like that after that trigger-happy Algie let fly. I've had enough of this benighted country and I'll be catching the first flight I can get on back to civilisation."

And in two days he was gone.

The remaining two continued to meet as many appropriate people as they could, finding it a frustrating and difficult task, though David's chess improved. They made further attempts to retrieve their parcel without success and finally concluded they were wasting their time and decided to follow Donald's example. They booked their flight, returned the hired car and fell back upon taxis once more.

On the evening before their departure the hotel receptionist drew their attention to a message for them from Monsieur Djourai, who had telephoned from the airport parcel office that afternoon. He reported the arrival of their parcel.

"You never can tell with Africans," said Ian. "One time it seems they are about as interested in you as a dung beetle in a moth ball, and the next you know is that one of them has your interest at heart after all."

"This," said David, "is where Oldacre may be able to earn his keep. As our flight is at three tomorrow afternoon we will collect the parcel tomorrow morning, leaving our luggage at the airport, and nip back to his office with it together with a list of those to whom copies of the brochure should be sent, leaving us time for lunch before reporting in."

They still had much to learn.

They entered the parcel office at ten next morning. Monsieur Djourai was not in. However, his colleague was all smiles, as though genuinely pleased that their quest was nearing consummation. No, the parcels were not kept in the parcel office: it would be necessary for them to apply to the parcel reception office, which was further down the road. This proved to be an office not unlike the first except for the number of jostling men and women on their side of the counter, behind which two clerks were verifying identities before rubber stamping tickets for, David and Ian presumed, the collection of parcels. When they had fought their way to the counter and satisfied one of the clerks over their identities they followed others to find where the parcels were kept. The trail now led them to the end of a long queue leading to a hut with a small opening not unlike a theatre box office. It took half an hour to reach it. Inside, a bearded Algerian stamped their ticket with a large rubber stamp and they moved on to another queue leading to another hut. It was depressing to observe that this queue was longer than the first and they soon understood the reason: it moved more slowly. By now they both realised the plan to employ Oldacre would have to be ditched. Nevertheless, they agreed that having come so far they might as well collect the parcel even though it meant carrying it back to England and posting the brochures back individually. They also agreed that it would be less tedious if they took it in turns to approach their goal and Ian went off to get a beer in the main airport building. When he returned he found David six or seven from the opening and they were able to observe why movement was so slow: the clerk was recording details of each ticket in a large ledger before adding another rubber stamp. Gratefully, David handed over to Ian and moved out of the heat into the main building. What he needed was a cool drink and a seat. His watch showed the time to be twenty minutes past eleven. A quarter of an hour later Ian hurried up to him with his long limping strides. He was waving a piece of paper in the air.

"We're there at last," he cried. "I had to go to yet another office for one last lingering stamp and to pay ten dinars before getting this, which the bloke assured me is the last hurdle. All we have to do now is to go to the building where the parcels are kept and collect. It's quite close."

"Ten dinars! That's a bit off. Why so?"

"To pay for the rubber stamps and ink, I suppose. Come on!"

They discovered the parcel store to be an enormous steel and asbestos structure rather like a gymnasium with a kind of bare ante-room where they recognised several of their fellow claimants of the morning waiting as patiently as ever. Every now and then a fat Algerian wearing a fez came through the large opening leading into the vast body of the building holding a parcel of one kind or another which the happy recipient then carried to a small office embodied in the ante-room where his or her ticket was rubber stamped, while the fat Algerian took another ticket and disappeared to collect the next parcel. The process was taking time and David became impatient. He pushed through the opening and looked about. The building really was immense and entirely empty save for the parcels. These were in a chaotic heap about fifteen feet high spread over a bay to the left of the opening. Two completely black men were picking through it in a desultory manner. How any person's parcel came to be sorted from that jumble defied David's comprehension. The fat man in the fez had disappeared mysteriously and there being no time to be lost David approached one of the black men ticket in hand. He took it without question and showed it to his colleague. Together the two began to rummage unhurriedly through the pile in random fashion. David quickly perceived that if the parcel was to be found some sort of method had to be introduced and joined in the hunt, placing each examined parcel to one side to avoid reinspection, a precaution not observed by the two official sorters, who picked up parcels aimlessly, frequently examining the same parcel several times. However, they made no objection to unauthorised assistance even when Ian joined in the hunt. After a quarter of an hour it became clear that the situation was desperate. It might take days to discover the prize. The whole affair became a challenge, even an obsession. They calculated that they had just over two-hours before they must leave to check in for their flight. It was a daunting task, but with two of them working systematically they might be lucky.

Obsessions invite miscalculations, and the loud wail of a nearby hooter rent the air. The two black men tossed aside the parcels they were holding and moved off towards the entry. They looked surprised when David and Ian continued their search.

One said: "Time for lunch: we have to lock up now."

Both friends had forgotten the two hour lunch break inherited from the French.

"But what about our parcel?" asked David.

"Come back after lunch and we will go on looking."

"That will be no good: we have to report for our flight soon after two!"

The blackmen smiled hugely showing shining white teeth.

One of them said: "Come back to Algeria. Then we will try again!"

Oldacre was in the transit lounge preparatory to taking the same plane.

"Leave," he explained.

They told him of their recent experience.

"Ah! Pity I didn't know. You should have had the parcel sent care of the Consulate. When the volume of parcels becomes too massive or when something perishable decays in the heap and the pong gets too strong they take the lot out, burn them and start again."

At the end of four months of concentrated work in both offices together with various experts they had their project drawn up in outline and costed. All were satisfied that they had evolved an exciting and viable scheme. David posted the drawings with a report to the Prince and waited.

Six weeks later the Prince replied.

"Dear Mr Drummond," he wrote. "Your proposals for the limited competition in Algeria disappointed me. Nevertheless, I submitted them with my own report covering matters of finance and contracting firms to the Minister. I have now received notice that the committee over which he presides has rejected the application.

"It is a considerable mortification to me that through your ineptitude I am exposed to this humiliation.

"If you will let my secretary have a note of your expenses while in Algeria he will arrange a refund.

"Yours truly."

It is one of the many burdens that an architect has to bear when, as frequently happens, considerable labour proves fruitless. It is not only the waste of time: far more, it is the bitter disappointment as dreams cannot be realised; for the artist in him cries out to see and touch his work, without which experience it remains mere "castles in the air". He grows accustomed to this non-fulfilment, though never immune to its bite, and in this instance, the Prince's harsh words rubbed salt into the wound.

Ian did his best by arranging a luncheon for all most involved, calling it a "wake", while emphasising the probable miseries in the event of success.

Later, they examined the scheme selected, published in the professional journals. A firm of French architects and engineers had been successful, and David and Ian wryly observed several features which they had included in their own submission.

It was a few years later that David met Donald McLeod again. It was at some City dinner where they were guests. Naturally they talked of their time together in Algeria and Donald chuckled over the tale of the parcel.

"It doesn't surprise me a wee bit," he said. "I can tell you it was my advice to my firm not to touch the country. You were well out of it yourselves and if I'd known then what I know now I would have brought you back with me when I left instead of leaving you there to waste your time."

"We would all act differently with the benefit of hindsight," said David.

Donald looked at him quizzically for a moment and then asked: "Did you never hear the truth about your work on that job?"

David was puzzled and said so.

"Ah well; I see no harm in telling you, though it will not improve your faith in human nature. I heard it from one of the directors of a refrigeration firm we work with from time to time. They got a contract to work in that Algerian development and he knew quite a bit about it. He got to be friendly with one of the architects, a Frenchie who spoke English. After a few drinks one evening this Frenchie let on that his consortium was being financed by your Prince Versky, or whatever his outlandish name might be, but under cover. Apparently your Prince got into the bad books of the Algies at the time of the war with France and thereafter they would have nothing to do with him. The Prince was dead keen to get into the act and he knew the Algies knew it. So, he planned to finance and run this consortium from behind the scenes. But, being a canny man, he wanted to make quite sure the Algies didn't investigate too deeply and he gulled them. It was your bad luck to be selected as the fall guy!"

CHAPTER 16

*"Modern education has devoted itself to the
teaching of impudence, and then we complain
we can no more manage our mobs."*

JOHN RUSKIN

David and Jill never regretted their purchase of the cottage in South West France, and I am not surprised having spent several happy times with them myself. At the beginning they spent family holidays there in fairly primitive conditions, gradually improving the place year by year. Eventually, when their children became independent, they sold their house in England and moved out to France *definitivement*, as the French say, to enjoy what they called their "long holiday".

Living in another country teaches much not otherwise observed and David and Jill had many experiences, some salutary some highly entertaining and all instructive. However, since that time some able writers, who followed their example, have recorded similar adventures with accuracy and wit, and because repetition is tedious I forbear recording them here.

Men and women granted good health and without close family ties may live contented away from their homeland until ripe old age, even adding their bones to the soil of other lands without compunction. A reversal of these chances draw them inexorably back and it was so with David and Jill.

They found a pretty cottage in West Sussex, the position selected for its beauty and not too near and not too far from their children and their young. It was, apart from an attic room useful to David as a place of work, on one floor, an essential feature owing to Jill's failing health, a shadow they both endeavoured to dismiss without significant success; for when two people have loved and lived together for many years the prospect of compulsory separation is an incubus that invades the mind as a sombre background to thought.

It might be asked what is meant by not too near and not too far, and

243

it is not an easy question to answer. In a gigantic country like the USA with advanced travel facilities the distance could be as much as one hundred miles, whereas in one of the Channel Islands such as Jersey or Guernsey with narrow winding roads and heavy traffic five miles would be nearer the mark. In David's case, fifty miles divided the two households of their young and the position of their new house roughly bisected them.

The unexpected twists and turns in life presented by fickle Fortune provide variety without which existence might be tedious, and it is essential to accept the rough with the smooth, prepared to extract lessons or comic aspects. These are usually hard to perceive at the time, emerging later to provide balm for bruises.

For example, mention of Guernsey brings to mind an event experienced by David in the company of his daughter, Carol, her husband Bob, and their two little girls, Anne and Emma, at the time in question aged ten and eight.

Bob is a thoroughly agreeable giant of a man, whose father, by dint of hard work and ability, had amassed a large sum of money before retiring to Guernsey to avoid the ill judged and punitive taxation applied to money spinners at that time. Bob is one of those quiet peaceable big men, whom it is dangerous to arouse. He works in television. It is wrong to have favourites amongst grandchildren, but inevitable, and David had to own that Anne was his. Perhaps it was because she reminded him of Jill when young.

Bob with his family had been on holiday in Guernsey and David had driven to Southampton airport to bring them back to have tea with Jill and himself, picking up their car left in the drive during their absence. It was explained to David on the way that Bob had started to make a video film for family consumption with Anne and Emma the stars. It was to be titled "The Mother Snatcher", unfolding a tale of a series of unexplained disappearances of mothers of young children, the brave hunt for the kidnapper involving magic by Anne and Emma leading to the discovery and destruction of the "Snatcher" and his witch accomplice with the consequential delivery of Carol and all the other missing mothers. Filming had started on location in Guernsey.

"The advantage of the plot," explained Carol, "is that most of the adventure can be adapted to different holiday places using peculiarities of the scenery to build the adventure round. For example, we spent a few days on a small island just off St Peter's Port. It is undeveloped except for a nice hotel which caters for children, and we used the bit of rocky coast as well as the wild middle bit."

"Yes," broke in Emma excitedly, "and Daddy is going to dress up as the monster and put on a horrible face he is going to buy."

"There," said Bob, "I may call upon you as camera man."

David asked how long it would take to make the film.

"It will have to be done inside two years," replied Carol. "The girls are growing so fast, though we are trying to film more or less from the beginning to the end so that alteration will be explained by the length of their journey."

Not much more was said about the matter until the following summer when Jill and David spent a weekend with Bob and Carol at their home. Bob explained that the filming had reached a point where scenes including "The Snatcher" and the witch were to be shot.

"I am to play the witch," said Carol. "Bob has got hold of the most gruesome masks and costumes for the witch and the 'Snatcher'. Bob is going to play the 'Snatcher'. We were contemplating a wild bit of the South Downs as a location."

It turned out that they had selected an area in the hills just south of the village where David's grandparents had lived and very familiar to him. It was a good choice because there was unfrequented open downland combined with dense woods of beech and yew all within walking distance from a road.

By good luck the Saturday chosen for the expedition was a beautiful day, the kind of day in early September that England occasionally presents, which cannot be matched anywhere else on this planet. The sky was blue with a few fleecy clouds to provide the occasional slow moving patch of shadow, the air was warm with a hint of approaching autumn in it, and away from the busy roads the rich, ripe smells of lush country towards the end of a fine summer filled the senses.

They drove up the village street that David had walked down on a similar day many years before with his grandfather, great uncle Charles, aunt Emily, uncle Edward and Mullen Tipping on their way to inspect his painting of Christ on the cross before hearing the momentous news of war from Violet Tipping. What alteration less than half a century had wrought! Then they had walked down the middle of the road, ignoring the rudimentary pavements, suicidal now as fast-moving traffic roared up and down between smartly "done up" dwellings, now occupied by a well-to-do middle class while the village folk lived in new housing nearby. Then it was possible to talk quietly to a background of gentle country sounds and the rooks cawing above the elms at the end of the vicarage garden, a pleasure now rarely enjoyed. No doubt, the violent changes were a mark of the new period of revolution and progress; but the elderly prefer more gradual transformation and David felt acute nostalgia. They passed "The Three Horseshoes", quite altered with a resplendent new sign and "Pub Lunches" lettered on a board. Along the pavement outside it a line of parked cars indicated popularity. Inside a crowd of men and women would be drinking wine, short drinks and bitter beer at nearly a pound a pint. David could remember drinking a pint of bitter in the old and musty bar for six old pennies, men only present since self-respecting country women did not enter bars. What would the publican, old Fletcher, make of it all if he could rise from his grave in the churchyard and look at it now?

They ate their picnic on top of a down, leaving the car amongst others in a car park where before the war David had picked blackberries. All round the grass was coarse and long, while thickets of thorn and bramble gave protection for ash and later beech. He yearned for the springy turf thick with thyme and "smelling like dawn in paradise", maintained for generations by great flocks of sheep and, when they were removed, the humble rabbit until myxomatosis swept them all away in turn to allow the steady return to beechwood, the climax vegetation of chalk downland. David explained this to the two girls. Emma soon lost interest, but Anne listened gravely. When he had finished she wanted to know why the original beechwoods had disappeared and he explained how early man had found the hills drier and safer than the dense and boggy oak forests of The Weald, their pigs and goats gradually forming clearings by preventing regeneration of the beech, leading eventually to the fine turf covering he had loved and never thought to see disappear.

"I shall like it when it is all beech woods," she said. "I love them, especially when there are bluebells."

"And scuffing through dry leaves."

"Mm, yes."

"You'll have to wait a hundred years."

"As long as that?"

"Nature is deliberate as well as patient."

"Lunch break over," said Bob. "To work!"

The plan was to find a suitable place in the woods where David would shoot some scenes involving the girls alone while Carol and Bob dressed up as the witch and the "Snatcher" by the car. They took a minor road and looked for a place to park. The first space contained two brightly painted powerful motor bikes and they moved on several hundred yards to another.

They selected a leafy clearing beneath some magnificent old beeches and after some rehearsal the two potential villains left to change.

Most children make natural actors when patiently guided, a golden rule being not to over rehearse. Within half an hour David was taking the last shot when the swishing scrunch of several feet approaching from behind him caused him to lower the camera and turn his head. Three youths and a girl came straight towards them. The leading youth looked muscular and broad-shouldered, with red hair cut in what is descriptively called a burr cut. He had handsome features and a strong mouth. Behind him came a smaller, wiry individual with head shaved smooth save for a central band from front to back like a cocks-comb. The third youth was tall and thin, and in contrast to the other two sported a hair style of thick black hair trained to stand out from his head, reminding David of Kipling's fuzzy-wuzzies. It made his pale face appear unnaturally small. All three wore jeans so tight that it was a wonder how they put them on. The leader's black leather jacket was zipped open to his waist displaying a gold coloured chain. His knee-length boots were cream with a floral pattern, high heeled and sharply pointed. The smaller companion's shirt was patterned with large white and red squares and he wore a yellow silk scarf. The fuzzy-wuzzy's coat was some dirty white woolly material reaching to his thighs. Enormous green buttons were left undone to expose a hairless chest and bead necklace. From one ear hung a large metal ring. They made a bizarre spectacle; but the girl outdid them. Her lips were painted silver to match the heavy silvering below her plucked eyebrows above heavily black-lined blue eyes. On each cheek she had applied doll-like patches of orange rouge in sharp contrast to the white powder over the remainder of her small round face. Her erect hair fell forward at the front to form a lock over her forehead and was dyed in two colours, pink and blue. Long silver chains hung from her ears. She had only to apply a bulbous false red nose to resemble a circus clown. Below a full cream bodice trimmed in front with pink lace her black leather mini skirt was inside a lace suspender belt supporting large mesh black net stockings that ended just above her knees to expose a quantity of naked thigh. On her feet were scarlet calf-length leather boots.

They came up to David and the two little girls.

"'Ullo, 'ullo," said the leader. "What 'ave we 'ere? A dirty old man, I do believe, taking pics of little dolls. Birthday suits next I s'ppose! Tche! Tche! Not very nice."

"They are my granddaughters," said David stiffly. Punks, as he assumed these to be, were, he understood, peaceable youngsters endeavouring to express themselves, and this coarse approach surprised him.

What came next was worse.

"Grab them kids," the leader ordered, and the girl ran forward with the fuzzy-wuzzy to stand behind Anne and Emma grasping their upper arms.

"Now then, granddad," he continued, facing David while the wiry youth stood behind him, "that's a nice bit of video you've got there. What about giving us a present?"

"It doesn't belong to me," said David at the same time realising what a fatuous reply it was. It was difficult to adjust to the ugly development that had so suddenly shattered the happy calm of the day.

"Pinched it, eh? Well! Well! 'Oo would 'ave thought it of a la-di-da bloody granddad?"

The fuzzy-wuzzy grinned and the girl tittered.

Without warning David felt his arm twisted behind his back in a painful half nelson and the leader took him by a lapel of his coat.

"First let's 'ave the bread," and he took David's wallet from his inner jacket pocket. Then removing its contents he tossed it into nearby bushes.

"Now the video."

David wondered desperately what he might do. The "old one two" RSM Stoner would have advised, meaning a swift jab with his left into the pit of his opponent's stomach followed by a right to the jaw, was impossible with his left hand held behind his back and his right holding the video. In films the prisoner lifts his knee sharply into his opponent's groin before twisting out of the arm hold, but David felt too old for such agility even if feasible without practice, and, anyway, he was anxious about the two little girls, whose white faces and big eyes expressed shock and fear, Emma held by the clown-like girl and Anne by the fuzzy-wuzzy.

At this tense moment something happened to increase David's sense of unreality. A newcomer joined them, his approach unnoticed. It was a skinny little man with a wispy brown beard streaked with white, bearing an enormous knapsack. He wore a tartan shirt, khaki shorts and black walking boots. He peered at the scene through thick-lensed glasses.

"I am loosing my way," he said in an accented piping voice. "Pleese to tell me the way to Cheechester."

It was as though the extraordinary spectacle made no impression at all upon him, possibly accepting without question all manifestations of the curious foreign country through which he hiked. Yet, without realisation he was the instrument that abruptly shifted the whole situation in the defenders' favour.

Turning to look at the newcomer with surprise, the fuzzy-wuzzy loosened his grip on Anne, who with a quick wriggle was free and scampering off in the direction of the car.

"After 'er!" shouted the leader and David's left arm was released as the youth behind him set off in pursuit ahead of the fuzzy-wuzzy who was slower both in uptake and speed.

"Not both of you, you stupid cunts!"

The fuzzy-wuzzy stopped, still looking after the chase, now out of sight.

The leader's head was turned in that direction, too, and David saw his opportunity. He swung the heavy video at the back of his head and detecting the movement the leader was turning towards him as it struck so that he received the blow on his ear. He stumbled sideways and fell amongst the leaves, blood pouring down his neck. With a shriek the girl ran to him, letting go of Emma, who bolted in turn.

"You fucking bastard!" cried the girl. "You've killed 'im." And she fell upon her knees beside him.

Concerned, David stepped forward only to see the fuzzy-wuzzy rushing at him.

He remembered being told that if charged by an enraged bull one should coolly face it and leap aside at the last moment to let it thunder past. This ruse seemed appropriate now and he took a hasty step backwards to balance himself for the manoeuvre. Unfortunately for his plan, probably over ambitious in any event, he tripped over a root concealed beneath the leaves and fell flat upon his back. He need not have worried. The fuzzy-wuzzy was not intent upon revenging his leader's downfall: he was making a rapid exit; and almost immediately the reason became apparent, for there burst upon the confused scene a huge and horrible creature with thick hair and distorted features roaring like a bull, followed by a hideous hag.

The kneeling girl uttered another shriek, though admirably making no move to desert her man, only putting an arm over his shoulder as if to protect him from further misfortune.

The monster stopped and asked David if he was all right. Its deformed face was fearsome and a hairy claw took his arm to assist him to his feet. The hag took a handkerchief from beneath her tattered cloak and applied it to the bleeding ear of the wounded youth, now sitting up and gazing round with glassy eyes.

"I might have caught the Apache," said the monster, "but thought you might need reinforcements. Anyway we've bagged a couple. How many were there altogether?"

Further discussion was interrupted by an accented piping voice: "Please to tell me the way to Cheechester."

EPILOGUE

The last time I saw David was when he invited me to spend a holiday on Herm Island with him, his granddaughter Anne, her husband and their small daughter.

For some reason or another I particularly recall to mind one sunny morning when we both sat upon folding chairs watching the little naked nymph playing at the water's edge. From time to time the gentle breeze would throw her rich chestnut hair across her eyes when she would cast it back with a delicate little hand while she collected shells in a brightly painted pail.

The beach was a mixture of clean white sand and dark rocks, upon which wherever they were covered by the tide various seaweeds grew. The sea was calm and only ripples curled gently along the shore. Across the water the island of Guernsey lay green and blue. Near us lay the shell and pith of a cuttle-fish, white and solitary. The spring sun warmed us.

"Look Geegee! There's a funny kind of fish in the water," called out the nymph, pointing.

David stood up stiffly and went to the rock pool she was gazing into. The water was so clear that it was invisible.

"It's a small crab, darling. It's been left behind by the tide."

"Is it worried, do you think?"

"No, it will probably wait there until the tide comes in again."

"Won't it get bored just sitting there for hours and hours?"

"It could climb out and run across the beach to the sea if it wanted to."

"Why doesn't it?"

"I expect it is quite comfortable where it is enjoying the warm sun and it is a safe place for it to stay."

"Why is it safe?"

"It is very small and if a seagull saw it running about it might pick it up for a meal. It is wiser to stay where it is."

The little nymph digested this information.

Anne smiled at me as she passed and approached them, her dark hair shining. She was wearing a simple pale blue and white cotton frock and looked fresh and very pretty.

Her shadow fell across the water and David turned to find her

251

smiling at them.

"You both looked so engrossed I wondered whether I should interrupt you," she said. "What have you discovered?"

"I found a fish called a crab and it's waiting for the tide to come in. Look, Mummy!" Her finger touched the surface above the crab and immediately ripples made the water visible.

"Why don't you both go for a stroll?" I said. "I'll stay and look after Julie."

"What about it?" Anne asked her grandfather.

"Thank you both, but I feel a bit tired this morning. I don't know why: the journey and the sea air perhaps. You take Julie and we'll wait here until you come back."

"I shall be just as happy to sit with you here for a bit," she said.

She took David's arm and led him back to his chair, seating herself upon a rock close by.

"I daresay all old people feel the same," he said, "but I find it most strange to watch Julie. It really seems only the other day that I was the same age beginning to discover things. At that age everything is so new and clean while time seems endless. When you grow old time closes up like a telescope."

"I can understand that," said Anne. "When I was bored in class at school the time dragged terribly and when I was enjoying myself it flashed by. What a pity it can't be the other way round."

"Yet, one of the keys to happiness is to be fully occupied. Do you get bored much now?"

"I don't get the time. What are the other keys?"

"To happiness?" David reflected and then said: "Don't repine over errors and failures gone beyond recall."

"Mm. Difficult. I often do."

"It is an affliction of sensibility."

"But I have met intelligent people who don't."

"Intelligence and sensibility do not necessarily go together."

He turned to me. "Do you not agree, my old friend?"

"It is complicated," I replied, "like everything to do with the human mind. Some may hide their care, often with damaging results, and others learn to master useless regret, which is, after all, a form of worry, and worry is a fearful obstacle to happiness."

"How do they master it?"

"Ah!" I said. "Have you the answer to that one, David?"

"If you mean, how do I avoid it, the answer is: without much

252

success; although it becomes increasingly less of a problem for us, does it not? We are nearer the safety exit."

"What I try to do," I said, "is examine worries in detail, carefully and deliberately, considering the worst that could happen. Then, take any possible action to deal with the source. It is rare for the worst to happen, which is a relief."

"We all should take a lesson from the East," said David, "and resign ourselves to the will of Allah."

"What else have you learnt?" asked Anne as she watched Julie who was now lying in a rock pool emulating, perhaps, the crab in order to discover what it felt.

"That old men who expound what experience has taught them are bores," said David with a wink at me.

"Socrates wasn't a bore," she said.

"He was in rather a different class and not old. And anyway, look what happened to him!"

"It wasn't his pupils who did him in."

"So, you did find some of your school work interesting! Probably he wouldn't be listened to today. He taught people to think for themselves, and for the last hundred years humanity has preferred to play follow-my-leader."

Anne laid her hand upon her grandfather's knee.

"But I'm listening to you and you don't bore me."

He looked into her kind eyes, so reminiscent of Jill's, and suddenly felt both very sad and curiously happy. He took off his glasses and wiped his eyes.

"The sea air sometimes makes my eyes water," he said. "Well, I'll just add: spread your interests as widely as you can so that if some things are denied there are others to fall back upon – the field is very wide these days. Be calm and gentle, though firm in the face of bullies: the hunting instinct remains just beneath the surface in many men and weakness indicates a quarry."

He turned to me. "What else I wonder?"

"Laughter?"

"Oh, yes indeed. Socrates left that out too, unless he has been misreported. A highly entertaining friend of mine, killed in Burma during the war, used to insist that one should not take life too seriously."

"Punter Parkinson," I said, and David nodded.

David touched Anne's cheek and smiled.

"That's enough of my limited philosophy. What would you stir into the dish, clever little cook that you are?"

She looked away out to sea for a while. Then she turned her eyes to his.

"Loving kindness?" she said.

"Ah!" he said softly. "That you have shown, my dear, that you have shown."